ARIZONA FOREVER

A love story

By Jaclyn M. Hawkes

Spirit Dance Books

Acknowledgements

Thank you to all of my team who always pull together to help me get a project done. Producing a book is a huge project. I could never do this without you.

Also, thank you to my family, especially my incredible husband, for trusting that something good is eventually going to come out of all the hours spent with my computer. On this project, they actually sent me a hilarious "Miss You" note. They have my back always and I so appreciate them.

Dedication

This book is dedicated to my dad. He was a veterinarian for thirty-two years. He was a brilliant surgeon, whose patients and clients alike loved him. He was known to say that veterinarians had to treat any number of species, all without any of them being able to actually tell him where it hurt.

He was a tough boss to work for because he expected excellence, but he also finished his long career without anyone ever threatening to sue him for malpractice—unheard of these days. He let us have any number of interesting pets, even when my mother was known to bring home wounded animals that were sometimes more dead than alive. At one time, we had a house broken mini lop bunny and a 150 pound Landseer Newfoundland, who actually got along great.

My dad spent years working with large, often dangerous animals, sometimes in the dead of night in bitterly cold, smelly, squishy corrals. He was once butted in the head by a bull, had a rank Appaloosa tear the chest pocket off of his lab coat with a front hoof, and was probably bitten by about forty-three German Shepherds and Chihuahuas.

He taught me to love horses, and he taught all eleven of us kids to work, and to me, those are both treasures. He passed away in 2005, but left behind huge legacies. Love you Dad.

Prologue

Six year old Jessie Benjamin did what she always did when she was afraid—she ran to her big brothers. Hurrying, she went two doors down the hall to Josh's room where her other brothers, Brennan and McCade, would most likely be as well. It was where the four of them usually met whenever there was something wrong. Only this time, she knew something was really wrong because her brothers didn't smile and tease her before they gathered around her like they usually did. They swallowed her into their jostling group hug, but this time there was the same scary feeling here in Josh's room that she could hear in her parents' raised voices coming from their room further down the hall.

She couldn't tell what they were fighting about. She only heard a word here or there, her mother's voice loud and angry, while her dad's had calmed down to sad and almost pleading.

This bickering had been going on for a couple of days now, but nothing like tonight's fighting. It was so strange. Her mother got fussy pretty often, but her dad never got like this. Ever. He was typically calm and soft spoken. Even when someone did something big, like when Brennan broke the garage window, he never got too riled. Whatever this bortion thing was her mother was hollering about had made him truly upset.

Jessie looked up into the serious faces of her brothers and hid her own face against Josh's chest. She wished her mother would calm down. That shouting couldn't be good for the baby in her mom's tummy. They'd just found out she was expecting. Jessie was praying it was a girl and couldn't have been more excited for anything! Ever since she was little, she'd imagined she had this little blonde sister named Jennifer who did everything with her. She'd even dreamed about her and it felt like she'd waited forever. Even a baby brother would be wonderful!

The fighting spilled out of their parents' room into the hallway and her father almost seemed to be begging as he said, "Please, Clara, don't do this. Just hang in there four more months. Even three and a half. Then you can leave and won't ever even have to see it. I know it's your body, but please . . . It's my baby too."

Storming past Josh's bedroom door, her mother shouted something they all clearly heard, "I'll do what I want! It's my body! In four months I'll have missed the two biggest shows of the season. I missed shows for years to get the four we have. They're plenty. It's too much to ask that I do it again. This was your mistake, Ken—not mine! I shouldn't have to pay for it and you can't make me!"

The front door slammed and a moment later Jessie heard a car squeal away and then there was only silence. For some reason, that scared her more than the arguing. Finally, her dad went into his office and stayed on the phone with someone for a long time and when he came out, he actually looked like he'd been crying. Of course, that couldn't have been true. Dads didn't cry. But he looked like it.

That night, after everyone else was gone to bed, Jessie snuck into Josh's room and sat on his bed and whispered, "Josh, what are they fighting about? What does bortion mean?" He was almost ten. He would know.

At her question, Josh began to cry. He pulled Jessie into a gentle hug. When he could finally speak, he said so softly and so sadly that Jessie could hardly hear the words that shattered her world into pieces, "Dad says it means Mom's going to have the baby taken out of her tummy and then it will die, Jessie."

Chapter 1

21 years later

Jessie slid onto the bench on the edge of the soccer field beside McCade and gave an exaggerated sigh of exhaustion as she began to unlace her cleats and said, "Man, you schooled me out there this morning, Muck. I thought I had you until that sweet juke before the half and then I was toast. My calves are killing me!"

McCade smiled and batted at her blonde ponytail. "That's what you get for working too much and playing too little. Juked by the king of jukage!" He reached a hand over her head to fist bump Brennan who sat on the other side of her sucking on a water bottle. "She's getting old and slow, Bren. Adulthood'll do that to ya if you let it!"

Brennan stopped drinking and squirted her in the face with the water bottle. "I don't know. She's still got some moves of her own. You forget she scored on me like I was standing still. She even got around Suki. And you know she's got some moves." Brennan winked at his wife Suki and McCade rolled his eyes.

Jessie opened her mouth to catch some of the water Brennan was squirting, then smiled and said, "Twice. That would be twice I scored on you, bro. And that second one was world class. Christiano himself would have been jealous. Old and slow? I may be overworked and under played, but I'll always be younger than the three of you. And we did win. I love this deal where the winners get taken to breakfast." She pulled off her socks and wiggled her toes. "It's already insanely hot out here. You two seem to be buying a lot lately. I'm having blueberry waffles. Think they'd care if I walked into the Wagonmaster bare footed? My feet can't face shoes yet. They need air."

As if on cue, all three of her brothers held their noses and Josh's wife, Lucy, laughed from where she was standing beside the bench. "Just ignore them, Jessie. They're only sore losers. Nice toenails, by the way. Love the polka dots."

Jessie stretched her foot out to admire her pedicure. "They are cute, aren't they? Ryley did them for me yesterday while I was finishing my patient log. You have a very artistic son."

Josh turned to her from the other end of the bench with a look of horror. "You let my son paint your toenails? Jessie!"

Jessie laughed. "What? He did a great job for a three year old. Well, once I'd showered the excess polish off my skin. For awhile there it looked like I'd been attacked by an ax murderer with a foot fetish. But he did much better on his own toes. I think mine gave him some practice. His didn't look nearly so gory."

This time it was Lucy who was horrified. "You let him paint his own toes, too? Jessie! That's a terrible thing to teach a little boy. You are never babysitting again!"

"Okay. Fine. I won't do it again. Don't ground me from your kids. They're my favorite nephew and niece."

"They're your only nephew and niece."

Jessie stood up and picked up her bag. "True, but they're still my favorites."She gave a wide smile. "So . . . Hustle up people. I'm starving and my fans are waiting. I have a 7:30. Justison is bringing in that boneheaded buckskin gelding of his with the speed index of 106."

Josh grimaced. "Some fan. He's likely to try to kick your head off. Justison thinks if they try to strike, they're just feeling good and ready to run."

McCade shook his head as they headed to their trucks. "There's probably nothing wrong with the horse. Justison just needs an excuse to visit Doc Jessie again. Don't take any of his crud, Jess. You know how he is."

At the restaurant while they waited for their food, Josh began fooling with his phone. After a second, he gave a low whistle and then said, "Unbelievable! You know that guy from my mission, my friend Riordan Kane? From up in Brisbane? The one we taught forever and got to be such good friends with, but he would never join even though he basically agreed with all the principles. He'd had that LDS girlfriend who had played him so bad and he always said it all sounded great, but he'd already been baptized and didn't need to do it again. Remember he came over for a visit a couple years ago? Elder Burton says the Wall Street Journal reported that he's selling his company for $168 million dollars! Holy crud! That's a hunk of dough! He's only like twenty-nine years old! How does a guy do that?"

Brennan only shook his head as he built sugar packets into a cube. "Apparently very deliberately. You said he was a business machine. Didn't you say he was ruthless? He was in software, right?"

"Oh, I don't know about ruthless. Well, actually, yeah, he was pretty ruthless in business. But I don't think he'd always been that way. He's a nice guy. I think he started out developing the software of some of his computer geek friends, but somewhere along the way he became ruthless. Awhile back his girlfriend, who he thought he was going to marry, started sleeping with the enemy—literally. So he wiped the other guy out. Apparently his company was built on solid technology, mostly phone apps I think, and it snowballed."

Brennan nodded. "Yeah. I'd say it pretty well snowballed. Why's he selling?"

"Who knows why Riordan Kane does anything he does? You'd think he had it made, but he doesn't seem very happy sometimes. Last time I talked to him he distrusted every woman on the planet. Talk about your disenchanted. He had tons of money, no smile, and no idea of his purpose in life."

Brennan raised his eyebrows. "I'd say if you built a company to $168 million dollars before your thirtieth birthday that you had some purpose in life."

"Well, that seemed to be his only purpose. Other than to fish. He does like to fish. I hope once the sale is final he throws himself into something else and doesn't just go all billionaire playboy. That's the last thing Riordan needs. He'll never join the church."

Jaclyn M. Hawkes

Lucy patted his hand. "Relax, honey. It's hard to go all billionaire playboy with only a paltry $168 million. He can hardly do much damage on that pittance." She smiled at him. "Didn't you say he was coming to the National Stock Show and bringing his fancy reining horse?"

Josh put his phone away and grinned. "He is. He's bringing a guy named Quinn something, who's some famous goalie for a pro soccer team over there. Riordan got him into reining as well. He says Quinn is a maniac."

Jessie accepted her plate of blueberry waffles from the server, smiled her thanks and then said sweetly, "Well, you'd better not have them stay at your house then. That's all Ryley would need is an aunt who lets him paint his toenails and a resident maniacal pro soccer goalie for role models. My, but this breakfast bankrolled by the losers looks wonderful, don't you think, Lucy?"

Lucy smiled just as sweetly. "Indeed it does, Jessie. Bon appétit, Bren."

****

Riordan Kane signed the last document his barrister handed him and then put the pen down, wondering why there was no emotion attached to the signing away of the company that had been his life for the past seven years. He felt nothing. No regret. No sorrow. No anticipation. Not even any satisfaction that he'd succeeded to a level he'd hardly even remotely considered. When he thought about it, it seemed slightly cold blooded, really. And thoroughly depressing. Crikeys, his life was perfect.

8

He was incredibly blessed, in so many ways. Why was he not happy? It made him feel like he was ungrateful.

He pushed back his chair, shook his barrister's hand and reached for his briefcase, then turned for the door without looking back. Geez, what was he going to do for the rest of the day? For the rest of his life? There wasn't really any need to work anymore and he could be officially retired. That had always sounded cool to retire early. But what did one actually do with himself when he no longer had a life's work?

It would have been crazy to turn down the offer for that much money in an economy as unstable as it was, but now that the sale was actually done and he was this blah about everything, he realized he needed to find something else to throw himself into quickly. Apparently he was someone who needed to have a passion for a project.

He hoped his accountant had a handle on all of this, so he didn't lose most of it to taxes before he figured out what direction his life was heading next.

Once out in the hall, he reached up and tugged at his tie then glanced at his watch. Three-twenty in the afternoon. If it wasn't pouring rain out there, he'd go fishing. But it was raining buckets, and Quinn was out of town at a game. If he'd told anyone else that he was cashing out today, they'd have insisted on having some big celebration, which to most people just meant a wild party—something he really, really wasn't interested in, so he hadn't mentioned the sale to anyone but Quinn.

He'd assumed that when he got the pay out, he'd be at least temporarily stoked. In fact, he'd made a decision not to spend any of the proceeds for a couple of months to give him time to ensure that he didn't foolishly blow any of it. But now he was completely bored with absolutely no plans and no real interest in hanging out with friends today anyway.

Just outside the conference room door he paused, still considering the rest of his day. Someone approached him from behind and he turned to see the two barristers who had been representing the firm that bought his company. The older man nodded and said, "Pardon me, Mr. Kane." Turning to his younger companion, he said, "I'll see you back at the office on Monday, Ms. Jarret. Have a good weekend."

The man left and the attractive young brunette quirked an eyebrow at Riordan, gave him a come-on smile and said, "So, Mr. Riordan Kane, what are you doing tonight to celebrate your new freedom?"

She pronounced his name Ree-or-dan instead of Rye-or-dun and for some reason that was irritating. Instead of answering, he simply gave her a lazy shrug and returned her smile, but then kept on walking. Women were all the same. Only interested in his money and their own agendas. He'd started learning that the hard way years ago with Sariah Hensley and then cemented that belief with Lydia. Even after being schooled earlier by Sariah, at twenty-seven he'd been still naïve enough to have believed Lydia really loved him—until he found out she was only trying to use him and his company to further her boyfriend's interests. The boyfriend she hadn't mentioned in several months of dating Riordan.

He'd known for years that people could be pretty mercenary, but that had been the first time he'd fully realized just how underhanded a human being could be. It had been the final wake up call. He'd thought he and Lydia were headed somewhere serious—like potentially down the aisle. What a fool he'd been.

The boyfriend's idea for an app had been a good one, but Riordan had slammed the door on him financially anyway. At the time it had eased some of the feeling of betrayal. Later he'd made a lot of money pursuing a similar idea for an app elsewhere that had gone huge. In a way, he probably should be grateful for Lydia's duplicity sending him in a different direction. It had made him wealthy. And it was a long time ago.

At least he wasn't stuck with Lydia. Hindsight made him extremely grateful for that. But since then, the knowledge that women wanted him only for his wealth had been consistently reinforced. It was another reason why he'd told almost no one about this sale day, although somehow it had made the financial news anyway. Still, only Kyra Beven had called him, so that was a good thing. She'd casually mentioned that she'd seen the news about his company and then suggested that maybe they could get some dinner together. He'd tried to be polite as he'd said no. Leave it to the princess of the money grubbing debutantes to watch the financial pages.

It made the future look ridiculously bleak, even for a bloke who had just banked a lot of money—especially for a bloke who just banked a lot of money. Which was sad. He'd loved those innocent high school and college days when he'd happily dated lots of girls. Then, he had thoroughly enjoyed being with girls. And he'd always hoped to someday marry one and have a family and the whole package.

Now, he wondered if that would ever happen. It seemed backwards, but having a lot of money seemed to make that idea of finding a decent girl nearly impossible. He took a deep breath and pulled at his tie again as he walked down the hall next to the attractive attorney.

At the door out of the building, he opened it for her and finally answered her earlier question, "I'm not really sure what my plans are right now. I'll see you around." He wouldn't, but he was fairly certain that she already knew that. Toying with women had never been his style anyway.

After driving around in the rain, he finally went to check on his parents. His dad's recent hip replacement surgery had made him realize that his parents weren't thirty anymore.

Letting himself in their back door, he called out, "Hello."

From somewhere in the interior of the house, he heard his mother call back, "In here, Ri."

He went in search of them and found his mother helping his dad out of a chair in the TV room where his dad said, "This woman is pestering me again, son. She won't leave me be and keeps making me get up and move."

Riordan shook his head and grinned at his mother. "You poor man. She's a brute. You should escape with me soon and go fishing."

He walked beside them through the hallway toward the kitchen as his mother said, "We're just going to have some lunch. Can you join us? It's nothing fancy. Just some chicken thing."

"Your chicken things are always to die for. I'd love some lunch."

Once his dad was seated, his mother pulled a glass dish out of the oven and set it on a trivet on the table as Riordan began putting plates and glasses out as well. When the table was set, his father asked, "Ri, would you say grace?"

After the prayer, his mother began to pass the food and casually, his mother said, "So, Kyra Bevan was just here looking for you."

Shaking his head, Riordan tried to keep the disgust out of his voice as he said, "Really? That's strange. Why would she be looking for me?"

His mother met his eyes and said, "Maybe because she'd read about the sale of your company."

Riordan made a sound of disgust and his mother laughed and said, "Do I take it that you aren't interested in Kyra Bevan, honey?"

"Not even remotely."

"Oh, good. I mean . . . Oh, that sounded so unkind. I'm sorry. It's just that so many girls, or women, these days seem to think tattoos and piercings are attractive. I don't know what the world is coming to. If my mother had seen me walking around with a trailer hitch in my lip and twenty-seven bra straps hanging outside my clothes, she'd have fainted away right then and there."

Riordan laughed, "Grandma Lily never fainted away over anything in her life, Mum, and you and I both know it."

"Well, that's true, but she never failed to remind me that nice girls wear slips and are modest, even if the current fashion says they need a nasty tat."

At that, his dad chuckled and Riordan totally cracked up and asked, "Grandma Lily did not say that about the nasty tat. No way. Now, how in the world do you know what a nasty tat is, Mum?"

She gave a sigh as she sat in her own chair. "Oh, Zoe is pestering Ashleigh to get one. She says all of her friends have them and it won't show anyway below her waistline. Which makes no sense. Why even get something that doesn't show? Anyway, apparently Warren nearly had a meltdown at the idea, and I can't blame him. I wish they could move home again. Hong Kong is just too cosmopolitan. Those kids are going to grow up with no moral foundation. They'd be so much better off here in Australia, although, I hate to admit it, but even Queensland is too worldly sometimes."

Riordan frowned. "Zoe is twelve. She's like a tween still. And she's talking about getting a tattoo? How does she even know what a tattoo is?"

At that, his mother rolled her eyes. "Don't be silly, Riordan. Kids grow up fast these days. It's a pity that they can't enjoy much childhood. But it's the way the world is."

"Mum, they'll be fine. Ashleigh is a good mother, and Warren is as grounded as they come. Someday they'll be able to move back."

"I hope so. I miss them. What's the point of having grandkids, if you can't be with them occasionally? Huh?"

His dad across the table said, "Here it comes, Riordan."

Grinning, Riordan replied, "I know, Dad."

Smiling, his mother said primly, "No. I'm not going to say a thing, Riordan. If you want to deprive your parents of the joy of more grandchildren, then you go right ahead. It's probably our fault for being such poor examples of a loving, happy family. I'm certain you're much happier up in your big, quiet house, all alone, and lonely, anyway."

Picking up his water glass, Riordan raised it to her. "Touché, Mum. You win. There's just that slight problem of finding a mother for my children, what with the girls these days pierced and with straps and all, and sporting those nasty, nasty tats. What's a bloke to do?"

His dad raised a hand and gave him a silent fist bump, while his mother swatted at them both and said, "Actually, that is an issue. And I truly sympathize with you about the dating world these days. Online profiles, and twits, and Snap chats. It might as well be called snapcheats for all the honesty involved. I don't envy you, Riordan, but I still wish you'd get with the program a bit more. You're a marvelous catch, you know. Handsome and sweet and hardworking."

"I think you meant tweets, not twits, Mum. Although most of those tweeting probably are twits, from the caliber of what they are tweeting."

His dad added, "You forgot that he's rich now, Caroline, to add to the husbandly attributes."

Nodding, his mother said, "Yes, but that actually concerns me. There are a lot of girls like Kyra out there. And Riordan is well aware of that. And while it's good to be cautious, Riordan has graduated to full blown cynical. I'm not so sure that is good."

Riordan waved his fork. "This chicken is fabulous, Mum. What's in it?"

His mother only gave him a patient smile and said, "Nothing you'd have the slightest knowledge of, Riordan. Would you like some dessert? I made custard."

He got up and began taking his dishes to the sink and said, "Dessert would be wonderful. And I'll clean up while you wrestle Dad. How did your new gardeners do?"

"They were excellent. But Riordan, you don't need to keep hiring people to help us. I can mow the lawn just fine while your father is laid up."

Riordan came around the table and hugged her. "Let me do things for you, Mum. Just like you've always done things for me. It's the least I can do."

She grinned, "No. The least you could do would be to find a wonderful girl and get married. I need some grandbabies who live on the same continent, you know."

"Really? How come you've never mentioned that to me before?"

His dad chuckled again and he shook his head and laughed as he cleared the table. His mother was probably never going to change. He hoped she didn't. His parents were the greatest people on earth.

That evening at his house, he poured himself a bowl of cold cereal, wishing he could hire his mom to cook for him occasionally. She was a marvelous cook. And a marvelous mum. What would be really cool was if he could find a girl like his mother. Or if he could truly pick and choose, a girl as nice as his mother, but in a black leather mini skirt.

Sadly, there were no girls like his mum and she would never have been caught dead in a black leather mini anyway—that's probably why she *was* so nice. He texted his mother and told her that he loved her, then changed clothes and went into his home gym to work out on the universal with the TV going in the background, hoping it would bring on some of the endorphins that he was seriously in need of right now. Maybe that was the key to being, if not happy, at least not unhappy. Maybe all the struggle and fuss, the money, the prestige was pointless. Maybe decent food and exercise were the secret.

After forty minutes, he was sweating, but not much more enthusiastic. He stepped off the machine, sighed and clicked the remote. He was already bored.

He got out his cell phone to call his assistant Rich and ask him to hire him a cook, then decided to call Elder Benjamin in America about showing up early instead. He and Quinn hadn't been planning to leave for a few more days, but if their trainer could get away there wasn't anything else to stop him. Maybe while he was in America he'd try racing cars. He'd heard there was a track in Arizona, and he'd wager that going a couple hundred kilometers an hour could fix boredom.

Chapter 2

Dr. Jessie Benn DVM, leaned down to adjust the lead plate behind the X-ray machine, sensed that the dappled gray racehorse beside her was going to move and she pushed away. She jumped back just in time to keep from getting kicked by both hind feet. One of the horse's aluminum racing shoes caught the lead plate and sent it flying across the room where it crashed against the solid cinderblock wall with enough force to clang like a cymbal. The spooky gray took that as a cue to rear violently back against the cross ties tethering its head and strike at the air with a front hoof. Its ringing neigh jarred with the sound of the lead plate and the horse's owner worriedly looked at her.

Standing safely back from the tied horse, Jessie wiped at her face with the back of the sleeve of her lab coat and glanced at the thermostat. It was eighty seven degrees in here, even with the air conditioning running on high. Such was high summer in Mesa, Arizona. At least she was in here where it was climate controlled. It was probably a hundred and fifteen outside the clinic at this time of the afternoon. Making farm calls at this time of the year was murder. She tried to do all of that kind of thing early in the morning if possible.

Giving the horse owner a reassuring smile, she said, "Well, Mr. Robson. It looks like Dapple here is going to have to be sedated." She drew several CCs of a mild sedative from a vial and glanced at her beefy assistant, Cal, who gave her a small nod and moved toward the horse's head. He rubbed the side of the horse's face and spoke quietly to it and she moved to its neck to quickly find the jugular and inject the drug. She almost got it all administered before the horse began to fuss. Cal swore under his breath and tried to literally hold the horse's head still by sheer force. Even for someone as big and heavy as Cal, hanging on to a nervous full sized horse was wishful thinking and it got dicey for just a few seconds until the horse miraculously mellowed out from the drug.

Almost instantly the horse put its head down and let out a big blustery breath and Jessie smiled and said, "Thank the Lord for modern medical research." She went across and picked up the metal plate and shot the X-ray. Standing back upright, she said, "This will take a few minutes, Mr. Robson, if you want to step into the waiting room." He seemed to release a deep breath of his own as she went into the next patient room and Cal went to process the digital image.

Ten minutes later, she was all smiles as she called Mr. Robson to come look at the films displayed on the screen and said, "Good news. It's not a broken seismoid bone like we feared. Just a tiny chip floating in there. We can take that out and with some proper medication to keep the swelling down and let

Jaclyn M. Hawkes

the damaged periosteum heal, he should become sound right away. We can't do it today because he was fed this morning, but bring him back on Thursday and he'll be in and out in less than a day."

As the relieved horse owner took his now much more well-mannered racehorse back to his trailer, Jessie pushed her hair off her forehead and rolled her shoulders. She really hadn't anticipated that her veterinary practice would blossom like it had as quickly as it had. In only eighteen months, she had all the clientele she could handle and then some, and more phoning every single day. She had been right when she'd figured a clinic would do well here attached to the Mesa Equine Facility. With the racetrack to the south, the arena facility to the east and her father and brothers' ranch sprawling out behind, she had what had proven to be a sweet set-up here.

Now if she just had a bit more spare time. Her life had become crazy busy and who knew what would happen next week with the National Stock Show opening. It was one of the largest reining shows in the world and life had the potential of getting even more insane.

She shook her head. She shouldn't be thinking that having a burgeoning practice was a negative, even if she had honestly expected to be long married and wrestling babies instead of horses by now. The successful practice was a blessing. Now she just needed to keep it well managed.

She looked at her next afternoon's schedule and squared her shoulders. She'd already advertised to hire another vet to take over some of her clients, and had three applicants flying into town next week to interview. It was going to take some time to train someone and bring them up to speed, but it would be great to lighten some of her workload. Especially if she ever did find her Mr. Right and got to have more of a personal life. Stretching her shoulders, she grabbed a cold water bottle from the fridge and went in to see her last patient of the day. Then she needed to get home, check on Pablo, and later Clay was coming to take her to a chamber concert at the Civic Center.

At home, she pulled her call truck into the usual spot beside her cottage, but went into her dad's house instead of hers to check on Pablo. When she walked in, the sight of his little dark head leaned over his homework at the kitchen table with a plate of cookies and a glass of milk parked beside him warmed her heart. This adorable son of one of her dad's hands was definitely doing better with a little extra attention from her dad's housekeeper, Polly.

"Hey, you." Jessie ruffled Pablo's hair as she went to the cupboard to get her own glass. "How's your mother today? Are you going to hog all those cookies, or can I have one?"

Pablo grinned and then sobered. "She is good. My mother. You can have all the cookies."

Meeting his eye, Jessie asked, "Honest? Your mother is good?"

He shook his head. "No. Today is a bad day."

Quietly, Jessie asked, "Where is Marcela?"

"Hermana Pasilla has her."

Nodding, Jessie said, "Good. She'll take care of her until your dad gets home." She ruffled his black hair again."Don't

Jaclyn M. Hawkes

worry. Your mom will figure it out. Things will turn out okay." She thought of her own mother for a second and then firmly pushed that thought from her mind. So sometimes troubled mothers never did figure it out, but she wasn't going to tell a sweet little boy that. Instead, she asked, "What are you studying?"

He almost sighed his answer, "Math."

Smiling, Jessie teased, "Oh, your favorite!"

Pablo shook his head gloomily. "No. Es not my favorite. But I am almost done. Then I'm going to draw a yellow bird for my teacher and go swimming."

His face perked up at the swimming part and Jessie laughed and ruffled his hair again. "You don't enjoy math, but it's important. Keep at it. You're a good boy, Pablo. And a smart one. Someday that math will help you to become a great scientist, or a doctor, or whatever you choose to be."

Polly came in the kitchen door. "That's what I keep telling him, but he says he wants to be a race car driver and that race car drivers don't need to do math."

Jessie gave Polly a one armed hug as she looked at Pablo and raised her eyebrows. "What about to be able to figure out all those millions of dollars you'll be making? Huh? See? Even race car drivers need math."

Pablo grinned at her. "Both of you against me. Ai yai yai. A boy has no chance here."

Jessie laughed again. "Nope. Not a chance. Where's Mr. Benjamin? Have you seen him?"

"He and Mr. Josh go to town to get feed and pick up some horses at the airport. He said he'd be back this evening."

"Oh, that's right. Josh's friend from his mission was coming in from Australia today. I almost forgot." She snagged a cookie and took a bite, then headed for the door and said, "The cookies are great, Polly. Thanks for watching over my little buddy here. Tell Dad I said hello. And I'm off to a concert."

"With Ryan?"

"No, tonight it's Clay."

Polly made a hrump sound and Jessie laughed again. "You fuss too much, Polly. Clay is a perfectly nice man."

"He's a lawyer."

Jessie shook her head and chuckled. "G'night, Polly. Tell Ralph I said hi. Enjoy that math, Pablo. Hug up Marcela for me." Jessie went out the door grinning. As if saying he was a lawyer said it all. And who knew, maybe it did. Clay was definitely a stuffed shirt, but at twenty seven, Jessie was in looking-for-Mr.-Right-mode big time and had made a deal with herself that she would at least consider any decent guys who asked her out, or who she wanted to ask out. And that included lawyers, even if Polly disapproved.

At her house, she gratefully slipped into a shower, lathered with melon scented body moisturizer and basked in the fragrant steam. It was heavenly to wash away the day's stress and feel halfway feminine again. She loved horses and she loved being a veterinarian, but it could be dangerous and draining for a huge man, let alone a slender woman.

Stepping out, she wrapped in a towel and without even dressing got a glass of grapefruit juice and went out the French door from her bedroom to her secluded patio oasis. Literally sighing with pleasure, she sat on her hammock and closed her eyes. Ah, all she needed was a recharging moment. Maybe a long one. Evening was just starting to fall and she could smell that subtle change that happened at dusk. She didn't even know what it was, but somehow the creek and her flowers smelled better in the evening.

In the waning light under the cottonwoods the water burbled and chuckled over the stones. It cooled the air and she could hear the birds and see the butterflies. Occasionally a bee from her dad's hives down the creek droned by, but even that sound was restful to her. She idly pushed off with a foot to move the hammock, wishing she hadn't accepted a date after all. She was tired. And it was incredibly nice to sit here and soak in the peace of the desert evening.

As the tiny twinkling lights she'd woven into the vines near the door started to come on with darkness, she eventually peeled herself out of the hammock. She went in, dried and styled her hair and got dressed. Opting for simply eye shadow and mascara, she was ready when Clay arrived.

He helped her into his Lexus with just a touch too much flourish, but she chose to ignore it. How was he to know that expensive cars meant nothing to her? But, she was definitely one who could enjoy chamber music even if her date turned out to be a dud. She turned to glance at Clay. Okay, so maybe dud was too harsh a word. Other than suing people for his life's work, he really was a perfectly nice man, just like she'd told Polly. Maybe, in time, some attraction would come. It could happen.

Chapter 3

It had been an insanely long flight, followed by a seemingly grueling few hours of loading horses and gear and a long drive across a sweltering huge city. Then it was topped off by finding his prize horse limping as they unloaded at the facility where it would be stalled for the U.S.A. National Stock Show. Riordan felt like limping right along with it as he watched his trainer trying to get his horse unloaded and stabled.

For a champion horse and trainer, the two of them didn't seem to work at all well together today—something he hadn't really noticed before. But what did he know? He could ride reasonably decently, but if he had tried to ride one of these reining horses, he'd have gotten dumped off in seconds. As animal athletes, they were incredible.

But that limping wasn't a good thing at all. At least Josh Benjamin assured him that they had a top notch veterinarian on call who would stop by in the morning.

When Riordan was shown into the guest suite in Josh's house and met his wife, with a toddler hanging onto her leg, and

Jaclyn M. Hawkes

carrying a baby with one sloppy finger in its mouth, he almost backed out and opted to check into the hotel with Quinn and the trainer. The wife and those two children were entirely more than he was up to dealing with just now. He only didn't go to the hotel because he didn't want to offend Josh and the house truly would be more convenient as Josh's ranch bordered the arena facility.

For once, he almost wished he was a drinker. Maybe that would have helped with the jetlag. But Josh didn't drink and he knew it. He didn't do a lot of things that the world typically did. It was actually refreshing.

Sometimes it was weird, but if he were honest, that was the main reason he'd chosen to accept Josh's invitation to come to America to this horse show. He would never have admitted it to Josh out loud, but there had always been something so reassuring and comfortable about Josh Benjamin. It was like he had this bubble of a comfort zone that he carried around with him. It was the most soothing feeling Riordan had ever known and heaven knew he could use some soothing right about now.

He knew he shouldn't go to bed this early, but the jetlag was thrashing him and he went anyway. He had a few days to settle in before the real competition started at any rate. At least here in America with these horse shows he had something to keep himself occupied.

****

Jessie had only just started her slew of morning appointments when Josh called to tell her they needed her to come see to a chestnut stallion in their barn A3 at the arena. She didn't think much about it except to consider that typically the horses in Josh's barn were the ones in training right then and were usually his most valuable.

After shuffling her schedule, she pulled in, parked her call truck and glanced around for Josh. He was usually there to help her with his horses, but not always. Occasionally he'd be unable to get away from something elsewhere and had one of his help handle it. She didn't see him anywhere. In fact, she didn't even see any of his hands. Oh, no, there was Pete.

But he was standing by watching two men working with a chestnut horse cross tied in the front of the alleyway. One of the men was taller, with crisp dark hair and tanned skin. The other was heavier and was wearing an unusual brown brimmed hat. As Jessie got out of her truck and went to gather up her equipment, someone near the horse shouted. She looked up just in time to see the horse rear against its tethers and then kick backwards with a hind foot. In response, the shorter, heavier man reached up to grab the nervous horse by the ear and twist it viciously. At the same time, he booted the horse soundly under the belly. The other man took a step back and looked at the one who had just kicked the horse and said, "Easy, Harper. Take it easy, man."

Jessie frowned. She hoped that wasn't the horse she was supposed to be treating. She hated it when some trainer tried to rough up a horse just before she got the opportunity to deal with it. It typically didn't go terribly smoothly. The man yelled again and twisted harder on the horse's ear and the horse responded by trying to turn its head and bite at him. Shaking her head, she thought, *Stupid man. Did he really not have a clue that a horse's ear was relatively fragile and intensely sensitive?* Treatment like that could easily deafen a horse in that ear permanently, and it certainly wouldn't ever want to have its ears handled again.

Walking closer, Jessie felt the nerves in her stomach tighten. She hated situations like this when her gut reaction was to rip into the guy and tell him to leave the horse alone. It wasn't typically something that endeared her to a loud obnoxious trainer. In fact, just the opposite—they typically wanted to turn all that aggression on her instead. She let out a deep breath and breathed a quick, silent prayer. No, this probably wasn't going to be pretty.

When the horse tried to bite the guy, he cursed it bitterly and then picked up a nearby buggy whip and snapped it wickedly at the horse's face. Jessie was horrified. He wasn't just going to make the horse deaf, he was going to take out its eyes as well. This man was crazy!

The stallion began to plunge and rear in full blown panic and the man only got angrier as his companion moved back to get out of the way of the lunging horse. The shorter man began to whip the horse in an all out fury. The man beside him stepped back further with the same concerned shock on his face that Jessie was feeling and shouted, "Harper! Enough!"

Pete was looking from one to the other of them and when he saw Jessie, he shook his head and shrugged to signal that he had no idea how to handle this guy. Jessie knew. She didn't really want to do it, but she knew what she had to do. And she didn't have any choice. Striding near, she all but shouted, "Stop! Stop whipping that horse! Stop it now!"

The man only glared at her, swore and snarled, "Back off, Sheila." He whipped the horse again brutally and said over his shoulder to Jessie, "Mind your place. This doesn't concern you."

The man whipped the stallion again. It lunged and one of the leads tethering it to the crosstie broke. It reared and turned on the man to strike at him. Now the horse could move around somewhat and faced the man holding the whip. The man only got madder, gripped the flailing partial lead and continued to whip. In complete panic, the horse reared back again and this time snapped the buckle that clipped it to the crosstie. At this point, the only thing containing the horse was the broken lead from its halter that the man held in his hand, but he still continued to abuse the stallion.

Jessie glanced around, stepped into Josh's nearby tack room and picked up another buggy whip. Striding back out, she snapped the whip just as brutally as the other man had, only she aimed it at the man's hat brim instead of the horse. It lashed at the hat, tearing through the fabric of the brim and sending it flying and she again commanded, "I said, stop whipping that horse!"

The man turned on her with white hot fury in his eyes and raised his own whip at which the horse jerked out of his hand. It ran down the alleyway in the other direction as the man moved toward Jessie. His companion turned to follow the horse and bit out, "Harper, knock it off!"

Fear tried to make her back away, but Jessie forced herself to hold her ground as the man bearing the whip advanced toward her cursing and then snarled, "You whipped me! Who do you think you are? And speaking to me like that?"

Jaclyn M. Hawkes

Even in his seething anger she could hear his Australian accent and as he raised his whip again as if to strike her, she said in a deceptively calm tone, "Stop abusing that horse or you can miss your flight back to the land down under while you're sitting in an American jail awaiting trial for animal cruelty."

The man called Harper narrowed his eyes and ground out, "Are you threatening me? Animal cruelty? Don't be absurd! Do you have any idea who I am? Or who that horse is? I said, nose out!"

He was still advancing menacingly toward her. The other man glanced back over his shoulder at him. He frowned when he realized his angry companion was still moving toward her, turned from trying to catch the loose horse and strode back to the man. He grabbed the aggressive man's arm to pull him back, saying something Jessie couldn't hear.

She kept the whip in her right hand and dug her phone out with her left and speed dialed her dad as she said to the man still glaring at her, "I don't give a rip who you are, quit whipping the horse!" As her dad picked up, she said, "Dad, could you send security to barn A3 immediately? Please."

In spite of his companion trying to calm him, Harper's eyes narrowed even more threateningly and she added. "Armed security. Right now." She ended the call and glanced to where the horse had run and was still wheeling and bucking in the alleyway and then looked back at the advancing Harper.

He pushed at the other man and took another step and Pete came to Jessie's side as the taller, darker man said stridently with a strong Australian accent, "Harper, back off! Leave her alone and catch the bloomin' horse! What are you thinking'? Back off!"
30

Glaring back at the other man now, the whip bearing man ground out through gritted teeth. "I'm thinkin' that no mindless Sheila is going to whip me! Or accuse me of abusin' a horse! Me, of all people. No woman whips me!" He turned back toward Jessie, took another slow step and growled, "Abuse! I know more about horses than you could learn in a lifetime!"

He spat out an expletive and raised the whip again, but the other man stepped forward to strip it from his hand, throw it aside and say with his accent, "Harper! She whipped your hat. Buy another. Get hold of yourself before you do get arrested! I said *leave her alone!*"

Turning back on the taller man, the one who'd been threatening her spat, "You don't order me around, Kane! I'm the trainer here! You're not calling the shots! And I'm not taking that from a woman!"

The one called Kane shook his head and very calmly and deliberately said, "Yes, I do call the shots, Harper. And yes, you are going to take that from a woman. She's right. Go take a walk and cool off. Now!"

A security guard in a Razor came speeding out of the end of a barn down the way and Harper swore again under his breath. Picking up his torn hat, he spun to walk in the opposite direction as Jessie took a huge breath of relief. Man, she hated confrontation.

The man he'd called Kane watched him go, then glanced at Jessie as if to ask if she was okay. She nodded after the horse and he shook his head and walked toward it. Turning to Pete, she swallowed and said, "Pete, can you get me a bucket of oats and a lead rope? Let's catch the horse. Thanks." He nodded and turned away. Her phone buzzed in her pocket and she literally had to will the shakes away as she pulled it out and answered, "This is Dr. Benn."

****

Heading to catch the horse, Riordan pulled up short when he heard the lethally beautiful blonde woman who'd just literally whipped his trainer answer her phone as Dr. Benn. No way! He turned around and tried not to stare. Slender, with long straight blonde hair bleached by the sun, tanned skin and strikingly blue eyes, she could have been a model. Surely this wasn't the veterinarian that Josh had so confidently recommended. She was way too young and far too attractive to be an experienced veterinarian.

Then he thought back to the way she had just fearlessly handled his out-of-control trainer without flinching. Scratch that, maybe she could be that good of a veterinarian. She'd certainly known how to handle that whip. He looked at her again. Upon closer observation, she wasn't as fearless as he'd first thought. Her hand shook as she held the phone and he could hear just a touch of little girl in her voice as she spoke to someone who must have been her father on the phone. She'd been scared, but she'd whipped Harper anyway. The idea actually intrigued him. Wow, intrigue was an emotion he'd thought he was immune to lately. It felt wonderful. Maybe this trip to America was going to help him finally perk up emotionally.

Josh came flying around the corner of a nearby barn and pulled up short. He was followed closely by a uniformed policeman and Riordan glanced toward where Harper had disappeared behind a different set of stalls and let out a breath. What the heck was going on with Harper? He'd never seen him act this way. Or the horse either, for that matter. Must be the jet lag. They'd both gone nuts.

Looking down at his clothes, Riordan brushed at where the horse had hit him when it was throwing its head. This little episode couldn't have helped the horse's lameness. He turned to go help Josh's hired man catch his horse, wondering how Josh had known there was a problem and hoping the beautiful vet would still be willing to treat the horse.

Well, he'd been hoping for excitement.

His horse was still in the alleyway. It had been stopped from running all the way through the barn and probably into the next territory by some men working over another horse at the far end of the building. It was still rearing and crow hopping nervously in the alleyway between. The limp was more pronounced, even in its fool antics, and as Riordan approached, he could see heavy welts on its head and haunches from the whip. Blood ran from a couple of places on its face.

Great. He had a supposedly champion trainer who blew a complete gasket and whipped a champion horse worth a mint and then threatened a woman. That had to be impressive to the veterinarian. And to the policeman and security guard who were just now conversing with her.

As he neared the horse, it raised its head threateningly, pinned its ears back and then spun and tried to kick at him and he backed off. What? Were they going to have to get a tranquilizer gun in here to catch the poor beast? This horse was typically a little spirited, but nothing like this.

Hearing steps behind him, he turned to see Josh's hired man and Dr. Benn approaching. She carried a red plastic bucket and a lead rope and as they walked up to him, he heard her say, "If he can't catch him, let me have a go at him first, Pete and see what happens. Just don't let him get out of the alleyway. The last thing we need is a loose stud in the complex. It's a thousand dollar fine." She slowed and began speaking in a low, calm voice as they approached the horse side by side.

At first, it raised its head again, but then, as she slowly put out a hand and continued the soothing speaking, the horse swiveled its ears forward and put its head down into a more relaxed position. She gently shook the bucket of grain and said, "That's the way now. Easy. Come on, boy. Nothing to fear. Come have a taste of these oatsies now."

Handing Riordan the lead, she gave the bucket another shake and Riordan wasn't even surprised to see the big chestnut take a tentative step forward and push its muzzle into the bucket. To be sure, it snatched a bite and then wheeled away down the alley again, but then it came right back and he simply reached up and clipped the lead onto its halter under its chin and then unclipped the portion of the other lead it had broken.

Slowly, the veterinarian reached up a hand to rub the horse on the face above its nose and continued speaking quietly. "Easy, buddy. There you go. Have a bite of oatsies now and settle down and let's take a look at what that big, stupid oaf did to you, huh? There's a good boy. Easy. Take a big deep breath now. Easy." Still moving slowly, she turned to Riordan and said, "Okay, now then, let's get out of this barn, shall we?" Beside Riordan, she slowly began to walk, still holding the bucket and said, "Let's just give him all the room in the alleyway and let him settle down."

Riordan nodded silently and walked beside her out of the barn leading the stallion. It was no wonder Josh Benjamin had hailed her as a good vet. She definitely had a way with horses. As they exited, he saw the policeman waiting to the side near Josh and wondered how this was all going to go down. There was no sign of Harper. The security guard was gone, but the blood and welts on the horse couldn't bode well for his trainer.

Riordan had to wonder just how much he would be included in any criminal charges. He hadn't done anything. In fact, he hadn't dreamed Harper would come unglued like that, but he had still been there, and in his shock at Harper's sudden violence, hadn't stepped in as abruptly as he should have. Moreover, he was the one who had hired Harper, although, in all honestly, had he known he could treat an animal that way, he wouldn't have.

Dr. Benn walked several meters away from the barn and then turned to ask, "This *is* the stallion Josh Benjamin called me about this morning, isn't it?"

Riordan nodded, "It is. He limped off the plane last night. Sorry for the insanity."

"Yes, me too. Will a couple extra quarts of oats hurt him? Or can I just let him eat and settle down for now?"

Jaclyn M. Hawkes

Riordan shook his head, "I've no idea what his eating regimen is to be. Harper was handling all that. I know he had the vet give him some kind of medicine before putting him on the plane yesterday, but I don't know what his plan was since then." He nodded at the eating horse."I tend to think from the way he's romping into the oats that he hasn't been fed recently."

She frowned, took a stethoscope from a pocket in what he now realized was a lab coat and slowly put it on the horse's ribs and was still for a moment. Finally, she put it back in the pocket and asked, "What did he give him for the flight? Was he sweating like this when you got to him this morning?"

Riordan turned to look more closely at the horse, considered that and nodded, "Yes, I believe he was. Seemed unduly nervous from the start. He's not usually this wild at all. But I have no idea what he gave him."

"Can you call Harper and ask him what they gave him? And if two extra pounds of oats will hurt him? I'm sure you're aware that horses have incredibly sensitive gastrointestinal tracts. I don't want to founder him."

Thinking about how Harper had just acted, Riordan doubted he would take a call, but he said, "I can try."

Harper didn't answer and Riordan shook his head and put his phone away. Dr. Benn nodded as if she had expected as much. She petted the munching horse again and turned to walk closer to a white truck with a custom modified bed. She slowly let down the tailgate, opened a compartment and pulled out a flat tray. She set it on the downed tailgate, opened it and put some kind of an instrument against the front of the horse's brisket. Several seconds later, she held it up to her face and looked at it, then turned back to Riordan and said, "Look. I know this didn't start out well. But right off, I'd say your horse is having a reaction to whatever your trainer gave it. Some sedatives cause anxiety when they wear off. Am I okay to start treating him? Your trainer isn't going to come roaring back and threaten me with a lawsuit or something, is he?"

"No. He would have no legal grounds. It's my horse. I don't handle the training." He shook his head. "At least I haven't been, but I can make any decisions. Josh Benjamin seems to trust you. That's good enough for me. You're the medical professional. Treat away."

"Even if I'm going to press charges against your trainer for cruelty to animals?"

Riordan took a deep breath as he considered what he should do here. At least she was being up front about it. Finally, he shook his head and said, "That would be my ex-trainer. I can't in good faith trust him to train for me anymore anyway. You're right. His behavior was cruel and frankly shocking. I've never seen him behave that way. Especially not with an animal this valuable. I'm sure that sounds completely mercenary, but . . . What shall I do to help you?"

Petting the horse's face one more time, she said, "Nothing. In fact, other than giving him something to help with the reaction to whatever he was given earlier, I'm just going to let him eat for a moment while I give my statement to the police. He's waiting. I'm sorry to upset the applecart on your first day here, but I have no choice but to report what happened. It would

Jaclyn M. Hawkes

be breaking the oath I took as a veterinarian not to. Please forgive me." Turning to the horse, she smoothly gave it a small injection in the neck that it didn't even seem to notice and then she gave Riordan a sad half smile and said, "Welcome to America."

He watched her walk over to where the policeman was standing next to Josh and his hand, then was floored when Josh came close to her and wrapped his arms around the vet in a surprisingly intimate hug. Riordan frowned as they held each other for a long moment, appearing to be speaking and then she nodded her head and casually pushed Josh away to turn to the policeman. Riordan frowned even more deeply. Would Josh really be fooling around on his wife? And wouldn't he at least try to hide it? Riordan shook his head, trying to figure it out. He would never have pegged Josh for a player. Something was definitely strange there.

It took her about fifteen minutes to finish with the policeman, who then handed her some paperwork, took photos of the horse and walked away with Pete. She came back over to Riordan's horse with Josh following her. Josh seemed to fall effortlessly into the role of veterinary assistant and Riordan simply watched the two of them work together like they'd done it all their lives, still trying to figure out what was going on.

Her diagnosis of a simple strain to his horse's pastern was at least somewhat comforting after the tumultuous morning. In theory, with rest, the horse could be ready to compete in a few days. At least its foot would be. When she'd finished with the horse's leg, she turned next to its still bleeding face and the

38

frown that creased her brow was nearly as disconcerting as her saying, "You know, he came within a centimeter of blinding your horse in this eye." She shook her head and made a sound of disgust with her lips and added under her breath. "What an idiot."

She gave the horse another shot that must have been a mild tranquilizer because it visibly relaxed and didn't seem to mind as she injected and then painstakingly sewed up a place on the corner of its left eye. She then stood on the overturned bucket to stitch another over its brow between its ears.

She was almost finished when Harper came sauntering back around the corner of the next barn. She glanced up to see him and then looked over at Josh who raised his head in a marginal nod. After that, she seemed to forget Harper existed as he stood back and glowered while he watched her work. When she took her last stitch, she disinfected both wound sites, smeared some kind of salve on top as well and then gently patted the sleepy horse's nose.

Stepping down from her bucket, she picked up a tablet and began to write on it with a stylus as she said, "You can put him back in his stall now, Mr. Kane. Rinse him off first to cool him down a bit and give him water and a minimal flake of whatever kind of hay he's used to. Not more than that for about another two hours and he's perked up. Then you can feed him his usual diet. Give him mild exercise on a lead or under saddle, but nothing strenuous. A trial of Bute, some liniment and massage will help as well, but be sure to stop the Bute at least forty-eight hours before he competes or he won't pass the blood tests. I'll print it all out for you. And sometime between now and the show, bring his health certificate into the clinic and I'll sign off on it. The stitches should come out in about a week." She finished writing, set the tablet down and asked, "Any questions?"

Riordan gave one short, humorless laugh, glanced at Josh and shook his head. "No. I think that will about do it."

"Perfect." She opened another compartment in her truck to pull a page out of a printer and hand it to him, then added, "Josh knows where to find me if he doesn't come around. Be nice to him. He's had a rough morning." She put out a small, calloused hand and shook his. "I'd say it was nice to meet you, but frankly, it was stressful, so I'd be lying. I'm sure you understand. I hope you have the rest of a nice day, mate."

Picking up one of the papers that the police officer had given her, she walked over to where Harper was still glaring at her and handed it to him and said, "I was asked to give this to you. It's American for you need to contact the police or they'll come looking for you. I'm pressing charges against you for animal cruelty."

He all but exploded, "You've got to be joking!"

Almost drily, she said, "Oh, yeah. Here in the states we think it's hilarious when people abuse animals. I can hardly control the chortles." With that, she walked around to the driver side of her truck and opened another compartment where she pulled out a frosty bottle of water, unscrewed the lid and downed half of it. Then she turned back to the three men who were watching her and asked, "Water anyone? Josh?"

He put out a hand and she deftly tossed him a bottle of water and looked at Riordan. He put out a hand as well and she tossed him one, too, then turned to Harper and raised her eyebrows. "Mr. Harper?"

He only swore at her. Mildly, she said, "Dehydration sneaks up on you. Watch yourself. Welcome to America."

She climbed into her truck and drove away and Harper began to swear again. He wadded up the paper she'd handed to him and tossed it. Then he swore again, picked it back up and put it in his pocket and stomped away.

Riordan didn't know whether to swear with him or laugh right out loud. After a second he glanced at Josh who only grinned, downed his water bottle and then repeated, "Welcome to America—Jessie Benn style. You wanna go grab some lunch?"

"If I go to lunch with you, will you train my horse? And Quinn's? He's going to be hot about this. I think our trainer is going to be arrested in the near future."

Josh grinned and shook his head. "Nope. You're both the competition. You like Italian?"

Chapter 4

Several times that day, Jessie caught herself in pause mode as she thought about her earlier meeting with Riordan Kane and his brutal trainer. Surprisingly, it wasn't the awful confrontation with the trainer that was so thought provoking. It was the insanely attractive horse owner who had her daydreaming. When Josh had spoken so often of his friend from Australia, she'd never dreamed that the friend was a complete hottie with the most beautiful deep blue eyes and dark slightly curly hair. And a dynamic combination of soft spoken, confident reining horse owner, with a sexy Aussie accent thrown in.

And seriously set on not joining the church. She kept reminding herself of that every time she caught herself thinking of him. After all, he was the guy Josh had worked with for nearly his whole mission, who hadn't joined. And she knew from experience that Josh could be a very persuasive guy when he wanted to be. He'd gotten someone as cool as Lucy to marry him, hadn't he?

She went through her appointments at the clinic half on auto pilot and then late in the afternoon when she was heading out, she stopped back into barn A3 to see how Riordan's horse had settled in. He was in his stall drowsing when she peeked in. He still sported some of the welts, but he had feed and water, so she assumed he'd begun to recuperate from his trip and whipping. As she climbed back into her truck, she wondered what had ever happened to the trainer, Harper. And his very attractive boss.

She shook her head and pulled out for home. *Don't go there Jessie. He isn't a member. He doesn't even qualify to open the eligible for husband tab, let alone see the drop down menu. Focus, girl.*

Tonight she was going to enjoy Caleb, an honorably returned missionary and sous chef from one of the restaurants in town whom she'd recently met through one of her girlfriends. She was trying to convince him that cooking wine was against the Word of Wisdom, but he wasn't really buying it. Technically, he was right, the alcohol did cook out, usually, and the Word of Wisdom didn't actually address that, but it was the spirit of the thing, wasn't it? Literally. And frankly, she didn't care for the taste of his wine cooked dishes. But how to tell a sous chef that?

At least he wasn't so caught up in what she liked to call the Portfolio Complex. He drove a comfortably broken in Ford Expedition that he used to pick up produce from the local herb farms where he went to find the freshest ingredients. And he plopped on a ball cap after work to deal with his messy chef's hat hair. Plus, tonight he was cooking *in* at her cottage, so she could relax while she searched for Mr. Right. That was always a plus as busy as her life had gotten lately.

She stopped at her dad's house again to see about Pablo and was glad she did when she saw the adorable seven year old juggling his nine month old little sister on his lap as he went over his vocabulary words at the kitchen table. Jessie came in, ruffled his hair and automatically took the little girl to hug her as she asked, "What are you up to today, Pab? And how is Marcela?"

The little girl gave her a smile as Pablo answered, "Just homework."

Marcela grabbed at Jessie's earring and Jessie carefully rescued it as she asked Pablo, "Are you all finished with your math? Or saving the best for last?"

He sadly shook his head. "Not finished. I still have ten problems, but it's too hard to do with Marcela. She grabs my pencil and I have to keep erasing."

Her dad came into the kitchen and Jessie said, "Well, how about if I take her for awhile for you, while I talk to my dad?"

Pablo nodded solemnly, looking as if the weight of the world was on his shoulders and Jessie patted his arm as she took the baby and followed her dad into his office off the front entry. As he shut the door, she asked, "Is Polly running errands?"

"She went to take Ralph to the ophthalmologist. He was getting his eyes dilated and couldn't drive himself home. Then she's going to the grocery store. Sister Pasilla couldn't keep Marcela today, so I volunteered to come in and wrestle her until Jorge finishes working those colts. She just keeps crawling in there to Pablo. It's kind of precious how much she likes him. Reminds me of how another little girl I knew worshipped her brothers. How did your day go? After the dueling whips this morning?"

Jessie rubbed Marcela's back and the baby laid her head against Jessie's shoulder and closed her eyes as Jessie answered, "My day was good. After that. Is Consuela doing any better?"

He shook his head. "No. Jorge is trying, but she keeps denying there's a problem. I think he's finally going to insist she go into an alcohol treatment program or he's going to kick her out, even though he loves her dearly. Which sounds tough, but I think it's what he should do. Not that it's any of my business."

Jessie nodded and kissed the baby's head. "It is tough. But sometimes tough love is what it takes. It's for her own good. And these guys'. They can't keep on like this. It's killing Pablo."

"He's been better since you talked him into coming here after school. But sometimes even tough love doesn't help when someone is truly messed up."

She gave him a sad smile. "I know, Dad. And Jorge will help his kids through whatever he has to. He'll simply do his best, just like we did when your wife blew. We're going to help him get through it, just like people helped us get through. Hopefully Consuela will handle this better than your wife did and will choose her family over her issue."

Her dad looked her in the eyes for a long moment and finally said, "You're going to have to forgive her someday, you know, Jess."

She turned for the door. "I forgave her years and years ago, Dad."

"Then why is she only 'my wife' still? And not Mom?"

Jessie shrugged. "Just habit. It's more comfortable. I can take these two to my house tonight if I need to. Caleb is cooking me dinner. I'm sure he wouldn't mind a couple more."

"Jess, you work in the same place your mother does, almost every single day. She's in that arena complex most days. How often do you speak to her? Or do something with her?"

Jessie turned back to him with confusion on her face. "You equate me not socializing with her as me not having forgiven her?"

"You could at least say hello when you pass in a barn. I saw you the other day at that Coke machine. You wouldn't even look at her."

"We have nothing in common, Dad."

"It's been twenty-one years, Jessie. Move on."

Jessie shook her head. "Dad, that's exactly what I've done. I don't hate her. I've forgiven her. But I don't typically hang out with people who do really heinous things like murder their babies. It's not that I have a beef with them. I just try to associate with people with more character. I wouldn't do things with a girlfriend if I knew she'd done something like that. That would be like hanging out with a serial killer. A tad awkward. Do you give the boys lectures like this occasionally?"

He raised his eyebrows. "Yeah. Occasionally. They can all at least say, 'Hi, Mom.'"

She shrugged. "Hmm. Well, they're obviously all more socially adept than me. I don't see you hanging out with her either."

"She divorced me, Jessie. That's a little different than a mother and daughter."

Jessie gave a completely humorless laugh and shook her head. "How in the world do you figure she didn't divorce us all? It's not like she asked you to move out of her house so she could have more quality time with her precious children. She wouldn't have done what she did if we were her burning passion. We can be honest here, Dad." She felt hot tears in her eyes and it made her mad that she couldn't not feel pain even after this long. She shook her head. "You know. I'd really rather not discuss this any further. Should I take Pablo and Marcela home with me?"

Her father looked at her and then wrapped his arms tenderly around her and Marcela and hugged her for a long moment before he pulled back and tried to smile and asked, "You really think Caleb wouldn't mind a couple of small people?"

"If he did, then I'd quit dating him. It would be an easy way to make sure he liked kids, wouldn't it?"

He nodded. "Yeah, it would. That's excellent logic, I have to admit. But unless you want the kids expressly for weeding out potentially poor husband material, they're fine here with me until Jorge shows up. You know I love children."

She wiped at her watery eyes. "Yes, Daddy. I do. I've never doubted you in my life and you've never let me down. Thank you."

Her father gave her a sad smile, "Well, there was the one time when I grounded you for changing into that mini skirt after you got to school and I made you miss the midnight showing of that vampire werewolf movie with the Hicken kid. I'm pretty sure I let you down that night. You were mad for days."

She finally laughed. "I wasn't happy with you. But I certainly knew you loved me. Keep the kids with you. If I actually decide there might be something to Caleb, I'll ask Jorge if I can borrow his children then."

"Good, because Caleb uses too much cooking wine in his food anyway. That's the last thing those two need right now. Have a good night, honey."

****

Fatigue hit Riordan like a brick wall at about three-thirty in the afternoon. Crikeys, he should never have gone to bed so early last night. He'd been going to go find himself a truck today, but there was no way. He'd just do it tomorrow.

He left Quinn at the arena complex and walked back down the lane to Josh's house, looking all around at the desert landscape. Australia had some great deserts, but the scenery here was amazing. There were some cactuses that were striking. Or was that cacti. He shook his head. He really needed to get some sleep. At least Quinn didn't blame him for the trouble with Harper.

He knocked on Josh's back door and then let himself in and was just about to call out to Lucy when she appeared with a finger to her lips and whispered, "Rylie and Bethy just finally went down for their naps. They've been fussing for hours." She paused to really look at him. "That might be a good thing, huh? Are you as tired as you look?"

He smiled at that and she back pedaled. "Sorry. I didn't mean it to come out like that. Uh. In case you might like a few moments of peace and quiet, now's your chance. Was that better?"

48

"Yes, actually. In fact, I'd love a nap. Would you be offended?"

She turned to go back into the kitchen and said over her shoulder, "Not at all. If they wake before you do, I'll try to keep them quiet."

"Thank you. I'd appreciate that."

Lying down in his guest suite, he picked up a magazine he'd purchased at the airport to finish reading an article he'd started about Matt Damon. The movie star had gotten involved with a project that was helping to supply clean water to parts of the world that didn't have any. Riordan was surprised at how much of the world still struggled with such a simple basic need. For some reason, he'd thought decent water was a given everywhere by now. It made him feel guilty that he hadn't even realized so many people were still dealing without something so vital.

Picking up his cell phone, he texted Rich, his assistant, to ask him to find out more about Damon's water project for him. Finally closing his eyes, he mused to himself that maybe that was what he could do with some of the money sitting in his accounts. Maybe he could sign on to some similar type of project. Pure clear water in underdeveloped parts of the world would certainly be a worthwhile way to invest. It was definitely something to think about.

When he woke up, the house was indeed completely silent. That surprised him, because Josh's children had been very energetic the times he'd been around them. He opened the

Jaclyn M. Hawkes

blinds in the guest room to see that the sun was almost down. That made him wonder where Josh's family was. He yawned and wandered into the kitchen and opened their fridge. He wasn't really hungry, but he seemed to be constantly thirsty here.

Pulling out a bottle of water, he stood in the coolness of the open fridge and thought back to how Dr. Benn had offered them all water earlier and grinned. She was definitely a pistol, that one was. Harper had been livid.

Man, she had looked hot drinking down that bottle. And it had had nothing to do with the temperature. The skin of her throat had looked like moist silk as she had swallowed. He shook his head. She had something going on with Josh. Something illicit. That negated any attractiveness. Or it should have.

What was up with them? And how in blimey was Josh still able to act like he was so in love with Lucy at home? For some reason, he'd never asked Josh about Dr. Benn this afternoon. Probably because he was in the process of trying to talk him into training his horse for him and was staying right in his home and hadn't wanted to alienate him. But it was so surprising for the guy who had spent two years literally preaching to people about the teachings of Jesus Christ and trying to talk Riordan into joining him.

Not that Riordan was seriously intrigued by Dr. Benn anyway. He was still too burnt out on women who all seemed to have an ulterior motive. At least he hoped he was wise enough to still be completely cynical where beautiful girls were

50

concerned. And Dr. Benn was definitely beautiful. Still, it would be nice to actually be intrigued and enthusiastic about someone occasionally and enjoy it.

A doorbell rang interrupting his thoughts and he shut the fridge and wandered in to the front entry. Opening the door, he was surprised to find Dr. Benn herself standing there on Josh's porch wearing a pink t-shirt and a pair of long wildly patterned shorts with her hair hanging loose down her back. She raised her eyebrows and grinned when she saw him and he glanced down at himself. He was only wearing a pair of pajama pants that were almost as wild as her shorts and he wondered for a second if his hair was wild too. Most likely.

Saying, "Hi, Riordan," Dr. Benn pushed past him to come into the house uninvited and he forgot about his hair in his shock that not only would she show up at Josh's house, but would invite herself in as well.

She headed for the kitchen, asking, "By any chance, do you know if Lucy has fresh Greek oregano?" Almost to herself, she mumbled, "Who am I kidding? No one has fresh Greek Oregano. Maybe just normal old dried, though."

He followed her without answering and almost laughed when he saw her walk to a cupboard and start unloading spice bottles out of it. She went through the entire two bottom shelves and then put it all back in. He finally did crack a smile when she kicked off her flip flops and climbed onto a chair to dig through the top shelf. She was unbelievable! Why didn't she just go to the store for her oregano instead of driving clear out here on a private lane to Josh and his wife's house and digging through their cupboards? She had some guts, by crikey.

Jaclyn M. Hawkes

"Bingo!" She apparently found what she had been digging for, righted the cupboard and hopped down. She slipped back into her flip flops and went toward the door, saying over her shoulder, "Tell Luce I'll bring it back in the morning. Thanks."

He only watched her go. When the door shut behind her, he said, "You're welcome." He ran a hand through his probably rumpled hair and shook his head and groaned. She would have to come by when he looked such a mess. Not that it mattered.

What in the world was going on here? Had he landed smack in the middle of some twisted Mormon love triangle? And why in the world was he still intrigued by a woman who seemed to be having an insanely blatant affair with his married friend? Geez, she looked good in shorts. Even strangely long ones.

****

Jessie heard Josh's door close behind her and took a deep breath. Holy my oh my! Had she just walked into a Soloflex commercial, or what! She took another deep breath and put a hand to her chest. Good heavens, even her heart was pounding! How ridiculously adolescent. But man, it was definitely warranted! Riordan Kane was positively sculpted! Not to mention, frankly adorable with rumpled hair and cartoon kangaroo jammies.

She giggled as she walked. Oh, he would be so offended if he knew she was thinking that. She had seen that in his eyes when he'd opened the door to see her there. Yeah, he'd definitely looked a little jet lagged. No wonder Josh and Luce had taken the kids and gone out. If she hadn't seen the light come on in the kitchen, she'd have gone back home after checking at McCade's and then at her dad's for the blasted oregano. But dang she was glad she had! The sight of him had definitely been worth her hiking all over the ranch in her flip flops.

Poor Caleb. He was going to seem sadly dull compared to the sexy Australian hunk of the year. Even if whatever he was making smelled marvelous. She paused and wondered if Riordan Kane could by any chance cook. Stepping up onto her own porch, she shook her head. *Not a member, Jessie. And not interested in becoming a member. Admire the pecs and leave it at that. He did have some phenomenal pecs.*

Chapter 5

The next day Riordan was helping Josh feed a row of two year olds he was starting to train. As they stood side by side, loading flakes of hay into hay bags, Riordan finally got up the wherewithal to ask, "So, what's up with you and Dr. Benn? She showed up at your house to borrow some kind of spice last night while you were gone."

Josh didn't even look up as he asked, "What do you mean, what's up?"

Riordan straightened and said calmly, "I'm not judging you, Benjamin. I'm just wondering. You seemed pretty chummy yesterday morning. And she certainly didn't appear to hesitate to come right to your house. But you have to admit that's kind of weird. I mean, what if Lucy had been home? Or does she know about this? Dr. Benn seems to be fully aware of her. You're not in some funky 'open' marriage or something?"

This time Josh definitely looked up, but he looked confused. "Open marriage? What are you . . . What do you mean, we looked chummy? And weird? And why wouldn't Lucy be aware of Jessie?"

Riordan shrugged and went back to what he was doing. "I guess I just don't understand American culture well enough yet. Sorry. But this doesn't really fit in with all those Mormon teachings from your mission. Or did I miss something about marriage back then?"

Josh didn't answer right away and when Riordan glanced his way, the confused look on his face had become even more pronounced. Finally, Josh asked, "What did I do to make you think I was too chummy with Dr. Benn yesterday?"

Leaning back down to the bale of hay he was working on, Riordan said, "Well, that was quite a hug. And it lasted a bit."

Josh gestured back and forth with his hand. "And you think Dr. Benn and I are . . ."He shook his head and laughed and stepped into the stall to hang the bag. "Jessie's my little sister, Kane. I hugged her because she was pretty shaken up about that shindig with your trainer. She and Lucy are the best of friends. She and I are the best of friends. I'm in love with my wife, Riordan. Madly. I'm most definitely not having an affair." He shook his head again and chuckled. "Open marriage."

Standing back up, Riordan was the one who was confused. "Your little sister?"

"Yup. 'Fraid so. My little sister. And let me tell you, it's been a project getting her raised and through vet school and all. A few heads had to roll when she was a teenager. She's an intrepid one, believe you me."

Riordan was shocked to his toes. "How could she be your sister? There wasn't a sister here when I came before."

"She was gone to Colorado to vet school."

Jaclyn M. Hawkes

"Well, she's short—you're tall. And she's blonde. And beautiful."

"Hey now."

"And has a different last name. Wait, is she married?"

At that, a sad look crossed Josh's face and he said, "No. She's never been married. She just shortened her name from Benjamin to Benn and added the extra n. She did it years and years ago. And women are typically shorter than their brothers. It's not like she's tiny. She's still probably five foot seven. And I'm not that unbeautiful, tall, dark, and handsome as I am."

"Oh, is that what you are?"

"Yes sirree." Josh laughed again. "You thought I was having an affair."

"Uh. Actually. Well, yes, actually I did. But I do get credit for being shocked. That should count for something. I couldn't for the life of me fit that idea in with your Mormon blarney, though."

Josh gave another laugh and shook his head, then laughed again, harder. After a minute, he put a hand on Riordan's shoulder and said, "Man, I'm so sorry. I thought you knew. I mean, Jessie. . . And everything. I've probably talked your ear off about her over the years."

"That must be what happened. I tuned you out. I'd like to just go on record as being thoroughly relieved. For a bit there, I thought Mr. Celestial had bitten the American dust."

Still chuckling, Josh said, "I'm no Mr. Celestial. Not by a long shot. But I do adore my wife and intend to be completely faithful. For my own self preservation. Lucy wouldn't just

56

divorce me. She'd torture and kill me. And Jessie would definitely help her. The two of them, now that's a deluxe combo." He was quiet for a minute, then grinned again and said, "Man, Riordan, you must have quite an opinion of me. You thought I could get a woman as fine as Lucy to marry me and have a fling with someone as excellent as Jessie, too. Dang, I must be epic!"

Blandly, Riordan repeated as he went back to work, "Yes. Epic. And full of wallaby euke. That's Australian for bull droppings."

"Are you saying I'm not epic?"

"Oh, no. Certainly not. You're the most epic fellow I know."

Josh shook his head. "Talk about your wallaby euke."

After a moment or two, Riordan casually asked, "So. Is this sister of yours involved with anyone? Who needed the oregano last night? She sounded like she thought it was strange to need oregano. Like she wasn't the one cooking."

Josh turned right to Riordan, folded his arms across his chest and said, "Oh no. No. No way. I love you dearly, man. But no way are you asking me that about my baby sister."

"She's a veterinarian. That's like eight years of university. Surely she's old enough that her stuffy big brother doesn't get to decide who knows if she's involved with someone."

Josh grinned, but he shook his head. "I slaved over you, Riordan Kane. I begged. I cajoled. I probably even tried to bribe you. I pounded the pavement. I wore the knees out of three suits praying like the Pope for you. Although, between you and me, I doubt the Pope really prayed for you. I mean, you are

Jaclyn M. Hawkes

Australian. I've been giving you my best shot for almost ten years, Kane. Ten. We were teenagers. I tried, man. But you weren't having any of it. So you can only thank yourself for the fact that you have no right to ask that question. And I am *not* stuffy."

"Australia is the greatest country in the world. And what do you mean I wasn't having any of it? I had some of it."

"Not enough of it."

"Oh, so you're saying that since I didn't join your church, you won't let me inquire about your short, blonde sister."

"You left out beautiful this time. And it's not me you have to worry about. You can inquire all you want. It ain't gonna happen. For twenty-seven years my dad's been drumming into her head that she's a princess in God's kingdom and not to even look at a male who isn't a prince with a temple recommend. Trust me, it's sunk in. She dates a lot. But not anyone who isn't headed for a temple marriage. She wants to be sealed to all of us in the eternities. Family is a big deal to her. But no baptism, no temple marriage. Sadly, you opted out. Not for the lack of being coerced in that direction. Plus, she's an LDS girl. An LDS girl was part of the reason you refused to join the church anyway. Remember?"

Riordan looked at him for a long moment, trying to process what he'd just told him. At length, he bent again to the next hay bag and said, "I don't remember any real coercion. Cajoling yes, to a degree. Begging maybe. But I certainly can't recall any bribes. How much are you willing to put up?"

****

They usually played soccer a couple of mornings most weeks, so it wasn't really anything new, until Jessie climbed into Josh's truck the next morning to find herself seated next to a very awake and more gorgeous than ever Riordan on the way to the field. Sitting this close, he even smelled good and his legs below his shorts were every bit as attractive as his pecs had been. Jessie suddenly wished she'd spent a little more time on her hair. Then, when they told her they were stopping at a nearby hotel to pick up the friend, Quinn, who was actually a pro soccer player, things got even more interesting.

At the hotel, Riordan's friend Quinn came walking across the hotel parking lot with his longish blonde hair styled just enough to look about half wild and with a huge diamond stud in one ear. He was handsome and tanned and obviously athletic and exuded attitude with his walk. When he got in and the first thing he did was give Jessie this world class flirty grin, the idea of a pick-up game took on a whole new meaning.

At the start of the game, she was a little intimidated until the natural competitiveness of growing up close to three brothers kicked in and she forgot to be nervous. She threw herself into the game the way she usually did and the extra, handsome players seemed to take her to the next level. At one point, she actually slide tackled Riordan, and she almost—not quite, but almost scored against Quinn in the second half.

Her team still lost, and in the truck on the way in to breakfast Quinn ribbed her, "You just couldn't help but shoot it straight at that bar, could you? You could have tied the game with that one."

She laughed and teased Josh in return, "I could have won the game with that one if Josh had been just a tad more cutthroat instead of so gallantly checking out of the game to pick his wife up off the field after he accidentally flattened her. What's a little blood when you're married? How is your nose anyway, Lucy?"

From the front seat, Lucy said, "Uh, tender. And leaning just a little to the right, but other than that, perfect. I say if you actually gave your life's blood for the game, then the other team should have to buy, even if you lost."

Quinn didn't hesitate to nix that with his Aussie accent topped with a touch of smart aleck. "Not if it was your own mate who fouled you. That would be rewarding stupidity."

Josh shook his head. "Hey now. Although, that is the American way. Have you seen our congress lately?"

Riordan laughed softly and Lucy groaned and said, "Don't even go there. I hope they have a strawberry Danish this morning. And a Tylenol."

Josh reached to take her hand. "I'm so sorry, honey. Are you okay? Really?"

Innocently, Lucy said, "No. I'm not okay. I don't think I'm going to be able to vacuum for a week."

Jessie added, "Of course not. Not with a nose injury like that."

Lucy put a hand over the seat to high five her and Quinn rolled his eyes and said, "Looks like a conspiracy to me. The girls are ganging up on you, mate."

Nodding, Josh said blandly, "No worries, Quinn. I'm on to 'em. They've been conspiring against me for years."

Jessie laughed, "You've known about our conspiracies?"

"Heavens yes. I can see it your eyes, Jess."

Jessie shrugged. "We're busted, Luce. Guess we're doomed to vacuuming. At least you don't have to muck out like we had to when he was laid up last winter. One little broken arm and he had us running around like nurses."

Lucy leaned to kiss Josh on the cheek. "Poor baby. Well, technically, I am a nurse. And honestly, I'd rather muck out than vacuum."

Josh patted Lucy's knee. "That is why I married you, honey. You got skills." He looked in the rear view mirror and added, "When you're shopping, gentlemen, be sure and find a wife with skills."

Beside her, Quinn gave Jessie a grin and asked, "So, Jessie, how are you with a mucking fork?"

"I can hold my own. Why?"

"Just wondering." He winked at her. "We would have the most adorable blonde children, you and I. They'd be great at soccer and they'd get your brains. They'd be fabulous!"

Jessie laughed and shook her head. "Uh, no. You'd better hold out for a wife who can handle a mucking fork *and* actually make that shot on goal. But thanks for considering me for your gene pool."

On the other side of her, Riordan shook his head. "First time I've seen you strike out with a girl, Quinn. You're losing your touch, man. I'm guessing it's because you hinted at that M word when you've known her all of what? Less than two hours."

"You think that's too fast?"

Jaclyn M. Hawkes

"Just a hair, mate. But your audacity is impressive. At least I'm impressed. I mean, who tries to marry a girl right in front of her big brother? Maybe next time. Who's up to going truck shopping this morning? You in, Quinn? Since you're not engaged quite yet."

"Sure, I'll go if Jessie will."

She shook her head. "Sorry, darling, but I have a full slate of patients this morning. I'm vaccinating at the Desert Blossom Farm. Maybe Josh could go."

"No can do, *darling*. I'm working colts all morning. But I can recommend a good dealership. We've bought from them for years. And we trade services so if you're with one of us it'll save you some money. Maybe Brennan or McCade can go with. McCade would love it. He's a car buff."

Quinn said, "Riordan's rich. He doesn't need to save money."

To that, Josh said, "He's also smart. That's how he got rich. Let him keep what he's earned. What are you looking to buy, Ri? Why don't you just rent something? You're only going to be here a month or two."

They arrived at the restaurant and as they got out of Josh's truck, Riordan said, "I don't want to have to worry about dinging it and keeping it all clean." Turning to Brennan and McCade who climbed out of McCade's truck beside them, he asked, "Either of you two up to helping me buy wheels this morning?"

Brennan shook his head, but McCade groaned and said, "Oh, man, I'd love to go, but I'm booked solid this morning with

62

Dad. Have you seen that sweet new Ram? It's got like a full office built right into the cab! Or those new Fords are great! The seats are heaven and the duallies purr. Yeah, I'd probably go with the Ford F350 diesel. Even that full size Toyota is slick, except I only buy American. Or Australian." He chuckled at his own joke and then continued. "Shoot. I wonder if Dad would kill me if I flaked on moving water on the west hills."

As they entered the restaurant, Josh said, "He wouldn't kill you, but he needs your help. He can't do that alone and it has to be done this morning. Maybe Lucy and Suki could go with."

At that, Riordan shook his head. "No. I'm not going to bother your wives for a few hundred dollars. Quinn and I will be fine. He'll probably try to get me to buy a Ferrari instead of a truck, but I can handle him."

Quinn slung a long arm around Riordan's shoulder. "A Ferrari would be an excellent vehicle for fine young playboys like us, Kane."

Riordan pushed his arm off and said, "Playboys. It might be just a shade difficult to haul the playboys' horse gear around in though, mate."

In concern, Jessie said, "It would probably save you a few thousand, not a few hundred if one of us was with you. Dad gives the dealer a break on his training fees because we buy so many vehicles. I'll try to hurry with my farm calls and at least drop by for you."

Riordan pulled out her chair to seat her at the table and said, "If you can, that would be fine, but don't trouble yourself, Doc. Especially since you're already buying my breakfast this morning, my little slide tackling friend. I owe you now, you know. Next time we play, you're going down."

Quinn elbowed Riordan as they sat down, but to Jessie he said, "He's so lying, *darling*. He would never tackle a woman. He may not trust girls, but he would never physically hurt one. He's far too nice a guy. He might do a hostile take over of your company, but he's relatively non-violent. Trust me."

Riordan only smiled as he picked up his menu and said, "All's fair in love and soccer, mate. I think I'll order the Arizona Skillet Scramble this morning. It sounds so apropos."

Chapter 6

When Jessie arrived at the Desert Blossom Farm, she was surprised to see that a nearby corral was filled with milling yearlings. As she and Cal got out of her truck, the farm manager came forward and said, "I had the boys bring the youngsters in this time so we don't have to try to catch them. We'll run 'em through the chute. I figured I owed you after last time."

She nodded, remembering the hours they'd wasted trying to round up the frisky yearlings. This was a much better plan. She might actually make it to the dealership after all.

It still took them almost three hours to vaccinate everything, but that turned out to be a full two hours less than it had taken her the last time.

In her call truck with Cal, on the way back into Mesa to see if Riordan and Quinn were still truck shopping, she called the number Josh gave her for Riordan and found they were indeed still at the dealership and she had Cal drop her off. Riordan and Quinn had narrowed the selection down to three trucks and as she walked up, Quinn gave her his come-on smile again and held the front door of a big black Ford dually for her and said,

Jaclyn M. Hawkes

"Doctor darling, I'm so glad you made it. I had the chauffer wait for you."

She laughed and climbed up into the truck beside where Riordan was already sitting in the driver's seat and Quinn climbed into the back seat and asked, "So, did you bail on your vaccinating?"

"No, actually. I was just able to get through faster than I had planned." She glanced across to where Riordan was quietly watching her and said, "So, you didn't opt for the Ferrari, I see. This seems nice."

He gave her his easy going smile. "No. No Ferrari. Although, they do actually have one here that one of the owners has been driving. They're a bit hard to pack bales of hay into. Quinn did try though. He said we could just make lots of trips carrying fifty kilo paper bags of hay pellets on the roof. I voted no."

Jessie nodded her head and grinned. "And he who signs the check has the deciding vote, I assume."

Riordan looked in the rear view mirror and shook his head as Quinn laughed and Riordan said, "In theory, yes. Bob, the sales guy, is still a bit confused about whether to sell to me or to Quinn. Quinn is much more enthusiastic about it all and that's a natural draw it would seem. I keep saying I need a truck to use with the horses. Then our celebrity truck shopper in the back seat there will say something about chrome and we're off to the pretty trucks again."

Jessie asked, "Well, what are your priorities?" She began to open the console and then checked out the dashboard and said,

"Really, a truck is just a very big, very expensive tool we use to get our work done. And they're about like people. Some vehicles are strictly work oriented. They're no-nonsense, comfortable, real. Some can't work at all and are completely frivolous, and some are middle of the road. Some know how to work and play. This is very roomy, and the console seems user friendly. I'd guess you could get all kinds of bells and whistles in here. I'll try to keep Quinn under control for you for awhile so you can have Bob all to yourself." She pointed to the man approaching with the set of keys in his hand and added, "I should sit in the back so he can sit up here and give you his pitch."

From the rear, Quinn laughed again when Riordan put out a hand to stop Jessie from getting back out and said, "No. Please. Stay up front. I'm sick of both Quinn and Bob. I'm actually thinking of giving them both a dose of that diet Pepsi commercial with the race car driver. Just tell me what your thoughts are as far as what you'd buy."

The salesman climbed in. He seemed surprised but pleased to see Jessie and handed Riordan the keys. "Here you go, Mr. Kane. I think you'll love this truck. Give it a whirl."

Riordan looked over at Jessie with a grin and Quinn laughed again, then said, "A whirl. That does indeed sound like the race car commercial. He's given you permission. Go for it, mate."

The salesman in the backseat got a worried look on his face and Jessie grinned back at Riordan as she reached for her seatbelt. As it clicked, she said, "Ready for lift off. All systems are go."

At that, Riordan gunned the truck's engine a couple of times, but then only smoothly pulled away from the parking spot and gave Jessie a bigger smile as he looked in the mirror at the hurriedly buckling Bob. Riordan turned back to her as he exited the parking lot and said, "You were going to tell me what you'd buy."

Jessie chuckled and shook her head. "Oh, right. Well, let me think. I'd buy the big engine and duallies to trailer with. They recommend diesel to pull as well, but they're just too loud. You can't hear yourself think even inside with all the windows rolled up. They make me crazy. I'd buy an automatic, and a bench seat with a fold down console, for when you have a girl in here. It's nice to be able to sit by each other. I'd get all the electronic stuff possible. It just makes everything more convenient which, to me, computes to safer. I'd get the custom floor liners right from the get-go so it didn't perpetually smell like a horse from the very first week. And black is hot."

In a silky voice from the back seat, Quinn said, "Hot is always good."

Jessie shook her head. "Not in southern Arizona, goalie darling. I meant the color. Get white. Or at least a lighter color. Black is way too hot in this climate unless you get the one with the automatic fans in the windows. They help. Although black is very pretty—especially with lots of chrome."

She smiled at Riordan and then at Quinn in the back and added, "What the heck. Chicks dig guys in pretty trucks. Plus, because it's a truck, you can avoid that whole portfolio complex. No one's going to think you're trying to show how much you're worth, like if you drive a beamer. But if you are going to spend this much on something, it might as well be a gorgeous expensive tool."

Riordan nodded thoughtfully, while from the back seat, Quinn asked, "And what about the gold package, love. Do chicks dig gold trim as much as they dig lots of chrome?" Riordan rolled his eyes.

Jessie thought about that and then shook her head. "No. That's over the top. That's like a guy in jewelry and earrings. It looks good. Maybe a little wild, but not quite so completely masculine."

At that, Riordan laughed and Bob glanced at Quinn's ear stud as Quinn laughed good naturedly and asked, "Are you saying my bling isn't masculine, darling?"

Jessie grinned back at him, "Oh, heavens no, goalie darling. You have the most macho bling I've ever seen. Really."

Quinn narrowed his eyes. "Is she serious, or is she teasing, Kane? I can't tell from back here."

Riordan looked across the truck and met Jessie's eyes and said lazily, "Serious as a school marm, Quinny. She's obviously thoroughly enamored."

Quinn looked suspiciously at the back of Riordan's head and said, "Yes. Obviously. You're both pitiful liars. Blast! I thought the girls loved my style."

Nodding with a smile, Jessie said sincerely, "And we do, Quinn. How could we not? You're patently adorable."

"Oh, good. You hear that, Kane? Adorable. And that coming from a woman who will slide tackle a guy and then buy the romantic bench seat and automatic transmission. I don't think they make women like that in Australia. At least none I've ever found. Are you sure you don't want to be the mother of my children, Jessie? The offer still stands."

Jessie raised her eyebrows and shook her head again. "As tempting as you are, Quinny. And as nebulous as whatever your offer is, I'm uh . . . No. I'm sure I'm flattered, but . . ."

Riordan interrupted her hesitant answer, "Sounds like American for no to me, mate. But I could be mistaken." To Jessie, he said, "Girls really still do that occasionally? Sit by their date, I mean? Here in America?"

"Do they not in Australia?"

"Do women still even date in Australia? Sorry, I'm woefully out of the loop. Ask Mr. Ferrari back there. He's the officianado of all things feminine. Not me. Quinn? What do the Australian girls do these days?"

Quinn got an exaggerated dreamy smile on his face. "Ah, the Australian girls."

He gave a sigh and this time Bob rolled his eyes and said, "So, this truck has best in class horsepower, unsurpassed torque, and a reliably efficient engine considering that. All the Benjamin boys drive something similar. Isn't that right, Jessie?"

She shook her head, "Sorry, I can't keep up with their trucks. It's like keeping up with Quinn's girls. What other rigs have you guys driven today?"

Riordan chuckled and said, "We tried the comparable Chevy and the biggest Toyota. They were both very *pretty*, but I think this seat is more comfortable. We're going to drive the

Dodge next. It's a lovely red. Tons of chrome. *Chicks* should love it. Although they'd have to ship one in from another dealership to get the dually. I wouldn't be able to take it today."

From the back, Quinn said, "But we can take the Ferrari today. That way we'd have wheels for sure. Hey, I wonder if they make Ferraris with bench seats. Talk about your romantic." He turned to the salesman. "He'll take one of each. We'll take the Ferrari today and you can send the truck tomorrow when you get it."

The salesman looked ridiculously hopeful as he looked up to Riordan for corroboration, but Riordan only smiled and shook his head as they pulled back into the dealership lot. When they got out, he said, "Okay, Quinn, you go drive the Ferrari, and take Bob with you. Jessie and I will take the Ram for a whirl and meet you back here in twenty. Then I'm going to grab something to eat while I decide. Is that all right with you, Jessie? Do you have anywhere you need to be?"

"You can have me for another hour and a half."

Quinn said, "How about if I take Jessie with me, and you take Bob in the Ram? I'm going to need her opinion on the romanticness of the seats."

Shaking his head, Riordan said, "Nice try, mate. But Bob already told you he couldn't let you take the Ferrari without him. Company policy, remember? And Dr. Benn gave me more solid input on the Ford in three minutes than you gave in three hours. She's concerned with more than how you'd look driving it. Plus, she'll need to weigh in on the romanticness of the Dodge's seat."

Quinn gave an exaggerated sigh. "Fine. But they all have four wheels and a cargo bed. They're all great vehicles. The bottom line really is how the thing makes you feel. You know I'm right."

"I'll keep that in mind. And pace yourself. We've already had one arrest since we've been in the country. Don't get thrown in jail for speeding." Riordan held out his hand and Bob put a set of keys into it. Riordan caught Jessie's eye and nodded at a big red Dodge pickup parked nearby. "After you, Dr. darling."

He helped her in and then went around to the other side and got in, but before he drove away, he pulled his ringing phone from his pocket, smiled and then said, "Good morning, Mum. You're up bright and early. Is everything okay?"

Jessie could only hear his side of the conversation, but it sounded like Riordan and his mother had a cute relationship as he said, "Yes, Mum. I'm behaving myself. Yes. No, not so far. Just the Benjamins. Yes, I'm eating. Yeah, actually. I don't know why, but you're right, I am happy here. Sure, I'll analyze myself. Mum. Is Dad up yet? Have him call when he wakes up. I will. Love you too, Mum. Talk to you soon. Bye."

Jessie couldn't help grinning and Riordan shook his head and grinned back and said, "She tends to forget that I've been grown up for awhile now."

All Jessie could say was, "She sounds like a wonderful mother. Enjoy her."

They'd been on the road for several minutes when Jessie said, "He's right."

Riordan glanced over at her. "Who's right?"

"Quinn. What he said makes sense. I mean beyond anything obvious like buying a car that you're too big to sit in comfortably, or buying a Ferrari to carry hay. They are all good vehicles. You really should buy what makes you feel best."

"And what is best?"

"That depends on you. Do you want to feel powerful? Or attractive? Wealthy? Flashy? Unobtrusive? Responsible? Earth friendly? What do you want?"

"All of the above."

"That would be a fantasy vehicle. You have to make a decision."

He slowed and flipped a u-ie and headed back to the dealership. Once they were headed the other direction, he asked, "Are you always that practical?"

"Practical? I just said to buy what made you feel good. That's not practical."

"I mean. Get all the facts, weigh the pros and cons, study it out and then go with your gut?"

She thought about that for a moment and then nodded, "Yeah, I guess I am. But that makes sense. It's logical. Mostly."

He grinned across at her. "Mostly." He chuckled. "That's the way life is. Logical. Mostly."

"Sometimes."

"That too."

"So, what are you going to buy?"

"The black Ford. With the big engine and the duallies. And the bench seat."

She looked over at him, wondering if she needed to read anything into what he had just said, but he didn't seem to be flirting. After a second, she said, "Should be a nice truck."

They stopped afterward at Caleb's restaurant for a late lunch. As they ordered, Jessie said to the server, "And could you ask the chef to make mine without any cooking wine in the sauce. Hopefully, he won't mind."

A few minutes later, Jessie saw Caleb look through the little window in the door from the kitchen. She waved and he came out the door and up to their table, checking out both Riordan and Quinn as he came. He came right up to her, put a hand on her shoulder, still looking hard at the others and said, "I wondered if it was you giving me grief about my cooking wine again, Jessie. What are you up to?"

"Just finally getting around to lunch. Caleb, these are friends of mine. Riordan Kane and Quinn Darling. They're from Australia. Josh knew Riordan over there and they've come for the U.S.A. National Stock Show."

Caleb gave them a stiff smile and shook their hands and then looked even harder at Quinn and said, "You seem really familiar to me. Are you related to a guy over there who plays soccer? The goalie for the Stingrays? His name is Quinn too. Only Quinn Montere."

Turning back to Quinn, Jessie asked, "You mean your last name isn't Darling? Really? It's Montere?"

Riordan shook his head and smiled as Quinn said, "You're a Stingrays fan? Clear over here? Yeah, I'm Montere. Dr. Darling here just thinks I'm so adorable that the darling thing took on a life of its own."

Caleb looked at her and raised his eyebrows. "Is that so?"

Grinning, Jessie said, "Apparently so. I thought that was his name. You know me. Ditsy, ditsy."

Looking positively skeptical, Caleb said, "You're the most unditsy woman on the planet, but whatever, Jessie. Still don't want the wine, huh? You're ruining one of my signature dishes, you know."

She shook out her napkin and put it in her lap. "I'd prefer no wine, but if it's a big deal, wine is fine."

"You know I'm your servant, Jessie. Always." Turning to go back into the kitchen, he said, "I'll get your entrées right out. I hope you enjoy. It was good to meet you two."

After he left, Riordan grinned over at Jessie and said, "I think he was lying, Dr. Darling. I don't think he really thought it was good to meet us. I think he wants to keep you all to himself and not share with us boys from down under. Do I detect a bit of the territorial in your friend in the poufy hat?"

She shrugged and said, "Oh, I'm sure not. After all, he knew that Quinn's last name wasn't darling. He's obviously a fan of at least Australian soccer. He was perfectly polite, wasn't he?"

Riordan picked up his water goblet. "Yes, dutifully so. He wasn't by any chance the reason for the fresh Greek oregano the other night, was he?"

"Actually, yes. How did you know?"

"He just had that confused boyfriend look to him when he saw us with you."

Jessie could feel her skin heat slightly and shook her head. "We date occasionally, but he knows we are definitely not an exclusive couple."

Riordan gave her the easy grin she was coming to expect from him. "But I'm guessing that's your idea—not his."

She had to think about that for a moment. While she considered, Quinn nudged her with a hand and said, "Oh, don't be modest, girl. Of course it's not his idea. He'd horde you all to himself in a Sydney minute. Just like me—if you'd have me. But apparently you won't. But I haven't given up. I can compete with a chef any day of the week. I can make a kicking grilled lobster."

"Really?"

He laughed and shook his head. "No, but I know a guy who owns a share of a private plane that will fly us out to the bay area for lunch and there's a great restaurant there for lobster."

She nodded, "I imagine that competes quite nicely with a chef, in fact. Who's the guy with the share of the private plane?"

Riordan just sat calmly looking on as they bantered back and forth, so Jessie was surprised when Quinn said, "Oh, yeah, sure. Now she's looking for the bigger fish than the pro soccer player, but it won't work. Mr. Kane here is the private jet owner, but he doesn't do casual socializing with ladies."

At that last, Jessie was confused. And concerned. Surely he wasn't inferring that a man as attractive as . . . Turning to Riordan, she asked, "What is he saying, Mr. Kane? Surely, you're not . . . You do prefer females—right?"

Riordan's eyes widened and he coughed on the water he was drinking. Quinn laughed and said, "Yes, Jessie. That's not what I was saying. Riordan likes women. He's just a tad disenchanted with the less honest females of the species. Or, well pretty much all of the females of the species. They're all after him for the wrong reasons. Right, Kane?"

When he'd cleared his throat, Riordan looked at her and asked, "Do I act like a guy who doesn't prefer females?"

Back pedaling as fast as she could, Jessie said, "No. Of course not. I just thought that was what he was saying. You let him take your private jet to the coast for lunch?"

"Only when he lets me borrow the new Ferrari to go to Tucson for dinner."

Jessie shook her head and laughed as she asked Quinn, "You're kidding! You bought it? Just now?"

Quinn grinned. "Leased it. For the month. I have to play here while I can because I have to fly home next week." He turned to Riordan. "Are you asking to borrow my car?"

Riordan shrugged. "Maybe."

At that, Quinn actually looked a little surprised and asked, "For a date? Do cynical old Australian business tycoons still do that?"

Riordan didn't even seem offended, just asked, "Are you saying I'm old? I'm two years older than you, Montere. I'm twenty nine. That's not old. By the way, Jessie, I don't own part of a plane. We chartered a private jet to bring the horses over. That's all."

Caleb appeared out of the kitchen door with their three plates and headed to their table as Quinn said, "It's not the years, man. It's the cynicism. Before I give you the car, who are you taking to Tucson? Because I have first dibs on Dr. Darling, the veterinarian here. If you'll recall, I'm nearly eight hours into a quest to get her to be the mother of my blonde, brilliant, soccer playing children."

At his comment, Caleb did a complete stall as he went to set plates down and looked over at Jessie who only rolled her eyes and said, "Thank you, Caleb. These look delicious. We're positively starving. Do you have time to sit down with us? Can you take a break?"

He shook his head as he put Riordan's plate down. "No, but thanks. I've got to prep for the dinner rush. Enjoy your meals."

He left and Jessie took a bite of her food, still watching Riordan to see if he was going to answer Quinn about who he was taking to Tucson, but all he did was taste his entre and say, "Mmm. Your chef is very good. But you're right. It would be better with less wine. I'll bet your Greek food the other night was excellent. No wonder you date him—non-exclusively."

She was watching Riordan's calm face and wondered what he was thinking at the moment as she took a bite of her pasta. He was remarkably implacable at times. She glanced at the kitchen door Caleb had gone through and gave an inner sigh. Caleb was definitely a nice enough guy, and he truly was a great cook. But seeing him here next to Riordan Kane made him seem painfully nondescript. She'd known there wasn't really any chemistry going there, but had still been trying to faithfully find Mr. Right. In that short moment, she knew now Caleb wasn't him.

She glanced back across the table to see that Riordan was watching her as well and she tried to smile at him through her suddenly discouraging thoughts. She had to look on the bright side. She still had her date with Ryan later that night. Ryan was an IT genius. That was supposed to be desirable, wasn't it?

And she still had Clay. She hadn't given up on him yet. Something could spark there eventually. It wasn't really his fault he wasn't all that much of a dashing guy. He'd probably worked hard to achieve that sense of professional stoicism. In fact, they probably taught it in law school. In time, maybe she could overcome it. Or get used to it.

Looking up, she saw Quinn watching her too and at her glance, he gave her another one of his thoroughly cheerful smiles and said, "You didn't completely brush me off that time, darling. Does that mean there's hope for our children yet?"

She gave him a teasing smile back and said, "No, Quinn. You're completely out of my league, literally. Not to mention the fact that you're completely ineligible. I'm planning to marry a nice, sober, boring Mormon guy. But don't let that stop you from your round-about way of trying. It's very entertaining. I'm sure it's great practice for you. Someday, another hapless veterinarian with skills is bound to take you up on combining gene pools. In the meantime, we'll go to the coast for lunch together and I'll keep trying to score a goal past you."

Quinn picked up a bite of his meal on his fork, pointed it toward Riordan and said, "Aah. I think that was American for not a chance. It happens to the best of all of us someday. Doesn't it, Riordan?"

Jaclyn M. Hawkes

Riordan Kane only calmly sipped at his water again and said blandly, "That's what I keep hoping, Quinn. Heaven only knows we need more scoring in this world."

Chapter 7

They played soccer again on Thursday and Jessie actually did score on Quinn, but it was probably only because he was pretty trashed from too much clubbing the night before. He was hung over enough that Jessie was frankly surprised he even got up to come with them. When she kicked the goal through, he groaned right out loud before falling to his knees. Then laying flat out in defeat he said to Riordan, who was on Jessie's team this time, "I gotta quit drinking, Kane. Playing with all these clean living religious zealots is going to kill me."

Jessie simply retrieved the ball around him and said sweetly, "Playing with us isn't what's going to kill you, buddy. And it feels incredibly good to score against you, even if you are a bit compromised."

Quinn groaned again, "More than a bit, darling. You win. I'll gracefully concede."

She laughed and snagged Quinn's water bottle from beside the goal, shot a stream at Riordan and then dribbled some on Quinn's face and asked, "You call this graceful?"

Jaclyn M. Hawkes

"Ah. American sarcasm. It's as graceful as it's going to get this morning. How do you people do it? Don't you ever miss partying the night away?"

She paused as if thinking and then said, matter-of-factly, "Nope. Now that you mention it. We never miss the drinking. We have a perfectly good time sober. Although, in all honesty, my veterinary practice tends to negate playing too late most nights. But yeah, we never miss being too drunk to know what we are doing and who we are doing it with. We are blessed to never have those aching head mornings like you're enjoying. So, was the night worth it?"

He had the energy to grin at her and say, "I don't know. I can't remember."

She laughed and booted the soccer ball out of the goal over Riordan's head to the center of the field and said mock tenderly, "Poor baby."

Riordan chuckled and Quinn said drily, "I'm sure you're awash with sympathy."

"Oh, yeah. Awash. Watch yourself. I may just try to score on you twice. I'll make it more fair this time. I'll point to where I'm going to kick it just before I do it."

Riordan grinned again and Quinn said, "Oh, now that's just rude." He stood up and leaned over with his hands on his knees. "Okay, darling. Give it your best go. No way are you scoring on me twice. I've got my second wind now."

Shaking his head, Riordan chuckled and said, "Good luck with that, mate."

82

Quinn only grimaced and rubbed his forehead and said, "I may have to join their church, mate. The clean living thing may be the key to a long pro career."

Laughing right out loud, Riordan said, "You join, and I will too, goalie darling."

Josh gave a rebel yell, high fived Jessie and said, "I heard that, Kane."

Quinn looked confused, and Jessie did a double take at Riordan as Quinn said, "Yeah, like you would even need to change much of your lifestyle. You're as clean living as they are. And you're already retired."

Riordan slapped him on the shoulder and said, "Don't remind me. What am I going to do with myself when we go home? Hang in there. No pun intended, mate. You'll feel better the second half."

Quinn ran a hand through his wild hair. "I'm holding you to that."

At breakfast, Josh asked, "So, Jessie, today's the day you've got the other vets flying in to interview?"

"It is. You want to come by and give me your professional opinion?"

"Absolutely. Would you mind?"

"Heck no. I'd love it. The first one should be in around ten. Do you have time?"

Riordan broke in with a grin. "He's got plenty of time, since he's refused to take on the training of any more horses."

Josh smiled back, "I'm not averse to training any more horses. I'm just not going to help you beat my own, self-centered man that I am. That would be brain dead. And why are you complaining? I've been helping you keep him legged up and exercised."

"Which is very nice, mate. But someone has to actually ride him in the ring or I'll have flown him over here for nothing. At least refer me to another good trainer. That's the least a self-centered guy can do. Who's good?"

Jessie was eating and watching their banter back and forth with seeming interest as Josh answered back, "Jorge's good, but he's already our guy. And Harold Sturt is coming on. He's hard in their mouths, but he's competing. He took a first place at Redding this spring."

Riordan shook his head as he chewed a bite of his breakfast and then said, "But he's not better than you. Is anyone?"

Josh only smiled, but Lucy proudly said, "Nope. Sorry. Josh is the best there is."

At that, Josh looked across and met Jessie's eyes and quietly said, "Jessie's better than me."

All eyes at the table turned to her and Riordan glanced back at Josh to see if he was serious, but Jessie only held Josh's eyes for a long second and then joked, "Yeah, right." To the others, she said, "He's joking. I don't train reining horses. I don't even usually ride reining horses. They make me motion sick." Back to Josh, she said, "So, if you have time, come in and hang out at the clinic with me and tell me what you think. Bring Dad or whoever. I'd love your insight."

Riordan was still looking at her, confused at Josh's obvious sincerity about her being a better trainer and Jessie glanced around and then said almost too brightly to Quinn., "You Aussie boys can come too if you're feeling up to it, goalie darling. How's the head?"

"Hanging a bit after being cheerfully scored on twice by a veterinarian." He raised his coffee cup and grinned. "I'll be fine in a couple hours and come in to defend my turf. I'm an excellent judge of medical character, plus I still intend to win you for my gene pool."

Jessie only rolled her eyes. Riordan laughed softly and nudged Quinn with his elbow and said, "My but you are the most romantic hung over Romeo I know. How's that gene pool line working for you, anyway?"

Quinn squinted against the sunlight coming in the windows of the restaurant, then grinned at Jessie and said, "Hard to tell with a woman this poised, mate. But I think she's warming up to me. Just give me some more time. She hasn't seen me at my best yet."

Riordan grinned from him to Jessie and then said, "No, I suppose not. Just keep in mind, this is a woman who routinely neuters things for a living. You'd better watch yourself."

Quinn winced, and said, "Oh, man, you didn't have to remind me of that, Kane. But a gentleman such as myself has no need to worry. Do I, Dr. darling?"

Sipping her ice water, Jessie shook her head. She wiped her mouth on her napkin and tossed it to the side of her plate as she picked up her tab and got up to go. "Certainly not." She grinned at Quinn and added sweetly, "It never gets quite that far when someone crosses the line. My brothers kill them first. Gotta go, all. I have an eight o'clock. Drop by if you can."

She breezed out the door and Quinn glanced around the table at her smiling brothers and asked, "She was kidding, right? That was only American joking with the Aussie, right?" Josh, Brennan, and McCade only raised their eyebrows and Lucy laughed as Quinn went on, "So, Riordan, you are gonna help me stay alive and keep all of my parts intact here in America, right, mate?"

Lazily, Riordan said, "Oh, I don't know, goalie darling. After all, you aren't the only one who needs to find a mother for his children. Having you out of the way might be a good idea."

Quinn grinned. "No way! The man of ice and steel wouldn't even joke about having children. You do realize that would require actually caring about a woman? At least for most people. You would never actually trust a woman enough to get that committed."

Riordan took out his wallet and tossed a twenty dollar bill onto the table. "No, you're right. I would never do that. Especially not a scalpel wielding woman. You can have all the American women to yourself."

Quinn watched him quietly for a long moment and then chuckled and said, "Geez, I have a hard time getting a take on you, Kane. So does that mean that you might actually have a heart in your chest, or not? Even after all this time I've known you, I still haven't figured out how to tell if you're kidding through that calm shell of yours. Okay, we'll go halves. I only want half the girls in America. And you can have all the surgeons. But that's it. Fifty fifty or no deal."

Riordan only smiled again and then added, "You'd better leave at least a couple for McCade to choose from. You riding with Josh and me over to the complex after we grab showers? Or do you want to go back to the hotel to recuperate some?"

"The hotel, definitely. I gotta do my hair before we screen her candidates. And put on more bling. One might be a fan. You go ahead. McCade will drop me, won't you mate?"

Chuckling, McCade said, "Absolutely, goalie darling. Just as long as you leave me a couple of American women to choose from."

****

On the ride over, when it was just him and Josh in the truck, Riordan finally asked, "So, is Jessie really better than you?"

Josh gave him a sad smile. "Better by a mile, Kane. She's an unbelievably gifted trainer."

"Honestly?"

"Honestly."

"But she doesn't ride?"

Josh shook his head sadly, but then added, "Oh, she rides. She has this sweet, old gelding named Bo, that she's had since she was four, who's too old to even muster up a trot, but he and Jessie wander all over the ranch bareback in the evenings or early mornings. She just doesn't ride professionally. Never has. Unless we have an emergency. Then she'll step up. But training doesn't even tempt her."

Josh pulled his truck into the shade of one of the horse barns and put it in park, but didn't turn it off as Riordan watched him, wondering what the story was here and why it made Josh so sad. Finally, he asked, "So, do you want to tell me? Or is this a family thing that's none of my business?"

Slowly, Josh shook his head. "No. It's not that it's none of your business. It's just a little painful. And maybe it's not my place to say anything. After all, Jessie's the one who has had the hardest time with everything. Only, she's still too bitter to be able to talk about it and it would make her cry her eyes out—if she could bring herself to tell it."

Riordan could feel his brow furrow in confusion. What in the world could make Josh this sad? Or the ever cheery and competent Jessie cry her eyes out? Still wondering whether to ask, or not, he sat there quietly, until Josh turned to him and said, "When Jessie was little, like really little, like two and three, she had this little imaginary friend named Jennifer. She was like this little ghost who went everywhere and did everything with Jessie."

Josh paused and grinned. "Whenever Jessie got into trouble, she blamed whatever she'd done on Jennifer. It was actually really funny sometimes. She couldn't quite enunciate and she'd say in this cute little baby voice, 'Jenny dood it, Daddy.' It was almost as if there were two of them running around together instead of just Jessie. I'm sure in her head there were."

There was a long, long moment of silence and then Josh went on, "My mother is a trainer. I'm not sure if you know that. I don't talk about her much. She left us when I was nine. I mean left us as in divorced us, but she didn't go far. She trains right here in Mesa. She's here at the complex most days."

He shook his head. "I'm not sure why my dad married her. They don't match very well. She was beautiful. But as far as character, she was—is, sadly lacking. Her career was everything to her. It still is. It's kind of pathetic actually, 'cause she's not really all that good, but it was way more important to her than Dad or us kids."

Riordan looked over at him, feeling the deep-seated hurt that Josh was trying to mask with his matter-of-fact telling of such a harsh story. After a ragged breath, Josh went on woodenly, "She found out she was pregnant when I was nine and Jessie was six. Our whole family was excited and Jessie was ecstatic. She just knew it was Jennifer."

After another long, painful silence, Josh shrugged and quietly said, "My mom had it aborted so she could keep riding."

Riordan was horrified. He'd expected that the baby hadn't made it, but he'd thought Josh was going to say there had been an accident. He all but winced, knowing what that would have done to a six-year-old Jessie as Josh sadly went on, "Dad tried to talk my mother out of it. He even tried to get a judge to order her to carry it to term, but by the time the ruling came, the baby was already . . . It was too late. And my mother didn't try to protect us from the ugliness of it. All of us had to learn early on just what an abortion was. My dad couldn't lie to us when she'd been hollering around about it and then the baby was gone."

Riordan looked away from the hurt in Josh's eyes and out the window at nothing. It must have been an awful, gut wrenching time.

Josh stoically finished, "Mom left. And Jessie closed up like a flower in the dark. We all tried to pick up the pieces as a family and Dad was great. He did the best he could. The ranch kept us together and our church kept us on track. The neighbors were amazing. Life goes on. Well, for everyone but Jennifer.

"Jessie took it the hardest. As she grew up, she didn't want anything to do with training professionally. When she was fifteen, she talked my dad into letting her change her name from Benjamin to Benn. I'd guess because she looks so much like my mom. To this day, she has a hard time even saying hi to her, although I hope that deep inside she still loves her.

"Jessie's not a hater. Or a grudge holder. She just still hurts inside. She still can't figure out how to process the betrayal. The viciousness and depravity of it. Because she's the exact opposite of my mother. She's the most gentle, loving, caring, invested human on earth. Her whole life, what she's wanted most is to be a mom. To help people. Comfort them. And animals. She didn't really ever want a career. I think she was actually a little surprised that she finished vet school. She'd started into it thinking she'd be married and with children before long. The only reason she's a vet today is just because she hasn't ever found her Mr. Right and she's too brilliant to not pursue a profession while she's looking."

Riordan looked back over and met Josh's sad gaze and Josh finished, "So Jessie doesn't train. Unless we're desperate. She's filled in a couple times when I've been hurt because she knows she's far and away better than any of the others. But usually, she just doctors our horses and smiles. Goes back to sifting through the LDS men she meets in hopes of someday finding him. And teasing the rest of us mercilessly."

Riordan raised his chin to nod marginally and gave a sad smile of his own. "I have noticed that she teases you brothers. And everyone else she meets, unless they're wielding a buggy whip. Then she's not so teasing."

Josh finally gave a real smile. "Nope. Jessie's a lot of things. Pushover ain't one of them." He turned off his truck. "Come on. Let's go train that horse of yours that we're not training."

Chapter 8

The first veterinary hiring candidate arrived at a little before ten. Dark brown hair going prematurely gray at the temples made him seem older than the thirty-two years his resume claimed, but he was trim and seemed fit. Bifocals roved up and down his nose, depending on what he was looking at, and lent him an air of maturity as well. Jessie took him straight back to examine a broodmare with her. The mare's hair coat had gotten rough and her hooves were fracturing to the point that she was lame. Jessie was relatively sure from the first glance that the mare had Cushings Disease, but instead of voicing her thoughts, she encouraged the other veterinarian to take over for her. She was quietly standing to the side, watching the vet and mare when Josh walked into the exam area wearing one of Cal's lab coats with the Mesa Valley Veterinary logo on it. She simply gave him a one armed hug and the two of them kept quietly watching.

A few minutes later, Brennan dropped in as well, wearing another lab coat and the young veterinarian began to look almost a little bit spooked at the three of them standing there.

For the next two hours, Jessie let the other vet handle her appointments as she watched with what ended up being a decidedly motley crew of assistants, all wearing the signature lab coat. At one point, when there were actually five on-lookers, it was all Jessie could do not to smile as Quinn attempted to solemnly ask the other vet questions about what kind of antiseptic he preferred to use during surgery. The other man looked up at her and she gave him what she hoped looked like an encouraging smile and not the start of the giggles over this spectacle. Her dad stopping in wearing yet another lab coat, was simply the grand finale of the whole deal.

The first vet left around lunch time, and the second one showed up a half hour later. Everyone but Quinn and Riordan had left by then. When it turned out to be a very attractive young female veterinarian, Jessie was tempted to smile again when this time, Quinn asked her about her preferred anesthetic, as if he was well versed in that type of thing. Jessie realized the young vet was on to him, though, when with a completely straight face, she named off a seven syllable disease instead of a drug as her answer and then gave Jessie the slightest hint of a grin.

Riordan Kane never did say much, even when Josh came back and the third and older candidate showed up. Riordan just stood by in his borrowed lab coat and watched both the candidates and Jessie with an almost somber interest. It would be interesting to find out what he was thinking as the veterinarians worked with their patients.

When the last vet left, and Jessie began to put a few things away, Quinn gave Jessie his signature grin and said, "Well, after giving it a lot of thought, I think you should hire the hot brunette. She would definitely have the best bedside manner. In fact, I could be coerced into trying her out at my bedside, if you need me to."

Finally, cracking up, Jessie said gushingly, "Oh, Quinn, how thoughtful. That's certainly going above and beyond the call of duty for me. Thank you." Drily, she added, "It's also going way into the realm of sexual harassment litigation, but who cares about something so trivial, right? Bless your little heart. Just like that, you're on to a new gene pool."

"Anything I can do to help out, Doc."

Jessie nodded. "Yes, I can see that. Always the server. Did you want to give me any specifics about her skills?"

Holding his chin in a thoughtful pose, Quinn considered that for a moment and said, "Hhmm. I'm thinking I'm going to have to do some more observation before I can answer that. The only thing I know for sure is that she definitely has a great figure for examination. When is she coming back?"

Jessie wandered into her office with the two of them following and said, "Yes, I'm always on the lookout for employees with great figure *skills*. Thank you so much for your astute research. What would I do without you?"

At that Riordan spoke up, "Probably hire the man with the expertise and the people skills, but the not so great figure. Quinn is back in the pretty truck mode. Why was the first guy not already in a practice? What was his name? And what did his resume look like?"

Jessie looked up at Riordan, intrigued that he was thinking along the same lines as she had been about the first vet. "Dr. Stettler. He's been working out of a clinic out in California he thought he was going to be purchasing, but the contract was pulled on him when the vet owner who was retiring because of cancer went into remission. His resume looks great on the surface. You thought he had enough expertise? The last guy has been practicing for fourteen years."

Quinn sprawled into the chair across from her desk and closed his eyes as Riordan went over to stand in front of her diplomas and say, "He may have had years more experience, but he was so brusque he made both the patients and the owners nervous. I'm not a vet, but I'd imagine that you'd need to be both more gentle and use more finesse to be a decent surgeon. He was less than soothing."

Nodding, Jessie said, "Well, Quinn was right, the woman was definitely soothing. Almost too soothing."

Riordan turned to look at Jessie without saying anything and she finally asked, "Would you be comfortable with her 'bedside manner' if you were a client in her clinic?"

Riordan shrugged and turned back to her diplomas as he said, "Maybe. But I'd probably always be wondering if she was more interested in making a house call."

"As opposed to a farm call."

"Exactly. How extensively can you research these people? Can you do background checks, credit reports, double check their credentials and the whole barrel?"

"Yes, although, sometimes it's less complex to simply go to their social media. I weeded out another group almost instantly by just checking their Facebook pages. However, Dr. Stettler didn't have much social media. Just a LinkedIn profile."

She sat down at her desk and clicked her mouse and Riordan came to stand behind her and asked, "May I? I've done a bit of hiring in my checkered past. Mostly learned what not to do."

For half an hour, Riordan stood behind her and they read through information on the different candidates. Occasionally putting a hand on her shoulder, he quietly asked pertinent, thoughtful questions, had her scroll through several different websites and within what seemed like seconds, he'd been able to pull up an amazing amount of information that she'd had no idea to even look for, let alone known where to get it. He did basically the same thing they had spoken of when truck shopping; research the facts, analyze everything, then make an educated decision and last of all, go with your gut instinct.

By the time the two of them left, she had a remarkably thorough amount of both knowledge and reassurance about picking Dr. Stettler. As well as a whole new appreciation for the Australian businessman who could have been in a Soloflex commercial in his cartoon kangaroo jammies. He may have looked like a playboy movie star, but he definitely had as much business savvy as he had muscle.

****

Two nights later, she was lying on her hammock drowsing, listening to the creek when Josh and Lucy stepped up onto her patio out of the darkness and sat down on the porch swing opposite her. Turning over, she said, "Hey, guys. What are you up to?"

Lucy leaned back and said, "Just an evening stroll. No dates tonight? I thought you'd be out."

Yawning, Jessie gave the hammock a small push off and said, "No. The stock show starts in a couple days. It'll be too busy to date, so I started my dating sabbatical early so I could rest up."

Josh said, "I know exactly what you mean. Are you dating anyone you even like, anyway?"

Blandly, Jessie said, "Of course, I like them. Why would I go out with someone I didn't like?"

"You know what I meant. Is there anyone you really like?"

She thought about that and then said tiredly, "Uhm. No. I keep hoping they'll grow on me. Did you need something, Mr. Nosypants?"

Lucy laughed as Josh admitted, "Yes, Miss Impatient Pants. But you're not going to like it. I need some help riding. With Riordan's and Quinn's extra horses, I'm in over my head. I haven't seen my kids awake in three days. Wanna ride a couple horses for a few days to keep them legged up? No training or show ring involved, I swear."

"Oh, sure. You bring in the wife to guilt me into this. Why not just bring the kids to really make me squirm?"

"Well, like I said, they're asleep, or I would have. I'm not above a little coercion."

"Lucy can ride. Why don't you just ask her?"

Jaclyn M. Hawkes

"Because she has two small people to watch over. Plus, that stud is a handful. He's too much horse for Lucy. I need you."

"I'm going to be as busy as you are."

"Riordan said he thought the new vet would be starting in just a couple days."

Jessie yawned again. "I hope so. I so could use shorter days. Just legging up?"

"Just legging up. The stud is actually already amazing. And there's only so much I can do with Quinn's horse in a couple of days, so . . . Just help me keep them show ring ready."

She blew out a long breath. "You try this every year, you know."

"Try what?"

"To get me back into the training end."

"I wonder why? You're the best and what, seventy pounds lighter than me? We could sweep every show if you'd just get on board."

"I'm a veterinarian. Give it a rest."

"In your dreams. Is that a yes? Don't make me drag Rye and Bethy out here."

"Okay. Two horses. For a week. I'll give you a week."

"'Til the end of the stock show."

"Nine days."

"Ten."

"Forget it. No deal. Now go away."

"Okay. Nine. You're my favorite sister. I don't care what they say."

"Nine. And you owe me."

"Anything in my power."

"I'll think of something. Something big. You'd better watch out."

Josh got up to lean and drop a kiss on Jessie's hair and then he pulled Lucy up from the swing and said, "Go in and go to bed. You've got to get up and slide tackle Riordan again in the morning. He's getting better fast and it's giving him an ego."

"What, like he wasn't confident before he got here?"

"Well, maybe Quinn will feel lousy again and agree to get baptized and we'll finally get to dunk Riordan."

Jessie yawned again and said, "Take him home, Luce. He's starting to hallucinate. We're not playing soccer in the morning anyway, are we?"

The two of them got up to go and Lucy said, "Goodnight, Jess. Thank you. The kids and I really appreciate this."

"You're welcome. Goodnight, you two. Kiss those babies for me."

Chapter 9

When Riordan walked into the barn after an early breakfast the next morning, he was surprised to see his horse's stall empty but could see Josh working at the end of the alleyway and went to find out what was going on. Before he even made it to Josh, he glanced ahead and realized that it was his horse that was being worked in the arena at the end of the alleyway.

He paused in mid-stride, marveling as always at the magnificence of his horse in action. That horse was a glorious beast. And today it was moving even more spectacularly than he ever remembered, which was saying something. As he watched, the horse tore off down the arena for a short sprint and then sat into a beautiful sliding stop that made his full, rippling mane swing forward into his face.

Even as his mane swung back, he abruptly turned into a left hand spin for three quick perfect rotations, each hoof beat like a perfectly choreographed dance move, then switched instantly into a right hand spin with his long mane still swinging wide into the air. He did three beautiful rotations then rolled back sharply to his left to sprint back down the arena toward Riordan.

It wasn't until the stud was headed straight toward him and then pulled up into another incredible abrupt sliding stop, that Riordan noticed that the rider, whose long blond hair swung in tandem with the big chestnut's mane, was none other than Dr. Jessie Benn.

For just a second, Riordan felt a strange squeeze in his chest as he realized that Josh definitely hadn't been kidding about Jessie being the best there was at reining. The horse was magnificent on its own, and Jessie was a strikingly beautiful girl, but with her aboard the horse, the pair was flat out glorious. Breathtaking, in fact, when he realized he'd all but stopped breathing to watch that exquisite girl working his stallion.

She glanced up and met his eye for the merest second and then turned the horse to lightly jog back down the arena away from him. She turned the horse into a slow circle, jogging for a couple of minutes and then pulled the horse up and let him settle into a true stop. Riordan saw both horse and girl take a deep breath and he heard her quietly speaking to the stud as she reached down to pat the big chestnut on its neck in front of the rolls of the saddle.

Glancing at her watch, she nudged the great beast forward and then let him simply walk the perimeter of the arena for a couple of laps. At length, she brought him back into the alleyway where she stepped off of him in one smooth, incredibly graceful motion and handed his reins off to Josh, who had come up beside Riordan without him even noticing.

Leaning into the big horse, she rubbed him gently down his neck again with another quiet word before glancing up at Josh and saying, "You were right. He's as good as it gets. But I gotta go. I'm already late. I'll come earlier tomorrow."

With that, she gave Riordan a small smile that seemed a little tired or something and then headed up the alleyway with him watching her walk all the way. Even though she was dressed simply in jeans, a lavender tee shirt, and well worn cowboy boots, she all but exuded feminine attraction and he wished her older brother hadn't been standing there with him as his eyes followed her. She made it almost all the way to the end and then went and leaned her head against the wall near the doorway.

Riordan glanced up at Josh with concern and asked, "Is she okay? What's wrong?"

Josh only shook his head and gave Riordan a slightly sad grin and said, "She's fine. Or she will be in a few minutes. She's the best rider I've ever seen, but they really do make her motion sick. She usually just gets off and goes to lie down on the cot in the tack room for a few minutes, but I'm sure she doesn't want you to see her sick. Go take her a cold water bottle out of the fridge in there. She'll probably just put it on her forehead, but she'll appreciate it. And you owe her for riding the horse. She's so busy I had to guilt her into helping me out for a few days so I could have a little time to see my kids."

Turning back to the horse that Riordan noticed was wet with sweat, Josh said, "She gave you quite a work out, didn't she, boy? She made you look good out there. It's probably a good thing she doesn't train. The two of you would beat all of us." He gently patted the big stud, slipped his bridle off and a halter on and then clipped him into the cross tie to take off his saddle and rinse him off before putting him on the horse walker to cool down. Riordan only half heard him as he headed for Jessie with the cold water bottle.

As he approached her, Jessie glanced up and gave him another hesitant smile. He only handed her the water bottle, saying, "Josh said this might help."

Taking it, this time she gave him a sincere smile and sat down on a nearby bale of hay that was stacked beside a stall door and indeed leaned her head back and put the water bottle against her forehead. "Thank you. I'll be fine in a minute. Which is good, 'cause I gotta get to work."

Riordan stood there quietly for a couple of minutes and then asked, "Does riding always make you sick?"

She gave a quiet groan and closed her eyes. "No. Just the reining horses. I'd be fine except for all those spins. It's worse than an amusement park."

Feeling guilty for making her ill, he said, "I can understand why you don't train, then. Although, as gifted as you are, you might consider some Dramamine. You were incredible. It's a pity to waste that."

She opened her eyes and smiled again, this time almost sadly then closed them again and said, "Thanks, but there are a couple of reasons I don't train. And Dramamine makes me a zombie. Josh is better than me, anyway."

Riordan sat down next to her on the bale of hay, realizing anew what the story Josh had told him about their mother had cost Jessie. Still, he had to be honest with her about how well he thought she rode and he said, "Mm. No, he's really not. As good as he is. Not even close. And I can't even believe that was the same horse who was acting so wild just a couple of days ago."

"He'd just had a rough morning, Riordan. If you were jet-lagged, and anxious from a strange drug and being whipped by a lunatic, you'd have acted up, too."

"Yeah, but even without all those things, that horse is usually still a handful. For you, he acted like an old plug."

"Old plugs don't spin and slide like silk like he did, Riordan."

"Still, he seemed happy to be spinning and sliding for you. He always performed for Harper, but he never liked it."

She sat up and turned to him, "You can't demand with a spirit as strong as that horse, Ri. The biggest human in the world still isn't going to be as strong as that horse. It has to be because he wants it. No one likes to be ordered around. You have to ask. That horse will give you his whole heart and then some if you ask. And if you reward him. Nothing big. All he needed was a gentle but firm hand and some kind words and a pat or two. You can't push a rope. You have to work together. You have to ask. We're all that way, really. Happy to cooperate if you're kind." She closed her eyes again. "It's a trust thing."

"Well, he certainly seemed to trust you. You rode him better than I've ever seen anyone ride him."

With her eyes still closed, she said drily, "I'm not riding your horse in the show ring, Riordan. Did Josh put you up to this? You needn't worry. He always takes first place."

"No. He didn't put me up to it. But he should have. He's

only keeping them legged up, anyway. I'm still trying to find a trainer to ride in the show."

At that, she laughed and sat up to pull the water bottle away. "He told you he wouldn't show for you?"

Riordan shook his head. "He said we were the competition."

Jessie laughed again. "He's just giving you the run around. The competition? That's American for of course he'll ride your horses. He doesn't have anything in the stud classes right now, anyway. And your horse will definitely win. He's phenomenal! Quinn's is up for discussion, but yours will win. Josh will ride for you. He's just hassling you. He has a habit of that."

She brushed her hair off of her forehead, sighed quietly and unscrewed the lid on the water bottle to take a long pull and Riordan couldn't help watching her again. Capping the bottle, she stood up, although she still seemed a bit nauseous and glanced at her watch. "I gotta run. Thanks for the water. It really did help. Have a wonderful day."

She hesitantly went out the barn door and disappeared around the corner and Riordan still sat for a long moment, considering the slender, very intriguing veterinarian and the fascination he was feeling since coming to America. Who would have realized the simple act of drinking could take on a life of its own? Especially for him—burnt out on all things female. And where did this interest in a girl come from? A Mormon girl? One who apparently didn't even consider him eligible to go out with, if what Josh had said the day before was true. And it probably was. Jessie was perfectly friendly, but hadn't seemed to truly

Jaclyn M. Hawkes

give either him or Quinn much thought. At least she hadn't taken any of Quinn's flirting banter seriously.

He went back down to where Josh was working and began to help him fill water buckets, thinking about what Jessie had said about Josh riding, and eventually asked, "So, you still not willing to ride in the shows for me?"

"Well, are you still the competition?"

Riordan decided to come right out and ask, "Do you even have any other horses in the stallion classes?"

Josh looked up with a grin. "Jessie put you up to asking me that, didn't she?"

"No. She just said you were giving me the run around. What exactly does that mean, that you're giving me the run around? In American speak? And do you, or do you not already have a horse in the stallion classes?"

Still grinning, Josh said, "*Giving you the run around* is American for I'm not really going to answer any of these questions—yet. Why don't you ask her to ride your horse in the ring? You saw how good she is."

"You were right, she's incredible. But she also looked like she wanted to lose it into the nearest dust bin. And I thought you said she doesn't train."

Standing, Josh gave him a full blown smile and said, "I've been trying to get her to train with me for years and years, but maybe—just maybe, you could be the secret weapon! I've never had a hunky, Australian gazillionaire playboy making the request for me."

Riordan shook his head and laughed. "Right. Your secret weapon. 'Cause she certainly seems to be swooning at my feet. Me being such a Mormon boy and all. I thought you said she wouldn't give me the time of day."

Cheerfully, Josh said, "Probably not. You're right. You refusing to be a Mormon boy and all. But it would be worth a try. I'd do about anything to get her to at least agree to ride in the show ring for me. I'd win everything! Please, feel free to literally haunt her and see if you can get her to give in. Turn on that legendary charm. I'll gladly supply pills for the motion sickness."

Then, with a more serious tone, he added, "I wonder if she could finally come to terms with what happened when she was six years old with our mother. I think she's forgiven her. But I think the specter of someone killing her little sibling for such a superficial reason still haunts her. Not training is her way of dealing with it, but it's not very dealt with, even though it's been twenty-one years."

As he turned off the hose, Riordan shook his head. "Even if I had legendary charm, I doubt it could be the way to deal with a hurt like that."

Grinning again, Josh said, "Oh, I don't know. Maybe your charm is more legendary than you think it is. The least you can do is give it a go. Tell you what. You try to convince her to ride your horse. Seriously give it your best shot. And if it doesn't work, I'll ride your horse in the ring. Deal?"

"Deal."

"But this is going to be a trust thing. So don't just keep

asking her to ride for you. Do other favors for her as well, so she'll want to reciprocate. She's fair to the bone, that one is."

"Other things like what?"

Turning to take the stud off the walker, Josh said over his shoulder, "Oh, big, ugly, hairy favors, like taking her a bottle of cold water when she feels lousy."

Chapter 10

Riordan was still thinking about what Josh had said late that afternoon when McCade asked him if he and Quinn wanted to go with the LDS Young Single Adults to do service at the Humanitarian Center for their Family Home Evening. Riordan had no idea what any of that meant and was just trying to figure out how to discreetly find out if Jessie was going to be there, when Quinn cheerfully asked, "Are there going to be any attractive sheilas there, mate?"

McCade grinned, "Other than my sister, do you mean?"

Quinn nodded his head. "Your sis is certainly a very attractive female. I'll give you that. But that Young Single Adult thing sounded like there might be more as well. Yes?"

"Oh, yeah! Why do you think I'm going, man?"

"Righteous! Then I'm going. What will we be doing?"

McCade laughed and shook his head, "Now what exactly do you think you're going to be doing with a bunch of righteous young single women?"

Riordan only looked between the two of them, wondering what he'd lost in the translation, but when McCade turned to him and asked, "You in, man?" Riordan nodded his head.

"I'm in. What time is this supposed to happen?" The least he could do is start trying to get Jessie to agree to ride their horses in the show ring. For Josh, of course. It had nothing to do with the fact that Jessie was beginning to intrigue him. Or the fact that he didn't really want Jessie hanging out with a bunch of young, single men without him.

McCade leaned across and opened his truck passenger door. "Right away, if you can. We'll drop by and pick up Jessie, and they'll feed us there. Hop in."

When they stopped and honked at the house on the other side of Josh's dad's house, after a minute, Jessie came out, carrying a nalgene bottle of ice water.

With a wave and a, "Hi, all," she climbed up into the truck to sit beside Riordan in the back.

He studied her for a moment, wondering if she was as tired as she looked, and asked, "Feeling better?"

She nodded. "Yes, thank you. Much. Sorry I was a little green around the gills this morning."

He shook his head and held her water bottle while she buckled up. "I should be the one apologizing. It was my horse's fault." He handed her back the water bottle when she was settled and added, "He asked me to beg you to ride him in the show ring, by the way. Said it was the most kind, gentle but firm, undemanding ride he'd ever taken and that he'd like to give you his whole heart, if you'll ride him."

Looking up from her seat belt, she laughed, in spite of her obvious fatigue. "Oh, he said that, did he?"

"Yes. He did. He was quite eloquent about it, actually."

"I'm sure he was. But I regret, I must disappoint him. You see, I'm actually a veterinarian. A very overwhelmed veterinarian for at least the next little while. I don't have time to show horses. During the show, I'll be the veterinarian on call as well, so there just won't be any chance of me riding. Please give him my apologies."

"He'll be so disappointed. But I'll tell him. Although, it's not going to stop me from haunting you and pestering you to give in and agree."

From the front of the truck, Quinn asked, "What are you two talking about back there? Who'll be so disappointed?"

Riordan winked at Jessie and answered, "Hugo."

At that, both McCade and Quinn turned around to look into the back seat and Jessie looked confused as she asked, "You named your horse, Hugo?"

Before she could answer, Quinn asked, "Hugo is disappointed about something? What'd you do to Hugo? And he talks to you?"

Before either of them could answer that, McCade, who had caught part of their earlier conversation, asked Jessie in total surprise, "You rode his horse? How in the heck did Josh talk you into that? You never ride the horses." Then he turned to Riordan with the same confused look that Jessie had and said, "You named a world champion stallion, Hugo? And he talks to you?"

To Jessie, Riordan said, "Well, actually, he came named. I just didn't bother renaming him." Turning to Quinn, he continued, "I'm trying to talk her into riding our horses in the

Jaclyn M. Hawkes

shows, Quinn. She worked them this morning and you should have seen it. Even Josh agrees that she's the best rider. But she won't agree to ride them in the show ring." He grinned and added, "Maybe you could help me persuade her—since you are trying to talk her into marrying you as well. Just add it to the list."

Quinn waved a hand. "Oh, sure. No problem. But no more talking to the horse. That's just weird, Ri."

That made Jessie laugh again and McCade chuckled in the front seat as well, but then he added, "That might just work, Riordan. Maybe the horse can do what the rest of us haven't been able to do. She's always been a sucker for a sweet horse."

At that, Quinn piped in, "Have you actually met, Hugo. Sweet is not exactly the word I'd use to describe him. He's about half outlaw."

With a mellow smile to Jessie, Riordan replied, "That's just because we haven't properly asked him what we want him to do, Quinn. Jessie has him all figured out and yeah, he was being pretty sweet this morning. You should have been there. Oh, but then you're not exactly a morning person some days. I forgot."

Quinn shrugged. "I'm getting better about mornings, mate. The more I hang out with these clean living blokes, the easier mornings are. It's quite miraculous. And here I am tonight, being not only clean living, but doing service as well. You wanna talk about your righteous!"

In the back seat, Jessie smiled and nodded her head. "You go, Quinn, darling. You go. You're probably going to attract tons of girls tonight for you gene pool with your newfound righteous persona!"

112

Quinn grinned back at her. "Yep. That's what I'm talking about." He fingered his diamond stud in his ear. "You think they'll like my bling?"

****

At the Humanitarian Center, they started out with a short tour and a movie presentation that explained some of the projects the Church is involved in. Riordan was surprised at how many young adults had shown up to help out, but he was more amazed at the scope of the service and supplies that the church was providing literally all over the world. And he loved the idea that they weren't just giving donations, but were also teaching the peoples they helped how to be more self-sufficient to overcome the poverty they often lived in.

It made him introspective later as he stood between Jessie and McCade and packed something called newborn kits for mothers in less developed areas of the world. He'd never seen anything like the cloth diapers, plastic cover, diapering salve, or huge safety pins that they were packaging, but when he thought about it, it made sense that they would need to provide items that could be re-used in primitive situations rather than the expensive disposable diapers he saw advertised on TV.

The more he thought about it, the more intrigued he became with the idea of working to improve the standard of living of people all over the world. Though they were only doing physical labor tonight in packaging the kits, the organization that the church had in place to facilitate this type of thing on a massive scale was impressive. He could see how one could donate to this effort and be assured that the help was actually making it to the people who truly needed it, instead of being caught up in a corrupt system somewhere. It made him think again of Matt Damon and of all the millions of dollars that were sitting in his accounts waiting for him to figure out what he was going to do with it. He left that night, actually kind of excited about doing something in the future for the first time since he'd sold his company.

Back in the truck as they were getting ready to leave, he asked McCade, "So, if someone wanted to contribute to this humanitarian aid, financially speaking, who would he talk to?"

McCade grinned back at him. "If *someone* wanted to contribute, they'd probably start with Church headquarters in Salt Lake. I'm sure there's a contact number on the website. And I'll ask President Glade for you as well."

On the way home, Jessie literally wilted from fatigue. It was after ten o'clock Mesa time and she had finished riding at least two horses before seven o'clock that morning. As her head banged against the window when she fell asleep, Riordan unbuckled his seat belt and scooted over next to her and gently pulled her head to lean against his shoulder. It would be much more comfortable than the hard window.

His phone buzzed and he looked down to see that he'd gotten a text from his mum saying, "Just checking in, love. Miss you. Call us." He texted her back and then thought about his mum as he breathed in the scent of Jessie's shampoo. His mum would have adored Jessie.

That night, he Googled the Church of Jesus Christ of Latter Day Saints' website and pulled some contact information off of it and sent it to Rich to begin researching how he could donate to their humanitarian efforts. He'd specifically like to be involved in providing clean water sources.

Chapter 11

The next morning, Riordan showed up at the barn at just a little after six a.m. in hopes of getting to see more of Jessie actually working the horses and he wasn't disappointed. She arrived minutes later, munching on a bagel and it was definitely worth the early morning to see her swing up onto both Quinn's and his horse and put them through a work out there in the cool of the morning at the arena.

She was the very picture of both grace and balance and she rode as if she were a part of the horses, even when they were at the height of a fast spin or run. She handled both of them quietly, but they gave her exacting obedience and it was like watching a complicated ballet or something as the girl and beast worked together. Again, both horses behaved as if they enjoyed being ridden by Jessie. You'd have thought she had been training these two horses for years instead of this being the second day.

Again, at a bit before seven, she dismounted Hugo and handed him off to Josh and this time Riordan was ready with the cold water bottle. Instead of leaving immediately, she went into the tack room and lay down and Riordan followed Josh into the tack room to talk to her a few minutes later after they had the stallion on the walker. Josh went to the fridge again and brought another water bottle. Approaching Jessie, he lifted up her head and pulled her hair aside and put the second water bottle under her neck.

His actions were gentle and the friendship between the two of them was sweet to watch, even as Josh began to tease her about her queasiness as he said, "You know, Jessie, we boys grew out of this car sick thing when we were about seven. You ought to be about old enough not to go here anymore."

With a small groan, Jessie said, "Watch it, bub. Or you'll be riding two more horses every morning and wondering what your kids look like for a few weeks. And I'm fine in a car—most of the time."

Josh laughed, "Yeah, right. As long as you're only going down the block. Who are you trying to kid?"

She groaned again and turned on her side. "Leave me alone or I'm going to hurl into your garbage barrel. Don't you need to feed something? Or groom it. Leave me in peace. Cal just called in sick and I need to get myself together to deal with everything without him today. Go away."

At that revelation, Josh glanced up at Riordan and gave a small nod at her and Riordan knew exactly what he was hinting at and said, "I'm usually an office guy, but I've spent my fair share of time in a veterinary clinic handling horses. Could you use my help today? To help out without Cal?"

Jaclyn M. Hawkes

She sat up and looked up at him and then looked from him to Josh and back and asked, "Why do I get the feeling that this is a vast right wing conspiracy? And why do I not care? Can you really spare some time today? I would absolutely love some help at the clinic. But I'm warning you, I've got a couple of completely boneheaded horses coming in. You might regret offering. Do you really have the time?"

Nodding, Riordan glanced at Josh and said, "I'll make the time. It's not like I have gobs on my calendar. Just tell me when you're ready."

Sighing, she pushed to the edge of the cot and slowly stood up. "We might as well go now. Do you want to follow me in your new pretty truck, or ride in the vetmobile?"

Grinning, he said, "The vetmobile, definitely."

****

They'd been working at the clinic through the morning and had, indeed, dealt with the two boneheaded horses, which Riordan handled admirably well, and were now deciding what to order in for lunch. They narrowed it down to Chinese and Riordan was calling it in, when they heard the outer door open. Knowing she didn't have any immediate appointments, she went to see to whoever it was and was surprised to see her attorney friend Clay standing in her reception area.

As she walked in, he gave her a big smile and said, "Hey, Jessie. I was in the neighborhood and decided to drop in and see if you have time for lunch. I was thinking the Della Fontana."

Of course, Clay would choose the nicest restaurant around, but it was also Caleb's restaurant. She knew from recent experience that that would be totally awkward. Thank goodness she already had plans to eat in with Riordan. At that moment, Riordan came through the door into the reception area and said with his sexy accent, "Chinese should be here in twenty minutes. And they did have potstickers today."

Even though he was wearing one of the Mesa Valley Veterinary lab coats, Clay's look soured markedly as he looked at the tall, handsome Australian. Turning to Jessie, he asked almost sharply, "New vet tech? Where's Cal?"

For some reason, his slightly dictatorial tone made a little rebellious spirit rise up in the back of her mind and she attempted to quell it as she calmly turned to Riordan and said, "Riordan, this is a friend of mine, Clay Caldwell. Clay, this is another friend of mine, Riordan Kane. Cal is out sick and Riordan is sort of interning today to see if this might be something he wants to pursue. He's here in the states with a horse to compete in the USA National Stock Show."

Riordan smiled cheerfully and stepped forward, a hand outstretched. Clay, on the other hand, hesitated for just that stupid, posturing second or two that men sometimes did that seemed so petulant and then took Riordan's hand as Riordan said, "Good to meet you, Clay."

Clay almost wrinkled his nose as he said, "Delighted, I'm sure."

Jessie rolled her eyes where Clay couldn't see and was grateful to feel her phone buzz in her pocket. To the two men, she said, "Excuse me. I need to get this." Then, to save Riordan from the awkwardness she was leaving in the reception area, she

Jaclyn M. Hawkes

said, "Riordan, would you mind putting those last x-rays up on the light wall. I'll be right there to read them."

She stepped into her office to answer the call, which was only to schedule an appointment. After putting it into the computer, she turned to go in to the light wall to explain to Riordan that she hadn't really needed him, when from the reception area, she heard Clay saying in a decidedly cold and very lawyerish voice, "I'm not buying the internship thing. I've dealt with your type before, loser blue collar weasel trying to slip in the back door as an employee to get close to her. Yeah, I'm sure she's something you want to pursue, but she's taken, so get lost. Now! If you know what is in your best interest."

Her eyes widened and the little rebel spirit mushroomed exponentially in less than the second it took for her to cross to the reception area door and open it. Standing there in the doorway, she looked Clay in the eye and took a deep breath to calm down so that she wouldn't rip his head off like she wanted to.

It actually took two deep breaths as she debated just how brutal to be as she assured him that she so wasn't "taken". Then, she decided to just dispense with all the drama and not take the chance that she would lose her cool. To that end, she simply said, "Clay, I heard what you just said. I'm sorry I've inadvertently given you the wrong impression. We won't be doing lunch today. Please leave. And don't contact me again. Ever."

He put out a hand and started to say something, but she only shook her head and to Riordan said, "Riordan, could I see

120

you at the light wall?" With that, she turned and walked out of the reception area, listening to see what was going to happen behind her, and wondering if this was going to be over that fast, or get ugly. Thankfully, all she heard was Clay swearing under his breath and then the door to the street slammed.

A second later, Riordan walked through the door to her and she let out a huge sigh and shook her head and said, "I'm so sorry about that, Riordan. He obviously misinterpreted why you're here. I had no idea he was going to show up today and certainly had no idea he would be so rude or threaten anyone to stay away from me. I've never given him any kind of inference that he has exclusivity. I'm sorry you had to be the target of such nonsense when you're being so kind to help me out today."

Riordan only raised a hand as if to brush it all off. "Not a problem, Jessie. I almost feel bad for the poor self-assured stiff. It can't be easy for him to be so thoroughly insulted in front of another man."

Rolling her eyes again, Jessie paced across the room and back, and then turned and started to do it again, grumbling to herself under her breath that she should have listened to Polly all along. Riordan smiled and put out a hand. "Jessie. Stop. Settle down. I know confrontation is unpleasant. But it's over. And it's okay. He didn't appear to be a keeper anyway. Let it go."

For just a second, she wondered if Riordan was trying to order her around in turn, and then she took another big breath and let it out and sat down in a nearby chair. Riordan was right. And he wasn't ordering her around. He was just hoping to get her to see that being stressed was silly here. As she sat, Riordan

Jaclyn M. Hawkes

came and dropped a gentle hand to her shoulder and gave it a light squeeze and asked, "Don't ya just hate the meat market?"

That made her laugh. "Yes. I absolutely hate it. Just not as much as I hate the thought of being single forever and never having a family of my own. So I keep trying." She looked up at Riordan's gorgeous face and physique and laughed again. "But surely, you know nothing of the meat market. How could you possibly?"

He only laughed himself and shook his head and asked, "What, is that American for 'you're clueless, Riordan'?" When they heard the outer door open again, he put out a hand as if to stop her from getting up and said, "I'll handle it this time. Relax."

"No. Riordan . . ."

She stood up and was just going to tell him that this was her responsibility, not his, when they heard a voice in the reception area say, "Chinese delivery."

Heaving yet another big sigh, she followed Riordan through the door and could have kissed the teenaged Asian boy who stood there holding a paper bag that smelled fabulous. She did actually put an arm around the kid as she took the cash out of her lab coat to pay for the food and then thanked him. Potstickers were exactly what she needed right now to forget Clay and this mix-up.

The afternoon passed relatively uneventfully until just as they were finishing up for the day, Jorge showed up with Pablo and Marcela. He rushed in the door with both kids and a diaper

122

bag and 2 car seats in tow and asked, "Jessie, can I ask you a mas favor, por favor? Can Pablo and Marcela hang out wi' you for while. Es emergencia."

He looked so stressed and Pablo looked so sad that Jessie didn't even ask, she just took the baby and put a gentle arm around Pablo and pulled him against her side as she said, "Absolutely. I'm just leaving here and then we'll be at my house whenever you get back. No worries."

Jorge nodded and rushed out the door as she felt little Pablo's shoulders begin to shake. Handing the gurgling baby to Riordan, Jessie took Pablo's hand and led him into the overstuffed chair in her office. She sat down and patted her knee and Pablo climbed up onto her lap and she began to rock him as she rubbed his skinny little back as he sobbed. At length, as he calmed down, she asked, "Do you want to talk or just rock, Pab?"

His tears started up again and he choked out, "My madre, she does not love us anymore. She is leaving us."

Jessie's heart squeezed in her chest and tears started in her own eyes, but she shook her head almost with a vengeance even though Pablo couldn't see her. This child wasn't going to lose his childhood. Not on her watch, and she said, "No. Pablo. It's not that she doesn't love you. Your mother loves you very much. She's just sick. But maybe she can get better. Even if she doesn't get better, don't think she doesn't love you. And your dad loves you. And we all love you. Mr. Benjamin, and Josh, and Brennan, and McCade and me and their families. And Polly and Ralph. And our neighbors. We all love you. Very much."

She rubbed his back again as she looked up to see Riordan standing in the doorway awkwardly holding Marcela who was drooling onto his arm. Still rubbing, she said again, "We all love you, Pablo. And we're going to be right here beside you to help take care of you. It's going to be okay. I promise, somehow, it's going to be okay."

He nodded, even though he was still breathing with little shudders. Finally, he looked up to see Riordan standing there with Marcela and he pushed off of Jessie's lap to go to her desk and pull a tissue to dutifully begin to mop up Riordan's arm where Marcela had slobbered on it, saying, "Sorry, amigo. Marcela, she is teething. Es very messy. At least she isn't grumpy bambina this time. So sorry."

Riordan's only reaction was to put a hand on Pablo's head and say, "She's just fine, my friend. She's a cute little girl. And it seems that you are a very good big brother."

Pablo climbed back onto Jessie's lap and cuddled into her side again, nodding solemnly. "Yes, I am a very good brother. And Marcela is a very good little sister." He looked up at Jessie and continued, but with a questioning lilt to his voice, "And we're going to be okay, together?"

Leaning down to him, Jessie said positively, "Yes. We're all going to be okay together. Now, I'm thinking about dinner. Do you think you would like to have some dinner soon?"

The little boy nodded against her, sounding very sleepy. "Si. Dinner would be good."

Jessie wondered how likely it would be that the two of them would be able to stay awake on the drive across to her house. On second thought, she took them into the refrigerator and let Pablo dig through her stash of yogurt and string cheese and fruit to pick something to eat just in case she lost them enroute and then they all went to leave.

However, at the door, she realized that she wouldn't be able to fit all four of them, including the two car seats into the front seat of her call truck. As she realized it, Riordan must have realized at the same time, because he set down the car seats he was carrying and said, "You stay with them and I'll run up and bring my truck from the barn."

Nodding wordlessly, she handed him her keys and took the kids back into her office and rocked them as they ate their snacks. And she'd been right. Before Riordan showed up just a few minutes later, both children were sound asleep on her lap. As he came in, Riordan only smiled down at the three of them, picked up the car seats, and then went back out.

He was gone for what seemed like a long time, and finally, Jessie carefully stood and left the children sleeping in the chair and went to see where Riordan had gotten to. She found him in the parking lot, working diligently to figure out how to install the second car seat in the back seat of his truck. As she came out, he looked up and shook his head and said, "Crikeys it's a good thing I don't have any children. These things are impossible. How is a mere human supposed to figure this out?"

She knew from experience exactly what he was talking about and together the two of them ultimately figured out that Marcela's seat was supposed to go in backwards. As they finally buckled both sleeping children into the pretty new black truck

Jaclyn M. Hawkes

and climbed in themselves, Riordan looked at his watch and made Jessie laugh as he said, "Well, that only took us twenty-seven minutes. It's a good thing we had nowhere we had to be in a hurry. I think I'm more exhausted from that than from the whole rest of the day."

As they pulled out of her clinic, she said, "Can you drop me at the barn and I'll grab my vetmobile?"

Riordan got a concerned look on his face. "And leave me with them alone? Without you?"

Jessie laughed again. "Riordan, it's like a three minute drive from there to my house. I think you'll be okay."

He nodded. "Okay. But come straight there. What should I do if one of them wakes up?"

"Tell them we'll be to Aunt Jessie's house in three minutes." She smiled and leaned across to pat his arm, to which he shot her a skeptical look, and she added, "You're actually kind of cute with a baby drooling all over you. You'll be fine, Riordan."

And he was fine. In fact, way more than fine as he walked into her kitchen carrying Pablo. Kind of cute was the understatement of the year as he gently put the little boy in her guest room bed and went back out to bring in the car seats and diaper bag. Somehow, seeing him with the kids that he was so obviously not used to, but still so willing to gently watch over, made the soft spoken Australian more attractive than ever. He would be a great father someday.

With the kids safely settled, she walked with him back out to her living room and to the door, where he looked all around and said, "Your house is great. It reflects the Southwest, but is still kind of feminine. It's beautiful."

126

"Thanks. I designed it and decorated it myself. Thank you for today. For all of it. Helping at the clinic, dealing with Clay, and helping me with these guys. I'd have died without you. Thank you."

"You're welcome. But will you be okay with them? Do you have any idea where their dad went?"

"No. But he's worked for my dad since I was ten. He's as rock solid as they come. Their mother is giving him fits, but he'll be back as soon as he can. Don't worry. If he's not back by tomorrow morning, my dad's housekeeper Polly will come and sit with them until they wake up, and then she'll take them over there. One way or another they'll be fine. But we should all keep praying for them."

He nodded and then said, "Your family is awesome. You are amazingly tight."

She thought for a moment about her own mother and then tried to push that thought out of her mind. Except for her mother they definitely were awesomely tight. Looking back up at Riordan, she said, "Yeah, my family is the best. We have our moments, sure, but we all love each other to pieces. It's the best feeling in the world."

Standing there with him at the door was too much like saying goodnight at the end of a date. It made her extremely conscious of the very attractiveness of Riordan Kane standing there in her home. It was silly, because they'd never so much as even gone out, but for some reason, she really wanted him to lean down and kiss her. Just at the thought, she felt her face grow warm and looked up, hoping he couldn't read her mind.

But then as she looked up, she saw him glance at her mouth. He wasn't going to kiss her. Certainly not, they were just friends, but maybe . . . just maybe, he wanted that too.

He stopped looking at her mouth and met her eyes for just a long second that felt longer and then turned away and said over his shoulder, "I'm just at Josh's. If you have any more emergencias, call me and I'll come help you."

"I will, thank you, Riordan. Have a good night."

She shut the door behind him and then leaned against it, thinking about the butterflies that were in her stomach, flitting around, thinking they were supposed to be all excited about a gorgeous Australian, when they weren't supposed to be—really. She felt silly and breathless all at the same time. She needed to be more careful where Riordan Kane was concerned. He wasn't LDS, and marriage obviously wasn't a priority for him, but he was pretty much lethally attractive and lethal was dangerous if her heart got involved. In his case, he could be especially dangerous, because her heart didn't seem to be listening to her head.

She sighed and left the door to go back and check on the children and then start settling in for the night. The big stock show started the next day and she was going to be busy enough that maybe she wouldn't have time to think about any sexy Australian businessmen.

****

Riordan really didn't even need to drive the short distance to Josh's, but he didn't want to leave his truck parked in Jessie's way. He was tired, but there was a restlessness upon him that he knew from experience would keep him from sleeping. Pulling into the driveway, he sat in his truck and watched Josh's son playing in the sprinklers on Josh's small front lawn while Josh and Lucy and the baby watched from the front porch as the sun began to set. It was an idyllic scene, but for some reason, it only made the restlessness he'd been feeling worse.

He wanted kids someday, and had even been thinking lately that he needed to get back to being more serious about finding a girl and settling down, but honestly, the whole idea was frustrating. Really, really frustrating.

When he was younger, he'd thought weeding out the girls who were superficial or materialistic would get easier the older, wiser, and more mature he got, but that hadn't been the case. He hadn't factored in how becoming wealthy would affect everything.

Then he'd been schooled by the couple of shonky girls who had flat out used him. Add to that the upwardly mobile show pony circle he'd landed in because of his business dealings, and the forecast for finding a truly nice, honorable, but attractive girl had become all but bleak because he realized now just how hard it was going to be to find her.

Lately, he'd all but given up, but then today watching Jessie with Pablo and Marcela had made it blatantly clear to him just what he'd been missing. Jessie was that truly nice, honorable and attractive girl—who only wanted to marry a Mormon, and so far hadn't really even so much as flirted with him. This evening, having her hand him that baby girl, right out of the blue had been mind blowing. He'd had no idea holding a baby would be that evocative. Then, her reassuring that little boy when he'd been so sad. And now watching Josh with his pretty wife and children—it left a frustrating almost hunger in his gut that was troubling.

On second thought, he waved to Josh and Lucy and backed back out of the driveway to go find Quinn. Quinn was usually good for entertainment. Instead of going home, he'd go hang with Quinn for awhile and see if he could shake this troubling introspection.

Two hours later, as he watched Quinn drink himself into stupidity and hang all over a couple of very willing but pathetic girls, Riordan realized he'd made a mistake in thinking that carousing with Quinn would make him less restless. It only made things worse.

He tried not to compare the loose and wild girls with Quinn to Jessie's open and honest, but truly classy and beautiful, and definitely modest and unpromiscuous demeanor. But as one of the girls leaned over against him, giving him a close up view of too much cleavage, and breathed Jose Quervo breath on him as she said something decidedly crass, he failed. He couldn't help but know that Jessie would never in her life lower herself to that level of trashiness. There was simply no way not to notice the difference in the two types of girls.

Pushing away his Coke that was starting to go flat, he got up from the table and went around to Quinn and said, "I'm leaving. You wanna come with? Or should I leave you to your princesses?" He couldn't contain the touch of sarcasm in his voice as he said the word princesses and Quinn was apparently still with it enough to notice, because he grimaced in confusion for a minute, then looked over at the girls and said, "No, mate. No more princesses tonight. Take me with you. Maybe I'll feel better in the morning if I leave now, huh?"

Dragging Quinn up and trying to steer him out the door to the parking lot, Riordan said to himself, "I think it's a bit too late for that, mate, but good luck to you." To Quinn he said, "Just try to make it to the parking lot, eh, buddy. And don't you dare throw up tequila in my new pretty truck. Especially not on that bench seat. I'm going to need that bench seat someday. Hopefully."

Chapter 12

The morning of the start of the big stock show dawned clear and bright and was hot from the second the sun topped the low ridge to the east. That blazing sunrise seemed a harbinger of the way the stock show was going to turn out because Jessie began getting vet calls before it was even seven in the morning. There were the usual sprains and strains, but for this area there were also the calls from trainers who hadn't anticipated how the extreme heat and dry desert air would affect the horses that weren't used to it. Even with air conditioned barns and humidifiers, if the horses were brought in trailers that weren't air conditioned in the heat of the day, they suffered from heat exhaustion and dehydration just the way humans did.

In addition, the very nature of reining could be dangerous to the animal athletes. It was a very demanding sport and Jessie was definitely looking forward to Dr. Stettler, the new vet, who was scheduled to show up later that day. He was going to get a baptism by fire straight into the thick of the stock show. That was for sure.

Jessie had been up late waiting for Jorge, who had called and said he would be by to pick up the kids at eleven. Then she had gotten up early enough to be to the complex by six to exercise the two Australian's horses before things got too busy. She'd finished in time to start the vet calls, but she was completely motion sick, and really missed Riordan being there to baby her for a few minutes. She'd gotten very comfortable with him hanging around off and on throughout the day, helping her out with whatever she was doing and occasionally badgering her to ride his horse in the show ring.

By nine, he still hadn't shown up and she wondered if she'd offended him the day before, or if something was wrong, but then he showed up as she was examining a horse that had come up lame after one of the show classes. The barn was busy and loud and there were people constantly going past and even ducking under the cross tie and the horse she was examining was becoming more and more nervous.

As another person went by and ducked under the cross tie, the trainer whose horse she was examining turned to the man and snarled a profanity laced comment. The cross tied horse jumped at the raised voice and the passing man turned and said something back. Jessie grimaced as she backed away from the horse for a moment. That had been a close one. The horse had barely missed landing on her foot as it hung back against the cross tie and she still hadn't even been able to examine it.

Taking a deep breath, she said to Cal, "Draw me some Acepromazine. Point three five CCs and see if you can keep these people back. I really don't want to be standing under this horse trying to examine a hoof in all this bustle."

Cal nodded and she stepped back before trying to pick up the horse's foot again and turned to the horse trainer and said, "Please try to keep your voice down. You're only making him more nervous and watch your mouth, huh? We're trying to work here. Have a little respect."

As she said it, the trainer turned on her and growled, "Don't tell me how to handle my own horse, lady. I know perfectly well how to deal with my own horses. Just do your job and keep your mouth shut."

His snarled comment was followed with more profanity and Jessie straightened up from where she'd been about to treat his horse. Turning to Cal, she said, "Forget the sedative, just give me some Bantamine."

He handed her a syringe that she smoothly injected into the horse's neck, then she turned back to her truck and picked up a stylus to scribble something on a tablet. The mouthy trainer tore into her again with more of the profanity, wondering why she had walked away from his horse. At his continued diatribe, she was surprised to hear Riordan's voice behind her say almost silkily, "The lady asked you to watch your mouth. If you want the horse treated, I'd suggest you do as she asked. She's not going to put up with it and the rest of us aren't going to let you disrespect her, either."

The trainer went off again and Jessie turned back to them, but Cal and two other men had already walked up next to Riordan and a small crowd had gathered around. Narrowing his eyes, the trainer glared at Riordan and said, "She's a horse vet! She oughta be able to handle typical horseman talk or get a new job! What does your vet with the tender ears say to that?"

Shaking her head, she reached for a sheet of paper coming out of the printer and handed it to the foul-mouthed trainer. "She says find yourself another veterinarian. Here's my bill for what I've already done and the Bantamine. Have a good day, sir."

She snapped off her exam gloves and tossed them into the nearby garbage can, glanced over her shoulder at Cal and then said to Riordan, "You coming with us, Ri? If you are, get in the truck, I've got five more calls lined up waiting for me."

The three of them piled into the truck and drove away and finally, Jessie took a big deep breath of relief and said, "You oughta watch yourself, Riordan. He'd been drinking and he had more guts than brains. You might have gotten yourself punched in the mouth. It would be a shame to mess up a face as pretty as yours. But thank you for backing me up. He might have punched me, too. Maybe you'd better wear a lab coat again. Apparently I need reinforcements."

Riordan grinned as he pulled off his golf shirt in one smooth movement and put on the extra lab coat that was hanging behind the seat, "You're welcome, but how do you know I wasn't trying to protect him? It was his pretty face I was worrying about. Maybe I was just worried you were going to take a buggy whip to him."

Cal laughed right out loud, but Jessie only rolled her eyes and kept driving.

Jaclyn M. Hawkes

At the next call, Quinn wandered into the barn looking thrashed and Jessie, assuming he was as hung over as he looked, cheerfully said, "Goalie darling, good morning! You're looking particularly chipper this morning. How are you feeling?"

Running a hand through his half wild hair, Quinn groaned and said, "Oh, chipper as . . . chipper as . . . oh, man, I gotta quit partying. Can you get all these people and horses to quiet down a bit? Does this mob have to be so loud?"

As she stitched up a sedated horse, Jessie said conversationally, "I never have quite understood how simply drinking alcohol until you're completely incoherent equated to partying. I mean, the word party used to mean like a party. Do you remember when you were in sixth grade and a birthday *party* meant games and cake and fun and laughing. And somehow, now, people don't even know if they're having fun because mostly they're just not cognizant. That's such a weird saying to me. It doesn't even look fun to me. Alcohol is actually a depressant, you know.

"I'd worry too much about what embarrassing and stupid things I was doing when I was out of it, if I was a drinker. And there's the consequences of what you did, that you don't remember what you did, or who you did it with. And then it seems extra stupid for famous people who are getting photographed all the time when they are oblivious and then somebody posts everything to Facebook or something. I personally have a hard enough time keeping my foot out of my mouth cold sober. That's not even taking into account the fact that it's highly addictive. And then the next morning looks so very, very pleasant."

136

She gestured toward Quinn, who had plunked himself down on a nearby bale of hay before shaking her head and saying, "I don't know. It just doesn't seem all that partyish to me. Not to be rude, Quinn darling, but to me it just seems kind of . . . dumb."

From his bale of hay, Quinn closed his eyes and said, "What? Is that American for you're a total idiot, Quinn? Why didn't you give me that little speech about twelve hours ago, Doc?"

Snipping her suture ends, Jessie said cheerfully, "Well, it wasn't really a speech. Just the musings of a long time partier observer. But let me know when you're planning to imbibe so festively again and I'll be glad to muse out loud to you before you head out."

Giving her a tired grin, Quinn said, "Ever the server."

"You know it, darling. In the mean time, there's some aspirin in the glove box of my truck."

Standing hesitantly, Quinn said, "I think it's going to take more than just aspirin to quash this pound, but that's a start." To Riordan, he said, "Crikeys, Ri, why didn't you stop me after that third round of grog? You weren't even drinking. You could have saved me. This is all your fault."

Chuckling humorlessly, Riordan shook his head, "Oh, no you don't. I am not your mum. You get to own your own decisions. And speaking of photographing famous people, your coach would kill you if he saw you like this. If anyone posted photos, he probably already has seen you. Why did you even come out this morning? Just go back to the hotel and have a lie down. Your horse isn't even competing today."

"I had to come and tell you that Kyra Beven rang looking for you. She keeps ringing my mobile to get your number. Says the one she has for you isn't working. Apparently, she has decided she loves Yank reining horses and wants to come to America and hang out with you. Since when are you and Kyra an item?"

Drily, Riordan said, "Since about a minute after the financial section of the newspaper got wind of the sale of my company. I'm not taking her calls. If she calls again, tell her she'll hate America and not to come."

Mimicking Riordan's earlier comment, Quinn said, "Oh, no you don't. I am not your mum. You get to own your own sheila issues. Tell her yourself. I'm not crossing Kyra Beven. She's too ornery for me. You're on your own with that one."

Jessie and Cal just kept working as Riordan replied, "Some friend you are. I did haul your butt out of that pub last night instead of leaving you to the mercy of the girls you were drinking with. That should count for at least dealing with Kyra Beven. I could have left you."

At that, Quinn sat up and asked, "Wait, I was with girls last night? As in plural?"

Nodding, Riordan said, "As in plural. But don't worry. They were totally respectable types. Mum Montere would have loved you hanging out with them."

Quinn winced. "I see. Okay. You're right. I owe you one. I'll tell Kyra about how awful America is."

Still working, Jessie said, "Hey, now. Don't be dissing my country. Tell her something else."

"Such as?"

Riordan broke in. "Such as Riordan doesn't want to see you. Why would I want to see a girl who is known to be ornery?"

Quinn shrugged, "Well, she is pretty."

Cal shook his head and interjected, "No. Pretty doesn't cancel ornery. Nothing cancels out ornery. If she's ornery, run away."

Both Riordan and Quinn nodded and Jessie rolled her eyes at all three of them and poor ornery Kyra Beven, who wasn't even there to defend herself, although Cal definitely had a point. Abruptly changing the subject, she said, "Speaking of lunch. Any of ya'll hungry?" She tossed her exam gloves and dusted off her lab coat. She hadn't had nearly enough breakfast before coming riding this morning. "Quinn, you up to facing all the folks up at the food trucks outside the Saguaro Arena? Or should we bring something back for you?" She grinned at the confused look on all their faces and went on, "We were speaking about lunch, weren't we?"

****

As the four of them stood in the line of a food truck outside the main Saguaro Arena waiting for smoked brisket sandwiches, Riordan realized he was hungrier than he'd thought. Beside him, Jessie took a deep breath of the aroma and almost sighed and he smiled as she said, "God bless whoever invented smoky barbecue."

Taking a deep breath of his own, he asked, "Is it that good, then?"

"Yes. It's that good. You're going to love it!"

For a few minutes, they all four small talked back and forth as they waited and then Riordan saw the smile stall off Jessie's face and she seemed to almost visibly stiffen and turn to face forward away from the other three of them. Wondering what was going on, he waited a moment and then casually glanced behind them to see a middle aged blonde woman who almost certainly had to be Jessie's mum standing a few people back in the line. She was wearing a lot more make up than Jessie ever wore, and was dressed in full show garb right down to the long fringed chaps that the riders wore in the show ring, but she was a dead ringer for an older Jessie.

The woman glanced up almost defiantly at Riordan and he realized she must have seen Jessie turn away from her. Josh had mentioned that things weren't dealt with here, and he obviously hadn't been kidding. It was still awkward enough that it even made Riordan a bit uncomfortable. How sad to not be able to speak to your own mum twenty-one years later.

Turning back to the others, he casually stepped forward a step to be between Jessie and the mum in hopes Jessie's easy smile would return. She'd already had a long morning; it would be a shame if she couldn't simply eat some lunch in peace before stepping back into the rat race of her busy afternoon.

They were in line for a couple more minutes and then had to walk past the blonde woman to leave, but still, Jessie never acknowledged the woman, and her smile certainly didn't make its appearance again for almost another hour after lunch.

140

They'd looked at two horses in the afternoon, and Quinn had gone back to his hotel when Jessie got an emergency call from the race track that was a couple of kilometers down the highway from the horse arena complex, reporting that they'd had a horse break a leg right on the track and they needed Jessie immediately. Apparently it was in a race that had been both televised and simulcast and the horse, with the obviously broken leg on all the cameras was creating a public relations nightmare. Not to mention that the horse was surely in excruciating pain. Jessie, Riordan, and Cal hopped into the front of the vetmobile with Jessie driving and went flying down the highway headed that way, going as fast as the vetmobile would take them.

About two hundreds yards from the off ramp to the track and just when Riordan had begun to wonder if he needed to be worried about how fast Jessie was going, he heard the signature wail of a police siren and heard Jessie start to grumble under her breath. She pulled over not far from the entrance to the track, still grumbling and Cal began digging in the glove box for the truck's documentation.

As the cop approached Jessie's window, they heard him calling for a tow truck and then Jessie's phone rang again. She answered it and they could hear her half of the conversation, "Dr. Benn. Yeah, Rick, I'm just outside the gate. I'm trying, but I just got pulled over. I'll be . . . "

Before she could even finish the conversation, the cop yanked open the driver's side door and barked, "Out of the truck! You're under arrest! Turn around and put your hands on the vehicle. It's going to be impounded. You were going a hundred and six back there, in a sixty-five! Get out of the vehicle!"

Still, holding her phone, Jessie repeatedly tried to explain, but the cop was having none of it and Riordan was horrified as the cop literally yanked Jessie out of the truck and shoved her up against the side, to which she let out a screech of complete outrage. Then the cop none-too-gently kicked her legs apart and had begun to pat down her sides when his radio went off. He swore under his breath, ignored the dispatcher, and continued to yell at Jessie, but almost immediately, the radio in his patrol car went off as well.

Snarling, "Stay right where you are!" the cop thumbed the radio at his collar and snapped, "Patterson! What? I'm right in the middle of an arrest! Can't it wait? What d' you need?"

A male voice exploded across the radio line, "Patterson, this is Deputy Chief Leifsen over at the track, and you let that woman go this second, do you hear me? We've got three TV cameras and thousands of people watching a horse with an obvious fracture laying on the track down the way and we need that vet stat! Do you hear me! Now you get back in your car and give her a police escort and you do it politely, or I'll have your badge and gun today! And we heard everything over her phone. Don't you ever treat someone like that again! I don't care how fast they're going! Do I make myself clear?"

Patterson literally stood up straight and paled as he replied meekly, "Yes, Sir. I'm on my way, Sir."

Turning back to Jessie, Patterson begrudgingly said, "You heard him as well as I did. Get in and follow me."

With that, he strode to his patrol car, turned on the lights and took off down the highway. Still visibly shaken from the rough treatment she'd just received, Jessie stood for a moment, her eyes tear bright.

Everything had happened so fast that Riordan had barely gotten his door open. Now, he hustled around the truck, seriously wanting to strangle the hot shot cop and instinctively wrapped Jessie in a hug and softly asked, "You okay, Jess?"

She nodded woodenly against him and he looked up at Cal, who was sitting in the middle of the bench seat of the truck and gently said, "Scoot over, Cal. Let her in where you're at, and I'll drive. She's a little shell shocked. Understandably."

Her phone, that was still in her hand, was still apparently connected to the track and as Riordan nudged Jessie to climb into the truck, he handed the phone to Cal. "Can you take the call, Cal? Give her a minute to try to regain her composure."

He climbed in and gunned the truck to follow the cop, then, still hoping to comfort her, reached for her hand and gave it a gentle squeeze and glanced down at her. "You okay?"

She only nodded again and he rubbed her fingers and said, "You're okay, Jessie. This isn't going to take very long. Just try to put the drongo cop out of your mind and get ready to take care of this horse. It's in a lot of pain, and you know how to help it. Focus on the horse and let your training just kick in. Okay?"

This time, she nodded more confidently, but she still gripped his hand and he kept talking to her, gently reminding her that she was okay and they'd help her through the whole situation.

Once inside the track property, Cal talked him through how to get right to where the horse was and then as they all jumped out of the truck, Riordan took just a minute to stand right in front of Jessie, get her to look up at him and say as he nodded his own head up and down, "You're okay, right? You're okay, and Cal and I are going to be right here beside you, helping you all the way. And the cop is going to stay clear away from you. All right? You're okay."She nodded back and reached for a bag of instruments and turned for the track.

When they got to the horse, it lay on its side in the dirt of the track with a mob of men around it trying to keep it calm as two leaned on its neck so it couldn't try to get up. Its foreleg was extended out in front of it with an obvious bend where there shouldn't have been one and the horse was damp, presumably from perspiring. Jessie took a moment to assess what was going on and then began to dig in her bag as she said, "Someone bring a hose, this filly is way too stressed and overheated. Get me some water. And I need the two of you here out of my way, please."

She knelt beside the horse's neck and ran her scan thermometer over the mare's brisket and then looked at it and shook her head. "Get me a hose, now! And could someone please let the announcer know that what I'm giving the horse is sedation, not euthanasia. I don't want this whole crowd to think I've killed this horse right in front of them."

Right away someone appeared pulling a hose spouting water and Jessie took it. "Okay, keep trying to hang on to her. She'll probably want to spook, but don't let her get up. We've got to try to get her cooled before I can sedate her. Cal, can you draw me point four five CCs of Acepromazine? Then can you find the owner or trainer and have him sign for treatment? Once you find him, I'll need the slings."

She carefully and quietly moved up next to the horse and slowly began to run the cold hose over the horse, starting at her hind legs. The horse actually stayed calm initially, but as soon as the water began to run over her belly and front shoulder, she began to kick and fight. A couple of the men who were trying to hold her got jostled away and they banged into Jessie and the hose sprayed several of them in the process. Water was flying, the race horse was kicking and groaning and the men holding her were desperately trying to hang on to her so she couldn't try to stand on her broken leg.

After a minute or two of struggle, the filly calmed back down and Jessie leaned up to take the syringe from Cal and inject it into the filly's jugular. Within seconds, the filly laid her head right down flat on the track and quit straining and everyone around took a deep breath of relief. In the relative calm, they could hear the announcer talking about how the horse wasn't being put to sleep. Slowly, the men who had been restraining her stood up and moved away until only Jessie was left next to the horse.

Hearing Cal take a big inhale of breath, Riordan glanced over at him and saw a look of almost panic on his face as he quickly nodded toward Jessie. It only took one look to understand what Cal was worried about. In the melee with the horse and the water, Jessie had inadvertently drenched herself and her white cotton lab coat was now effectively a wet tee shirt, revealing every little detail of the under clothing she was wearing under it, right down to the little flowers that trimmed her pale blue bra.

In the quiet of the sudden silence, the whir of the closest television camera became suddenly loud and Riordan almost knocked the camera man over as he stepped in front of him. With another quick yank, he pulled off his lab coat and quickly draped it around Jessie's shoulders. She glanced up, questioning, but it only took her one look down to figure out what was going on, and her face flushed red as she hurriedly snapped the lab coat. Riordan could practically see the wheels turn in her head as she looked around to see who all had seen her in her transparent wet shirt. It wasn't hard to imagine that between the crowd in the stands behind her, the jumbotron, and the news crews, it was a lot. Her face flushed even more as she looked up to Riordan and said, "Thank you. I had no idea."

"No problem." He gave her a small smile and then tried to get her mind off of her wardrobe malfunction by asking, "What now, Doc?"

Switching right back into veterinary mode, Jessie turned and asked the people standing around, "Where's the sled? Where's Rick Morgan? I need the sled and a fork lift."

A man stepped through the circle around the race filly. "I'm right here, Doc. Vern is on his way with the forklift and sled."

Jessie nodded. "Awesome. Come on in here and help me. Cal, can you and Riordan help as well? We need to get these webbing slings underneath her and secure them. Just make small trenches under to slide the webbing through, then the fork lift will gently pick her up and lay her on the sled to take her out. We'll actually take her right to the clinic to operate. Where that break is, she won't ever race again, but she'll be fine as a broodmare."

Riordan said, "I'll be right there." Feeling just a hint self-conscious shirtless, he went over to the cameraman who had been filming the whole thing and leaning close, he said quietly, "Turn it off for a second." When the camera man complied, Riordan glanced at the man's press badge and continued discreetly, "I'm assuming, Phil, that you're going to do the decent thing, and remember that she's a highly respected veterinarian and delete the footage where her lab coat is wet. Am I correct?"

At the slight hesitation from the cameraman, Riordan raised his eyebrows, wondering if he was going to have to hint at accidentally tripping and smashing the guy's camera, but the cameraman shook his head. "Of course, I'll delete it. There's no story just there anyway. The rest of the footage is enough."

Riordan pressed further, "Do I have your word, Phil? Because it would be extremely unprofessional if it happened to get leaked."

Looking squarely at Riordan, Phil said, "No, it won't get leaked. And not because you're threatening a member of the press, either. Because I'm also highly respected. Trashy paparazzi shots are not my style."

Nodding, Riordan said, "Glad to hear it, Phil. Just making sure." With that, he turned to go back to help get the horse ready to transport. It wasn't really his style to strong arm someone, but girls as upstanding and respectable as Jessie were few and far between.

In only minutes, they had the slings rigged and the filly loaded onto a low, flat bed trailer. When they finally pulled the trailer off the track, the crowd in the grandstands erupted into applause and the announcer said, "That, ladies and gentlemen, is our track veterinarian, Dr. Jessie Benn, in action. She's the best in the business. Horses are her entire practice and I'm sure that filly will be up and galloping again in no time."

Walking along with Riordan beside the sled as it exited, Jessie waved to the crowd. To Riordan, she said, "I don't know that I'd say no time, but she'll live to run another day, anyway. I didn't have a major orthopedic surgery slotted into my plans today. This might turn out to be a long night." She sighed and rolled her neck. "Thank you for the lab coat back there. I'm sorry you had to go shirtless."

"Better me than you."

"Definitely true. That's one way of taking your mind off of being half assaulted and almost being arrested for the first time in your life."

Riordan nodded in agreement, but then said, "Speaking of that, I don't want to upset you again, but I think you need to file a formal complaint. I know that police brutality is pretty commonplace these days, but that was ridiculous. And apparently someone with authority heard the whole thing through your phone. Which means it's probably on record and if Cal and I give statements, along with yours, hopefully Officer Patterson won't ever treat someone like that again."

Jessie sighed again. "I know. I already decided that, but I really would just like to leave it all behind me and forget it. I am going to forget it for at least this evening. This surgery is going to take a couple of hours as it is. Then this filly is going to need monitoring tonight as she comes around. Cal will keep watch, but if he has any problems, I'll need to go in to the clinic."

Wishing he could do something to help, Riordan said, "Well, I'm not much of a surgical tech, but I'll be at Josh's if there's anything I can do."

She grinned up at him as she handed him his own shirt off the truck seat. "Are you still trying to get me to ride your horse in the show ring?"

Honestly, that thought hadn't crossed his mind all day, but it was a good excuse and he said, "Of course."

Shaking her head, she laughed and climbed up into the cab of the vetmobile and said, "Give it up, Riordan. You can see how busy I am. It's not going to happen. Get in and we'll drop you back at your truck on the way to the clinic."

Chapter 13

Riordan had only barely gotten into Josh's house, where Josh and Lucy and the kids were cleaning up their dinner, and was in the guest room slipping out of his horse boots when Josh came and said, "Hey, Riordan, my dad's here to see you with some men from our church. Have you got a minute?"

Riordan went back into Josh's living room to meet and shake hands with Ken and three middle aged men in business dress and asked, "What can I do for you, gentlemen?"

Ken asked, "Josh, could they have some privacy?"

At that, Riordan was surprised. After all, it was Josh's home, but he didn't seem to mind and he and Lucy and the kids went down the stairs.

When they were gone, Ken explained, "Riordan, your assistant, Rich contacted the headquarters of the church and they, in turn contacted several departments. The long story short, is they actually sent someone here to see if they could meet with you in person. This is our stake president. That means he's in charge of several of the congregations in this area, and this is the area representative for the whole church in this part of

Arizona Forever

the country. And this is Brother Maples. He's a liaison for the church in third world countries that have a need for infrastructural improvements. They are very intrigued with your interest in potentially helping to fund projects to produce clean water in lesser developed parts of the world. They're here to discuss that in more detail. Do you mind taking the time to meet with them?"

Actually, Riordan was thrilled that they'd come to meet him in person and said, "Not at all. Thank you for coming."

Ken said, "I'll leave you to your discussion, then. If you need anything, please just call my phone. I'll be right next door."

Ken left and for the next hour and a half, Riordan and the other three men discussed the issue of Riordan potentially financing humanitarian projects. They showed him more than two dozen different projects that they could consider, what was already being done, how the projects were being handled in regards to encouraging the indigenous peoples to help invest in order to feel more responsible for the long term success of each project, and the ultimate scope of each project.

By the end of the ninety minutes, Riordan was thoroughly impressed with what was being done and the integrity of the organization, and he agreed to allocate two million dollars to the West Africa area if the church agreed to match his funds.

After seeing the organization and the work that was already being done, he was frankly more than impressed with the Church's system. It seemed far and away more well run than what he'd been reading about with Matt Damon's project. He'd still have Rich do some checking into legalities, but he was excited to be able to take some of the money he had available to do something that felt truly worthwhile. It felt far more vital than creating phone app software. In addition, because it was working with established international charitable organizations, he would be able to use his donations to offset some of the taxes he was going to end up paying to the Australian government on the proceeds he'd received.

By the time he shook hands with the three of them and saw them to Josh's front door, he was thrilled with the outcome of this subtle, but far reaching meeting.

A few minutes later, Josh and the others came back up the stairs and finished getting dinner put away. They still didn't appear to be either offended, or surprised at the meeting that had just taken place.

Later that night, he had an in-depth Skype meeting with Rich back home and worked out the details of what he wanted him to handle for Riordan's end, including a provision for anonymity. Somehow, it felt even better to be able to do good things in secret.

****

Jessie had been right. It had been an incredibly long night monitoring the race horse filly even though she'd finally gone home and left Cal to stay at the clinic with her overnight. She only had to warm up the Australian horses the next morning, but she went and lay down on the cot in the tack room afterward anyway and actually fell asleep. She was still sleeping when she was awoken by the buzz of her phone in her pocket.

It was Lucy, sounding frightened as she said, "Jess, Josh got hurt. His horse spooked on the way out of the arena gate when a truck backfired, and his ankle was crushed against a gate. We don't know how bad it is, yet, but he can't put weight on it. But he has a horse in the class after this one. It's Riordan's stud. I can't handle him, and he's not used to any of us but you and Josh. I know you're tired but could you come help him out? It's an emergency."

Trying to wake herself up, Jessie said, "Yeah, sure, Luce. Now what? Where are you guys?"

"We're over at the Saguaro Arena. I'm going to take Josh up to the Instacare. Your dad and Brennan and Riordan are heading back there to A3 with the horse he was riding and they'll help you get ready. Your class starts in thirty-five minutes. Sorry for the late notice, but we've all been helping Josh and it's been chaos here."

Jessie nodded to herself. "Thirty-five minutes. Wait, Lucy, I don't have any show clothes here. I'm in a t-shirt. I can't possibly be ready in thirty-five minutes. We'll just have to scratch. I can't run home and back fast enough."

"Dig in one of the cabinets left of the saddle racks. Josh said some of your things are hanging there. Riordan came all the way from Australia for this, we can't let him down. I gotta go. Good luck."

Still dazed about it all, Jessie said, "Okay, you too." She hung up, looked down at her jeans and slightly wrinkled t-top that she'd planned to wear under her lab coat after the fiasco yesterday and said to herself, "Okay. I guess I'm riding in the stallion class in . . ." She glanced at her watch and said, "Now thirty-three minutes. Holy my oh my, this is going to be a photo finish!"

Hopping off the cot, she grabbed a halter and went across to get Riordan's horse. Normally, he would have been warmed up and all groomed and polished and tacked up, but there just wasn't time. She cross tied him and quickly ran a finishing brush over him and was working on his mane and tail as her dad and Brennan and Riordan came hustling in with the other horse.

They took over saddling the stallion and she ran back into the tack room to see what she could find in the way of show clothing. Surprisingly, her best show clothes from other shows she'd had to help with over the years were hanging, neatly pressed in the cabinet. It almost made her wonder for a second if Josh had set this all up until she glanced back out at her dad, rushing to get the horse ready. No, Josh hadn't preplanned this disorganization.

All three of the men were coming in and out of the tack room, and she didn't have time to go change in a restroom, so she went across to an empty stall and whispered, "Brennan, come guard this stall for a second so I can change."

Without blinking an eye, her older brother came and stood with his back to the stall and she hurriedly changed out of her jeans and t-top. As soon as she was decent again, she said, "'Kay, you can go. I'm modest. All I have left is chaps and boots and doing my hair."

With that, Brennan went back to finishing getting the horse polished and she hurriedly pulled on the rest of her ensemble.

Miraculously, between them all, they pulled everything together. The horse was a bit flighty, probably from the air of urgency they were all working with, but Jessie hoped he'd settle down in the last few minutes they had before the Open Stallion Reining class. A class full of stallions was always a dicey proposition simply because stallions were stallions, even under the best of circumstances, so the last thing she needed was for her mount to act up.

As her dad put the last finishing touches of show polish on the stallion, she unclipped the big red horse from the cross ties and said, "Okay, Hugo, here goes nothing. Work with me here today, buddy, okay?"

She put her foot in the stirrup and went to step up, and Hugo took that moment to quickly side step three fast strides straight to his right. The only thing that kept her from going flying was years and years of time in the saddle. By sheer arm strength and balance, she pulled herself up onto the horse and quickly put her other foot in the off stirrup as Hugo continued to prance animatedly and even gave a small crow hop.

Shaking her head, she gave the men a small smile and said, "Under the circumstances, don't say break a leg. I wish we'd had time to warm him up again and get him to settle down. Dad, will you be there to take him as I come out of the class?"

"Absolutely, sweetheart. Go in there and shine! You both look fabulous! We're right behind you."

"And please pray for us."

"Always, Jessie."

She headed out toward the main Saguaro Arena and several times had to pull the big stud into a tight circle to get him to slow down. He kept wanting to prance and trot as she made her way past barns and pedestrians enroute. Once there, where several other horses were in a pseudo line waiting to be called into the ring, Jessie took Hugo slightly to the side and just kept walking him in a circle to try to get him to settle down.

A few of the other stallions waiting were also acting a bit nervous and occasionally as she went past, one would pin his ears back, or paw and neigh. One even put its head over as if it was going to bite her horse and Hugo crow hopped again as he jumped aside. She wished he would settle down, but she was glad he'd gotten away from the other stallion's teeth. She'd seen stallions fighting before and knew just how devastating a bite from a stud could be. She'd sewn up a number of horses who'd been the victims. Shaking her head, Jessie thought to herself, *Oh my, this might be quite a horse show.* She'd be lucky if she didn't get bucked off at this rate.

****

Riordan Kane watched Dr. Jessie Benn ride his horse out of the alleyway and toward the main arena with mixed feelings. As he and her dad and brother followed her to the arena, he recognized that the horse was being a complete handful, and honestly, he worried that such a slender, beautiful young woman couldn't control such a big, powerful, nervous beast. But on the other hand, she'd walked into that empty stall a sweet, tired, and probably stressed girl in a t-shirt, and had come out looking and acting like a queen. Dressed all in the fancy show garb, even her demeanor had changed to a proud, confident, and polished show woman. Even with the horse acting like a bonehead, between the exquisite girl and the phenomenal horse, together they were magnificent!

And fascinating! Jessie Benn was the most lovely, fascinating, and intriguing woman in America and Australia combined. She continually surprised him with the different traits of who she was, from the tender woman who comforted small boys, to the gifted surgeon, to the little sister who teased her older brothers, to the gutty woman who could control a half wild stallion, to the tired girl who got motion sick when she did her brother a favor, but did it anyway, to the stunning beauty who was just about to ride into the show ring—if she didn't get bucked off first. He watched her keep her seat and her poise, even as Hugo pranced and he knew there wasn't another girl like Jessie on the planet.

She was also on another planet as far as the likelihood of them ever becoming more than friends. She was devout LDS and determined to marry in the church. She was an integral part of a tight family in the desert of Arizona. She didn't even consider him as eligible to list in her dating pool, and they lived on different sides of the world, for crikeys sake! He knew they would never be more than friends, but frankly, that disappointed him greatly. Still, it was probably for the best. The last LDS girl he'd gotten close to had totally used him before he'd wised up, although he couldn't imagine Jessie being underhanded by any stretch of his imagination.

Jaclyn M. Hawkes

The class started, and as the first horse went into the arena to perform, Riordan followed Brennan into the stands to find a nearby seat and actually prayed for her, something he'd learned from Josh years ago, but probably didn't do nearly enough of.

One after another, the horses came into the arena and went through a reining pattern of spins, loping circles, side passes, flying lead changes, and slides with rollbacks or backing. At this level, they were all remarkably good and Riordan sat there, more nervous than he had expected. Of course, he'd been expecting Josh to be riding. It wasn't that he worried Jessie wouldn't do as well as Josh would have. It was that he knew the horse wasn't exactly acting like the old plug he had been for Jessie the other day, and in the mix of twenty something other stallions, the potential for a situation certainly existed.

When the third horse was announced, Riordan's head came up. Clara Benjamin. This had to be Jessie and Josh's mother. Riordan had never heard her name, but how many Benjamins trained reining horses? It brought a whole new level of tension to this situation. As he leaned forward in his seat, glancing at Brennan who sat uncharacteristically stoic beside him, he wondered if Jessie had known her mother would be one of those competing against her.

Clara was mounted on a beautiful dark palomino horse, but as she began her pattern, Riordan remembered back to when Josh had said his mother wasn't that great of a trainer. As sad as it was under the circumstances, it was true, and she finished her pattern and headed back out of the arena without impressing Riordan.

158

After the eighth horse, the announcer called Jessie's name. Riordan held his breath, knowing she was just outside that entrance and thought to himself, *Well, this is it. She'll either do very well—or not.*

After a long moment, they appeared and for the first couple of steps, Hugo still seemed to be cutting up. Before they even made it into the ring, Jessie pulled him to a full stop and just sat there for a moment or two. Riordan tensed, wondering if she had decided not to compete after all before she even started. Miraculously, as they paused there, the big stallion seemed to take a big breath. He put his head down and his ears up and appeared to click into show mode because when Jessie nudged him to move forward, he was behaving himself perfectly.

They walked out into the center of the arena so slowly that Riordan felt like everything was in slow motion, and even when the horse stopped front and center before the judges, he wondered what the hold up was. Finally, Jessie gave the horse an invisible signal and all manner of magic started to happen. Hugo all but leaped left into a spin and made four fast and flawless rotations, his hind feet stepping so smoothly underneath him that he didn't even appear to be moving them. When he came around the fourth time, he stopped abruptly, sat quietly for several seconds, and then lunged right into another series of four beautiful spins the other direction.

With out even realizing it, Riordan took a deep breath, leaned back in his seat and began to thoroughly enjoy watching the magnificent girl on the big red horse. They loped so smoothly that the horse's mane barely even moved and then

Jaclyn M. Hawkes

their side passes looked almost like Hugo was dancing. His flying lead changes were virtually undetectable unless you remembered to specifically watch for them, and then as he slid, the arena dirt flew up on either side of him like the wake of a boat. Instantly, he rolled back to the right and then came around to do it again to the left, just as beautifully.

Finally, he came flying down the arena a third time, slid forever and then without a second of pause quickly backed up, stopped and spun again, even faster than before, his long thick mane and tail swinging out beside him like a living thing.

At the fourth rotation, he stopped abruptly and Riordan rose to his feet as the crowd began to cheer and clap around him. He didn't even have to wait for the judges. He knew that she had just smoked the competition by a mile.

Brennan was whistling and cat calling beside him, but Riordan simply stepped past him and headed back out of the stands to where her dad was waiting for her. She and Hugo walked out of the arena just as slowly as they'd walked in, and as soon as she cleared the doorway, her dad stepped up and reached up to her and literally caught her as she slid off the horse. He seemed to be holding her up for a second, with his arm looped through the reins.

As Riordan approached, he could tell they were talking quietly as they stood there and he was just going to step back when Hugo decided he'd had enough conversation and nudged her with his head. At his bump, her dad gave her a last one armed hug, looked up at Riordan and motioned toward Jessie and then turned to lead the horse away.

160

As she turned toward Riordan, he was actually shocked at how pale her face was. Instead of congratulating her like he was going to, he put an arm around her and asked, "Jessie, are you okay? What's the matter?"

She only leaned her head against his chest and then groaned and hurriedly turned and ran for the nearest garbage can and leaned over it. Completely at a loss as to what to do, Riordan slowly followed. The only thing he could think to do was to put an arm around her again and try to keep the tendrils of her hair that had come loose during her ride back from her face. How did you help someone who probably just wanted you to not notice that she was being so sick?

When she was through, he led her through the walkway until they found somewhere for her to sit down and then he quickly went in search of a damp paper towel and a frosty bottle of water. It was the very least he could do after she'd ridden his horse in the ring, even when, as he knew, she was crazy busy.

Returning with the water and paper towel, he sat down beside her, handed her the damp towel and put the water bottle up under her hair like he'd seen Josh do. With his other hand he gently rubbed up and down her back. Eventually, she leaned her head back against the wall and gave him a tired smile and said, "Sorry."

He shook his head, and brushed her hair off her forehead. "No. I'm sorry. You were fantastic, but if I'd realized it was going to be this bad, I'd have scratched him."

She sighed, "No. A touch of motion sickness is no reason to scratch a creature that marvelous. He truly is a champion. He ought to have the ribbons to prove it. I'll be fine in a little while. Just give me a minute. Actual shows are worse because I get kind of nervous too."

He leaned back against the wall with his shoulder touching hers and said, "Well, you didn't seem nervous. I've never seen him perform as well."

"Did we place?"

"They haven't awarded the ribbons, but I'm sure you took first. None of the horses before you came even close."

With another sigh, she said sadly, "I've never gone head to head against Clara like that. It made me kind of uptight to see her lined up out there. Do you really think we beat her? She's my mother, by the way."

He only nodded at her and she added, "It's kind of sad really. She gave up her family and even more to be a trainer. I almost wish she was really good at it. As it is, it seems like a pitiful waste."

For a second, he thought about that and then said, "It is a waste, Jessie. A heartbreaking one. But try to forgive her. She just didn't understand. She may still not understand. Some of us take longer to figure it out than others. But try not to let it keep harming you after all these years. Try to forgive her."

Looking up at him, she asked, "Josh told you, didn't he?" Again he only nodded. Jessie was quiet for another few minutes. Finally, she said softly, "I think I have forgiven her. I think. It's not that I haven't forgiven her. It's just that it still makes me so sad. My heart is still broken over it all."

He reached for her hand. "I don't know how it couldn't be, Jessie. I can't even imagine."

162

Shaking her head, she sighed again and said, "My dad wants me to get to the point that I can say hello to her when I see her. But, even though I feel like I've forgiven her for killing . . . For the abortion. I still feel totally uncomfortable being cordial to someone who I know has done something like that. It's just too cold blooded. It's like being cordial to an admitted and unrepentant murderer. That's just weird. You don't be cordial to someone who has admitted to murder and isn't sorry. You stay away from them—whether you have forgiven them or not."

You couldn't really argue with that and he only nodded again. After another minute or two, she closed her eyes again and they just sat like that, hand in hand.

His phone buzzed in his pocket, and he answered it with his other hand, "Hi, Dad. What are you two up to?"

On the other end of the line, his dad said, "Not much, son. Your mum keeps me too busy going to rehab for the hip. And now they're making me use a cane. I look like a complete old wrinklie. I'm going to lose it if I can."

Riordan laughed, "Well, I think you should still be using the cane if your doctor says to. You'll never get away with that with Mum. She's a good wife. Be obedient."

Then his father's gruff voice said, "Do you have any idea why a brand new pick-up showed up here today?"

"Yes, I'm having so much fun with one here, I decided to send you one. You've always wanted a pick-up truck, enjoy it."

"You don't need to buy us a truck. I'm not keeping it."

"Okay. I'll come home and we'll take it down south fishing. Or we'll go to the coast."

Jaclyn M. Hawkes

"Well, I'm not bringing this bloomin' cane, if we do."

Riordan laughed, "Take care, Dad. Love you. Let me talk to Mum."

"Hello? Riordan?"

"Hello, Mum."

"How are you doing, son. Are you having a good time?"

"Yes, I'm having a good time."

"Did your horse win first place?"

"Yes, we think the horse won first place, but we're not sure yet."

"Can you send us the video?"

"I didn't have any video taken. Maybe the venue filmed it. I'll check."

"Do. He's such a lovely horse."

"Thanks, Mum."

"You sound happier, Ri. Don't you?"

"Probably. I have been happier here. And no, I still don't know why." He glanced down at Jessie, still looking like she didn't feel great and he felt a bit awkward having a loving conversation with his mum, while Jessie struggled so much just dealing with hers.

Into the phone, he said, "I'll call you later. I'm right in the middle of something."

"Okay, but you take care of yourself, Ri."

"I will. Love you, Mum. Goodbye."

He put his phone back in his pocket and leaned his head back against the wall and just sat there quietly with Jessie again, wondering what she was thinking. At length, she let go of his

164

hand and opened the bottle of water to take a long drink and then say, "I'd better go. I still have a huge day ahead." She glanced at her watch. "My new veterinarian, Dr. Stettler should be here in another hour or so. I'd better get back and get changed. I've got several more scheduled appointments."

As she got up, he got up with her and said, "I'll walk back to A3 with you. Then I'm going to go check on Josh. What will you do if he's out for awhile?"

She shrugged. "I'll do whatever I can do to help his little family keep on trucking—including showing his horses. My dad rides better than I do, but if he rides too much, his back stiffens up from an old injury. And I'm so much lighter than Brennan and McCade that it's really my deal if Josh can't. And yeah, I'm busy, but Josh has never once let me down when I needed something. It's the least I can do. He's the best brother I could ever ask for."

Riordan thought about that as they walked. Josh really was the epitome of the best a brother could be, both as a sibling, and as a fellow child of God. And Jessie was even more Christlike than he was. His mum would love Jessie.

Chapter 14

Riordan had been watching from Josh's big front window out toward Jessie's house to see when her vetmobile pulled in, as he'd been talking to Rich about arrangements for his water projects, but she hadn't shown up by the time Quinn pulled up in the Ferrari at a little before seven. Wandering outside to meet him, when Quinn rolled down his window, he gave Riordan a big grin and said, "I knew that red horse of yours would win, but even my horse won. Mine never wins. Jessie is an amazing rider!"

Nodding, Riordan, who had been there for her class, had to agree, "That she is, mate. What are you up to?"

"I'm just thinking of heading in to town to get some tea. Are you up for it? Or do you have other plans? It might be the last time we get to hang out before I have to fly out in the morning."

Shaking his head, Riordan said, "No. I'm not up to partying tonight, man. I tried to keep up with Jessie today and I'm tired. This heat takes it out of me. I just want to relax. Go on without me. I'll hang out with you when I get home."

Quinn shut off the car. "I didn't say anything about partying, mate. I just said food. No drinking involved."

A hair skeptical, Riordan asked, "Why no partying tonight?"

Grinning, Quinn said, "I've turned over a new leaf."

"Oh, yeah?"

"Yeah."

"And what brought this new leaf on?"

"It was a combo, actually."

"Yeah?"

"First off, you all seem to feel so much better than me in the mornings. And Jessie's musings about partying actually kind of made sense. I've had a veritable epiphany. Drinking like I did *was* dumb, when you think about it like she put it. And then I've been thinking about the girls I couldn't remember the other night. It's not a good thing to not remember what you did, or who with. You know?"

Riordan laughed. "Yeah, I know. Stuff like that can get you in all kinds of trouble."

"Exactly what I was thinking. Just a couple of months ago Staehli, our striker, got served with paternity papers. Turned out he had a kid he didn't even know about. Completely freaked him out. The kid was like six months old already and he'd never even been there for her. He felt terrible about it all."

"I'm sure."

"Not to mention it cost him a bloomin' boatload of money. Those attorneys see a pro athlete coming a mile away. They do."

"Naturally. 'Cause you're all bloomin' rich."

"Says the tycoon millionaire. So, yep. Thus the new leaf. Plus, once you've been around the likes of Jessie and Lucy and Suki, those other girls seem a trifle. . . I don't know . . . How do I say this kindly. Less than classy. The Mormon girls don't have tattoos and piercings everywhere and all those strappy bras hanging out all over. No filthy mouths. But totally attractive. Just not cheap. Those three just seem to be on a whole different level. Almost regally so. Like Princess Kate. It's like they know inside themselves that they are something precious or valuable or something. Does that seem stupid?"

"Not at all. They do have a much more innate sense of who they are. And they are truly much, much classier than the girls you didn't remember the other night. But you do realize that you and I are still ineligible for these Mormon girls' gene pools — right?"

At that, Quinn grinned at him again and said, "Believe it or not, I'm considering getting eligible."

Confused, Riordan asked, "Meaning?"

"Meaning what do you think? I'm thinking about joining their church. I'm going to check into it when I get home."

"Just for the girls? Mate, don't do it. First off, two of the three girls you mentioned are already happily married. And you won't even be here with them. You have no idea what joining their church would entail. They have standards, and serious rules. Covenants with God himself. This is a bigger commitment than you're thinking."

"They have happy, honorable, respectable, healthy, comfortable lives. What more do I need to know? Can you even imagine how cool it would be to have your spouse as confidently committed as Josh and Brennan's seem to be? And they know what the point is to this whole life thing. Which is very comforting to me. There needs to be a point. Otherwise, everything is, well, pointless."

"Well, you might want to be a bit more informed than just knowing and admiring that they have happy lives. Joining isn't something to be taken lightly. They want exactness in some things. Whole hearted commitment. And once you commit, you're going to have to stay committed or it would be better for you if you never did in the first place. God won't be trifled with. Why do you think I've hesitated this whole time?"

"What? You'd question my commitment? If I truly decided to do it? I wouldn't do it if I didn't intend to be committed. And what do you mean, you hesitated? I just assumed you weren't interested. It's that heart of ice and steel thing. Are you saying you've considered getting eligible for the gene pool, as well?"

"Of course, I've considered it. They do have a happy life. They are fantastically comfortable to be with. I just always feel inadequate. And I hate the whole coercion to be baptized thing. It seems to me that just being good should be enough without having to knuckle under and be baptized again."

"You're just being a rebel head, mate. But you've outgrown that now. You're adult enough to realize sometimes it's all in."

Riordan smiled tiredly. "I should be, at least. But it doesn't matter anyway. I could never be good enough for their church. I'm not exactly Josh material."

Quinn shook his head and laughed. "Yeah, you are, mate. You of all people could compare with Josh. Plus, you need to talk to Brennan. He was explaining some things to me. If you think you aren't good enough, then you've missed the main point. Their whole church is about something called The Atonement. The Jesus Christ bit. The main principle of all of Christianity is that Christ helps us to become good enough—in spite of ourselves. That's the crux of the whole thing, mate."

Riordan couldn't believe what he was hearing from Quinn and just stood staring at him for a long moment until finally, Quinn started his engine and said, "Get in the car, mate. We'll go find Brennan and Suki and take them as well. He can try to explain it to you while we eat."

As they drove, Riordan considered everything that Quinn had been saying, as well as his own growing fascination with Jessie and wondered how serious Quinn had been about Mormon girls, Jessie in particular. Quinn was a good friend. A really good friend. But after the last three weeks, so was Jessie. And as much as Riordan appreciated Quinn's friendship, he was almost as protective of Jessie as her brothers and didn't necessarily think Quinn deserved Jessie. Just the thought of her and Quinn together made Riordan almost a bit territorial—not that he himself deserved Jessie. Far from it.

With all of that in mind, he casually asked, "So, you're serious about Mormon girls, then? Or is this only about one Mormon girl? You think you really might be interested in Jessie?"

Quinn glanced across the car and then back at the road and then back at Riordan again for long enough that Riordan gestured toward the road ahead. "Uh, Quinn."

Quinn turned back to driving, but shook his head and said, "Oh, I'd be interested in Jessie, absolutely if she didn't already have her head completely wrapped around another guy. Not that I could even begin to deserve her with my back story. But I would be anyway in a Sydney minute! She's fabulous! She's beautiful, and smart, and nice, and funny, and nice, and . . ."

The idea of Quinn seriously with Jessie was frankly irritating and Riordan interrupted, "Yeah, yeah, yeah, Montere. Is there a but coming, here—or not? Enough with the endearing adjectives. Which other guy are you talking about? I didn't get the impression she liked any of the guys she's dating."

"No, you're right. It's not one of the poor boomers she's dating, unfortunate blokes that they are. How could she be? They're all stooges. It's someone else we're bloomin' familiar with—who is apparently also a stooge if he doesn't realize Jessie is totally into him. Come on Ri. You can't be serious. You think I might be interested in Jessie when she looks at you like a lovesick wallaby? Crikeys, mate! Don't be stupid!"

At that, Riordan abruptly turned to stare at Quinn. "Me? Are you inferring that it's me? Oh, come on, mate! You can't be serious. I'm firmly in the ineligible gene pool group! Remember? She doesn't know I'm alive. In fact, she told me I'm comfortable because I *am* ineligible! Remember?"

Quinn only glanced across at Riordan again and shook his head and then said, "Well, her words may have said that, but her eyes, when she looks at you sure don't. Surely, you're not completely blind, Kane. And stupid to boot. Even if the only reason you joined their church was to get eligible, I'd do it in a heartbeat, to have a girl like her, look at me like she does you."

At his words, something warm and sweet rolled over in Riordan's chest. Not that he believed Quinn's incoherent ramblings for a moment, but the thought was really, truly tempting—for the second or two that he let that intriguing thought enter his brain. How nice would that be—if it could have been true?

But it wasn't. Quinn was just temporarily mad as a hatter. It couldn't be true. The only times Jessie had ever acted remotely like she was flirting, she was just teasing him, like she teased her older brothers and Quinn himself. Quinn was simply mistaken. At least Quinn wasn't going to stake a claim for himself with Jessie. That would have been incredibly frustrating to watch, or hear about once Quinn went home. And that was the other thing. He was leaving the country in less than a week. He was an Australian, for the love of Pete. And he was a good Australian. He loved his mother country with a passion. He could never leave Australia permanently.

Turning back to Quinn, Riordan only said, "You, my friend, have imbibed just a bit too much grog. And anyway, that would be a crazy thing to make commitments to God himself, just because you had a thing for a girl—one who lives more than half way across the world from Australia. Don't you think?"

Surprisingly, Quinn said confidently, "No. I don't think that. Not for a second! I think Jessie Benn would absolutely be worth all manner of commitments, and even changing countries for, much as I know you love Australia. She'd be worth it and then some. It's not like you can't afford to visit home. Plus, I think, deep down, you believe in their church. I think it's why you live the way you do. You already live all the principles. You're what Brennan calls a 'dry Mormon'. The only thing missing is the baptism. The committing out loud to someone else that you're all in. Your rebel head is keeping you dry. But it might come back to bite you."

He paused and then said, "Why do you think I'm seriously considering all this? I've been watching you live their standards all the years I've known you. And it's been good. You've side stepped all the land mines I've landed myself on from not living them. I just didn't get it until I got over here and saw the whole mob of them living happily ever after. And I've had a couple of wake up calls. I didn't realize it was a lifestyle. I just thought it was your personality that was so comfortable."

Riordan stared over at Quinn again in confusion. What was up with Quinn tonight? He was being all fervent, or heartfelt, or something. And his usual smart alecky sarcasm was there but even the direction of his sarcasm was strangely pointed.

And comfortable? There was that word again. Jessie had said he was comfortable because he was ineligible. Which made sense—if you weren't a dating option. There wouldn't be any pressure or awkwardness, because he *was* ineligible.

Not sure at all how to answer Quinn, Riordan simply leaned across and put a hand to Quinn's forehead, grinned and said, "Nope. No fever. I can't imagine what's causing your delirium, mate. But I'm starting to worry."

Jaclyn M. Hawkes

Pulling into Brennan's driveway, Quinn put the Ferrari into park and replied, "I know exactly what you mean, Kane. You're starting to make me worry too, that you can't see what's in front of your face. You need to turbo charge your intuition here, mate, or it's going to be too late and you're going to go right back to being a rich, lonely, unhappy, and unfulfilled bachelor in Australia again."

It was a good thing Quinn got out of the car just then, because Riordan wanted to reach across the car and pop him one for just the image of himself as he'd been back home in Australia. Until that very moment, he didn't realize just how much happier he'd been here in America and the thought of going right back to the same place he'd been back home, was flat out depressing. Even that was reason for introspection. What was different here? His mum had noticed it immediately. What had caused the change?

Jessie.

Beautiful, strong, smart, funny, intriguing, sweet, fascinating Jessie. Crikeys, how had he fallen in love with an American Mormon girl? At just that thought, he felt himself instinctively back pedal.

Opening his door, he got out and called, "Montere."

When Quinn turned to look at him, he said, "We are not saying a word about Jessie and me, or you, or anyone in front of Brennan. Not a word!"

Suddenly grinning, Quinn said, "Whatever you say, mate. But it's not as if Brennan can't see the way you look at each other as well as I can."

174

Riordan got back in the car. They did not look at each other. Quinn was being ridiculous.

****

At nine-thirty that night, Jessie finally pulled her vetmobile into her driveway and shut off the engine, but still sat there for a couple of minutes, trying to find the energy to drag her body out of the truck and into her house. She hadn't had dinner, but she was far too tired to even consider cooking and was just planning to go to bed hungry. Dr. Stettler had shown up, but even that had only made more for her to do as she and Cal had begun to train him and help him figure out what would be required of him during the big stock show.

Mid-afternoon, she'd ridden Quinn's horse in its class, then gone back to more appointments again, finishing with checking on the race filly at the clinic. Thank goodness Riordan had shown up off and on throughout the day to either help, or bring her food or cold drinks, or pull her hair back and rub her back when she'd been sick after Quinn's horse's class. She was still a little embarrassed that he'd seen her sick again, but it was incredibly nice to be babied for a few minutes. Riordan was very considerate that way on what had been a huge, tiring day.

Finally getting out of her truck, she let herself into her house and then felt absolutely loved when she found a plastic covered plate of chicken fettuccini alfredo and a salad sitting on her kitchen counter with a note from her dad. She sat right down at her bar and ate it all without even reheating it. Then, she walked straight into her master bath and turned on the water for a shower. On second thought, she turned it back off and started the water for a bubble bath in her jetted bathtub. Maybe melon scented bubbles would rejuvenate her. Shedding clothes, she eased her tired body down into the warm, sweet, frothing water.

It had been a very long, very full day. At least the prognosis for Josh had been good. He had a badly sprained ankle, but nothing was broken and he'd be back to training horses within a couple of weeks. In the meantime, she'd have to find the time to fit in riding for him in the show ring. He had seven other horses than Riordan's and Quinn's and that equated to at least two classes most of the next eight days. Just thinking about it made her a little car sick and she decided not to go there. Instead, she considered that she'd taken first place in the open stallion reining class with Hugo. That was a good thing. That was usually the most competitive class.

It made Hugo even more valuable internationally and Riordan had been so sweetly grateful for her riding. She thought back to how gentle he had been with her when she was so sick and it made her heart do this funny little somersault thing, even as she was embarrassed that he'd seen her throw up. That was about the kindest thing she'd ever heard of, to help her be sick. She was having a hard time not falling into a silly school girl crush with him. Riordan was a remarkably nice, and ridiculously handsome man. It was too bad he wasn't interested in joining the church-or staying in the country. She had to take a moment and remind herself just how far away Australia was.

Chapter 15

Riordan woke up with a headache. So much for feeling better in the morning because you hadn't partied the night before. He sat up and almost immediately grabbed for a tissue from the nightstand as he gave a sneeze. Crikeys. A head cold. It was like two thousand degrees outside right now and he had a cold? But then that happened occasionally when he didn't sleep. Like he hadn't last night. After Quinn's and Brennan's thought provoking conversations.

He'd lain there awake, thinking about a mob of subjects from all things Jessie, which, in the bright light of day seemed ridiculous again, to personal salvation, which frankly he'd never really believed could apply to such a hopeless soul as himself, to such crazy and far fetched ideas as moving to America, which was insane. He loved his country.

Stretching, he stood up and yawned and headed for a warm shower. Maybe the steam would wash away this cold and help him to think more clearly than he'd been thinking last night.

Last night in the weirdness of the dark, after awhile, he'd actually begun to listen and believe some of the things Quinn and Brennan had been saying.

When he walked into the barn thirty-five minutes later and met Jessie coming in at the same time, it was pretty obvious instantly that she was dealing with the same cold he was. She gave him a tired smile and then sneezed as if for proof and he returned her smile before sneezing himself. She got on the horse McCade brought her, and Riordan went to help Josh who was hobbling around in a walking boot trying to fill hay bags.

When she got off the horse after working it, instead of getting right up on the next one, she said to Josh, "Josh, do you guys have time to give me a blessing? I came down with something nasty last night and I really don't have time to have a cold right now. Would you mind?"

Josh shook his head. "No, of course not." He called down the alleyway to McCade and Brennan, who were both working there. "Muck, Brenn, will you guys grab Dad next door and come here for a second?"

Both of the other brothers nodded and McCade went around the other end of the barn and then they all three came toward the tack room and McCade asked, "What's up?"

Josh said, "We're going to give Jess a blessing if you want to stand in."

Riordan wasn't completely sure what was going on, but when Josh motioned to him, he followed all of them into the tack room to where Jessie was sitting on a trunk. To Riordan, Josh said, "You're welcome to come watch, Ry. Have you ever been around when a blessing is given?" Riordan shook his head and Josh went on. "Have a seat on the cot right there. It will only take a minute or two."

As Riordan watched, Jessie bent her head and folded her arms and Josh put a drop of something on her head and then all four of the men put their hands on her head and Josh said a short prayer. Then Ken said a slightly longer prayer, asking for special blessings of health for Jessie.

It only lasted the couple of minutes that Josh had promised and then Jessie got up and hugged her brothers and Ken in a group and said, "Thanks, guys. Now maybe I can get through this day."

They all went right back to work and Riordan got up and followed them out, not exactly sure what had just happened, but definitely sure that this family were tight and happy to be helping each other out however they could. He watched Jessie leg up onto Hugo and take him into the arena at the end of the barn to exercise him and hoped she didn't get as motion sick as usual on top of a head cold. If she felt as lousy as he did, she'd be miserably nauseous as well.

Surprisingly, when she got off Hugo after working him, she actually looked better. Her smile wasn't as tired looking and her face wasn't as pale as it had been the other times she'd ridden. Not only that, but she only took the bottle of water Riordan handed her and smiled again and went out of the barn toward her vetmobile instead of crashing on the cot in the tack room like she usually did. He watched her walk away, noticing how pretty she was with her hair hanging down her back and her faded jeans and then wondered aloud to Josh, "Whatever you guys just did, must have been pretty miraculous. She didn't even need to lie down like she usually does."

Grinning, Josh said, "Apparently. And if you sneeze one more time, I'm going to ask you if you want a blessing as well, you old heathen."

Returning the grin, Riordan shook his head and said, "I'm fine, but thanks. Just let me wake up a bit."

A couple of hours later, when he came into the main Saguaro Arena to watch Jessie compete on one of Josh's other horses, he wished he'd taken Josh up on his hinted offer because he felt awful. Jessie, on the other hand, seemed to be one hundred percent healthy as she again took the blue ribbon in her class on an energetic four year old gelding. She still stayed near the garbage can for a bit afterward, but then she only sat, resting for a few minutes with Riordan watching over her before she got up and went back out to finish her veterinary calls while he headed back with Ken to help him put the horse away. He'd have to check into this priesthood blessing thing. It truly did seem miraculous. In the meantime, he checked in with Rich who was coordinating conference calls that evening with his accountant and attorney for the water projects before flying over here for a few days.

****

Jessie was almost back to the vetmobile after changing her clothes, when an announcer came over the PA system for the whole complex, saying, "Would the attending veterinarian please come to the Saguaro Arena? We need the attending veterinarian at the main arena, please. Stat." Wondering why they hadn't just called her cell phone, she jogged the last fifty feet to her truck, wishing she had Cal with her instead of him being with Dr. Stettler in another part of the complex working over a horse with a severe case of colic. As she climbed in, she called them to let them know she was responding to the call, and then she called her dad to ask him if he could come back to the Saguaro Arena to assist her.

His response was classic Ken Benjamin. "Riordan and I are already here, hon. Hustle back. It's a compound fracture. Bring your slings. The horse went down in a roll back." Then he added, "It's your mom's, by the way. She's hurt as well. It landed on her left leg when it fell."

Nodding even though he couldn't see her, she swallowed and then asked, "Is she okay? Does she need an ambulance?"

"Probably, but she won't accept one. Just keeps standing here, one legged, worrying about the horse."

Jessie nodded again and grimaced, but she sped up. Clara's horse. This was going to be really awkward.

In the Saguaro Arena it was eerily reminiscent of the horse on the track those days before with a handful of people gathered around trying to both keep the horse calm, and seeing to her mother, while the crowds in the stands waited and worried. This time, however, there was an ugly, blood red piece of bone protruding from the horse's front cannon. Jessie shook her head. This wasn't an injury that should be repaired. It would be needlessly painful for the poor horse. Unless this was a ten million dollar stud, this horse should be put down. It was a stud, but Jessie had seen this horse before and it really should never have been left as a stallion. It just wasn't stud quality at all. Still, who was to say that someone had to geld a lesser quality horse?

Jaclyn M. Hawkes

Glancing up at her dad, she met his eyes and he looked steadily back at her. Knowing that he knew exactly what she was thinking and feeling, she shook her head again then glanced at Riordan, who gave her an encouraging smile as she gave the horse a shot of sedative and anesthetic to relieve its pain until they figured out what to do with it.

Squaring her shoulders, she went to her mother and hesitated for only the merest second before she said, "How are you doing? There's an ambulance on call here. Should we send for it?"

Her mother only grimaced and said, "I'm fine. Let's just get the horse taken care of."

Nodding slowly, Jessie said quietly, "About that horse . . . It has a compound fracture of the cannon bone . . . That's a bad break."

Almost sharply, her mother replied, "I'm well aware that it has a compound fracture of its cannon bone and that that is indeed a bad break."

Squaring her shoulders, Jessie said gently, "I recommend that the horse be put down, Clara. For humane reasons. It will never recover enough to compete again, and it will be a long, and miserable recovery—if it does recover. It will have to be completely immobilized and that often results in secondary problems like an impacted bowel, or pneumonia, or laminitis that still end up with euthanasia. Even if it does recover, it will be unable to be ridden except possibly for some mild pleasure riding. Definitely no more reining. It would just be too strenuous. He will really only be able to be used for breeding purposes."

182

She wanted to point out that this particular horse wasn't even breeding quality, but could never have said that. She also wanted to add that it was going to be several thousand dollars worth of veterinary work, but couldn't bring herself to mention that either.

Nodding sharply in response, her mother replied, "I'm aware of all of that." Almost as if she had to defend her horse, Clara added, "This horse is a valuable stallion that was well on its way to becoming a champion. It would be a shame to put it down. Go ahead with the surgery. Immediately!"

Taking a big deep breath, Jessie gave her dad a look of resignation and said, "Dad, can you print an authorization form packet that explains everything and have her sign it?" At least with a signed packet, her mother couldn't come back and say she hadn't understood, and Jessie wouldn't have to worry about being sued by her mother if things went south. Although maybe that was not something to worry about with Clara. Who knew?

She turned back to the horse, trying not to bristle at the tone her mother had used. This was a bad decision, but she was going to let her mother make it. And she was going to try not to wonder who was going to pay for all of it in the crush of things.

She called again for someone to bring in the facility's sled, and then knelt beside the poor horse to begin the process of rigging up the slings to lift the horse, mentally prepping for a surgery that would last at least a couple of hours. You couldn't always get a client to make the choice you considered best. That was just the nature of being a veterinarian. She needed to not over think this, or it would only make her upset. Instead, she

Jaclyn M. Hawkes

tried to make this just another client and just another surgery on just another poor, hurt horse.

Riordan knelt across from her and met her eyes as he worked to get the slings passed under the horse in the arena dirt. Softly, he said, "Just do what you do so well, Dr. Benn. Just take it one step at a time. It's what you do. I'll help you any way I can."

He grinned at her and she couldn't help smiling back at his incredibly handsome face and saying, "I've already been riding your horse, Riordan. You don't have to keep haunting me."

With another smile, he said, "Now I just have to figure out how to make it up to you." She knew he didn't completely understand the dynamics here, but he understood enough to be just the encouragement she needed. She wished he wasn't going home to Australia in a matter of days. He'd become a wonderful friend to her in the short time he'd been here in the states.

By the time Riordan had stayed with her through transporting the horse, prepping, and through the entire surgery, in spite of obviously feeling lousy, she was more grateful to him than ever. He'd been a huge help while Dr. Stettler had seen to the other appointments and to the stock show.

Orthopedic surgery was incredibly strenuous and as she was using the power drill to place the screws that would hold the plate she had placed to secure the horse's cannon bone, she could have truly hugged Riordan for bringing a paper towel and wiping her brow. It was still miserably hot and she'd taken to wearing a light shirt under her lab coat, which made it even hotter, and Riordan's care was very sweet. She gave him a tired smile and said, "Bless you, Riordan. We're almost done here. Thank you."

It was obvious that he didn't feel great either as he said, "You're welcome." He was truly kind that way and she had a bigger school girl crush on Riordan than ever after standing beside him, smelling his aftershave as he assisted. He had been incredibly competent as he had worked beside her and Cal, even occasionally sneezing into his mask.

Finally finished, she snapped off her surgical gloves and mask, rolled her neck and stretched her back with a small sigh. Since her priesthood blessing early that morning she'd felt immensely better, but that seemed like days ago. She was incredibly tired and had sneezed a couple of times in the last half hour of the surgery. Her patio oasis was all but calling out to her.

She was supposed to go out with Ryan tonight. Knowing she wasn't up to it, she took a moment to try to call and cancel, but he didn't answer. She left a voice mail and turned back to the horse and Riordan and Cal and said, "Now we only have to tackle getting studly here strung up in a stall. Bless his heart. Cal, can you bring the forklift back in?"

She pushed a button to lift the nine foot wide door and said to Riordan, "Honestly, this will be nearly as much work as the surgery. We have to put him into another sling set-up to keep him immobilized and weight off of his leg. And the misery is just starting for him. Poor horse. She really should have put him down. Horses aren't made to be immobile. They hate it and it usually makes them sick somewhere else."

Jaclyn M. Hawkes

It took them another forty minutes to get the horse satisfactorily settled into a wide canvas sling that went under his belly from his front legs to his rear legs to support his weight, and then have him cross tied at both his head and rump. Hanging from the chain hoist above him, was an IV system administering antibiotics and pain killers. Yawning again, Jessie said to Cal. "Are you okay to stay tonight with him? Or should I ask Dr. Stettler to come back in?"

"I'll stay. Stettler doesn't really know his way around the clinic alone yet. Go home and rest and I'll call Dr. Stettler if there's a problem."

Jessie shook her head. "No, call me. You're right. Dr. Stettler doesn't really know the clinic yet and with this being Clara Benjamin's horse, the buck had better stop with me this time. Hopefully, there won't be a problem, but if there is, I'll come back."

Cal nodded. "Will do. Get some rest. Both of you. We've nearly killed Riordan. I'll watch over studly."

Slipping off her lab coat, she tossed it into the laundry hamper and said, "Thanks, Cal. Good night. Can I give you a ride again, Riordan?"

"Yes, thanks," His adorable Aussie accent sounded tired as he pulled off his own lab coat he'd put on for the surgery and tossed it in the hamper as well. Incidentally, he wasn't wearing a shirt under it and was walking beside her, shirtless and looking like a Soloflex commercial, when the outer door opened and Ryan walked in.

He took one look at Riordan, standing there beside her in all his glory, and Jessie could see the confusion, chased by the accusation, that crossed Ryan's face before he said coolly to Jessie, "You sounded tired in your message, so I was going to drop by and check on you on my way home, but I see that apparently 'not being up to doing something tonight' was just an excuse."

As Cal came into the outer office as well, Ryan shook his head and continued, "I never thought you'd lie to me, Jessie. I thought you were the one honest girl on the planet. I guess not, huh?"

As tired as she was, his instant accusation made her want to roll her eyes and say something cutting back, but she didn't have a chance to before Riordan shook his head and said just as coolly, "She wasn't lying, and this isn't what it looks like. She's just done a grueling bone surgery and deserves a little respect, mate. You owe her an apology."

Putting a hand on Riordan's beautifully sculpted arm, Jessie shook her head as she handed him his shirt that was draped over the back of a chair. "It's okay, Ri. If he's going to believe the worst about me at the slightest provocation, then there's no point in our dating anyway." She grinned tiredly at Riordan and said, "Keep your shirt on."

Turning back to Ryan, she said, "I wasn't lying about not being up to going out, Ryan, but in light of this . . ." She gestured with her hand between them, "I don't think there's any point in . . ." She gestured again. "Let's just . . ." After floundering for a second trying to figure out what to say, she only sighed and said, "Let's don't plan on any more plans. We had fun, but . . . Have a good night, Ryan."

To Riordan, she said, "I'll drop you at Josh's on the way home. I'll be in the vetmobile. Goodnight, Cal." She walked out the door without looking back and headed for her call truck, stretching her tired neck as she went. Geez, guys were idiots sometimes—most of the time. And now in less than a week she'd told two of the men she'd been dating not to call her again. Crud, her gene pool was down to only Caleb. And realistically, she already knew he wasn't her prince charming. And now she had a stupid, foolish crush on one very attractive, but not interested or even eligible Australian hottie—who now made every other guy seem boring and plain in comparison. Great, she was actually going backward in trying to find her Mr. Right.

Getting in the truck, she leaned her head back against the headrest and sighed. Twenty-seven. Who'd have ever thought she'd be twenty-seven and apparently terminally single? Even as tired as she was, having Ryan accuse her of lying to him made her mad. She didn't play head games. She wasn't a lying person. She was humbly trying to give even the dweebiest guys the benefit of the doubt. And where did it get her? Accused by the dweebs! McCade had been right when he'd called Ryan a gravyhead after he'd met him the first time and told Jessie to stop with dating a computer geek. At the time, Jessie had told McCade to be nice, but now, she totally agreed. Ryan *was* a gravyhead geek.

Starting the engine, she shifted into reverse as Riordan came out and climbed into the truck. Ryan followed him out, but

Jessie didn't even look at him, just dug out in the gravel and headed for home. Oh well, who wanted a computer gravy head anyway?

She sighed again. Maybe she should just take a sabbatical for awhile from dating. After being around Riordan, every other guy seemed colorless and drab. Maybe for the time being, she'd just take a break until Riordan was a distant memory and she could get back into the meat market without him skewing her view of every guy. Maybe she'd just stick to taking leisurely rides around the ranch, or go hang out with Pablo and Marcela, instead of dating. At least her old gelding Bo and the kids didn't make her feel as frustrated as dating did lately.

Across the truck, Riordan sneezed and she glanced over at him and asked, "You okay?"

He sneezed again, but said, "I'm fine. A little congested. I'll live. Sorry I keep paring down your dating gene pool. Maybe he'll call and grovel and you can take him back."

The thought made Jessie sigh again and she said, "Nah. Life's too short to deal with that kind of flack when you don't really even like the guy." She changed the subject. "Do we need to stop and get you some cold pills before I drop you? I've got some at my house, if you want them."

Riordan shook his head. "No, but thanks. Why do you even go out with someone you don't really like?"

That was an excellent question. But she was pragmatic enough to answer it honestly, even to Riordan. "I don't know. I have two options, Ri. Keep shopping, or grow old alone. I keep hoping someone will grow on me. But a lot of guys don't seem very smart, compared to my brothers. Still, even as frustrated as I am tonight, shopping still seems the best of the two options. No?"

He seemed to consider that for a long moment and then nodded, "Yeah, you're right. Good for you for staying patient and open minded."

Smiling, she asked, "Is that Australian for 'you're pathetic'?"

"No, that's Australian for good for you for staying patient and open minded—in the face of male boneheadedness."

She pulled up in front of Josh's house next to Riordan's pretty black truck. As he got out, she watched him, enjoying the way his shoulders filled out his button down shirt. He was definitely not colorless or drab. More like beautiful. Trying to rein in the attraction, she said, "Rest and fluids, and call if you want the cold pills. Thanks for your help today. You were a lifesaver. Have a good night."

Chapter 16

Riordan watched Jessie pull away in her vetmobile until she went around the corner from Josh's house. Taking a big breath, he turned to go inside, but wasn't really in the mood to face Josh and his family. Instead, he stopped beside his truck and leaned on the edge of the truck bed and looked at the last of the rays of the sun going down behind the ridgeline to the west.

He's been around Jessie Benn every single day for almost three weeks, and he'd been admiring her for every one of those days. But today, this afternoon actually, he'd become something totally and overwhelmingly more than admiring. He wasn't sure what this feeling was, but it was fairly overpowering. And seriously troubling.

That it was because of a bloody, gory compound fracture surgery on a big, smelly horse didn't make much sense. But the fact was, he'd never been more attracted and intrigued by a woman than he'd been standing beside Dr. Jessie Benn DVM as she performed the intricate, but at the same time, very strenuous task of pinning and putting a steel plate inside that horse's leg. She had been incredible!

He'd known she was beautiful, and strong the first time he'd laid eyes on her. He'd come to know that she was gentle, and compassionate, and funny and smart over time, but somehow, finding out that she was so brilliant, and such a gifted surgeon had done some crazy thing to his heart. Jessie was amazing!

He leaned his head back and groaned. Crud. This wasn't good. He'd fallen in love with a girl who was completely wrong for him. Or he was all wrong for her. He was Australian for crickey's sake. Happily Australian. And not LDS. And definitely not good enough for Jessie. And even if he could somehow become good enough, she had three uber guardian brothers and a seriously protective father. And a wonderful life in Arizona! And a plan that only included a nice, boring Mormon husband. She'd said those exact words herself!

Not to mention the fact that she had shown not one drop of interest in Riordan—really. Oh sure, right from the start there had been those moments where they'd recognized the mutual attraction. Lots of those moments, but Jessie had never once tried to go beyond that. She was always eminently poised, in even the most stressful situations.

This whole time, he'd known he was ineligible for the gene pool, and he'd gone from mildly disappointed to truly regretful about that, but tonight . . . Crickeys what had happened tonight?

He shook his head. Nothing. Nothing in particular had happened tonight. He needed to keep telling himself that. He was just tired, that was all. Or it was his cold. It was messing up his judgment. He just needed to keep everything in perspective.

Lately, he'd been seriously considering joining her church. Just biting the bullet and letting Josh baptize him. Especially after working with the people about the water projects. But only because he felt it was the right thing to do. It wasn't about Jessie. Even he was astute enough to realize that that decision had to be made irrespective of what he felt about Jessie. But even if he did, it was going to take him a royal while to get good enough to do it. And once he was back in Australia, away from the Benjamins' constant, clean living influence, that might be even harder than it appeared it was going to be.

But now what did he do? Tonight? And how was he ever going to be able to go back home to Australia and find a way to be content again? He was going to be more of a head case than he'd been before coming here. And that hadn't been pretty, even before he'd met Jessie.

Oh, he and Jessie were friends. Possibly even very good friends after the last weeks. In spite of the whipping incident, they'd hit it off well, right from the start. But they'd never crossed the friend zone barrier into even flirting zone. And at twenty-nine years old, with what suddenly felt like a total emotional upheaval in the region of his chest, he had no idea how to deal with this weird disappointment about his and Jessie's relationship never going beyond platonic. Certainly it was for the best that he enjoy his time here, but then be able to walk onto a plane in a couple of days and go home, unencumbered by any seemingly primal attractions for unattainable girls. Of course, that was for the best.

It was just that after literally years and years of not trusting women, and therefore not getting very close to any of them, he was frustratingly unfamiliar with this baffling urgency. Somehow, something here tonight felt critical. More than critical. Suddenly, he didn't think he could go back to Australia and be at peace. Whatever this angst was, it was actually troubling.

This wasn't like him. He was a reason things out, logically, analytically, and wisely kind of a bloke. A planner. A plotter— not a fall in love irrationally kind of a bloke. Things were done intelligently, with purpose. This wasn't intelligent. It was nuts! And therefore, he just needed to redirect his thoughts. Rethink these urgent emotions, and fix this . . . this . . . whatever it was.

Leaning against the cab of his truck in the deepening darkness, he closed his eyes and yawned. Jessie was the most comfortable person in the world to be with, but he was leaving in just days. He needed to squelch this feeling in a hurry. Only, he wasn't sure how—especially since he didn't want to squelch it. He wanted to enjoy it. But enjoying it wasn't an option. It would make him miserable in the long term back home, and no way was he toying with someone as wonderful as Jessie.

Still, how did he overpower the desire to take this friendship into more, and instead back away? Groaning again, he sighed. This was all wrong. Maybe he should just make it a point to stay away from Jessie for the rest of his time here. That would be best, and maybe it would actually be easiest in the end.

He was still standing there, leaning on his truck when his phone rang. Taking the call, he heard Josh's voice on the other end say, "Riordan, where are you? I need a huge favor."

"I just got to your house and haven't come in yet. What do you need, mate?"

"Oh, man, Ri, Jessie just got home awhile ago and she found her old gelding hurt. Bad. Apparently it needs to be put down. Lucy and I are in Mesa, Dad and McCade are moving water up the south canyon, and it's Brennan and Suki's anniversary. They're out of town for the night. Even Polly and Ralph are gone to the movies. Jorge's there, but he's got his little kids. I hate to bother you. I know you don't feel good, but could you go help Jessie? It shouldn't take very long. You don't really even have to do anything. Just let her cry. And help her not be alone as she puts him down."

Nodding, though Josh couldn't see him, Riordan said, "Sure, mate, whatever I can do. I'll go right now. In fact, is this something I can do? Or does she have to do it?"

"No, she'll have to do it. But it's going to break her heart. She's had him since she was four. She'll cry her eyes out, but she'll get through it. Just help her and we'll be home in a few hours. Tell her I'll take care of burying him in the morning."

"Right. I'm on my way."

"Thanks, man. We'll hustle home."

Well, so much for steering clear of Jessie. But this was an emergency, so he could just go help her and not stress over what he should be doing. Getting into his truck, he drove around the corner, got out at Jessie's house and went in search of her. He'd just have to start keeping away from her later.

Assuming she wasn't in the house, he went down a path to the side and emerged into her backyard and looked all around for just a second in wonder. Her backyard was amazing! Flowers and plants and a deck with a porch swing, and a hammock to

195

the side, with tiny lights that made her little oasis a fairyland in the deepening dusk. The sound of water from the creek behind made it sound like a fairyland as well. It even smelled fantastic with the scents of the flowers and creek. The only thing that would have made it better was if there were fish in that creek. Maybe there were.

Walking past the beautiful oasis garden, Riordan headed for the small barn further back, wondering where Jessie was and how the horse had gotten hurt. When he didn't find her in the barn either, he went further back still, and stopped at a fence line, trying to figure out where to go next. As he was pulling out his phone to call her in the relative quiet after he stopped, he could hear her crying somewhere in the trees near the creek. The sound made his heart squeeze. She was absolutely strong in some ways, and sweetly tender in others.

Coming up on her standing in front of a big dark horse with its face leaned down to hers, Riordan softly spoke her name and moved up beside her. When she turned to him, he wrapped both arms around her and pulled her into a hug and whispered, "Oh, Jessie, I'm so sorry. Josh told me your old friend is terribly hurt."

Nodding against him, she quivered as she leaned into him and continued to cry, and at length she said, "He's cut up his whole pastern. It's not that it can't be operated on, but . . . He's old. There's no reason to make him go through all that. I've known I was going to have to put him to sleep one of these days anyway. It's time."

She paused and took a shuddering breath and then went back to crying against Riordan for a few more minutes before continuing. "I just didn't know it was going to be this soon. I thought I had a few more months. He's been such a dependable old friend. He was born when I was four. He was little, and I was little." She sniffed. "And he's so patient. He never tells me I'm being stupid, or . . . That I'm wrong. He just listens. He's never impatient or critical."

She shook her head, "It's my fault that he's hurt. I thought he was safe here. But I didn't notice there was a hole rusted in the culvert. And he stepped through. I should have noticed." She began to cry even harder and Riordan gathered her more closely into his arms and began to rub her back with the flat of his hand, wondering if he was supposed to help her stop crying, which was his first inclination, or just let her cry on him, like Josh had said. He had no idea what was best here.

He finally decided that Josh probably knew best and just continued to hold her and stroke her back and her hair. He'd pulled her hair back several times when he'd helped her when she was sick, and he'd come to love it. Straight, and streaked by the Arizona sun, it was soft and silky in his hands and smelled of strawberries and melon. Putting his fingers into it, he smoothed it back from her face and leaned his cheek against it as he whispered how sorry he was about her sweet old horse.

After several minutes the horse shifted his weight but his knee buckled and he let out a big whoosh of breath. At that, Jessie seemed to straighten her shoulders and stand up away from Riordan and said, "I should just do this. He's hurting."

Riordan nodded and let her go, asking, "Is there anything I can do to help?"

She sadly shook her head and he could see the shine of tears still coursing down her cheeks in the near dark. Sniffing, she said, "No. I just need to give him a shot." Almost as if she was trying to convince him, she said, "It's the kindest thing to do for him. He's old."

Riordan put a hand back on her shoulder and gave it a small squeeze as he said, "It is. It's much better for him than being in pain. Josh said he'd help us bury him in the morning."

She nodded without answering and then took a big breath that he knew was to hide a sob as she pulled a large syringe out of her back pocket. Talking quietly to the horse, she petted his neck for several long moments, then gently, but quickly, inserted the needle into his jugular vein. For another long moment, she hesitated, and Riordan put his arm around her shoulder. Then, with another big sigh, she began to push the plunger of the syringe. When she finished, she recapped the needle and tossed the syringe to the side on the ground.

At first, the old horse just stood there. Then, his head lowered slightly and his knees buckled and he slowly went to the ground. For another long moment, he sat there, and then, slowly, he collapsed to his side, laid his head out flat, and gave a long groaning breath and was still.

At that breath, Jessie let out a soft cry of utter heartbreak and burst into tears again and Riordan pulled her tightly back into his hug. She clung to him almost desperately and this time her crying was even more poignant. Riordan continued to rub up and down her back, completely at a loss for how to comfort her in her obvious sorrow. All he could think to do was stroke her hair and shoulders again and again, and keep whispering unintelligible words of comfort against her silky hair. After several minutes, when she didn't seem to be winding down, he pulled her into an even tighter hug and kissed her hair once between whispers.

She was slender, and fit perfectly in the circle of his arms, and she was firm, but oh so femininely soft against him. In spite of her sorrow, hugging her felt exactly right as she held onto him and her tears slowly became more quiet. He knew she was devastated, and his heart ached for her, but he also wished he could hold her like this forever. His decision to stay away from her was completely forgotten as he cradled her close, doing anything he could to comfort her heartbreak and sooth her tears.

Eventually, after several more sad, but heavenly minutes, her tears seemed to lesson. Pulling her even tighter, he kissed her hair again and continued his whispers of comfort that were really too soft to be heard. They were mostly just understood as he held her there in the sweet smelling darkness with the sound of the creek lulling him into near mindlessness. This girl was amazing. She was such an exquisite blend of strength and femininity and grace.

He should never have kissed her hair. It was completely innocent, and meant only to bring solace, but it completely stalled the plan to stay away from Jessie for the duration. It completely stalled every brain function he'd ever hoped to have in his life as well and it made the most amazing, sweet, warm sense of . . . of he didn't even know what well up in him. It made him want to comfort her, and protect her, and heal her heart, and find her smile, and hold her, and kiss her, and watch over her, and kiss her, and heavens she felt so good against him. It made him think about kissing more than just her gorgeous, sweet smelling hair. Like her smooth, warm temple as she lifted her head from where it leaned against his mouth. Like her sweet beautiful mouth as she raised her sad eyes to meet his. It made him want to kiss her beautiful, tempting mouth. A lot.

Her tears wound down to a shuddering breath that made his own breath catch in his throat as she looked up at him, her eyes still bright, her breath still unsteady. He glanced down at her lips, and she glanced from his eyes to his own lips with a look that completely quieted the guilt he was feeling for wanting to kiss her. If he was honest, those lips had fascinated him from the first moment he'd seen them.

Moving a hand from her silken hair, he gently brushed a thumb across her cheek and breathed out, "I'm so sorry."

She gave a miniscule silent nod and watched his eyes as he felt himself drowning in her own blue ones. As he watched her, he could swear she lifted her face a bare fraction more, and he breathed the words again, "I'm so sorry."

Then, somehow, he was kissing those soft, firm, beautiful lips that were miraculously kissing him back.

He could taste the salt of her tears and it made that warm, sweet need to protect her even stronger, and he felt her mouth quiver slightly as she inhaled a shuddering breath against him. Her hands gripping his shirt at his back clung even tighter and she closed her eyes and tilted her head. Every sense faded into the background in a warm, sweet, breathy swirl of the most exquisite pleasure. There was only Jessie hugging him deliciously close, and her mouth making him forget anything except the feel of her kiss.

Jessie this close smelled like flowers and grace and eternity. He breathed deeply, wanting to inhale her scent into his soul. Her gentle kiss was a heady breath of pure, sweet oxygen that wafted across his senses like the most delicate misty night wind. He wrapped his arm around her waist tighter and cradled the back of her head in his other hand, her hair sliding between his fingers like warm blonde strands of spun silk. How had he never realized a simple kiss could feel like this?

He'd have been fine except for her soft moan. Just when he knew he needed to back away and let Jessie go, she made a moan of pleasure so quiet that he almost wondered if he'd imagined it. It made something in the back of his brain shut off and he gave a low moan of his own and forgot all about letting Jessie go, or staying away from her for the next few days, or pretty much anything else he should have been remembering. That delicate little sound heightened every sense he owned and the swirl of pleasure in his brain heightened and he very willingly kissed her again. Somehow, Jessie's sweet mouth had all but enslaved him in a few sensuous hidden moments there under the trees by her creek.

A truck pulling down the lane finally brought them back to reality. Jessie opened her eyes and for a second there, he saw raw wonder before sadness filled back in. Slowly, she let go of his shirt where she had been clinging to him and took a step back, still looking up at him and then down at her dear old horse and she sighed. Shaking her head, she said, "Sorry, Riordan. I didn't mean to do that. I guess I was pretty upset. Please forgive me for taking advantage."

She leaned and picked up the syringe she'd tossed and then knelt beside the dead horse to wrap her arm around him one last time. As she stood back up, her eyes bright with tears again, Riordan only reached for her hand and gently said, "Don't. Don't say you're sorry. That was the nicest kiss of my whole life. Please don't be sorry about it."

"But it was probably a mistake. I was upset."

He shook his head. "It was fabulous."

"Or foolish."

She tried to pull her hand out of his, but he didn't let her as he said, "Hey, stop dissing our kissing."

In spite of the tears in her voice, she laughed, but said, "I am sorry, Riordan. That's not very fair of me to take advantage of you on a bad night. I'm sad, and you're exhausted, and sick."

At that, Riordan rounded on her and put both hands on her shoulders, then raised them to her face. He looked into her eyes for a long moment, then leaned down to kiss her gently again, smiled and said, "If it was anyone's *fault*, it was mine. And I didn't mean to take advantage of your sadness. But then I didn't mean to kiss you either. But I don't regret it. Can we just leave him here until morning?"

"Yes."

"Then come on. I'll walk you home."

He could tell she'd started to cry again as they walked and

he let go of her hand and put his arm around her shoulder and pulled her close and again said, "I'm sorry about your horse."

Her voice sounded like a little girl as she said, "Me too. Thank you for being here."

"You're welcome."

At her little oasis fairyland, they paused, and he said, "Your garden is beautiful. What are you going to do right now? Can I hang out here with you for a little while? So you don't just cry alone? Or would you rather have some time alone?"

This time, she sounded like a tired little girl as she said, "I'll be fine. Go home and go to bed and kick your cold."

"Is that American for I want to be alone? Or American for I don't want to bother you?"

She hesitated for a moment before answering him and he encouraged, "Be honest, Jessie. You want some company? Or not?"

She didn't look up as she said, "Honestly, I'd love some. Do you mind?"

Tipping her chin up, so he could see her eyes in the faint glow of the little lights in her vines, he asked softly, "Would I have offered if I minded?"

She pulled out from under his arm and went to sit in the cushioned porch swing before she answered him and even though he knew she was thoroughly sad, he could still hear the smile in her voice as she said, "That would depend on whether you were still trying to haunt me into riding your horse for you."

He came and sat beside her in the swing. "Ah, but my horse's classes are finished, so there's no need to haunt you anymore. Now I just need to repay you."

"Riordan, don't be absurd. You've spent most of everyday helping me, somehow. I feel guilty about how much you've helped me, but I'm hesitant to offer to pay a multimillionaire. And you forgot about the Grand Champion class. Because your horse took blue ribbons in his classes, he's eligible for the Grand Champion class. If he wins it, it could make him worth even more than he already is."

He put an arm around her and tugged her to lean against him and then pushed off gently with a foot to rock the swing and said, "That's American for you know the two of you will win and I'll be in your debt even more, isn't it?"

"No, that's American for your horse is going to be worth a gob and I hope you are making arrangements for some big fancy stud farm to stand him so you can reap what he's earned."

"What the two of you have earned."

"Whatever. I hope you have him insured. It would be a shame if something happened to him."

He could tell that she'd made herself think of her old gelding again and he put his other arm around her as well to hug her again and gently rocked the swing one more time. Rubbing gently down her shoulder, he agreed, "It would be a shame."

They just sat like that for a long time, with her leaning against his hug, listening to the sound of the stream burbling over the rocks and the occasional creak of the porch swing. Every so often she would quietly cry, and when she did, he would hug her closer, and stroke her arm, or her back, and then feel guilty for wanting to kiss her again when she was so sad.

But he couldn't help himself. Her little oasis garden was a magical place, and she smelled wonderful, and touching her, even so innocently, was absolute heaven. It made him seriously consider postponing his flight home. Crud, what was he thinking?

Along about where he was seriously questioning his sanity for wanting to pursue something with her—he wasn't even sure what—she turned slightly in his arms and looked up at him with those lethal eyes that still had traces of tears in them. That's all she did, for several long seconds, look at him, almost as if she was searching for something. Finally, she quietly asked, "Riordan, why did you kiss me tonight?"

Blast women and their need to dissect everything. Couldn't she just leave the foolish, but incredibly nice moment alone? Why did they always need to make sense of everything? Although it was an excellent question, actually. One he didn't for sure know the answer to and finally, all he said was, "Because I couldn't not."

That made her obviously confused and he added, "Well, you were so beautiful, and intelligent, and soft, and sad, and . . . I tried, but I couldn't help myself. But, was it just me? I thought you were a part of that whole moment. You didn't back off any when I leaned in. Didn't you kiss me, too?"

She nodded almost solemnly. "Yes, heaven help us, I did."

"Well why did you kiss me back?"

She considered that for another long moment, then gave him the merest hint of a grin and said, "I completely plead that I was distraught and you tempted me in my moment of weakness."

Riordan rolled his eyes and shook his head. "That answer was absolutely as obtuse as mine was."

She laid her head back against him again where he could no longer see her eyes and said, "Yes, I believe it was."

Now, what for wallaby's sake did that mean? She hadn't shed one iota of light on why, after weeks of being friendly, but only friendly, she had just kissed him back until his brain completely short circuited. Now what was he supposed to think? Or do? Or not do? Or want? How was a bloke supposed to know what was going on here? She didn't make any sense. And why "heaven help us"? What had that meant? Did that mean she'd liked the kiss? Or regretted it? Or both? And what now?

He put a hand under her silken hair and lifted her chin and this time, he studied her, wondering what she was thinking, and what in the world, he was thinking, because looking into her eyes only made him want desperately to kiss her again. Her gaze was steady and honest, even if he had no idea what was going on inside that beautiful, brilliant mind.

He looked at her, and considered that he really ought to get up off this porch swing in this magical fairyland oasis and go back to Josh's house where he could once more try to rationally make decisions about his orderly life back in Queensland, but somehow, his body wasn't listening to his pragmatic psyche. Instead, his body leaned forward, staring into Jessie's beautiful eyes, being drawn toward her tender mouth that seemed to be reaching for his, until finally, his lips touched hers again. Softly, gently, almost tentatively at first, and then more firmly as his arm instinctively pulled her closer as she kissed him back. She was definitely participating and her kiss stalled any introspection. Logic was really overrated anyway.

He closed his eyes and felt his body sigh with pleasure as he forgot all the shoulds and simply let himself revel in the sweet hypnotic power of her incredible kiss. Her mouth absolutely felt like pleasure and peace and fireworks all at the same time. Her scent and flavor and the touch of her warm, firm lips made his intellect completely shutdown and belly deep sensation rolled over any remaining logic. Pleasure rolled through his soul again, and he breathed the fragrance her kiss evoked clear into his brain. Crikeys, why had he waited all these weeks to kiss her?

He should have been kissing her and being with her, and enjoying every second he could with her from the very first. Why hadn't he realized?

Suddenly, there was an urgency upon him that made him question why in the world he'd been wasting this visit to America without savoring every second with Jessie Benn. He should have realized just how fabulous, and unique, and special, and . . . and now he'd blown his chance to enjoy being with her while he could. He only had a couple of days left.

That realization made him want to hold her even closer and he felt himself kiss her with even more emotion than he'd been. Even the urgency he felt was warm and sweet and seemed almost surreal in her fairyland oasis with the music of her creek lending its magic. If ever there was a perfect place to kiss the perfect kisser, this was it.

Jessie didn't exactly push him away. And she actually gave a small sound of pleasure just as she was easing back, but she definitely eased back. She was still in his arms, still a little breathy, and still warm and soft and incredibly tempting when she looked up at him with eyes almost a bit spooked as they glanced from his eyes to his mouth and back. He took a deep breath, wondering why he was a bit breathy himself and met her eyes, wishing she hadn't pulled away. Wishing he could have gone on kissing her, honestly, a little mindlessly, and not questioning if he'd completely lost his marbles. The urgency began to have a tug of war with good old fashioned guilt.

He leaned his head back against the cushions of the porch swing and took another deep breath, wondering if she was going to ask him again why he was kissing her, and hoping that she didn't. Because he wouldn't have any better answer for her this time than he had had the first time. Yeah, he'd felt like he couldn't help himself the first time, and felt even more like that just now, but that was a terrible answer to her question.

If he really analyzed things, he had no business kissing a girl as good as Jessie Benn. She was a much better person than he was and she'd been very forthright about wanting an LDS guy, which all computed to he should have been stronger and not given in to the urge to kiss her—so frankly, he didn't want to delve there.

And he certainly didn't want to analyze himself either. He wasn't a guy who kissed a girl just because he was physically attracted. In fact, he wasn't a guy who kissed a girl he wasn't emotionally invested in at all, but in this situation, he couldn't be emotionally invested, on a number of levels, so then exactly why had he kissed her—and wanted to keep kissing her?

When he would have started in listing to himself all the reasons he shouldn't kiss Jessie, something within him hung back and he consciously decided not to consider all that right this second. After all, tonight Jessie was having a legitimate crisis and wasn't it his responsibility, as a friend of her family and an all around decent person to be there in her moment of need? Okay, so maybe kissing her until he was delirious was going above and beyond the call of duty, but he was going to just chalk it up to being a server. Not a user.

And certainly not a guy who seemed to be toying with the idea of postponing his flight home over a beautiful, talented, intelligent, strong willed, spirited, LDS American girl. If he went there, first off, he'd have to face the fact that yeah, he had indeed lost his mind. He so didn't deserve to think about Jessie that way. And two, even if he could somehow convince himself that he could be good enough for Jessie, there were a hundred reasons why it would never work, starting with living thousands of miles away from each other.

He caught himself starting once more to list all the reasons why he shouldn't kiss Jessie and put on the mental skids again and looked back down at her. She was still looking at him and he could see the questions in her eyes, even though she wasn't asking. It made him need to reassure her. On what level and to what end he didn't even know. All he knew was that he wanted to smooth away that hint of distrust he could see deep in her eyes. He'd stay in America and then some, before he'd let Jessie Benn wonder if he'd been using her.

Jaclyn M. Hawkes

Leaning back closer, he gently ran a finger over her bottom lip and then smoothed back one finely sculpted eyebrow. With absolute regret, he squeezed her shoulder softly and whispered, "You're beautiful, Jessie. And bloomin' tempting. Much as I'd love to stay here, we're both tired. Send me back to Josh's."

He stood and pulled her to her feet and into a sweet tight hug that lasted and then, watching her eyes again, gently leaned and kissed her one more time on the mouth, long and slowly. Pulling away, he sighed with both pleasure and regret and softly said, "Jessie, I wish I was your boring Mormon guy. You were amazing today."

****

Jessie watched Riordan Kane walk around the corner of her house from her patio oasis and marveled again at just what an incredibly gorgeous man he was. And what a fabulous kisser. She was exhausted, and deeply sad, and felt herself sigh like a teenager and touch her mouth as she thought about the last little while with Riordan. She glanced at her watch. Make that the last more than a little while with Riordan. She'd apparently lost all track of time.

She smiled against her fingers and shook her head. Riordan was a phenomenal kisser. His kiss had made her think of shimmering apricot and pale mauve sunrises. Or lavender velvet night skies. Never in her life had colors washed over her brain during a kiss. How in the world had they ended up snuggled here on her porch swing? Straightening the cushions, she glanced around her little garden one last time and then went inside to go to bed. It had been a long, full, heartbreaking day with an utterly surprising ending. Part of her wanted to cry and part of her wanted to smile, and part of her wanted to analyze what in the heck had just happened, but frankly, she was too exhausted. She settled for a warm candlelit shower and the occasional sigh when she thought about his kiss. Kissing him had been really, really fabulous. She put on a soft light blue night shirt and gratefully slid between her cool sheets. What in the world was up with them?

She was still feeling ridiculously like sighing the next morning when she walked into A3 to exercise horses. Seeing Riordan there, looking magnificent in a pair of well broken in jeans and a sky blue polo shirt that showed off his eyes and his muscles didn't help. He looked like he'd just woken up as he came to her in the alleyway and she was actually a little nervous about how things would be between them, but all he did was give her tired, gorgeous, concerned smile as he said, "Good morning." He searched her eyes for a long moment and then asked, "How are you this morning? Were you able to rest?"

Nodding, she said, "I was exhausted, so yeah, actually I did. Did you?"

At that, he gave her a more cheeky grin and said, "Off and on. Between dreaming about your mouth."

Jessie felt her eyes widen at his tease and truly hoped she wasn't blushing as well. It was a good thing Josh led Quinn's horse up to them just then, because she had no idea what to reply.

When she got off of Riordan's horse forty minutes later, she was too motion sick to be nervous as Riordan came and smoothed her hair back and gave her a cold water bottle, then wrapped an arm around her to help her back to the cot in the tack room. He ran a gentle hand over her forehead as she lay down before going back to help Josh feed, and she closed her eyes. She hadn't a clue what was up with them, but Riordan was the sweetest guy she'd ever known anyway. She'd hardly been able to focus on riding this morning for thinking about those color-changing kisses.

Her phone rang only several minutes later, and she took a call from Cal. Her mother's stallion had finally begun to come fully out of the anesthetic from his surgery and was not taking well to being immobilized. Cal had had to sedate him again, but in the interim, the horse had stepped on himself and injured another different pastern. Promising to be right there, she sat up and gave a small sigh—this one not a dreamy one. She'd be lucky if she wasn't ill on the way into the clinic.

She was still sitting on the cot, trying to talk herself into standing up, when Riordan came back into the tack room. Coming up to her, he put a hand on her shoulder, looked into her face and gave an empathetic smile. "Your fans need you?"

She nodded. "Yeah. I gotta go. Clara's horse is acting up."

He touched her cheek in a way that seemed just a hair more of a caress than just friends and asked, "Do you need someone to drive you? You okay? You're still looking a little green around the gills."

"I'll be fine. But thanks." She stood and walked out to her truck, still absolutely wondering what was up with the two of them after last night. At least he'd said that quip about not being able to sleep for thinking about her mouth. Somehow, that had been very reassuring.

Between Riordan's nebulous answer to why he'd kissed her, to their, uh, kissing, a lot, to what he'd said about wishing he was her boring Mormon guy, to his care this morning, but including the fact that they'd never been more than really good friends, and certainly never professed any feelings, she was completely confused. Heck, she didn't even know what she wanted from Riordan. In some ways, he was her dream man. In others, he was still completely ineligible. All morning, as she worked, she found herself vacillating between dreamy and frustrated.

Chapter 17

For some reason, Riordan felt he had to tell Josh that he'd kissed Jessie. He just had no idea how to go about it, or how Josh was going to react to it. Finally, he just decided to get it over with and as he and Josh were mucking out stalls that were adjacent to each other, Riordan simply blurted out. "I kissed your sister."

All movement in the other stall stopped, but Josh never said anything and after another second, Riordan decided to confess even more and added, "Actually, it was a bit more involved than just a single kiss. Or several single kisses."

Still, no comment from the other stall and he glanced up to see Josh's eyebrows raised next door and said, "Oh, for wallaby's sakes, Benjamin, say something, or come over here and punch me. Something. What are you thinking?"

Conversationally, Josh said, "Just trying to decide which I should do. Exactly how many single kisses are we talking here, Kane?"

Riordan hesitated and finally said, "Well, technically, a gentleman should never kiss and tell, so I don't exactly know why I'm telling you this, because I am definitely a gentleman . . . Uhm . . . You should probably just come over here and punch me. But only once. It was all perfectly respectable, I swear it."

Nodding, Josh said, "I'm sure it was, Kane. Or Jessie would have already horse whipped you or something. Why in heaven's name did you kiss my sister?"

Going back to shoveling, Riordan said, "An excellent question. She asked that too, in fact."

"And?" After a pause while Riordan hesitated, Josh added, "What did you tell her when she asked?"

"Well, I told her I couldn't not. Which was true. I mean she was there, all sobbing, and I had to hug her. I mean, any decent human would have hugged her. I literally had to, under the circumstances. And . . . well . . . But I didn't kiss her right when she was so sad. I mean, I didn't take advantage of her sadness. It wasn't like that. It was awhile later. Josh, you do realize that your sister is fabulously attractive, right? You know it's true. And she's brilliant, and competent and, well, after assisting her with your mother's horse yesterday, and then seeing how crushed she was over her old friend, it was hopeless."

Josh looked confused. "What was hopeless?"

"*It* was hopeless. I simply couldn't not kiss her. That was just more than a mere human could withstand."

Nodding slowly, Josh hesitantly said, "I see. And what did Jessie think of your answer?"

Riordan considered that, remembering how he and Jessie had done that lovely dance around saying anything substantial when she'd asked. To Josh, he said, "I honestly have no idea.

Which is a bit disconcerting, actually. But she didn't seem to mind the kissing. I think in a way, it was medicinal. Therapeutic. She didn't seem nearly so sad."

"No, I'd imagine not. That's definitely an innovative way to get her mind off her horse. Way to think outside the box on that one, mate." Then, almost as if he was speaking to himself, Josh said, "What's weird is that she kissed you back. That doesn't sound like Jessie. She did kiss you back, didn't she? In your 'more than several single kisses'."

Riordan rolled his eyes and shook his head. "Yes, Benjamin. She kissed me back. She is the girl with the buggy whip, after all. And don't you dare tell her I told you any of this. I do so love your confidence in me."

"Hey, I haven't come in there and punched you. What are you complaining about? But you have to admit that's kind of strange. You being the heathen prince charming without the temple recommend. I never saw that coming. Of course, I never saw you needing to kiss her either. You also being the man of ice and steel that Quinn talks about."

Riordan shook his head. "You and me both, mate."

Then Josh mumbled to himself, "But I should have seen it coming. You two have had that electricity thing going right from the start. I should have suspected." He wiped the back of his hand across his forehead and picked his fork back up.

They mucked out some more while Riordan thought, *well, that went better than I thought it would.* But then, Josh asked, "What are you going to do now?"

"What do you mean?"

216

"Well, was last night a one time, 'medicinal' kissing? Or do you intend to kiss my sister again?"

Riordan stopped mucking again and literally groaned and said, "Geez, Josh, I have absolutely no idea. I mean, I honestly couldn't not. I had no intention of ever kissing your sister to start with. I'm not good enough to even consider kissing her. And she's made it perfectly clear that she wants a good, solid, boring Mormon guy—her words, not mine. She actually said I was comfortable because I'm not eligible. So, as fascinating as she is, I had no intention of becoming so intrigued. And I was holding my own. Or so I thought. But then yesterday, when she operated on your mum's horse. It's crazy, but you have no idea how attractive a brilliant surgeon is. She's so smart. And so competent. She was fabulous! After the surgery, I was vegemite in her hands."

Obviously skeptical, Josh said, "So, you're saying it was her surgical skills that put you over the top?"

Shaking his head at himself, Riordan gave a short humorless laugh. "Yeah. Who knew?"

Still questioning, Josh asked further, "Not her figure, or her perfume, or her lips? Her surgical skills."

"The world is full of beautiful, perfumed girls, Benjamin. They all want something. And she is definitely beautiful. She absolutely is. But there are no girls like your sister. Not that I've ever met."

Grinning, Josh said, "Okay. Her surgical skills were the distraction that drove you over the cliff."

Riordan sighed as he leaned on his pitch fork handle and said in a more serious tone, "Yes. And now I've buried myself.

Because I don't want her to believe I was toying. I wasn't. I swear. You just have no idea how incredible it was to hug her and when she looked up . . . But I'm not a good, solid Mormon guy. Believe me, if I was, I'd move to America tomorrow. But how in the world do I explain any of this to her?"

"You know, you could just become a good, solid Mormon guy. You must be at least somewhat open to the church to be hobnobbing with the big brethren from your meeting the other day. You'd probably never be able to pull off boring, but the rest of it is doable."

"Be serious, Josh. She's the nicest girl I've ever met. Getting baptized wouldn't make me good enough for her. I could be Saint Patrick and not be good enough for her. I'm a ruthless, grumpy, old business man, remember? I have skeletons, and hang ups, and a reputation for being uncaring and harsh, and rebellious. You've read the headlines. So, now what do I say, or do, with your fabulous sister?"

This time, Josh leaned on his fork handle and was thoughtful for a long moment. Finally, he said, "You know, Riordan, I've been trying to help you know who you really are for ten years now. And apparently, I've failed. You haven't listened to me so far, so I'm not going to keep trying to convince you. But, I will say this. If you're willing to walk away from someone as incredible as Jessie—if you really, truly want her, just because you're unwilling to try, then you're right. You don't deserve her. She's the best of the best."

He shook his head and went back to mucking. "If I were you, I'd figure out what you want, Riordan Kane. What do you really, truly want? Because if you want something bad enough, you go after it." He shrugged, "If you don't, you settle. Your choice. You can hang out single for the rest of your lonely, ruthless, grumpy old life."

****

After seeing him in the morning at the barn, the whole day, Riordan never showed up to help out at the clinic, or even to check on Jessie after she rode another one of Josh's horses in an afternoon show class, and she couldn't help but wonder what was going on. Not only did their kisses not seem to make Riordan more fond of her, they seemed to have made him steer completely clear of her. Which was probably for the best. It wasn't like they were a match made in heaven. Still, she was ridiculously disappointed. She really needed to get her head on straight where Riordan Kane was concerned.

As she was lying on the cot in the tack room again, feeling sicker than a dog, Josh came in and brought her a cold soda this time, and said, "You look like you could use some caffeine this afternoon. How are you doing? After having to put Bo down last night. You okay?"

She teared up and it took her a second to answer and he said, "Sorry to bring it up. But I've been worried about you all day."

Sniffing, she said, "I'm fine. Or I will be. It was awful, but you know how that goes. Riordan being there helped. He was very kind."

Sounding skeptical, Josh said, "Yes, that's what I heard."

Jessie looked up at him. "What does that mean?"

Jaclyn M. Hawkes

Shrugging, Josh said drily, "He said he basically kissed your face off after."

At that, Jessie sat up in sudden, total outrage. "He said what!" She breathed out in a huff. "He said that? He really said that?"

Apparently realizing that he'd not handled that revelation very smoothly, Josh back pedaled. "No, of course he didn't say exactly that. He said some drivel about how he couldn't help himself. That watching you in surgery had been amazing and that he simply couldn't keep his lips to himself after he'd hugged you. Quit fussing and lay back down. Or you're gonna hurl. And I don't want it all over the tack room."

Somewhat mollified, Jessie was still completely disgusted with Riordan telling her brother about their little interlude in her garden. She lay back down grumbling, "He's a total jerk to go blabbing around the very first second! Did he tell everyone? Do Brennan and McCade know too?"

Sitting back up abruptly, she asked worriedly, "Did he tell Dad? Please tell me he didn't tell Dad!"

"No. He didn't tell anyone but me. Stop freaking out."

She closed her eyes and groaned and lay back down, grumbling again, "Oh, I am so going to give him a piece of my mind!"

Calmly, Josh said, "No, you're not. You can't spare part of your mind. He told me not to tell you that he'd told me. He'll kill me if you tell him I told you that he told me. Geez, what am I saying? Never mind all that. The bottom line is . . . Geez, I don't even know what the bottom line is. When did you and Riordan decide that you had a thing? How did I miss this? I mean, I knew he was intrigued right from the start, and I noticed the way you two look at each other and the occasional sparks. And I knew he was watching over you and helping you. But I thought it was to get you to ride his horse. When did this happen? How did this happen? He's not LDS."

Jessie put her hands over her face and groaned softly. Maybe she was going to throw up after all. Josh brought her a frosty bottle of water from the fridge and lifted her hair to put it behind her neck. Then he just stood beside the cot.

After a second, she looked up at him and said grouchily, "What?"

Josh shrugged. "I'm listening. Just waiting for you to say something."

She shook her head. What was she going to say? That they weren't a thing? It had just been a non-committal make out? That they were a thing, but she didn't know what kind of thing? Even though she'd spent her whole life deciding not to have a thing with a guy who couldn't potentially marry her in the temple? That she didn't know if they were a thing? That they apparently weren't a thing because Riordan had chosen this day after 'kissing her face off' to quit haunting her? Which, even though she knew that she and Riordan were a bad idea, made her really, really disappointed.

As much as she'd tried to keep Riordan firmly in the ineligible territory, she realized today, now that he had stopped haunting her, of course, that she liked him way, way too much.

Being brutally honest with herself about that made her

suddenly royally tired. She finally just shook her head at Josh and closed her eyes again. After a moment, she said sadly, "We kissed. We're not a thing. Now leave me alone, Mr. Kiss and Tell's sidekick."

Surprisingly, Josh didn't have a comeback and while she was glad he didn't, it wasn't like Josh. She was fully expecting to get either a big brotherly lecture, or that he would just keep picking at her until she let down and had a heart to heart talk with him about what was going on. She opened her eyes to see why he wasn't saying anything and it was to realize that Riordan was standing there in the doorway of the tack room looking back and forth between the two of them. It didn't take much deduction to realize that he'd heard what she'd just said to Josh.

Riordan shook his head and frowned at Josh and said accusingly, "You told her. Why did you tell her that I told you?"

Jessie rolled her eyes and then turned onto her side facing the wall and said, "I don't think him telling me something was the problem here, Riordan." Oh, she really hoped she didn't throw up right now, because she felt like it.

Turning back she asked, "Did you really tell him that you kissed my face off?"

At that, Riordan got a confused and very concerned face and turned back to Josh and said haltingly, "No. I never said anything remotely like that."

Josh put his hands up defensively and said, "You know, I think I've made plenty of mess here. I'm just going to run and pick up a load of shavings. You two can iron this out without my, uh, interference." With that, he limped out the door on his walking boot.

In the awkward silence that followed, Jessie rolled back onto her side toward the wall and said, "You're a jerk, Riordan."

She heard his boots crossing the floor and then felt his gentle hand on her hair and turned to look at him. She was sick, and disappointed, and she either wanted to tell him royally off, or burst into tears. Or throw up. That was still a distinct possibility.

He smoothed her hair back almost tenderly, which made her sad and she pulled her head away. After hesitating a second, Riordan said humbly, "I wasn't trying to be a jerk, Jessie. I'm sorry I told him."

Shaking her head, she said, "Why would you even do that? You're not a guy who has to have an ego trip. Why did you tell him?"

He smoothed her hair back again. "It's hard to explain. And I know this is going to sound backwards, but it was a bit of an honor thing."

"Yeah, right."

"Well, think about it, Jess. He'd trusted me with his precious baby sister."

"I'm twenty-seven years old, Riordan."

"And you're still his baby sister."

"It wasn't like we were doing something wrong. We kissed. Okay, so it was quite a bit of kissing, but it wasn't something you were honor bound to report to my big brother."

Riordan looked at her quietly for a long moment, but then said, "I'm sorry I hurt your feelings, Jessie, but I did feel like I owed it to your brother to tell him. He trusts me. Trust is kind of sacred. I needed to tell him. Does that make any sense?"

He met her eyes steadily and she finally took a deep breath and said evenly, "Okay, Ri. No. I honestly don't get it, but I can tell that you truly believe what you're saying. But do you have to tell anyone else?"

He smiled his beautiful smile. "No. Of course not. And hopefully Josh will figure out to keep it to himself. I swear I didn't tell him I kissed your face off."

"Yeah, well, somehow that's what he got in the translation."

Riordan shook his head. "No. I don't think I intimated that. I'm not taking any blame for that little gem. I think that's just his inept communication to you. What I said, was . . . Actually, let's just don't even go there. Instead, tell me about your day. Sorry I wasn't around. I had some conference calls earlier. How is your mum's horse? Or would you rather simply rest for another while?"

She was nauseous, and confused about everything with Riordan, and still a little mad, and considered for a second what to say to him, but then her phone made the decision for her. It buzzed in her pocket and when she looked at it, a text from Cal said, "Clara Benjamin is here. Giving Dr. Stettler fits." That's all it said, and she sighed and sat up, but then rested there for a minute, hoping to keep the world from spinning.

Riordan was watching her in concern and she handed him her phone to see before saying, "I gotta go."

He only nodded and said, "I'd offer to come with, but I have to go to Mesa this afternoon for some meetings. Will you be okay? Do you want me to call your dad or something?"

She shook her head. "No. We'll be fine. Thanks though."

He gave her arm a gentle squeeze and she took the water bottle and went out to her vetmobile, hoping she was right that they'd be fine, and wondering what her mother was doing to give Dr. Stettler fits. All the way to the clinic she prayed that she would be able to know how to treat her mother and somehow figure out what Jesus would do in this situation. She could almost hear Riordan's voice in her head encouraging her to forgive and forget the past so that it wouldn't continue to harm either of them.

It turned out that Clara had, for some strange reason, adopted an air of ownership of her clinic and was making herself at home and basically ordering Dr. Stettler and Cal around when Jessie got there. As Jessie walked in, she followed the sound of voices back into the surgery suite where her mother said, "Oh, Jessie honey, I'm so glad you're finally here. These two don't have a clue what they're doing with my prize stallion."

Her mother hadn't called her Jessie honey in probably close to fifteen years and Cal was well aware of the strain between the two of them, as well as the fact that her prize stallion wasn't really champion stallion material. Jessie only looked at him and gave him what she hoped was a reassuring smile as she said to her mother, "Clara, I'm sorry, you'll have to go up in the front away from the surgical suite. Our insurance won't allow anyone but staff in here, and it's supposed to remain sterile. And I assure you, Dr. Stettler and my tech are both eminently competent veterinary professionals. What seems to be the problem? How is your leg, by the way?"

Rather than going into the reception area of the clinic, Clara headed with a Clayed limp back toward the patient stalls and said over her shoulder. "Well, my horse is in even worse shape than it was when it was brought in. Now another of its legs is injured as well and he's completely drugged. He can hardly even respond to me."

At that, Jessie had to swallow the desire to remind her mother that the horse had had a broken leg and bone protruding from it when they'd brought it in.

Instead, gently taking her arm, Jessie literally physically pulled her to a stop before she made it clear into the stalls and said, "You need to not go back there. It needs to stay as sterile as possible. Yes, your horse interfered as he was coming out of anesthetic this morning and scraped up his other pastern. I'm sorry about that, but even though his legs were all wrapped to protect them, he's a very powerful large horse. If he tries to fight the sling he's in, he will injure himself. That's why he's so sedated."

Jessie turned back toward the waiting room and put out a hand as if motioning forward and continued, "That is part of what I warned you about yesterday when I recommended the horse be put down. Immobilizing a horse goes against every instinct a horse has and causes other problems. The horse hates it, and it tends to shut down things like circulation and gastrointestinal action as well. The paperwork you were given yesterday should have explained all of this. Would you like some cold water, or a soda? Come inside and sit down. How is your leg?"

Clara went into the waiting room, but she stood and waved with her hand. "My leg is fine. How soon can I take him home and how long will it be before he can be ridden?"

Jessie shook her head, "Clara . . ." Riordan's voice in her head made her start over. Feeling totally awkward, she said, "Mother . . . your horse is going to have to stay here in the clinic for a couple of weeks at the very least. Then, he's going to be weeks, rigged up just like he is back there when he gets to your place. Then months in a stall and rehab. It's going to be a good year—if he doesn't get laminitis, before he'll be rideable. And then he will only be able to be ridden for light pleasure riding. He'll never be able to be a reining horse again. That leg will never be strong enough."

Clara was horrified. "A year! There's no way I can wait a year to begin showing that horse again! He's my best horse! My business will be devastated!"

Trying to be patient, Jessie said, "Clara, you're not listening. The only thing this horse would be able to be shown in is halter, which with that scar probably wont be an option. He will never rein again. He broke his cannon bone. It has a plate in it. I explained that yesterday, but maybe you didn't hear in the hubbub. Did you read any of the paperwork you signed yesterday?"

"Yes. No. I can't remember. But I need to be able to show this horse." All Jessie could do was shake her head sadly.

As a professional, Jessie wanted to roll her eyes at the theatrics, because she hadn't so much as mentioned payment, that for any other client would have already been in the thousands of dollars. How this played out as far as payment was going to be interesting.

Still working to find some kind of a comfort zone, Jessie went to the filing cabinet that held the authorization form and information packet her mother had signed the day before and she inserted it into the printer and pushed start. As it dumped out the other end, she gathered the copies and stapled them together and handed the copied set to her mother and said, "These are your signed forms with all of the information. Your copy may have gotten set aside somewhere yesterday. This will explain the procedures we'll be following."

She flipped a couple of pages and showed her mother a place that was highlighted. "These are the possible complications from this surgery, explaining why it is usually best to put an animal with this type of fracture down. Read through this, as you're resting your own leg, and if you have further questions, please feel free to call me. In the meantime, we'll be doing everything we know medically to see to it that your horse is recuperating as well as possible." She gave her mother a smile that she knew was stiff and handed her the packet and added, "It's going to be a long haul, Clara. And possibly not a successful one. You'll notice only about 30% of these horses come through well. But we'll do the best we can. Any other questions?"

Her mother scanned one of the pages, and then looked up and asked, "What about the other 70%?"

Jessie gave her a sad frown and said, "They develop a secondary condition like laminitis or pneumonia, and have to be put down."

At that, her mother's shoulders seemed to droop and she folded the packet of papers and turned for the door. Just before she went out, she turned back and said, "Thank you, Jessie, for all that you're doing. I'll bring you a check tomorrow."

Jessie nodded and her mother went out. She felt her own shoulders come down a couple of notches and relax as well.

Seconds later, Cal poked his head out of an exam room and asked, "Is she gone?"

"Yeah, what do you need?"

"Doc Stettler wants you to come give him your opinion on a broken seismoid bone."

"Tell him I'll be right there."

She got up and went in to the light wall to stand beside Dr. Stettler and look at an x-ray. They studied it for a few moments, and then turning to her, he asked, "What do you think?"

"It has to come out."

"Can we do it with the scope?"

"Most likely."

"How soon can he run again?"

Jessie shook her head. "Best case scenario—eight weeks. More likely, twelve."

"That's what I already told him. It's not the timeframe he wants to hear."

She shrugged, "You're good, Doc, but you're not a magician. Tell him the truth and give him the option of taking his x-rays somewhere else for a second opinion. Who is it?"

"Glen Justison. A big buckskin that's about half wild."

She shook her head again. "Tell him best case scenario twelve weeks. That horse is more than half wild and is prone to strike. Justison keeps him on such hot feed he'll never stand still long enough to let it heal. Hopefully he will take him somewhere else so we don't have to deal with him."

Dr. Stettler went to go out the door and she added, "And I'm not available to speak with personally, if he asks."

He nodded, "Got it," and let the door close behind him.

A few minutes later, he poked his head into her office and asked, "How did you know he was going to ask to speak to you personally?"

"Uh, I just know Glen Justison. I always make sure Cal is between him and me when he comes in. Did he take the x-rays?"

"No. He said he's been a loyal client for years."

She shook her head. "I only opened this clinic eighteen months ago."

Chapter 18

She was in her hammock that night, her hair still damp from her shower, trying to get up the energy to go back inside to bed, when Josh materialized out of the darkness and sat down on her porch swing. She let the hammock rock a couple more times before she asked tiredly, "What are you up to tonight, Josh? Have you come to grovel?"

"Heck no. But since you mention it, please oh please oh please forgive me."

"That's the worst groveling I've ever heard."

"It's never been my forte."

"You can say that again. What do you want, really? I honestly can't take on another horse."

"How tired are you? Should I hassle you for a few more minutes, or get right to my point?"

"Oh, hassle me for a few more minutes. Please."

"That is what big brothers are supposed to do."

"And you do it well."

"How much do you like Riordan?"

She turned to look at him in the dark. "It hasn't been a few

Jaclyn M. Hawkes

more minutes. I think I'd rather have more hassling, thank you. Why?"

"I just want to know how serious you are."

"Why, so you can tell each other?"

"Maybe. Probably. It depends on what you tell me."

"Gee, I can't wait to spill my guts."

"Why did you kiss him?"

"Because I wanted to."

Josh laughed softly. "At least you're honest."

"Only to a certain extent now that I know that what I say or do can be used against me in a vast brotherly conspiracy."

"Well, please don't stop being honest just yet. That's actually why I'm here. We never really got to discuss your whole kissing scene."

She rolled her eyes even though he couldn't see her and said, "And we're not going to, Josh. At least not any more than we already did. This may come as a surprise to you, but I do not have to report any and all lip action to you. And frankly, I didn't appreciate Riordan's need to tell all—even though he swears it was an issue of honor. It seems to me that kissing and telling equates to an issue of dishonor, but what does the kissee know, apparently? But, I'm really not discussing anything with you. For heaven's sake, I'm twenty-seven years old."

When she finally wound down, Josh said, "Are you about through? Or what?"

"Yes, I'm through discussing my personal stuff."

"Jess, it's not like I want to know any gory details about kissing. It's not about the kissing. It's about what are you thinking about Riordan."

232

"What I'm thinking about Riordan is firmly in the my personal stuff realm, bro. Why would you need to know what I'm thinking about Riordan, or any guy?"

"Well, Miss Snippy Pants, maybe because we could be talking about your eternities here. Am I just imagining that you two are totally into each other? You get along great, and I swear sparks fly between you. Riordan isn't just another gravy head guy on the list."

She yawned. "Actually, Riordan can't even be on the list. Remember? He's not LDS."

Josh shook his head in the dark. "Yeah. That's what I thought. Until someone kissed his face off. Then suddenly, apparently he is on the list, in spite of not being LDS—yet. In fact, he must be right at the top of the list, because of all that kissing. You never kiss anyone—really. I mean like kiss their face off kissing."

"And what makes you think you know who I kiss, or not?"

"Ryan, the gravy head, really? Or Clay, the stuffed shirt lawyer?" The way he said lawyer actually came out as liar and then he added, "You don't even like them to help you on with a jacket, let alone getting into your lip territory. I'll bet you fifty you don't kiss either one of them. And I can't imagine Caleb is any more tempting, although honestly, I do like him best of the three."

She sighed just at the thought, but then said, "Don't bother betting, because I am never going to admit to you who I do and do not kiss."

Jaclyn M. Hawkes

"Well, it doesn't matter anyway, because I know I'm right because Cal told Brennan that you already told both Clay and Ryan to hit the road permanently."

"Brennan? And Cal? Cal is now in the middle of this mess? I thought Cal had my back always. He's jumped ship, too, now? Geez, is anyone on my team anymore?"

"We're all on your team, Jessie. That's why I'm here. Because we've all been thinking about it, and we've been comparing notes. You like Riordan way better than any of the other guys. Plus, you kissed him—apparently quite thoroughly—although Riordan and I are the only ones who know that."

Jessie sat up in her hammock. "Who's been comparing notes? You've all been gossiping about me behind my back?"

"We're your brothers. Well, and Cal, but he's kind of a brother. It's not gossiping. It's being brotherly."

"You're being idiots. Who I kiss is none of you all's business."

"We weren't talking about who you kissed. We were talking about who you didn't kiss—until you did kiss Riordan—but I didn't tell anyone else that. Because we've all noticed that you're not really into any of them. Except Riordan. And frankly, we think you've got good taste. He's way more marriage material than the rest of those morons."

Jessie frowned in confusion. "He's the only one who isn't LDS. What are you talking about? Josh, just stop. Stop right there. Stop being such busybodies in my love life, and nose out. This isn't your deal."

"Of course it's our deal. We're your big brothers."

"No, you're my big meddlers. And no thank you. Now go home and leave me alone. But why are you even putting Riordan into the pot? He can't be in the pot. Which is a pity, frankly. You're right. He's by far the most intriguing of them all. But that's beside the point. Go home. I'm tired."

"Ah hah! See, just as we thought! You do like Riordan."

"Of course I like Riordan, Josh. He's your friend and he's very nice. What's not to like? But that has nothing to do with it. And honestly, this whole subject is a little painful for me right now. I've about decided I'm just going to take a dating sabbatical. The only one I even have left is Caleb, and he's nice and all, but I can't marry him."

She blew out a discouraged breath. "Now I have to figure out how to tell him. I hate that part. But it's not fair to him to keep stringing him along."

She lay back down on the hammock. "I was even going to finally get on some on-line sites, but I can't bring myself to. I know everything on there is all lies anyway and I just don't have the time to try to sift through all the baloney to find the decent ones right now. I'd be the person who had to do like background checks and stuff to dare to go out with someone."

Josh shook his head at the idea of her on-line. "Jessie, tell me again why Riordan can't be in the pot?"

"Well, duh. He's not LDS. No temple marriage, and I'm stranded alone in the eternities, remember? While the rest of you go on to live happily ever after with eternal families and mansions in heaven without me. I don't think so. You should be the one reminding me of all of this, Mr. Big Brotherly Meddler. Plus, Riordan isn't the slightest bit interested in me, anyway, so it's not really an issue. We're just friends."

"Oh, so you were just using Riordan for some friendly making out?"

"Funny. And not really your deal, as I recall."

"I'm just hassling you, Jessie. And yeah, Riordan is the slightest bit interested in you. He on the other hand wasn't just using you for kissing. He kissed you because you fascinate him."

She rolled her eyes again. "Oh, yeah, right, Josh. That's why he was so attentive to me today. He's positively smitten."

"Jessie, he was helping me this morning so he could talk to me, because he felt honor bound to admit he'd kissed you — which I appreciated, frankly. And this afternoon he's been doing conference calls and meetings for some projects he's got going. Which is somehow connected with the church. I'm not sure how, but I think Dad knows. He has a life of his own, you know. Don't be a drama queen."

"I'm not being a drama queen. I'm not being anything. He's not a member, and he lives in Queensland, Australia, which, in case you aren't aware of it, is a fairly long way from here. There's a reason he's staying footloose. He's leaving in a few days. You're being silly."

Josh stood up and came over to stand next to her hammock. "Okay, Jessie, I'm through joking around now. I'm tired, and I want to go home and climb into bed beside my wife. You listen to me, and listen well. I'm telling you, as a brother who loves you dearly and wants the best for you, Riordan Kane is a good man. He basically lives the gospel already. If you are at all seriously interested in Riordan Kane, I think he's honestly considering the gospel. I could be wrong. I've been wrong occasionally in my life. But I think he knows it's true. He just thinks he's not good enough to either belong, or deserve you, and he has that stupid baptism hang up. But I also think he was serious when he used words like 'fabulously attractive, and fascinating, and intriguing' to describe you."

He put up his hand."Now, I'm not trying to meddle, but I've seen the way you two look at each other. I really don't think he would have kissed you if he wasn't emotionally engaged. Even if he was that kind of a guy—which I don't think he is, I just don't think he would do that to my sister."

Jessie got up from the hammock to stand beside him as she considered what he was saying. At length, she said, "I could be interested in Riordan Kane in an instant, Josh. Words like fabulously attractive and fascinating can describe him too. But I also remember how many years you've been trying to convert him. Even if we could put aside all the other issues like the fact that he lives in Australia, isn't that totally putting the cart before the horse to seriously consider letting yourself become emotionally vulnerable with someone who may never be able to be sealed to you?"

He thought about that for a few minutes as well and then said, "Jess, we know as surely as anyone, how heartbreaking a bad marriage can be. And Dad married a Mormon girl—in the temple. It didn't guarantee bliss. Now, that doesn't mean that shouldn't be the goal. It definitely should. But after finding Lucy, and knowing just how truly joyful a good marriage can be, I can tell you what I for sure don't want for you. I don't want you to marry some nice, steady Mormon guy, whom you aren't madly in love with, just because he was a member. That would be miserable. You'd honestly be better off married out of the temple. Caleb is nice. I truly like him. But you aren't the slightest bit attracted to him, really. All the checklists in the world won't help if there isn't chemistry."

He shook his head and went on, "Marriage is heavenly, Jess. It truly is. I've never been happier. But it isn't all roses. There are stressful moments, just like in all of life. I believe you have to more than like, or even love someone, to have a truly great marriage. I believe you need to be in love as well. You can't settle for nice. Or steady. You need to be head over heels. I just don't want you to walk away from possible fireworks and regret it for the rest of your life. You don't have to pursue Riordan, especially if he doesn't get baptized. But if the sparks that seem to be arcing there are real, at least allow yourself to see what your options are. Are you brave enough to do that?"

She ran a hand through her hair and sighed and asked, "What are you suggesting here, Josh?"

He grinned at her as he turned to go. "I have no idea. I just know you have until next Tuesday to come up with something. That's a week. And Riordan is flying to Salt Lake City for the day for some meetings on Monday. So you'd better get cooking. You're a smart girl. You'll figure it out."

She was so tired she didn't know what to think except that she knew he was being sincere. Sincere and insane. This whole idea was crazy.

Except for those incredible sparks that he was right about. She thought back to those lavender velvet kisses with Riordan, right here on her little patio. In all her life, she'd never felt chemistry like she felt with Riordan Kane. Beautiful, sweet, attractive, brilliant—and not LDS, Riordan Kane

Chapter 19

"What do you mean, my parents are coming with?"

On the other end of the line, Rich said, "Your parents. You know, the two people who begat you? Caroline and Roy Kane. The two who you gave me cart blanche to do whatever they wanted, whenever they wanted. They called me a few days ago and asked if I'd make arrangements to get them to Arizona before you left. Your mom said they wanted to come and see what it was that had made you so much happier than you'd been back home. So, I'm bringing them with me. I figured I could sort of watch over them and help your dad in the airports and stuff. I thought it made more sense than sending them separate. I can change their itineraries if you want me to."

"No. No, they're fine. It's just that this Monday is going to be busy with us flying to Utah and back. But they're more than welcome. It will be nice, in fact. I can't believe they're doing it. It took them years to decide to up and leave the country to go see Ashleigh and Warren."

Rich teased. "They're worried about their baby."

"Curious, you mean. I'm just glad they had their passports.

Be sure and cushion his hip. That's an exhausting flight for anyone. Find out if they want to go to Utah with us, or just hang out by the pool here in Arizona until I get back, and make whatever plans they would like. I'll meet you at the airport. I'll still have you get a car, but I'll take them to their hotel. Thanks for the heads up."

He hung up and looked over at Josh and shook his head. "My parents are coming over. They've lost their minds." He laughed. "I told them years ago to do whatever they want and have Rich arrange it, but they've never taken me up on it before. Good for them. Seems they want to know what has made me happier here than I was back home. Apparently they think I'm different in America. Am I different here?"

Josh shook his head. "I don't know, mate. I wasn't with you back in Australia. Were you unhappy?"

Riordan tipped his head back and forth. "Eh. Burnt out, more than unhappy."

"When will they get here?"

"Tomorrow. Their flight arrives in the morning."

Limping along filling water buckets, Josh said, "My dad will be offended if you put them in a hotel. They're your parents. He'll want them to stay with him in the ranch house. They can have the whole north wing and Polly can watch over them. We'll all entertain them if they decide to stay while you go."

"I can't believe they're doing this. They're not typically spontaneous. That's a long flight for someone with a brand new hip."

Grinning, Josh said, "Your mom has heard about your wild lifestyle here and wants to check up on you."

"More likely, she's hoping I've met a girl over here."

Josh turned and looked fully at him. "Have you?"

Riordan looked back at him for a long moment and then grinned. "I'm not talking to you about anything to do with a girl, Josh. I'm still in deep wallaby euke from last time."

"Ah, speaking of Jessie, I need to get her horse tacked up for the two o'clock class. Then she's got another at three thirty that she's taking for me. She'll be toast, poor girl. I hope she can go home after. She's been so busy, what with taking over showing for me. It's a good thing the stock show is almost over. That reminds me. Your horse is in the Best of Show class tomorrow afternoon. What are you going to do with him in the long term? Do you already have arrangements to stand him next January somewhere?"

Hanging the hay bag he was working on, Riordan said, "Two farms down near Sydney have approached me, but I haven't decided. Why?"

"Would you consider letting us keep him here in the states and standing him here?"

"Possibly. If the price was right."

Grinning, Josh said, "That's why I'm approaching you today, because after Jessie wins Grand Champion on him tomorrow, he'll be worth even more and I might not be able to afford him."

Riordan laughed, "You're a terrible negotiator. Are you trying to get me to charge you less, or more?"

Josh came out of the tack room with a tote full of grooming gear. "It'd be a good excuse to come back to Arizona and check on him often. Among other things."

"What are you hinting at, Benjamin? Are you the same brother who told me just a couple of weeks ago that I couldn't even ask if Jessie was seeing someone because I wasn't a member?"

Josh pulled a black horse out of a stall and cross tied it. "Well, based on the big hoss brethren who came to see you the other day, I keep hoping you're considering becoming a member. And, not just using my sister for kissing."

Riordan picked up a wire brush and began working on the horse's mane as Josh began to brush its body. "Would I have opted for full disclosure if I was using your sister?"

"Nope, because you would know I'd have to whoop up on you. Does that mean you're finally seeing the light about the gospel?"

"It's not you I'm concerned about whooping up on me. But McCade is a bit of a beast."

"We were talking about the gospel, not McCade."

Riordan went around to begin grooming the horse's tail and asked innocently, "We were?"

Josh only sighed and moved to the other side of the horse and said, "You're making me old, Kane." He looked over the top of the horse's back and caught Riordan's eye and added, "Just make sure, Riordan. You just be darn sure that Jessie isn't the girl you've always dreamed of before you walk onto a plane out of here next week. That'd be a big, ugly regret to live with if you figure it out too late."

****

Riordan thought about what Josh had said the whole time he was sitting in the stands waiting for Jessie to ride, and while watching her. She rode fabulously, and her horse won again. That would be the eighteenth blue ribbon to join the others now hanging from the Benjamin Reining Horses sign in barn A3.

He was still thinking about it when he and her dad met her outside the ring where her dad took the horse. She pretty well wilted when she slid off and Riordan caught her around the waist and let her lean on him for several long moments. When she finally looked up, he handed her a bottled water and took her hand to lead her to sit down again. Holding her small calloused hand made him think even harder about Dr. Jessie Benn, and why he truly was happy to simply hold her hand.

They sat quietly on a bench in the concourse of the arena for more than twenty minutes without saying much until her dad showed up with the horse she needed to ride in the next class. She was still visibly ill from the last one and Riordan kept his arm around her waist, worried about her as sick as she looked and asked, "Can I take you home for the day after this one, or do you have more vet calls?"

She gave him a tired smile. "In theory, I can go home."

Smoothing her hair back from her brow, he nodded. "Good. I'll take you straight home whenever you're ready. Good luck out there."

Turning to her dad, she said, "Pray for us, Daddy?"

Putting a big hand on her knee, he said, "Always, sweetheart."

Riordan was a bit surprised when she turned back to him and asked, "Will you pray for us, too, Ri?"

He grinned. "Absolutely, sweetheart." Surprisingly, he was perfectly comfortable with that.

That second class, was the only class so far that she took second place in. This time, she slid off and probably would have gone right to the ground if Riordan hadn't caught her as her dad caught the horse's reins. She was sick into a nearby garbage can and then smiled gratefully at Riordan as he handed her a damp paper towel and a piece of gum before leading her away to sit down. Finally, he loaded her into his pretty black truck and took her home, then thought again about what Josh had said as he let her out. He knew she was embarrassed, and she was pale and not looking exactly her best, but she was still every bit as intriguing as she'd ever been to him and it made him wonder how you knew if someone was the girl of your dreams. As he drove away, he grimaced. Not that it mattered if he wasn't the nice Mormon guy of her dreams.

****

Jessie had gone straight to the shower and then laid down when Riordan had brought her home and had been able to sleep off the motion sickness. But by nine thirty that night, she was starving and dragged herself out of bed and ordered a pizza. She put on a pair of soccer shorts and a stretch t-shirt and wandered out to her patio oasis to listen for the door bell in her hammock. It had been a long, busy couple of weeks and Josh had kept her up thinking about Riordan way too late last night.

It was nearly dark and the little twinkling lights had begun to come on in the flowering vines. She closed her eyes and pushed the hammock with a bare foot and thought about how nice it had been to kiss Riordan here two nights ago. She'd told Josh she'd figure out if the sparks between her and Riordan were real, whatever that meant—and however a person did that exactly.

She couldn't just ask Riordan. Even if she did somehow manage to ascertain that Riordan felt something for her, she was still right back at square one as far as him not being a member. And honestly, she'd known him a month. She really didn't know him all that well.

When she thought about it, before she needed to know if the sparks were real, she needed to get to know him better. It was just that she didn't have much time—so maybe Josh was right. Maybe they just needed to figure out if the chemistry was as potent as it seemed and then they could take steps to figure everything else out. At any rate, if there was any chance that they'd be friends beyond the next week, if she had the opportunity, she probably ought to at least see if she could get to know him better. If she got the chance, there were a million things she'd like to ask him—if she got the chance.

She wasn't sure how Riordan felt about the sparks, but in thinking about his kisses, she certainly knew they were real where she was concerned. That night with Riordan had been the perfect blend of heady emotion, and sweet, safe restraint and it had been kissing nirvana. She yawned and stretched like a kitten in the fragrant deepening dusk and listened as the stream burbled and the crickets started up. Now, if only that pizza man would hurry. She was ravenous and still really tired.

It was the aroma of basil and Canadian bacon that woke her up. She slowly came awake, and then opened her eyes, wondering how the pizza man had found her back patio. It turned out to be the most attractive pizza delivery she'd ever encountered, actually. Riordan, wearing shorts and a t-shirt he'd cut the sleeves out of and deck shoes, was standing beside her hammock, holding the opened pizza box in front of her face and carrying a six pack of A&W root beer and some napkins in his other hand.

For a moment, she only blinked, wondering if she was dreaming. The faint light from the vines setoff each ripped muscle and the cut off sleeves showed off his arms and shoulders and hinted of the muscles on his chest and back as well. This had to be a dream. He was simply too attractive to be real. She put out a hand and touched Riordan on his very cut, solid bicep and then pulled her hand away and mumbled, "You're real."

That made him laugh and say, "Yes. Completely real."

She gave him a sleepy grin. "For a second I thought I was dreaming about you. How did you get my pizza?"

He set the pizza box on the small table beside the porch swing. "I was just walking into your driveway when the pizza bloke drove in. I take it your nausea is better."

"It's gone. Now I'm just starving. Would you care to join me? Have you eaten?"

"I was just on my way here to see if you would be interested in coming with me to get something. Do you have enough for two?"

She laughed and sat up in the hammock. "Do you really think I can eat a whole large pizza? Of course there's enough. Would you ask a blessing over it?"

When he didn't hesitate, just bowed his head and said a short, simple prayer, she had to wonder if maybe Josh wasn't right about him being more open to the church, but then decided that was silly. Lots of people outside the church prayed over meals.

He sat down on the porch swing and she got up from the hammock, picked up a napkin and slice of pizza and then sat down beside him with a happy sigh. "I love fresh, hot pizza."

Getting his own piece, he took a bite, chewed for a minute and then asked, "And what is it you like about fresh, hot pizza?"

Stretching a string of cheese out until it broke and landed on her chin, she swallowed her bite and said, "Oh, I love it all. The cheese." She wiped off her chin and continued, "The flavors, the so undietness of it, and the fact that they bring it right to you, and then clean-up consists of throwing the napkins away. It's perfect for nights like tonight when you're too tired to cook and clean up, but you're hungry for something real."

"As opposed to fake?" He looked confused and she laughed.

"As opposed to snacky stuff, or cereal, or fruit or something else quick and easy but totally lightweight. Pizza is easy, but substantial. You know, real? Real food. It makes your mouth and your tummy smile."

That made him smile. He took another bite and then said, "I do have to admit American pizza is fabulous."

She laughed. "Pizza is Italian, silly. Although, I have heard that American pizza is way better than Italian pizza." She picked some pineapple off, ate it, and made a sound of pleasure. "Plus, I think Italians think pineapple on pizza is a sacrilege. Personally, I think it's marvelous. Do they have Canadian bacon and pineapple pizza in Australia?"

"They have pizza, but I'm not sure about the Canadian bacon and pineapple."

She popped the top on an A&W root beer. "Do they have A&W root beer? Cheers, mate."

He grinned at her. "I'm sure, somewhere. But mostly, they drink the more stout kind over there. Australians tend to love their beer."

Nodding, she said, "Yeah, most Americans do too. We're definitely in the minority. Us Mormons." Getting her guts up, she said, "But I've never seen you drink here this last month. Back home, do you love your beer, too?"

"Nah. I'm not really a beer drinker back home."

She started into another piece of pizza and waited for him to continue, but he didn't. Finally, she asked, "What do you love to drink when you're back home?"

"Water mostly. A few juices. An occasional energy drink. Milk. Grape pop. RC Cola."

"None of those are alcoholic. Do you not drink drink?"

He met her eyes. "Not for years and years."

Being brave again, she asked, "Why not, if most other Australians do?"

He shrugged and took another piece of pizza as well. "Alcohol is a mind altering drug. It tends to turn perfectly decent men into scoundrels. Isn't that what Miss Swan said in Pirates of the Caribbean? I'm scoundrel enough when my wits are about me."

That made her smile and she tipped her head over against his shoulder. "Scoundrel? If only all the men in this world could be as unscoundrelly as you."

Chuckling, he popped the top on a root beer of his own. "I'm quite sure unscoundrelly is not a word. But thank you, Miss Benn. Sorry, Miss Dr. Benn."

She shook her head. "Miss Dr. isn't a word either, I'm afraid, Mr. Kane. Can I ask you a serious question?"

"Do I need to be worried?"

She considered that and said mellowly, "No. No worries, mate. It's just me. You certainly never have to worry about me. Well, unless you tell someone else you kissed me. Then you should worry."

Riordan chuckled and said, "No problem. I am never again going to tell a soul about any such thing."

Smiling, she said, "See that you don't."

He nodded. "What was your question?"

She looked up and met his eyes this time. "Well, I've known you a month or so. And in all that time, I've never seen even a hint of something that would go against the teachings of our church. But Josh mentioned years ago that no matter how hard he tried, you weren't interested in joining. Do you think you would ever be interested in joining the Church?"

He kept watching her as he was apparently thinking about her question and then finally, asked one of his own. "If I'm already behaving like a Mormon, then what's the urgency to make it official? Isn't living the gospel more important than the details?"

She nodded her head slowly, and then shook it sideways and said, "Yes, mmm, no. Yes, the spirit of the law is important, but then there are overt acts of obedience, too. It's kind of like witnessing to God that you're all in. On the team. Completely committed. Baptism is uh, absolutely vital. It's about the biggest thing every prophet has spoken about. It's not optional. It's the foundation everything else is built on for the eternities. It's one of the saving ordinances."

He leaned back against the swing again. "The God I pray to is concerned with my heart, Jessie. My intentions. How I treat my fellow man and neighbors. Not in fussing about the details. I was baptized as a child. I'm a Christian. Most of the time, I'm relatively well behaved. God seems to love me. I'm sure I'll be fine."

They sat there quietly for a few moments and then finally, Jessie quietly asked, "Riordan, in your company, if one of your trusted top guys behaved most of the time, but there was one thing that you'd emphasized over and over that you wanted done, but he kept blowing it off because to him it seemed trivial, would you have known without a shadow of a doubt that he was loyal to the death?"

He was quiet for another few minutes and then at length asked, "Do I have to answer that?"

She smiled tiredly at him. "No, Ri. You don't have to do anything. You're right. God loves us, no matter what we do. Thank goodness."

Pushing off softly to make the swing move, he wrapped an arm around her shoulders and gently pulled her to lean against him. After another second, he rubbed a hand up and down her forearm and said, "Yes, thank goodness. Us scoundrels would be in so much trouble."

She leaned there against him and considered what he was saying. Yeah, he would be just fine. In a manner of speaking. He was obviously a good person. And he had a wonderful kind heart. But she also knew that at some point in the big picture, his seemingly trivial refusal to be perfectly obedient would have consequences. She swallowed an inward sigh that was infinitely full of regret.

The sparks that were arcing off her arm where Riordan was touching it were definitely real. Incredibly real. Tantalizingly real. And oh so sweet. She loved when he touched her. It made her feel more alive than she'd ever felt. It was the chemistry she'd hoped for her whole life. And he was the most comfortable friend she'd ever had.

But it would be foolish to seriously pursue this friendship across oceans if she could never even hope for a chance to end up in eternity. Much as she definitely felt that Riordan was fabulously attractive, and fascinating and intriguing, he was also, sadly, not someone she dared fall any more in love with. From the time she was a little tiny girl, she'd known all too well how important being sealed together as a family was. For years, knowing that baby Jennifer was sealed to her family was the only thing that had helped her deal with the heartbreak of what her mother had done. There was no way she could ignore that knowledge now just because she'd finally met the interesting man she'd been hoping to someday meet.

She turned in Riordan's arms and put her cheek against his neck and chest and took a deep breath. He smelled as nice as he felt. She was so tired. Knowing for sure that she needed to just let Riordan go home to Australia next week was ridiculously sad to her. She'd miss him a lot.

He wrapped his other arm around her as well and she wondered if she should just wean herself away from him now, or totally enjoy him for the rest of the week, in spite of knowing that they'd never be more than dear friends. He put a gentle hand to her cheek and caressed it with his thumb and she decided to go with enjoying him. It was probably going to break her heart come Tuesday, but being here beside him tonight was insanely comfortable. She smiled to herself over that word. Yeah he was comfortable. And still fabulously attractive. There was no doubt about whether the chemistry was as potent as it had seemed. It was. Dang it.

Jessie closed her eyes and breathed in again. The crickets played their melody and the stream burbled and the softest of breezes brought the smell of the creek to mix in with Riordan's aftershave. It was a heady potion to her tired brain. It was probably a good thing that she had another huge day tomorrow, or she'd be tempted to stay here in Riordan's arms indefinitely. At least tomorrow was the last day of the big stock show. She could finally have her life back again.

After her fifth yawn, she finally gently pushed Riordan's arm aside and stood up and said, "I'm turning into a pumpkin, Ri. Send me inside."

He stood up beside her and they both came together into a sweet, tight, comfortable hug. She gave a sigh of pleasure and looked up at him and said, "Thanks for coming to eat with . . ."

His mouth coming down on hers interrupted her sentence and she felt her eyes widen. Then she closed them in sheer wonder and sighed again. Happily, she kissed him back. So what if this kiss would probably haunt her when he climbed on that plane next week? Right here and now, the feel of his warm firm mouth was evoking frissions of lavender and apricot electricity that she'd been daydreaming about for days.

His arms tightened around her waist and she put a hand up into his hair and felt herself inhale his scent. Somehow, at the very back of her mind, she registered that his mouth made colors shimmer and swirl through her head again and the skin on her neck tingled with chills. She'd wondered if she had somehow convinced herself that his kiss was better than it actually was after thinking about it so much, but no, it was every bit as heavenly as she'd believed it was. Chemistry was a perfectly marvelous thing.

Somehow, she found herself on her tiptoes, pressing into him, craving oxygen and yet needing to be even closer to him and he made the same nearly imperceptible sound that was almost a moan of pleasure that she'd heard herself make a few minutes before. It made something warm roll inside her chest to know that he felt the arcing as much as she did.

She took another deep almost shuddering breath, and slid her hand back down to his neck and put her other hand up to his cheek. Under her fingers she could feel the five o'clock shadow on his jaw as he kissed her and reveled in how very masculine it was as he moved his mouth over hers. Riordan Kane was a masterful kisser. A heavenly masterful kisser. Man, she was going to miss him.

The thought brought her back to earth and she relaxed off her tiptoes with a sigh that was more sadness than pleasure this time. She opened her eyes and his came open too and he gave her just a hint of a smile. Slowly, still watching her eyes, he lowered his head and gently kissed her on the neck below her ear and then came back to her mouth for one long last kiss before he pulled his face away and hugged her against him.

He rubbed a hand slowly up and down her back and took a deep breath that she felt him inhale and then softly said, "I wasn't going to do that, but crickeys you're tempting."

Nodding, she murmured, "Says the forbidden fruit." She gave him a hesitant smile. "But I couldn't not. It was hopeless."

"Yes, I know exactly what you mean. Goodnight, Jessie. I'll probably dream about your mouth again."

"Again?"

He gave her a grin and raised an eyebrow. "What, you didn't believe me last time?"

"No. I didn't."

"Well, you should have. See you in the morning, Jessie."

Chapter 20

Even after taking extra care with her makeup and hair, Jessie was a little more nervous than usual as she walked into the barn at quarter after ten the next morning. In spite of giving herself a pep talk the entire time she was dressing and doing her morning calls about how she and Riordan were destined to be nothing more than dear friends, she was still a trifle flustered about seeing him today. Not to mention the fact that it was the Best of Show class. If she was able to win this class for Riordan, it could mean tens of thousands of dollars in increased stud fees and the value of his horse.

She came in wearing her show clothes and fringed chaps and boots and hugged Josh and then began to help him finish grooming Hugo, who must have known he was being shown this morning, because he was side stepping and antsy.

Josh had just run to his truck to retrieve some more Vaseline while Jessie was working on Hugo's mane, when an attractive man who was probably in his early thirties appeared around the corner. He approached Jessie and the huge red horse and said with a distinctly Australian accent, "I'm looking for Josh Benjamin. Do you happen to know where I can find him?"

Looking up, Jessie said, "He just stepped outside for a minute. He'll be right back. Anything I can help you with?"

He looked her up and down unabashedly and smiled and held out a hand and said, "Yes, I'm sure there is something, although meeting a girl as lovely as you has completely addled my mind until I'm not sure what. I'm Rich Langford. Riordan Kane's personal assistant. He told me to meet him here this morning, but he didn't tell me that Aphrodite would be here to greet me. I am honored to meet you, Miss . . ."

Jessie couldn't help smiling at his over the top flirting. She took his hand and answered, "Benn. Jessie Benn. I haven't seen Riordan, but Josh just ran to his truck. If you remember how I can help you in the next . . ." She glanced at her watch, "Seven minutes, I'd be glad to be of assistance."

Hugo chose to crow hop just then in the cross ties and then hang back and Jessie instinctively put an arm around Rich's chest and forcefully pushed him back away from the antsy horse, saying, "Watch yourself."

She'd shoved him back against the stall wall and had to move close to get herself out of Hugo's way as well and Rich looked down at her standing close in front of him and grinned.

Trying to stay out of the still crow hopping horse's way, she said, "Sorry about that. Hugo here is a just a tad too rambunctious this morning. Stand back from him. Riordan would not be impressed if we maimed you on your first morning in America. You did just arrive this morning, didn't you?"

257

Still grinning, Rich said, "Yes, Miss, I did. And I can tell right away I'm going to love America!"

Jessie hurriedly moved sideways away from him as she said skeptically, "I hope you do, Mr. Langford."

"Oh, please, call me Rich."

"Certainly. Rich." Approaching Hugo again with her hand held out, she said, "Easy, Hugo. Hold still, buddy. We still need to do some work on you."

Josh hustled back in and Jessie made introductions as they tried to quickly finish polishing the horse without getting killed by his antics in the process. Shaking his head, Josh said, "What is up with him? He's acting like he's on race feed this morning."

Her dad showed up as well and immediately put a stud chain lead over Hugo's nose to try to quiet him down and said, "This might be an adventure this morning, Jess. Let's hurry and take him into the practice arena and try to settle him in some. Then I'll pony you up to the Saguaro Arena. I'd hate to have you get thrown in the Best of Show class."

They unclipped him from the cross ties and she legged onto him and did indeed just about get thrown before she even made it into the saddle when he hung back from her father who was holding him. She quickly took him into the nearby arena and as soon as her dad let go of his head, he bolted. She let him run half way down the arena and then pulled him into a big circle and held him to a long lope for several minutes, hoping to take some of the bluster out of him. Unfortunately, before he'd settled down, her dad called from the gate where he was on a pony horse, "We need to head out, sis. Hopefully he'll settle down some before class time."

When her dad went to clip the stallion chain lead he held onto Hugo's headstall, the big stud bared his teeth and lunged at the pony horse who in turn spun away. Her dad, spinning with the horse, calmly said, "Okay then. He'll be wearing a muzzle until class time this morning."

He slid off his horse and left Josh holding it as he strode into the tack room and returned with a heavy leather stallion muzzle. Attaching it over Hugo's nose, he then got back on the now extremely leery pony horse and said, "Okay then, let's try that again."

With Josh's help, they got the chain lead clipped onto Hugo's headstall and headed out with Hugo dancing and crow hopping all the way down the alleyway and Rich Langford standing by big eyed.

Jessie held the big stud in as best she could and gave her dad a grin and said, "Now you know why I'm a veterinarian. Eight years of rigorous exams is nothing compared to dealing with some of these boneheads."

Hugo tried to rear just then and her dad hauled the big horse back down and said, "Oh, but hey, the adrenaline rush can't begin to compare. Hang on to him, sis. And it's not like some of your patients don't behave the same way. Look at Justison's horses."

"That is true."

To Jessie, it felt like a long, long way down to the Saguaro Arena and once they were there, her dad kept his lead on Hugo and they walked slow circles near the other waiting horses. That is, they tried to walk slow circles near the other horses. Of course, Hugo would be the last contestant this time.

Riordan and his parents appeared while they were still trying to get Hugo to settle in and when he saw what was going on, he gave Jessie a look fraught with concern. He walked over as close as she dared let him and asked, "Jessie, is this going to work? Do we need to scratch him? I don't want you to get hurt."

Focusing on hanging onto the horse, Jessie said, "I think we'll be fine. If I need to, we'll scratch. Just say your prayers."

She had to crack a grin as he said the exact words he'd said last time. "Absolutely, sweetheart." And Hugo did indeed settle down some, but Jessie worried that it wasn't nearly enough. He was still all but dancing when they called his name to enter the arena.

****

When Riordan and his parents came through the portal from the stands to see Jessie and Ken ponying an all but wild Hugo, his heart skipped a beat in his chest. Jessie looked like a cowgirl super model astride the big proud horse, but the horse appeared to be ready to either bolt or buck as they struggled to contain him. Riordan's first inclination was to simply scratch him from the class. No amount of money or fame was worth risking Jessie getting hurt.

Hugo had settled down marginally by the time it was his turn and as Jessie headed into the arena, Riordan shook his head and went to go in and sit by his parents. This might turn out fabulous, or it might be a disaster.

The horse and rider came through the portal, Hugo still throwing his head and prancing and Riordan shook his head again and said another prayer. Once inside, Hugo reared up and Riordan decided to definitely scratch him.

As he was trying to catch Jessie's eye to make the call, Jessie never looked up, just pulled the horse right to a dead stop and simply sat with him again for several long moments, much as she had that first class. And again, it seemed to do the trick. Hugo fought the bit for a couple of seconds and then put his head down and his ears up and seemed to take a big deep breath and relax.

Jessie looked up and caught Riordan's eye and gave him a minimal nod, then started forward into the center of the arena. Riordan leaned back and ran a hand through his hair and then swore under his breath when Hugo crow hopped one more time just after she started him in.

Until Riordan felt his mum reach up and take his arm a few seconds later, he hadn't even realized he was holding his breath. He took in air and registered his mum's murmur of approval and glanced down at her to see a huge smile and her hands clasped tightly together in front of her. He had to agree when she whispered, "They're beautiful."

Miraculously, when Jessie finally started him into their pattern, Hugo behaved like an old plug again. They smoothly loped in circles for a few moments and then slowed to a stop and sat momentarily. Then the audience erupted into cat calls and applause when he suddenly spun hard to the right for what seemed like days, then abruptly rolled back, and pulled up into an impressive sliding stop, sending the arena dirt flying. Afterward, Hugo performed nearly invisible flying lead changes before doing it all again the other direction. It was like horse ballet. Not a step was out of place or off balance. He looked like he was dancing, his feet flashing and his mane swinging in a great red wave, while Jessie balanced atop him magically, her own shining golden mane swinging along in perfect sync with the horse's.

If Riordan thought she'd been magnificent in previous rides, he was blown away by this one. Jessie and Hugo made a phenomenal flawless pattern and then regally seemed to float as he headed out of the arena. The crowd instantly came unglued, which made Hugo start acting up again Someone behind Riordan slapped him on the back and he finally took in a huge breath. Man, she'd nailed it in spite of Hugo being a bone head!

He turned to his mum and patted her hands, and then hugged her for a second when he saw that her eyes were bright with tears. But, he couldn't stay with her. Saying, "Be back in awhile, Mum," he got up and hustled down to the portal out of the arena to go get Jessie. She had to be sicker than ever what with Hugo's antics.

She was. He could see it in her face as she glanced up at him before he even got close and he strode faster, glad for her sake that the stock show was over. She'd been a fabulous trooper.

Hugo was cutting up again from all the noise inside the arena and Ken wasn't able to get close enough to catch him with the pony lead because his horse was afraid of the big stud and kept sidestepping away. Josh was trying to help, but couldn't get around in his walking boot and Hugo was baring his teeth at the pony horse anyway. Finally, Jessie leaned forward and slapped Hugo hard on the neck and hauled on his reins and that seemed to help in getting his attention.

Inside the arena, another huge cheer went up and Ken shook his head and smiled, in spite of all the hoopla and said, "I guess we aren't going to be ponying him anyway, sis. Way to go! You took grand champion!" He slid off his horse and looped its reins over the nearby rail, and finally hooked the stud chain over Hugo's nose and asked, "Can you stick him for a couple more minutes to go in and get his ribbons? I'll be right here beside you all the way."

She grimaced, but she nodded and said to Riordan, "Come on, Ri. This is what you came to America for. Come on and get in the pictures." To Josh she said more quietly, "Josh, get me a barf bag. Something. Anything. Just in case."

They went back into the arena and as they came through the portal, the crowd got loud again. Hugo took that as a cue to try to rear up again, in spite of Ken hauling on him with the stallion lead. When he couldn't rear, he arched his neck like a circus horse and began to prance and sidestep instead, with Jessie sitting her saddle like she was glued to it and as if his antics were nothing out of the ordinary.

At the head of the other horses in the class, Ken glanced up at her. She gave him a minimal nod and Riordan was surprised when her dad reached up and unclipped the stallion lead and let Jessie have him by herself to walk up into the center position in the line, with Hugo still prancing like a show off all the way.

Once there, for one long second, he appeared to pose while the ring steward attached the ribbon to his headstall, and a photographer with a humongous camera snapped photos. But that only lasted until the steward stepped away.

Some slight breeze made the tails of the ribbon flutter and Hugo reared up again like a Hollywood stunt horse right in front of the camera that was shooting away. Still sticking him, Jessie only pulled on the bit and patted his neck, speaking to him and he settled back down to stand like the respectable show horse that he was supposed to be and they stood there posing again. Riordan shook his head and thought, *man, it's a good thing he's already been awarded his ribbon.*

As the class stood, there was one last round of applause and then the announcer made some final closing comments, thanking the audience for coming and giving the dates for the next year's show and then it was finally over.

As Jessie came to the side of the arena, the photographer followed her. Ken and her brothers joined Riordan and they all walked toward them to be photographed in front of the huge USA National Stock Show banner for individual photos. Riordan looked at Jessie's pale face smiling bravely there and frankly didn't care a bit about a photo. He just wanted her off that horse and safely in his arms where he knew she was okay and he could start to baby her back to feeling better. He so owed her for this.

As they were finishing with the photos, his parents and Rich showed up and Ken motioned for them to join a photo as well, and then Riordan politely but firmly stepped up to Hugo and reached for Jessie. As the cameraman finally left she stepped off the horse, still acting like a professional horse trainer, but then she handed the reins to her dad and all but wilted. When Josh would have spoken to her, Riordan took the air sickness bag he was carrying and stuffed it into a pocket and then nudged him away. Instead, he pulled Jessie into a hug against his chest and asked quietly against her ear, "Are you okay?"

She nodded against him, but then shook her head and murmured, "No. I need to get out of this arena. I'm afraid I might throw up in front of this whole crowd. And your parents. I'd die of embarrassment."

Putting his arm around her shoulders, he pulled her tight against him and practically carried her away from where the others were still standing visiting. Outside one of the portals, he bought two icy cold bottles of water at a concession stand as they passed it and then sat down on a bench out of the way of all the people walking past them.

Pulling her to lean against him, he put one bottle of water behind her neck, tenderly smoothed her hair back off of her forehead and asked, "Better?"

She nodded against him again and he put an arm around her and began to rub up and down her back, murmuring against her hair. "Just take it easy, Jessie. Some big deep breaths, and think about how awesome you did. Not how green your tummy feels. You were fabulous in there. You made my mum cry."

She rolled her head and looked up at him in concern and he said, "No. In a good way."

Jaclyn M. Hawkes

Jessie groaned and put her head back into his neck and said tiredly, "Oh, good. I couldn't imagine what I'd already done to offend her."

He smiled with his chin against her hair. "She's always loved horses, but she hasn't been to a lot of these horse shows. And she's certainly never seen anything like you and Hugo. The big lout. What got into him this morning? But as big of a pain as he was, he looked bloomin' beautiful prancing around like a showboat. Mum thought you were magnificent."

She leaned her head back against his shoulder and took a deep breath and he put the other bottle of water against her forehead and gave her a sad smile. "I'm so sorry, Jessie. But thank you for riding him. I'm sorry he was acting so beastly."

Shaking her head tiredly, she said, "It's okay, Ri. We got him his grand champion ribbon. It will make him even more valuable. As well as his babies."

He squeezed her shoulder and rubbed up and down her arm. "Yes. You were phenomenal. But now I need to make it up to you even more."

She blew out a breath and said, "No, Riordan, you don't. I'm still way in your debt for all your help while you've been here. Are your parents okay? That's a long trip. Are they thrashed?"

"Yes. But they still wanted to get back here to see you and Hugo. I'll take them to your dad's to rest in a minute when I take you. Can you go home? Or do you have to go to the clinic?"

She closed her eyes and turned her face back into his neck and answered against him, "Mmm. I should go into the clinic.

We're still busy, even though a lot of the stock show trainers have already pulled out. I'll check with Cal in awhile and see how they're doing. I'd love to go home and lie down in front of the air conditioner."

At that, he rubbed her back again and they just sat there, quietly, almost hugging while people continued to stream out of the arena and walk in front of them and he thought about the amazing girl he held.

Jessie was a singular individual. She had so many fascinating twists to her. Strengths and vulnerabilities, gifts and idiosyncrasies. He'd seen the resolute look in her eyes last night when he'd given her that blarney about not joining her church and he'd known that she was discouraged, but he couldn't lie to her either about something as important as joining her church. Until he knew for certain what he wanted and what he was going to do, he couldn't toy with her.

Although that's probably what she thought he was doing when he'd kissed her again last night. Thinking about her kisses made him want to kiss her again, and he closed his eyes and breathed in her perfume. What was he doing kissing Jessie Benn? Truth be told, he'd probably been hoping to kiss her again when he'd gone looking for her to take her to dinner last night. And why not? She was incredibly nice to kiss.

In a way, he absolutely wished he could take her home with him next week. But they both knew that in reality, it would be impossible. She had her life and he had his. He smoothed her hair back again and gently kissed her temple and wondered what in the world he was going to do about Jessie Benn.

At length, Ken and his parents, with Rich tagging along, appeared down the concourse and if Riordan hadn't been so concerned about Jessie, he would have smiled at the way his mum was looking at him with this incredibly beautiful girl. His mum's eyes had an insanely speculative gleam to them. His dad didn't even try to hide his smile as he looked at them.

When they approached, Ken leaned down to speak quietly to Jessie, "You okay, sis?"

She looked up and nodded at him, even though she looked pale and miserable, and said, "I'll be fine."

By way of explanation to Riordan's parents, Ken said, "Motion sickness. Poor girl. He really gave her a carnival ride this morning."

Riordan's mom made a sound of sympathy and Jessie looked up and gave them a tentative smile and a tired wave and then leaned back against Riordan again. Riordan knew she was embarrassed and he brushed a hand down her back again and said, "She'll be good as new in awhile and will be a bit more enthusiastic to meet you, Mum. Dad. Just give her a moment."

Nodding, Ken said, "In the meantime, can I do anything for you? Have you all had lunch? The boys and I are going to put the horse away and go grab a bite. Would you join us?"

Riordan's mum looked a bit hesitant, but his dad was apparently hungry and said, "Food would be wonderful. Thank you. Can we help with the horse in any way?"

Smiling, Ken said, "Absolutely! We never pass up good help around here. Just come with me. It won't be long and then we'll head out to lunch. Brennan, could you contact security and round up a Grizzly to transport us? I'm sure Mr. Kane has gotten plenty of exercise on that hip already today." To Riordan and Jessie he said, "Watch over her, Ri, and then if she's up to it, come eat with us."

Turning back away, he waved a hand down the concourse toward the doors and as they started walking, Riordan heard him ask, "What are you in the mood for? We've got Italian, Mexican, down home family style. Chinese. What would you like?"

He heard Jessie chuckle and glanced down at her with a smile and said, "I think our dads are going to get along fabulously."

With a smile in her voice, she said, "My dad gets along fabulously with everyone. It's because he loves everyone and it's easy to tell. He probably loves having someone his own age around, as well. Your parents seem very nice."

"Oh, they are. Unless you're sixteen and have just pulled some shenanigan or the other. Then, not so much. Especially my mum. She was usually the bad cop when I was in trouble."

Jessie laughed again against his neck. "I can't picture that elegant woman ever being the bad cop. What did you do?"

He chuckled. "Nothing I'm going to divulge to you. Feeling better?"

She leaned up and nodded. "Some. I think I'm going to live. At least until next year's stock show. Hopefully, Josh will stay whole and healthy next time and I can go back to being blissfully motion sickness free."

Riordan shook his head. "I know you're sick, Jess, but not having you compete would be a pity. You're fabulous at it. Incredibly gifted."

With a tired voice, she said, "Thanks, Ri. I appreciate that. But there are reasons that I'm a veterinarian. Haul me up and I'll go get changed and check in with Cal, while you eat with them."

He tipped her face up to look into her eyes and said, "We can hang out here for a bit. Can't we?" He put a gentle hand on her cheek. "Are you up to leaving already?"

"Not really. But your parents have flown all the way from Australia to see you. You should go be with them."

"I will. And I want you to officially meet them when you're up to it. But I'm okay here for a bit. Just get your legs under you first."

She nodded and snuggled back into him without saying anything.

21

That afternoon, in the sitting room of the north wing of Ken Benjamin's house, Riordan visited with his parents, surprised that they were actually up to visiting after their long flight. His dad was sitting on the end of the couch with his leg stretched out on it and his mum was sitting beside him in a wing chair, sipping fruit juice and gesturing with her hands as she talked about the Arizona climate, and their adventures in the airport where his dad had set off the metal detectors with his new hip, and how kind the Benjamins seemed to be to invite them to stay with them like this, and how Warren had been asked to transfer to either Thailand or the United States.

Eventually, his mum began to wind down and his dad said, "Caroline, did you remember to give Riordan the card from that woman?"

At that, his mum jumped up and said, "Oh, dear. I almost forgot, Riordan. Kyra Bevan sent a note to give to you."

She began digging in her purse and handed him an envelope. "She said she could have just emailed, but she wasn't sure if her messages were getting through, so she brought this by the house last week. She originally wanted the physical address here, but I figured you'd rather have the note than have her actually show up." She gave Riordan a small smile as she handed it to him.

Opening it, he glanced at the picture of Kyra in all her tattooed and pierced glory, then at the note it contained and tossed it on the end table. His mum picked it up and shook her head and tossed it back again. Sitting back down, she said, "Speaking of girls, why haven't you mentioned Jessie in any of your phone calls?"

He'd known this conversation was coming and said innocently, "Hmm. I didn't know I should have. Why should I have mentioned Jessie?"

His dad laughed and his mum rolled her eyes and said, "Oh, for heaven's sake, Riordan. It didn't take ten seconds of seeing you with that girl to realize that she was . . . important to you. Why do I have to come clear to America to find it out? She seemed like a very nice girl. A very brave nice girl to ride that half wild stallion of yours and come through it. Does he always behave like that?"

Drily, Riordan said, "Only during the most important show class of his career. Most of the time he's relatively well mannered."

"So, what about this Jessie girl? Have you been dating her the whole time you've been here?"

"We actually haven't dated even once, Mum. We're just friends."

His dad laughed again and his mum said sarcastically, "Yes, and I'm the Pope, Riordan. Be serious, please. I'm your mum. You can level with me."

Riordan smiled and shook his head. "I'm being serious, Mum. We're just friends. Very good friends, but just friends. She actually only dates Mormon blokes, so I'm out of luck with her. Plus, she's been crazy busy since I got here. She's the on-call veterinarian, as well as taking over showing Josh's horses for him when he got hurt. In addition, she has her vet clinic. She's really only had time to date her regular blokes she was dating before I got here. Although I do think I botched it with a couple of those. Accidentally, of course."

His mum frowned. "Are you telling me that the girl you were so very comfortably hugging, dates other men? And refuses to date you?" She made a small sound of outrage and Riordan chuckled, even though at times, he kind of wanted to make that same sound of outrage.

He nodded in answer to her question and his mum went on. "But she seemed so nice. Not like that kind of girl at all."

"She is nice, Mum. Not like what kind of girl?"

"Well, the kind of girl who hugs one man and dates another."

"It's not like we were behaving inappropriately. She was sick. Because she'd just done me a huge favor and ridden my very ill behaved horse to a Grand Championship of one of the biggest reining shows in the world. That ranks higher than nice in my book. She's dating to try and find someone to marry. It's like some sacred quest to her. She said she doesn't want to grow old alone."

His mum looked confused. "How in the world could someone as drop dead gorgeous as that girl was, worry about growing old alone? Is she bad tempered or something?"

Riordan laughed out loud at her and said, "She's the nicest, kindest, most even tempered girl on the planet from what I've seen, Mum. She is beautiful, isn't she?"

His mum got that speculative gleam in her eye again and asked, "You say she's a veterinarian? Is she old enough to be a veterinarian? They must not need as much education here in the states."

"She's a veterinarian. And they actually need more education here. Not less. She owns her own thriving practice here."

Putting her hands on her hips, his mum came to stand directly in front of the chair Riordan was sprawled in and said in an exasperated voice. "Then what, Riordan? What is going on between the two of you? Level with me now. What you're telling me, and what I saw out there today, don't add up."

Riordan rubbed the back of his neck and shook his head and said almost sadly, "They really don't add up, do they?" He sighed and added, "I don't know what's going on between the two of us any more than you do, Mum. It's a complete mystery to me as well."

Looking even more confused, she asked, "Well, is she the reason you're happier here in the U.S.?"

He nodded absentmindedly. "Yup. She is. But she's a Yank veterinarian with a thriving practice, in Arizona, USA, who wants to marry a nice, comfortable Mormon bloke. So, you see, I'm completely ineligible."

His dad laughed again and his mum made another hurrump sound, and said, "I'm trying to have a serious conversation with you here, son. Could you please stop with the sarcasm and engage?"

Mildly, Riordan asked, "Mum, which of those three items can I overcome here?"

"Well . . ." She considered for a moment and then said, "She could sell her thriving practice. Or you could move here. It's not out of the question."

Chuckling, Riordan said, "I thought you wanted grand children on the same continent."

Sounding thoughtful, she said, "Yes, I do. So, talk her into selling her practice and moving to Australia. You're rich. Dangle some money in front of her."

Riordan gave a short, humorless laugh. "Money doesn't equate with her, Mum. She's already reasonably well off, anyway. Did you hear the part about nice, comfortable Mormon? She came right out and told me I was ineligible since I wasn't LDS. And when we haven't so much as dated, I can hardly ask her to sell her practice and move down under with me. I mean, not with me, but sort of with me."

"Well, how bad is their religion, anyway? They seem very nice. Would it hurt to join their church if she might be the girl you want to marry?"

From the couch, his dad chuckled again and said, "Caroline, the last thing he wants is a gold digger. And who said anything about marriage? You've taken him from putting his arm around a girl, to saying the M word. That's a bit of a stretch, don't you think?"

She flounced back down into her chair. "Yes, I suppose so." She wagged a finger at Riordan. "But, you and I both know that that's the most friendly we've seen you be with a woman in years. You were obviously very concerned for her. Maybe she could be the one. You've got a couple of days still. Ask the girl out, for the love of Pete. And kiss her. I always say that you need to really kiss someone to find out if you there's any magic between you."

Riordan only smiled a mellow smile and then realized he shouldn't have done that when his mum stood back up from her chair and came over to him and said knowingly, "You've already kissed her! Haven't you? I can tell by that ridiculous grin. Why, Riordan Kane, you floozy. How can you have kissed a girl, but never taken her on a date? How does that work?"

Still grinning, Riordan said, "Now, Mum, don't jump to conclusions. Remember what happens when you assume things? And I am not a floozy."

She laughed good naturedly. "Well, the look on your face says you are something like that."

His dad piped in again. "Caroline, kissing a girl does not constitute flooziness. Good for you, son. She's a beautiful girl. Kiss her all you want."

"Roy! Don't tell him that! Riordan is a gentleman. He doesn't kiss girls indiscriminately."

"Of course he doesn't, Caroline. So when he finally does kiss one, it must be kind of a big deal. Let him have some latitude here, woman, or you're never going to get those grandkids you've been praying for."

"Well, I don't want grandkids just because he's been kissing someone all he wants."

"Relax, Caroline. Riordan isn't going to suddenly start having kids with anyone. Just let him enjoy kissing someone – who he obviously cares about.

Riordan looked from one to the other of them and shook his head. They were funny, but in truth, he didn't want to discuss any of this. Teasing his mum about Jessie was a good time, but the truth was, he truly did wish he could find a way to be with her beyond next week.

He decided to change the subject. "So, what would you blokes like to do while you're here? You want to go road tripping around here? And do you want to go to Salt Lake City with Rich and me on Monday? Or stay here and relax around the pool? Or a combination of the two? What are your plans?"

His mum sat down next to him again and said enthusiastically, "Actually, we've been thinking about that. Since you don't have to be anywhere in particular at any certain time right now, what would you think about touring around a little while we're here? We could go see the Grand Canyon! And then go north and drive through the four national parks in southern Utah on the way to Salt Lake City! What would you think about driving, instead of flying there? Then after your meetings, we could go further north and go see the national parks in Wyoming. Grand Teton and Yellowstone. We think it's only another few hour's drive north of Salt Lake City. The tourist sites say they're some of the best places to visit in the country. We could take a few days and fit in what we could. Then we could fly out of the airport in Jackson Hole there. What do you think?"

He looked at his mum and her obvious enthusiasm and for some reason, his heart suddenly wanted to implode. Here he'd been trying to intimate to his parents that he wasn't totally caught up in Jessie Benn, but if they decided to do what his mum had just suggested, they'd have to leave Arizona almost immediately. And if they flew out of Jackson Hole, he wouldn't be back to see Jessie afterward either.

It made sense. It would be a fun trip. His parents would probably not come back to the United States again anytime soon. And he knew they'd enjoy it. They loved that kind of thing. But, he so wasn't ready to tell Jessie goodbye permanently. Which was absolutely foolish, if he really analyzed his relationship with Jessie—but if he got gut honest with himself, that was how he felt.

Slowly, he nodded. "That would be fun. If you think you're up to it."

His mum must have seen his hesitation, because her enthusiasm level dropped dramatically as she said, "Well, hon, we don't have to. Your father and I would be perfectly happy doing anything you want to do."

He nodded more positively this time. "It would be fun, Mum. It's a wonderful opportunity. We should do it. You figure out the route and what you want to do, and I'll have Rich find us a motor coach. Let's plan to leave Saturday morning. That will give you tomorrow to relax and get organized. Then we'll have two days before I need to be in Salt Lake on Monday afternoon. We can at least see the Grand Canyon. If I have to, I'll fly up and back down to the national parks in Utah after my meetings."

Glancing over at his dad, he grinned and added, "And make sure you add in a fishing trip or two to this adventure. I want to fish the Firehole River in Yellowstone before I die."

He pulled out his phone to call Rich, wishing he was more excited to go with his parents. It was probably for the best not to get any closer to Jessie anyway.

Chapter 22

That evening, Ken Benjamin threw a barbecue to celebrate the end of the very successful USA National Stock Show. Benjamin Reining horses had taken eighteen blue first place ribbons, one red second place ribbon, and one blue Grand Champion Best of Show ribbon. They'd always done well, but this was their best year ever and they invited all the hands, and their closest friends, and of course Riordan's parents and Rich.

Ken had Jorge smoke ribs and brisket and they gathered around big picnic tables on the stream bank in his back yard and laughed and visited and ate. Jorge's wife, Consuelo even came and Jessie was thrilled to see that she seemed to be doing better. Pablo gave Jessie a big smile and a hug when he got there and Marcela reached for her with a big smile of her own.

They all ate too much, and her brothers teased her the way they always did. They enjoyed getting to know Riordan's parents, and it was a wonderful evening. Right up until after dinner when Riordan's mother, Caroline, beamingly announced that starting early Saturday morning, the three Kanes were all going to "go walk-about" for a few weeks in the United States through several western national parks and then fly out of the airport in Jackson Hole, Wyoming.

The announcement caught Jessie completely off-guard as she was holding Marcela and she was actually glad when, in the second it took Jessie to process the announcement, the baby got hold of her water glass and upended it all over the two of them. The ice filled water shocked the adorable little girl and she gasped and then burst into tears, which was incidentally, exactly what Jessie wanted to do as well.

Jorge took the crying baby to begin to mop her off and Jessie used her soaking wet clothing as an excuse to make an exit of her own. Tugging at where her peasant blouse was sticking to her chest, she quietly slipped around the corner of her dad's house and headed for her own to change clothes.

Saturday? That was one day away. Barely.

She'd already been struggling to figure out what she really wanted with Riordan before the Tuesday of next week, the way Josh had encouraged her, and had thought that was going to be impossibly too short of a time. Now she had one day!

Or maybe not. Apparently Riordan was able to pick up and go road tripping and then leave without giving her a second thought, so maybe there wasn't really anything to decide after all. Maybe his travel plan—that he hadn't even mentioned to her, was the answer. Because obviously, if their friendship was to blossom into anything more, it would need both them wanting it to. It was suddenly painfully clear that she just didn't matter as much to Riordan as he did to her. She'd inadvertently let her feelings for him get way out of balance with his feelings for her.

She tried to analyze the whole walk-about revelation unemotionally as she peeled her damp clothing off, but honestly, it felt like a grenade to the chest on a day that had already been exhausting. Suddenly, she was tired to the bone.

On second thought, maybe she wouldn't change clothes and go back. Maybe she'd just have a quick shower and call it an early night. It had been a long, long stock show.

****

He should have spoken to Jessie about leaving earlier than planned with his parents. He just hadn't had a chance.

He'd been planning to talk to her that night after the barbecue, but then his mum had been gushing about their plans and Jessie had gotten soaked by her water glass and disappeared. When she hadn't answered her phone later, he'd been worried, but Josh had assured him that she'd probably just gone to bed early. For some reason, that hadn't comforted him.

And now, her call truck had been gone since before he even got up and it had become pretty obvious by three o'clock in the afternoon that she wasn't taking his calls. He'd tried calling six times and left two messages and she hadn't so much as texted him back.

He got back into his pretty truck to go by her clinic again to see if she was there. She hadn't been when he'd gone by earlier.

Her call truck still wasn't there, but Dr. Stettler's truck was and he parked and got out. Maybe Dr. Stettler could tell him where to find her.

Inside, he had to wait for more than twenty minutes before he got a chance to ask the other doctor between patients, "Do

Jaclyn M. Hawkes

you know where Dr. Benn is this afternoon? She's not answering her phone."

Looking slightly harried, the other vet said, "Yeah, she hasn't had time to answer phone calls. Some high end barrel racing horse is colicking down in Gilbert. They found it cast upside down in its stall. She's been down there for a couple of hours now. They're going to bring it in for surgery—they just can't get it stable enough to trailer, yet. And then it keeps rolling and she's worrying about a full torsion. Hopefully, she'll be back here within the hour. If they can't get it trailered, she'll have to just open it up down there, which drops the surgery success rate dramatically. I'm sure she'll call when she gets a chance."

Frustrated, Riordan got back into his truck and went back to Josh's. If he couldn't find Jessie, he might as well get all his gear packed and then go find Thank You gifts for the Benjamins. His parents were still a bit jet lagged and were resting at Ken's and Rich wasn't feeling much better.

****

Jessie brushed the hair back from her forehead and wished she had a moment for a bottle of water as she watched the light fade from the sky in the west .Man, she wished Riordan's reassuring quiet confidence were here with her tonight. She hated to try to operate on this horse on a farm call, but it wasn't looking like she'd have any choice. They'd been at this for several hours now and she'd tried everything else she knew to do and nothing had helped.

She had to open it up and she had to do it now and trucking it in to the clinic wasn't going to happen. They couldn't even get it to stop trying to lay down when they were walking it around. Twice it had nearly fallen on her as it went to its knees.

At least the owners were experienced enough horse people to realize that it was either surgery or the horse would die. And even with the surgery, it might die anyway. Sometimes colic was just that way. She hoped it wasn't that way tonight. They understood, but this was a champion barrel racer and was probably valued in the seventy thousand dollar range.

Sighing, she nodded at Cal and then went to her truck and began to draw the anesthetic she'd need to put the horse under. Cal had already rigged up a makeshift operating table with a trailer divider panel on a platform of hay bales inside a well lit barn in case it got to this point. It wasn't her state of the art surgical suite, but it was the best they could manage.

Now she just had to perform this incredibly delicate surgery as quickly as she could. She had a much higher success rate than most surgeons, but even in the clinic, about twenty percent of these horses didn't make it. The equine gastrointestinal track could be a terribly unpredictable thing. She prayed as she snapped on her latex gloves.

Fifteen minutes later, she glanced up at Cal as he was monitoring the horse's vitals and he met her eyes as she untwisted the horse's bowel where it had gotten wrapped around itself. It was just as she had diagnosed. A full torsion where the secum connected to the colon, and from the size of the obstruction, they were lucky that this horse hadn't already died on them. Not only was the bowel obstructed, but the blood flow to the whole area was disrupted as well and part of the intestine was black and damaged.

She untangled the offending organs and proceeded to remove the dead tissue and then carefully sutured the section and stabilized the horse's guts as well as she could. Finally, she disinfected the whole of the area with a stout mix of chemicals. Anytime you opened the bowel, or had it rupture, the danger of infection and scarring went through the roof. They were what typically caused an abdominal surgery to go south.

With the horse ultimately sewn up, she and Cal carefully administered a drug to help the horse begin to come out from under the anesthetic and then she finally got her cold water bottle while they and the owners stood by, watching the horse. So far so good. Now they just needed to get this horse to successfully wake up and stand up and be able to withstand all the stress that a full torsioned bowel could inflict on it.

When the big bay gelding finally opened its eyes and let out a huge blustery groan, they all took a deep breath with it. That was a good start. They let it lay quietly while the owner sat next to him and gently petted the horse as it came more fully awake. But horses weren't like humans. Lying still could only last for a short while because it wouldn't be able to breathe well enough lying there on its side.

As it finally struggled to its feet a few minutes later, Jessie closed her eyes and said another quick prayer. At least it hadn't died in surgery. But they still weren't out of the woods. The worst was yet to come as the horse's system would need to be able to process all the toxins that had built up and would now begin to flush through its GI tract and bloodstream. Not to mention how the stress of it all would often cause additional colic and laminitis.

As soon as the horse showed any inclination to want to move, Jessie began to slowly walk with it again. It was just what they'd been doing for hours, trying to keep it moving, but it was the best thing for that huge mass of intestines that were causing it so much pain and trouble. They had to get that bowel moving again or the horse would still die.

In addition, walking would help ease the pain, but it also kept the horse from wanting to lay down and roll, which was what horses in pain did, but rolling had, no doubt, been the cause of the full torsion in the first place.

For nearly an hour, she was encouraged that the horse was doing well, and she just kept on slowly walking, and praying. But then, the obviously exhausted horse began to show signs of distress again that were very disheartening.

The pain came back, slowly at first, but then more obvious as the night turned into early morning. The gelding wanted to stop walking and lay down and it was all they and the owners could do to prevent it from laying down.

Jessie and Cal administered every drug and treatment they knew to give it, but its heart rate went up as well and the distress became more overt. It began to sweat as if it was being exercised even as they walked more and more slowly.

Feeling a cold dread, Jessie gave the gelding something more to fight inflammation in the bowel and wracked her brain to remember every little thing she knew to do in this situation. And she ramped up her prayers. This horse could still make it through. Maybe it was just a temporary setback. Such a surgery was incredibly hard on an animal. But it might perk right up in

Jaclyn M. Hawkes

time. Even as her body dragged from exhaustion, she tried to give herself a pep talk and will the horse one as well. Man, she missed Riordan.

Ultimately, as the horse became more and more lethargic, she began to talk to it, openly trying to speak healing to it, still trying to encourage it and her and its owners. But she knew in her heart that in all likelihood, this horse wasn't going to make it.

At ten minutes to three, even the four of them couldn't keep the horse on its feet and it lay down heavily, almost dragging them down with it and catching Jessie on the side of the shin with a heavy hoof as it collapsed.

As the horse lay fully out with a groan, its eyes cloudy with pain, the exhausted owner leaned down to stroke the horse that she'd ridden, and traveled with, and competed on through hundreds of rodeos, and asked, "What now?"

Sadly, Jessie shook her head, "Well, we go back in and try again, which, honestly, probably won't change anything. Or just let him rest for the time being and see if he somehow perks up — which is very unlikely. Or put him down."

Nodding, the two owners looked at each other and the wife's eyes teared up and she said, "No more surgery. If you don't think it will help for sure. He's been through enough."

At that, the husband said, "Then let's give him awhile, hon. Maybe he'll come around. Let's don't give up completely yet." He came to her and hugged her and it made Jessie think about Riordan again. A strong, gentle shoulder to lean on was such a blessing sometimes.

286

Looking to Jessie, the husband said, "Can we leave him to you for a minute or two? I'm just going to go up to the house and get her a drink. We'll bring you something back as well."

Wanting to cry herself, Jessie nodded. "Certainly. We'll be right here." She knew exactly what this kind man was doing. He fully expected the horse to die. They all did. But he was trying to give his wife a short break from the gut wrenching sorrow that Jessie knew she was feeling.

They left, and Jessie sighed as she began to pack her instruments and supplies back into her call truck. She could feel blood trickling down her leg inside her boot from where the horse's hoof had caught her on the side of the shin as it went down that last time, but honestly didn't have the energy to take her boot off and examine it. You didn't always get what you wanted, no matter how much you want it. She'd come to know that in this life. But it still hurt like the dickens to lose a patient.

Cal took another heart rate and then shook his head at Jessie. "Lower now. He's not perking up."

Looking at the horse that was now laying almost still, his shaved and sutured side, barely lifting and falling with his labored breathing, she knew that this horse wasn't going to perk up. It would probably be dead within minutes.

Wondering if she should go get the owners to be here as it died, she glanced to the house where they'd disappeared. The husband was walking toward them carrying two Cokes. Coming into the barn, he said sadly, "She's decided to put him down, Doc. Go ahead and put him out of his misery. She doesn't want to be here when you do. Honestly, I don't want to be either."

Jaclyn M. Hawkes

Nodding sadly, Jessie asked, "Do you want us to dispose of him? It will be tomorrow before I can get someone here to pick him up."

Considering, he asked, "Can we bury him here? Legally?"

Jessie shook her head. "Not in Gilbert. Not unless you put him in the pet cemetery. For a horse it's fifteen hundred dollars. Otherwise, he needs to be cremated or taken out into the county."

He thought for another moment and then said, "Let me ask her. Do you need to know tonight?"

"No. The morning will be soon enough."

He came close and shook Cal's hand and then hers and said, "Thank you for trying, Doc, Cal. We really appreciate you. You've been a superlative vet for us. I'm sorry we kept you all day and night and still lost him. It happens. We know that."

Sadly, Jessie agreed. "It does. But it's awful. I'm sorry. Tell her I'm so sorry."

Turning back toward the house, he said, "I will. Thanks again."

Cal rolled his shoulders and resolutely headed to the truck, saying, "I'll get the euthanasia."

Jessie knew she was either going to cry or cuss. She opted for cussing, but then never actually swore, just started to cry as she gave the horse the shot. Man, she was tired. Cal gave her a bleary eyed squeeze on her shoulder and then picked up a nearby tarp and pulled it around the dead horse.

She finished cleaning up and cracked the cold Coke as she headed for the Vetmobile with Cal following. Four fifteen in the morning. It had been a long day. Some days, she wished she'd become a stock broker.

And Riordan was leaving in only a few hours.

As she was letting herself into her house, she found a Post It note attached to her door that read, "I'm in your hammock. Please wake me up when you get home, Riordan"

She finished unlocking her door and smiled to herself at the thought of Riordan in her hammock. She'd known he'd been trying to get hold of her, but she'd been too busy all evening to stop and call. Honestly, she'd still been too offended by his mother's walk-about revelation to even want to call anyway. But, here, tonight, when she was tired beyond thinking, she was kind of happy that he'd wanted to talk to her enough to crash in her hammock.

Dropping her keys and gear in the kitchen, she got another cold drink and wandered in to glance out the patio door. Riordan wearing basketball shorts, was indeed dead asleep in the hammock, his skin magically lit by the glow of her twinkling fairy lights. Heavens, he was a gorgeous man, but he looked way too comfortable to actually wake him up. She was tired enough that she wouldn't know what to say to this adorable Australian anyway. In the heat of the desert night, he'd kicked off his deck shoes, and his shirt was in a wad next to the hammock and he looked good enough to eat lying there.

She glanced at her watch. It was after five in the morning and the sun would be coming up soon. She took a swallow of her juice and dug in her kitchen desk for another Post It and

Jaclyn M. Hawkes

wrote, "It's 5:07 in the morning. I just got home from an emergency call and I don't have the heart to wake you—but please don't leave without telling me goodbye in the morning. I'm going to miss you, Jessie"

Man, was she going to miss him. She took the Post It and quietly slipped out and stuck it inside his shoe. Standing there, she watched him for a long moment, then felt like bawling again. She kissed her fingers and silently blew it toward him. *Dang you, Riordan. Why couldn't you have at least been interested in being eligible?* Sadly, she knew the answer to that. She simply hadn't mattered enough. The one guy who was truly intriguing was hopelessly out of reach. She already missed him.

She sat down on her porch swing and put her head back against it. The sound of the stream was exactly what she needed tonight to try to lift some of the weight of failure she was feeling. She stretched to put her juice glass on the little table and left her head resting on the arm rest. Picking up a throw pillow, she hugged it and blinked tiredly out at the stars. It was a lovely calm night. Just her and the stream and the crickets. And one sleeping unattainable Australian hottie.

She yawned and considered that she needed to go in and shower. She was still wearing her lab coat and it seemed to hold the stress of the day and long night. Plus, she still needed to check out her shin to see how badly it was cut.

She was really tired. She decided she'd just rest there for one more moment and then go back inside and shower and go to bed.

Chapter 23

It wasn't the sun hitting him in the face that woke Riordan. It was Josh Benjamin pulling on the edge of the hammock and dumping him out that woke him. He shook his head and blinked in confusion. Looking up at Josh from where he'd landed in a lump, he saw Josh's finger to his lips and looked up to see Jessie, still wearing a blood spattered lab coat and her jeans and boots, dead asleep curled up on her porch swing. She was probably going to have a stiff neck when she woke up.

Looking back at Josh, he whispered, "What did you do that for?"

Josh only shrugged and whispered back, "I do that to all the guys who sleep over at my sister's." He handed Riordan a yellow Post It note. "This was in your shoe."

Riordan read the note and then shook his head. "Five oh seven? Crikeys. That's a long day."

Josh grimaced. "Yeah, it's even longer when the horse dies after everything. Cal texted me. Stinking valuable horse, surgery at the barn, and it went south."

Shaking his head, Riordan said quietly, "She'll be devastated."

"You mean more devastated than she was already going to be because her favorite person is going away today? What are you doing sleeping half naked in her hammock? Don't you know she has three big, mean brothers? I was a bit worried when you didn't come in last night."

Riordan groaned and sat up to reach for his shoes. "Well, she was screening my calls all day yesterday. And I'm leaving today. I had to talk to her. It was too hot to not be half naked. It's already hot out here."

Still whispering, Josh said, "You should have told her you were leaving sooner than planned before your mother announced it. Stuff like that will get your calls screened."

"Geez, don't I know it? I didn't realize Mum was going to do that. They'd only barely talked me into it and I hadn't had a chance to speak to Jessie."

Josh gestured at her. "Well, I know she's dead tired, but you'd better wake her up and let her get cleaned up. She'll be totally embarrassed to have your parents see her like this."

"I'm not worried about how my parents see her. Poor girl, she's only been asleep an hour. I'm worried about how to apologize."

"Which is only prudent. Considering that she might be the girl of your dreams. You better get to groveling, mate." He turned to go back down the path to his house. "And don't sleep over at my sister's again. Or I'll tell McCade on you."

Riordan rolled his eyes. That's all he needed was Jessie *and* McCade mad at him. He leaned up onto his elbow and looked at Jessie. Even exhausted and rumpled, she was a rare beauty.

He rolled up to sitting and ran a hand through his hair and then stood up and stretched. How to apologize to Jessie?

Sitting down beside where she lay curled up on the porch swing, he put a gentle hand to her back and began to quietly rub up and down. For a few minutes, she didn't even notice, but then she finally gave a small sigh and opened her eyes to look up at him. She glanced down at his still shirtless chest and then back up at his eyes, then to her own rumpled lab coat and blinked and said, "Oh, I was just going to sit and relax a moment before I went in and showered. Sorry."

He only brushed her hair back from her cheek. "You don't need to apologize to me, Jess. I'm sorry to wake you, but you should go in and get in your bed so you can really rest. It's going to be way too hot out here in a few minutes. You'll roast."

Watching his eyes, she asked, "What time are you leaving?"

"Around nine."

She nodded and he could see the shutters come down in her eyes and he went on. "I wanted to talk to you about that. I'm sorry I didn't tell you I was leaving sooner than planned. My parents had just sprung that on me before your dad's barbecue."

She closed her eyes and stretched and then turned onto her back and said, "It's okay. I understand. It will be a fun trip. Those parks are fantastic."

"But it isn't okay. With me. I was already feeling like I didn't have enough time here. With you."

Opening her eyes, she didn't reply, but he could practically see the wheels turning in her mind with all the rebuttals he knew could be valid. The silence felt almost damning. Surprising even himself, he said, "Come with us."

Jaclyn M. Hawkes

She shook her head tiredly. "What do you mean? Come with you?"

He took her hand and said earnestly, "Come with us to go walk-about."

Still obviously tired, she only looked at him for another long second that was finally interrupted by her phone ringing in the pocket of her lab coat. She answered it and arranged for a farm call about an injured Welsh Pony. Hanging that up, she immediately called Dr. Stettler to see if he would take the farm call, and would cover for her and Cal so they could rest.

When that was settled, Riordan asked her again, "Well, what do you think? Can you come to the Grand Canyon with us?"

She still only looked at him and then ultimately shook her head and said, "I can't go walk-about with you and your parents, Riordan. For so many reasons."

"Like what? List them and we'll try to work through them."

"Like my work. The stock show is over, but now I need to clear up the backlog of routine appointments that got put off over the last couple weeks. Plus all the emergencies. Even with Dr. Stettler, now isn't a good time to take time off. And your parents want to enjoy road tripping with their son. You've already got Rich. You certainly don't need me in the motor home mix."

"We're taking a motor coach. It's much bigger than a motor home."

Sitting up, she used one foot to push the heel of the other boot off, wincing as she did it and added, "Honestly, I'm too tired to go to the corner market, let alone to the Grand Canyon."
294

Pulling her jeans leg up, she began to pull her sock down and grimaced again, and he noticed the sock was stained with dried blood. She gingerly pulled it away, still wincing and when it finally pulled off of her leg, it pulled a scab with it. Her leg began to bleed again from a deep gash to the side of her shin. She quickly pulled her sock all the way off and doubled it over to apply pressure to the wound and added drily. "Plus, I need to go put a couple stitches in this. I really can't go with you. Would you mind getting me a couple of clean paper towels from my kitchen?"

Somewhat stunned at the size of the cut she had nonchalantly revealed, Riordan went inside the patio door and returned with the paper towels and asked, "How did that happen?"

She sighed. "Well, in the mix of a farm call last night—early this morning, I guess, I wasn't able to stay out of the way of a stray hoof when a horse fell on us. Would you mind helping me take off my other boot? You're right, it's getting really warm out here."

After pulling the other boot and sock off, he asked, "Are you wearing anything under the lab coat?"

That made her look confused. "Yes, why?"

He gestured with his fingers toward himself. "Then let's have it as well. You weren't saying you were going to stitch up your own leg, were you?"

Leaning forward, with his help she began to remove the lab coat. "Well, yeah. It'll only need a few stitches and it's not like it will need plastic surgery."

Jaclyn M. Hawkes

His gut reaction was to be horrified, but then if he thought about it, she definitely was a gifted surgeon. Still, that didn't make him need to baby her any less. He studied her face, considering for a minute and then said, "Jessie, you're tired. You've been up all night. And I know you're tough enough to stitch up your own leg and do a fabulous job of it, but let me run you into a human doctor who can do it for you and let you relax during it. Huh?"

She pulled the paper towels away to check the bleeding but pushed them back again, then leaned her head against the back of the cushion. "Nobody relaxes as they're getting stitches. You're leaving in just a little while. And human doctors take forever for stuff like this. Maybe I'll just shower and put a couple of butterfly bandages on it and call it good."

Riordan shook his head. "No, Jessie. That's a nasty cut. And with legs as beautiful as yours, you definitely need to get it stitched or glued or whatever it is they do these days." He stood up and pulled his shirt on and reached for her hand. "Come on. Up we go. Out to the pretty truck."

She looked up at him as if she was confused again and then shook her head and laughed. "You need to leave, Riordan. Plus, you really don't want to be seen with me looking like this. I can take myself."

"I have two and a half hours, and if we're late getting away, who cares when you're on walk-about? Let Dr. Stettler and Cal handle things and come with us."

She only gave him a sad, tired smile and said, "You're cute when you're being unrealistic, Riordan."

Arizona Forever

Three hours, seven stitches, and one LDS Dr. Collins, who Riordan thought was just a tad too interested in his patient later, Riordan brought Jessie back to her house in his pretty truck. Getting out, he came around to her door and let her out and then took her hand to walk her up to her door. She smiled up at him, but said, "I'm not an invalid, Riordan."

At the door, she turned back to him and let go of his hand to run it through her hair and said, "Thank you for taking me. It probably was better to have an MD do that. Thanks."

He nodded. "You're welcome." He took her hand again and when she looked up, he said, "Please come."

She smiled, but her eyes were sad as she looked back at him and at length shook her head and said softly, "Oh, Riordan. I wish I could. I really do. But I can't. You know that. And even if I could—what's the point?" She leaned up to kiss him once gently on the mouth. "Go with your folks and have a good time. Send me a postcard."

With that, she gave him another sad smile and let herself in her door and then gently, but firmly closed it behind her.

Standing there, looking at that closed door, he felt his shoulders slump. He knew that the story of Jessie and Riordan wasn't destined to have a fairytale ending, but this felt . . . it felt wrong. Just bloomin' wrong.

He sighed and walked back to his truck. He needed to go load up his parents and gear into the big motor coach waiting in front of Ken Benjamin's house.

He'd thought he could leave. He'd thought he had to leave. He knew he wasn't good enough for Jessie. He knew he wasn't Mormon enough for Jessie. But he hadn't known it would feel like this. This felt all wrong.

****

Inside her house, Jessie didn't even turn on any lights or open blinds as she headed for her bathroom. She was just going to shower and go to bed, and the darkness matched her mood anyway.

Even in the bathroom, she left the lights off and climbed into the steaming shower in semi darkness. The water felt like nirvana against her tired body and even soothed her gritty eyes. She closed them and let her tears slide out. She didn't cry very often, but sometimes she did if she was really tired. Or sad. Maybe the horse last night was God's way of helping her deal with Riordan's departure today. As tired as she was, she would hopefully be able to go back to bed and sleep through some of this devastating disappointment. She was really going to miss Riordan.

Twenty minutes later, she was out and pulled on some shorts and the exercise tank top she slept in on hot summer nights. She was in her kitchen, pouring cold chocolate milk into a glass when her doorbell rang. Setting the glass on her counter, she headed in to answer it. It was probably one of her brothers, or her dad. Cal tended to let someone know if she'd had as rough of a situation as last night's was, and it was kind of him to be concerned. But this morning she just wished she could rest in seclusion. She didn't want to be pitied for losing the horse—or Riordan.

She was rehearsing in her mind what she would say to her brothers or her dad as she opened the door to see Riordan standing there again. She glanced out to see that not only were his parents and Rich standing on her front lawn in front of a gigantic shiny motor coach, but so were her dad and Josh and Lucy and McCade. *Oh man, her hair was still wet and she was so not dressed to see his parents and Rich.*

Looking up at Riordan questioningly, she asked hesitantly, "Was there something you needed? What are you all doing out here?" She waved and did her best to smile at the entourage in her front yard.

Looking back at Riordan, she waited, but he took a moment, looking as if he wanted to say something, but nothing was coming out. Finally, he just said, "I, uh, I didn't feel like we really said goodbye."

Not knowing what to say to that, she simply waited and he actually looked strangely hesitant. At length, he asked, "Are you sure you won't come?"

She glanced back out at the others and then almost stuttered, "I . . . Riordan, I . . . I can't go. I really can't. Go have fun with your parents. And Rich." She smiled out at them again and then turned back to Riordan, wondering what he was doing standing there awkwardly on her porch. "It will be a fun trip. Enjoy it."

Nodding, he stood there, looking into her eyes. Not wanting him to see the sadness she was trying to hide, she looked away, but then looked back when he took a half step forward. Still watching her eyes, he wrapped his arms around her in a tight hug and she realized he was going to kiss her, right there in front of everyone. She could feel her eyes get big in something akin to panic, but then as his lips met hers, her eyes closed in sheer bliss.

She hadn't expected this, and it was foolish, and totally awkward with their families right there, but somehow, it was marvelous that he needed to say goodbye more . . . more . . .

His lips moving over hers stopped every thought process and she was too tired to try to think through what was happening anyway. She felt herself inhale a deep, sweet breath of pleasure and she kissed him back.

There was no thought of who was watching. There was no deep, sad disappointment that he was leaving. There wasn't even any wondering about why he was kissing her. There was only that fabulous lavender and apricot pleasure that washed over her brain and made her skin tingle to the tips of her toes. Riordan's kiss was incredible that way.

It was a decided "Ahem!" that brought them back to earth. She opened her eyes and they slowly pulled away, and realized that McCade was standing beside them on her porch giving Riordan an icy glare. For some reason that made her laugh, which only made McCade's look icier, but it made Riordan grin back at her. He hugged her tightly again and then leaned in for one more firm but short kiss that made McCade literally growl.

Ignoring McCade, Riordan looked down at her for a long, long moment and then finally glanced up at the other onlookers and said, "Goodbye, Jessie. I, uhm, I . . ."

For a panicked moment, she thought he was going to tell her he loved her, but he only said, "I'm going to miss you, Jess. I'll send you that postcard."

All she could do was nod. Finally, Riordan turned and strode off the porch back toward the others and the motor coach. Jessie looked out and to a man they all looked shell shocked. For that matter, so was she. She was suddenly too shy to face them all and went back into the house and closed the door, leaving McCade still standing on her porch looking growly.

Leaning back against the door, she let out a huge breath and closed her eyes. Holy Toledo. Riordan had just kissed her face off right in front of his parents and her dad. And McCade. She knew she was going to get a lecture for that one from McCade. And probably a good questioning from her dad. Not that she had any answers.

Sighing, she went back into the kitchen and sat down woodenly in a stool at the bar. Now why in the heck had Riordan come back and kissed her like that? He'd made it pretty clear a couple of nights ago that he was not interested in being part of her dating gene pool. But he didn't kiss like he wasn't interested. And in front of his parents. Crud. She blushed just thinking about it. His mother probably thought she was a . . . a . . . She didn't even know what a nasty girl was referred to in Australian.

She rolled her eyes and shook her head and got up to go pick up her glass of chocolate milk. She was wide awake enough now that she might as well get dressed and go to work. At least that way she could put off McCade's lecture. If she tried to rest now, she'd just lay there and wonder what was up with Riordan. She licked chocolate milk off of her top lip with her tongue. Man, he was a fabulous kisser.

Chapter 24

After some rather awkward goodbyes were said in front of Jessie's house, and they all loaded into the motor coach and drove away, Riordan settled into the passenger captain's chair in front next to Rich and reached for the printed itinerary Rich had put into the console. He'd seen his mother's raised eyebrows as he'd come back across Jessie's lawn, and his dad's grin and knew an inquisition was coming, but he wasn't really in the mood for it right now. He wasn't even in the mood for this trip. The thought of driving away from Jessie made him about as irritable as McCade had looked. He should have pestered her until she gave in and came with them, although in all honesty, she hadn't wavered even once when she'd turned him down both times.

Looking across at Rich, he tried to assume an amiable face and asked, "You're sure you're up to driving here right off, mate? This is rather like taking the mother ship out for a spin, isn't it?"

Rich waved a hand. "Ah, I've driven air craft carriers before, Ri. No worries. Just keep me on the right side of the bloomin'

Jaclyn M. Hawkes

road. That's what I'm concerned about. Well, that and that kiss I just saw. You should have warned me that you two had a thing going, mate. Then I wouldn't have flirted like a sailor when I met her the other day. She probably thinks I'm a half wit."

Riordan rubbed a hand over his jaw. What did he and Jessie have going, anyway? He had absolutely no idea at this point. Opting to ignore the unasked questions, Riordan only joked back at Rich, "That would be because you are a half wit and you'd have to have been a sailor at some point to have driven an air craft carrier. No?"

Rich only looked over at him and then glanced at his parents and replied, "Whatever you say, mate."

To his mum, Riordan said, "You'd best buckle in, Mum. Rich's other car is an Audi. Things could get a little racy."

Settling into the seats behind them next to his dad, she replied drily, "Yes, that's exactly what I was thinking when I saw that kiss, myself."

****

Jessie only made it through until two thirty that afternoon before she decided to call it a day and drove the vetmobile back home. Between no sleep to speak of, and no peace of mind because of Riordan's kiss in front of everyone, she was exhausted. She was just letting herself into her house when Dr. Collins called to check on how she was recovering from her stitches. She was taking a moment to assure him she was fine, when McCade let himself into her house behind her and immediately went to her fridge.

304

Getting off the call a few minutes later, she said, "Hey, Muck. What are you up to? There's nothing in there worth eating. I haven't had time to go to the grocery store lately."

Surfacing with a carton of yogurt, McCade said, "Yeah, I noticed you were too busy kissing Riordan this morning to find time for much else. How long have you been making out with Riordan?"

Raising her eyebrows, Jessie, said, "Excuse me?" When McCade refused to be intimidated by her look, she added, "It was a kiss—maybe a little bit drawn out one, but it wasn't like we were making out. Not that it's any of your business."

McCade gave a single humorless laugh and opened the yogurt. "That was making out and then some, Jess. And the fact that it was right in front of everyone makes it ten times worse. How long has this been going on?"

"You're not my kissing police, Muck. So nose out. You don't see me giving you the third degree about you kissing."

"Yeah. Key word is you don't see. Because most of us don't actually kiss like that with the entire western and southern hemisphere looking on. Since when are you and Riordan on kissing terms?"

Rolling her eyes, Jessie dug in the fridge for another yogurt and sat down at the bar beside him. Almost sadly, she said, "Riordan and I aren't on kissing terms, Muck. He was telling me goodbye, remember? He left this morning and that southern hemisphere is a bit far to pop in for a kiss."

"How long, Jessie? Quit beating around the bush."

"A week or two. Now nose out."

Jaclyn M. Hawkes

"Is he going to join the church?"

"No."

"And you kissed him anyway?"

"It was a kiss, McCade. Something maybe you need to do a little more of so that you aren't so involved in mine. Was there something you needed? Or did you just come over to give me the kissing inquisition?"

Finishing his yogurt, McCade tossed his carton toward her kitchen garbage and when it went in, he raised his hands and said, "Nothin' but net!" Then he continued, "I just wanted to know if I need to head up to the Grand Canyon to give Riordan the older brother glare. Or worse. How much should I lean on him? Do I need to take Josh and Brennan?"

Rolling her eyes again, Jessie muttered, "Oh, for heaven's sake." She slid off the bar stool. "I'm taking a nap. Let yourself out when you're done with the kissing inquisition."

"Who was that on the phone that you were so chatty with?"

"Nose out, McCade."

"I haven't heard you mention a Dr. Collins. And neither have Josh or Brennan. And when did you get stitches?"

She headed down her hall and said over her shoulder. "Love you, Muck. Have a nice life. And tell Brennan I don't want to be inquisitioned until at least tomorrow morning."

Behind her, she heard McCade say, "What about Josh? Wait! Josh knew about you kissing Riordan? And he didn't mention it? He's a dead man. He knows we're all three in charge of watching over your life."

Jessie only shook her head and laughed as she let herself into her master bath. She was actually surprised that Josh hadn't said something to the others. But she was glad. This whole mess hurt ridiculously, and the less people who knew how much she cared, the better.

She peeled off her clothes, tossed them into the hamper and turned on the shower, wondering if she could like Dr. Collins. He wasn't bad looking, and seemed nice enough. Maybe she could get involved somewhere else and forget all about that gorgeous, intriguing Australian, in spite of his fabulous kisses. Fat chance.

She rolled her neck and leaned into the warm spray. McCade was right. She should never have kissed Riordan.

****

The scenery at the Grand Canyon was every bit as spectacular as it had been touted, and being with his parents was thoroughly enjoyable. Even Rich and the motor coach were fun. But Riordan was as irritable as a grizzly bear.

He was trying to mask it. He'd smiled politely and agreed to whatever the others wanted, whether it was a side excursion, or which restaurant to have lunch at, but he wasn't fooling anyone. Especially not his mum.

At least so far, she hadn't called him on it. Which was more than he'd expected. After kissing Jessie goodbye, he'd expected a full out interrogation, but so far, it hadn't materialized. However, he knew from the way she was watching him so closely, that his mum was aware he was troubled. Maybe she just knew, like he did, that Jessie was simply something he

Jaclyn M. Hawkes

needed to get over and that it was going to take some time. It had been two whole days since he'd said goodbye to her. He hadn't been able to stop thinking about her, or stop wondering what she was doing, and wondering if she was missing him back since. At least tomorrow would be filled with meetings with authorities from The Church and hopefully, he would be too busy to miss Jessie—and wonder if he'd just walked away from the girl of his dreams.

****

The Church had accomplished an amazing amount in the couple of weeks that Riordan had been working with them. For that matter, they'd accomplished an amazing amount just in their meetings today. The Church was a phenomenal organization and the more familiar he became with it, the more comfortable he was that his money would be going to a wonderful work and managed astutely.

With their meetings over, as he walked down the hallway toward the exit beside the man they'd given him as a liaison, he finally asked the question that had been bugging him for days— ever since that night when Jessie has asked him if he thought he would ever join the church, and then had looked so resolutely sad when he'd said no.

Turning to his companion, he asked, "Can I ask you a question?"

"Certainly, Mr. Kane. I'll do my best to answer it."

Hoping he was putting it correctly, Riordan asked, "Do you know what a saving ordinance is?"

Nodding, the man considered it for a moment and then said, "In our church, there are a handful of ordinances called saving ordinances. I could take days to explain them to you, but the short answer is, they are the crucial, vital ordinances necessary to attain the highest degree of glory in the hereafter and achieve Eternal life and get to live with our Father in Heaven and Jesus. If we have received the saving ordinances, as long as we have lived righteously enough, we are able to be sealed to our families for eternity."

"And what does sealed mean?"

"Sealed means that if we are righteous, our marriages, our families, our relationships will last into eternity."

Wondering if he was understanding correctly, Riordan asked, "And if we don't have the saving ordinances? What happens to our families when we die? Take for instance, a baby who dies at birth? Can we be reunited after we die?"

Sadly, the man shook his head. "In most instances, without the saving ordinances, we can't be sealed to our families forever."

Nodding, Riordan thought about that. This was what made Jessie so resolute. After what had happened with her mum and her little sister, this concept was what had made Jessie so sure that she needed to be with her family forever. Sure enough that she would never even consider marrying someone who couldn't be sealed to her.

He was back in the motor coach with Rich, still pondering saving ordinances and hoping that his parents were enjoying their guided tour of the Church facilities when his mum and dad arrived back. He grinned in spite of himself when he realized his mum was thoroughly lit with enthusiasm. Immediately upon coming inside the coach, she began to regale him with tales of all she'd seen that day. For several minutes, she gave a rave revue of all the many departments and facilities she'd discovered that day

As she finally wound down, she said airily, "I like this church! They are organized and efficient, and do tons of service, and seem to be truly concerned about both their fellow man, and their members. I think they actually must be led by Jesus Christ like they claim! And they actually treat their women wonderfully—I'd heard they were against women, but it's not the least bit true, and you should see all the wonderful programs geared toward strengthening families! It's no wonder the Benjamin's seemed so close!"

She sat down on the sofa, but then popped right back up to dig in her purse as she said, "I'm calling Ashleigh to tell her she should encourage Warren to take the job here in the United States. If she could get Zoe and Kace involved with some of the programs this church has, it would be wonderful! Do you know they actually have a whole set of programs for teenagers. Just look at this little booklet! It's called For The Strength of Youth. Just the title is uplifting, don't you think?" She pushed the little booklet into his hands.

As she pulled out her phone and began to scroll to call Ashleigh, Riordan said drily, "They actually probably have the same programs in Hong Kong, Mum. Or Thailand. It's a global church now, you know."

Waving her phone, she said, "No. I think I'll recommend they come here. If you could have met some of those people today, you would have loved having Zoe and Kace around them. Such nice people. And I think your father and I would be much more comfortable traveling here than in Thailand. I've heard that it's very liberal there. Francie Hale said you could hardly tell the men from the women there. That's the last thing Zoe and Kace need is this new weird gender ambiguity. Plus, I think that food would get old fast."

Riordan laughed even though he was still in a pensive mood. His mum was a live wire, that was certain. Did she think Thailand only had one kind of food?

Speaking of food made him hungry, so while his mum was on the phone with Hong Kong, he asked his dad, "What are you in the mood for for dinner, Dad? If Thai food isn't your thing, what would you like?"

Lounging on the other end of the sofa with his leg elevated, his dad said, "I think I'm too tired to care about food tonight, son. Even though they shuttled us around with golf carts and drivers, I'm bushed. I'd rather rest this hip than go out. How about cold cereal here in the motor coach?"

In concern, Riordan got up to come and stand next to his dad and put a hand on his shoulder. "What would help, Dad? We've got ice, or a hot pack. Or how about another pillow under? And we can order all kinds of food in or leave you right where you're at and pick something up?"

Putting his head back against the sofa, his dad said, "Do you suppose they have any of that type of pizza they had in Arizona? That would be wonderful."

Catching Rich's eye, Riordan said, "Pizza it is. What kind did you like?"

"Oh, I loved the one they called the Hawaiian, with the ham and pineapple. Would that be all right with you?"

Riordan nodded. "Hawaiian would be fabulous. Do you fancy the thick crust or thin?"

In the middle of her phone call, his mum interjected, "Thin crust please."

She went back to her call and his dad said, "Thin is fine. That woman has two sets of ears, I swear it."

Rich opened his laptop and began to order the pizza and Riordan got his dad an ice pack out of the little freezer and handed it to him as well as a bottle of over the counter pain killers, then sat down beside him. Hawaiian pizza had been Jessie's favorite as well. She had been adorable that night eating pizza and talking to him.

It was Monday evening. She was probably getting ready to go out with the young adults to their Family Home Evening activity. The thought of his beautiful Jessie hanging out with a bunch of single men, didn't help his irritability factor a bit.

From across the coach, his mum asked, "What's wrong, Ri? What is it?"

He looked up at her in confusion and she pulled her phone away from her mouth and whispered, "Why are you frowning?"

He only shook his head and got up to go get a drink. If they didn't have any A & W root beer, he'd have Rich order some with the pizza. Man, Jessie had looked good drinking down her root beer that night. It was probably why he'd kissed her. How good she always looked drinking. Looking back, he'd been pretty much a goner since that first time seeing her with his horse and watching her drink down that frosty bottle of water. He hadn't really even known her then, but she'd already become intriguing.

Why her? Why someone completely out of reach? Why not one of the hundreds of non-Mormon Australian girls he came in contact with?

His mum ended her call and he could feel her eyes on him, but he didn't look at her. She was too good at seeing things he didn't want to admit to her. Instead, he just glanced down at the bottle of water in his hand and wondered again if Jessie was meeting any new guys for her gene pool tonight and unconsciously gave a sigh.

That was another thing his mum would love about the church—the way they were literally organized to help people find someone to marry. He hoped that obnoxious Dr. Collins wasn't in her singles group. He'd admitted that day that he was new to the Mesa area and that he was LDS. At the thought, Riordan wished he'd just let her stitch up her own leg after all. He hoped it was healing okay and wasn't sore. She was such a good sport about stuff like that. And she had amazingly beautiful legs. She had beautiful everything.

Chapter 25

By the time Riordan had been gone five days, Jessie was actually lonely enough that she finally let Lucy talk her into setting up a dating profile on-line. She had no idea how you would ever trust someone from just what they'd written about themselves, but she had to do something to help her forget about Riordan Kane.

Dr. Collins had called and asked her out, and she'd accepted, but she knew her heart wasn't in it. And she'd accepted another date with Caleb, but she'd already decided to cut him loose as gently as possible when they got together. He was way too nice of a guy to string along when she knew she'd never fall in love with him.

Ten days out, she even sheepishly approached Josh and asked him if she could help him out riding again. She assured him it was just until she found another saddle horse of her own, but Josh knew that it had less to do with riding horses, and more to do with staying busy enough that she didn't make herself miserable missing Riordan.

He laughed and teased her and then seriously asked, "Is he the one, Jess?"

She considered that for a long moment, but finally shook her head. "He couldn't be, Josh. He doesn't have a couple of the biggest items on my checklist."

Josh only looked at her steadily and at length said, "He's a good man, Jess. Maybe the checklist will come together in time."

Shaking her head sadly, she asked, "What if it didn't? Would you have married Lucy if she hadn't shared the gospel with you?"

He shook his own head. "No."

With a sad smile, she admitted, "You're smarter than me. You wouldn't have even let yourself fall in love without the gospel." Turning to go, she said over her shoulder. "But since I'm not that smart, now I just need to ride enough horses to fall back out of love with someone."

With that hint of smart aleckness he was famous for, Josh said, "Looks like I'm going to need to start breaking a bunch of new green colts. That'll keep your mind off any Australians."

The sad truth was that even a bunch of green colts didn't fix her heart. It just made her miss Riordan babying her when she ended up with a sprained wrist. Riordan had been wonderful to watch over her.

****

Rich flew home to Australia after the meetings in Salt Lake City, and it was just Riordan and his parents as they went back to southern Utah and wandered through Zion National Park and Bryce Canyon National Park. The scenery was phenomenal, and

Jaclyn M. Hawkes

Riordan was glad to be able to road trip with his parents, but the struggle to find the point in his life that he'd been dealing with in Australia amped up to full blown gloominess by the time they made it to Arches National Park.

For the whole nine days, his dad had only tried to be a little more cheerful, and his mum just watched him more closely without saying anything, until finally, as they were moseying up a paved path toward one of the more accessible arches in the park, she asked him a tricky question, "Other than Jessie, what's in Arizona that made you happy?"

He shrugged, loathe to admit to his mum what was bothering him and why he couldn't help it and said, "For awhile, Quinn was there. He always makes me laugh. And the other Benjamins."

She shook her head. "Quinn has been in Australia with you the whole time. It wasn't him. And you have friends back home who are as close as the Benjamins, don't you?"

He nodded and kept walking. It was Jessie who had made him happy, and he was pretty sure his mum knew it. But he didn't want to try to explain to her about his stubborn hesitation to join the Church because of a stupid girl when he was a teenager who had so hardened his heart, or his current feelings of inadequacy about being righteous enough to face totally committing to his Father in heaven.

As he walked, he did some more of the self examination that he'd been doing a lot lately. He'd been seventeen when Sariah Hensley had flirted with him just enough to make him decide she was the most desirable and angelic girl in all of South Elson

316

Prep School. They'd dated off and on for most of three months in which he'd finally let his guard down and decided they were formally a couple and that he'd found the love of his seventeen years.

Then had come one of the hardest times of his life. She'd literally shocked him speechless one night. He didn't know she'd ever even tasted alcohol and then she'd gotten drunk at a party. Then when he'd tried to take her home, she'd all but demanded that they detour into the back seat of his parents' car and it had gotten ugly when he'd refused. That awful wake up call only ended in a bigger ball of fire because the next day, when he didn't much want anything to do with her anymore, she'd begun to back stab him around school and tried to turn all his friends against him for being too chicken to finish what she'd tried to start that night.

It had been an ugly, scarring episode in his life that made him distrust all girls, especially the Mormon ones who he'd originally thought were supposedly more trustworthy. And virtuous. It hadn't taken him a whole lot longer to realize that what he'd at first thought was Sariah's sweet innocence must have been simply the influence of her parents who had tried to raise a sweet and innocent girl. Sadly, he'd also learned that a lot of other guys were more than willing to take what Sariah had offered.

In the end, he'd become thoroughly bitter toward the seemingly hypocritical Mormon Church. Only Josh's truly kind and serving patience over nearly two years of his life had softened that bitterness, and originally only toward Josh. In

Jaclyn M. Hawkes

Riordan's stubborn young mind, every other Mormon was still not to be trusted, no matter how much Riordan felt drawn to the Church's doctrine. In some ways, Sariah had changed Riordan's happy spirit forever.

It had been more than a decade since then. Long enough for Riordan to slowly, but finally realize that he couldn't blame all Mormon's for Sariah's lack of character, but probably not long enough to completely soften Riordan's ridiculous stubbornness. Even his wonderful mum often called him pig headed.

By this time, even if he could rationally admit that the Church of Jesus Christ of Latter Day Saints was right and good and what his heart craved, he felt like after all these years of bitterness toward the Mormons he would never be good enough to join it.

He wasn't the most horrible person. He knew that. But he'd been both hard hearted and stiff necked for so long that he didn't deserve to join the Church. By now, he was one of those who had become hopelessly stuck out of the fold. He hated it, but he'd come to believe it. The closest he could come was to try to stick to his set of personal values, which incidentally looked a lot like the principles Josh had so patiently taught him over all these years, and try to be a decent, honest citizen.

Coming to that conclusion one more time, which again, left him firmly outside Jessie's gene pool, was incredibly depressing and he frowned as he walked beside his parents in this place of incredible beauty. If only he could relive the last twelve years again with the perspective he'd gained with maturity. There were a lot of things he'd do differently so that he could be worthy of Jessie.

318

Josh was right. He knew that now. Jessie was definitely the love of his life. Only he didn't deserve her.

****

After Jessie's sprained wrist from breaking colts, and the on-line listings didn't seem to be panning out, McCade got this hair brained idea to drag Jessie clear across the greater Phoenix area to a new singles ward. In McCade's delicate eloquence, he said, "Jessie, what you need is fresh meat. For your gene pool. I could use some, too."

It hadn't been a very refined way to put it, but he was definitely right. Only it didn't work very well. They went to both the ward on Sunday and to the family home evening activities for three whole weeks, wondering why the people they introduced themselves to didn't seem very interested in getting to know them until finally, they figured it out.

At family home evening of the third week, a tall, slender young man who looked to be fresh off a mission hesitantly approached Jessie. After small talking for a moment asked, "So, how serious are you with McCade?"

Confused, Jessie asked, "What do you mean?"

The guy blushed, but he bravely pushed on, "Well, are you guys exclusive? Or what? You're always together, but you never hold hands or anything. Are you taken? Or can someone else ask you out?"

Looking at a guy who she knew had to be at least six years younger than her, for one moment, she wished she didn't have to be honest with him. At first glance, he definitely didn't feel like Mr. Right. Wishing she could just sidestep the question, she asked, "People here think McCade and I are a couple?" She shook her head. "McCade is my brother."

After a completely awkward date request, that she gutted through accepting, she and McCade left the activity a few minutes later and she explained to him on the way home what had happened. Off course McCade thought it was hysterical and automatically dubbed the guy Calvin Cowlick, even though his name was Parker and he didn't have any cowlicks that Jessie had noticed.

Unfortunately, their date was just as awkward as him asking for it had been.

They did try one more singles ward after that one, but it was more than an hour drive and had a heavyset girl with long, light brown braids and buck teeth who took an instant liking to McCade when they first were introduced. Needless to say, McCade decided that their old singles ward would be fine for the time being, and Jessie agreed. Her spirit was so tired from missing Riordan that she decided to just stop dating for awhile and give herself a break anyway.

****

In September, McCade got hit by a drunk driver. It was absolutely frightening at the time, and left him hardly able to help out around the ranch, but one good thing came from it. He injured his rotator cuff and a disc in his neck, but he met Sophie, a kind hearted, soft spoken blonde nurse who happened to live not far from them. They hadn't met her at the singles ward because she attended a family ward with her widowed mother. Miraculously, she knew just how to deal with McCade's teasing and they hit it off almost immediately.

320

Jessie was genuinely thrilled for McCade. Sophie seemed to be perfect for him. Even their dad and Sophie's mom seemed to enjoy each other's company. But, in a way, the whole situation took the energy out of Jessie's spirit. She'd completely lost her mojo. Sometimes she couldn't even remember what her mojo used to feel like. Literally, the highlight of her week was watching Marcela while Jorge and Consuela took Pablo paintballing for his birthday.

She didn't even really enjoy soccer anymore because it just always made her think about Riordan. And she couldn't fit any more flowers near her patio.

Ultimately, she decided to look into getting a new hobby. She'd heard that painting was very therapeutic. Or maybe kick boxing. Some aggression might do her good.

Or maybe just something like knitting. It would be safe and calming. Her grandmother used to make stocking caps for all of them. Not that you needed many stocking caps in Mesa, Arizona—which made it a stupid idea. She didn't have the patience for knitting anyway.

Maybe ant farming. Ants were more native to Arizona and her cousin had told her they were fascinating to watch—until they died. She'd said that was actually pretty traumatic. Apparently the ant family just walked around their dead sibling until they decomposed.

When she realized that a grown professional woman was considering ant farming, she decided that she was the most pathetic thing she'd ever seen and decided to get a lot more serious about accomplishing something of substance. With that in mind, she doubled her family history work and temple attendance. When that wasn't enough, she helped the guys wean and halter break all the year's crop of foals.

In the end, she signed up for a pottery throwing class as well. She'd always loved mud, and theoretically, if you made a mistake, you could smash your project and start over. With the shape her heart was in right now, smashing something and starting over was sounding really good. Who knew? Maybe she'd meet a handsome sculptor who would make her forget Riordan Kane. It could happen. Okay, so that wasn't very realistic, but she wasn't giving up hope. She couldn't give up hope.

Chapter 26

Riordan's mum had been remarkably closed mouthed about the marriage/grandkid topic while they were on walk-about, which he so appreciated under the circumstances, but it hadn't been like her usually loving but pestering way. So, he actually wasn't surprised when one day, as they drove in the southern entrance of Grand Teton National Park, she finally decided to face his lack of enthusiasm.

He had just pulled the motor coach into a turnout on the highway straight across from literally the most beautiful scenic view he'd ever seen in his life. Those huge, craggy, rugged, snow capped Grand Tetons of Wyoming rising straight up from the valley floor with the wide Snake River winding below them were easily the most glorious mountains imaginable and the view was breathtaking.

His mum had been sitting at the little kitchen table making sandwiches for lunch as he stopped and she looked up and drew in a breath of awe and said, "Oh, my gracious! Look at them!" When she glanced up at him, all he did was nod. They truly were the most amazing mountains in the world. They had to be.

Even in the Snowy River Mountains in Australia, he'd never seen anything like them. They were breath taking. He wished Jessie had been there to see them with him.

His mum watched him for a moment, then patted the little bench seat between her and where his father was snoozing on the other end and said, "Come sit by me, Riordan. For heaven's sake, come sit here and tell me where in the world your smile has gone. Even the most glorious sight on earth can't drum up some emotion. This can't go on."

Swallowing a sigh, Riordan reluctantly got up and moved to sit next to her and look out the big picture window at the mountains. The view truly was the most striking thing he'd ever seen. But he didn't want to talk about the view. He honestly didn't want to talk about anything, but he wasn't going to be rude to his mum just because he was discouraged about his life.

Still quietly watching him with that seemingly all-knowing wisdom she always seemed to have, she paused for a long, long moment before she said, "We came to the states to find out what had made you seem so much happier here. And it was so nice to see you finally at ease and cheerful. I'm sorry we took you away from her."

Shaking his head, he said, "You didn't take me away from anyone, Mum."

"Well, I've given this some thought—a lot of thought—and I've come to the only obvious conclusion that it was that lovely blonde veterinarian, whom you kissed so thoroughly when we left, who had made you happy in Arizona. What I can't figure out, is why in the world you don't seem to have any obvious

324

plans to continue being happy with her. Have you even given her a phone call?"

He leaned his head back against the couch cushion. "Mum, she lives in Arizona. She's worked hard to build her veterinary practice there. I live in Queensland. And I wasn't joking that she said I wasn't eligible to date her. She wants to marry a Mormon."

Nodding as if she was thinking, his mum said, "And so what you're saying is that you love Australia more than Jessie and aren't willing to relocate to be with her. Right? Have you asked her if she'd be willing to sell out here and move down under?"

"No. What I'm saying is . . ." He sighed again. "I'd stay in America in a heartbeat, Mum. She wants a Mormon. I'm not a Mormon."

Again she considered what he was saying for a few moments before she asked, "So, then, why don't you become a Mormon?"

He looked at her in surprise. "Just like that? Why don't I become a Mormon? Mum, did you happen to notice that the Benjamins take their religion rather seriously?"

"Yes. Of course. I think it's fabulous! They were hard working, and clean living, and loyal to each other, and very nice, decent people. Frankly, I thought they were a bloomin' wonderful family in a world that is sometimes crass and coarse. So, then what you're saying is that you would rather be without Jessie, than live a devoutly religious life?"

"Mum, I'm not a devoutly religious person. I'm one of the crass and coarse ones. I can't be a Mormon."

Jaclyn M. Hawkes

Nodding slowly, she looked confused. Finally, she asked, "So, what exactly do you do that is so crass and coarse? I know you've been on your own for years and years, but I've never known about any egregious sinning going on. What have I missed that is so unredeemable? If you don't mind my asking."

He shook his head, wondering how in the world to answer her. Finally, he simply said, "Mum, I hated the Mormons for years. Years. After Sariah Hensley made my life so miserable in school, for years I believed that what she did was the Mormon Church's fault. I know now that wasn't true, but becoming a Mormon after all that would be the most hypocritical thing in the world."

With another thoughtful nod, she said, "So then what you're saying is that you would rather hang on to your misconceived bitterness, than be with Jessie? Or are you saying the Mormons have refused to let you in? They didn't seem exclusionary to me, but maybe I missed something. Help me understand. Do they not believe in Jesus' grace?"

"Of course I wouldn't rather be bitter than be with Jessie. And they haven't actually said they would reject me. Very much to the contrary. But they don't understand how . . . how much . . . how long I've rejected Jesus' grace. At this point, I'm just not Mormon material. Trust me, Mum. I'm not. You have no idea how incredibly wonderful Jessie is. I could never deserve her."

Nodding again, she still seemed thoughtful and said, "Hmm. I see." After considering another few moments, she asked, "And Jessie? Is Jessie on board with this idea of you being undeserving? Is she fine with you leaving and never looking back?"

326

Sadly, he said, "Yeah. She's fine with it. When I told her I was never going to get baptized, she was obviously sad. But she was also obviously very sure that she had to marry someone who she can be sealed to for eternity. It's a long story, Mum, but her mum found out she was pregnant when Jessie was six. Jessie was so excited. She'd apparently had this little imaginary friend named Jennifer that she'd hoped for for years and she was absolutely convinced that the baby was going to be Jennifer. Sadly, her mum aborted it so she could keep training horses. I think it must have almost destroyed Jessie. That's why she changed her name and became a veterinarian instead of a trainer with the rest of them. You never met her mum when you were there, because she is kind of estranged over it all. In Jessie's mind, her mum killed her baby sister in a heinous manner for a career. She still can't really deal with that."

He shook his head sadly and continued, "The bottom line is, all Jessie has of Jennifer is the sure knowledge that they are sealed in heaven and can be together in the hereafter. It's a big deal to her. Huge. I think she honestly loved me, even after just a few weeks, but I could just never be enough for her. She is afraid of being left out of the family in the eternities if she doesn't marry in the temple to someone with all the requisite saving ordinances. So yeah, Jessie is fine with me leaving and not looking back. It was actually kind of her idea. Not mine."

Now his mum looked a bit angry. "Jessie really said you're not good enough? To leave and never come back?"

Riordan sighed. "No, of course not. I told Jessie I wouldn't ever be joining the church. So she felt like she had no choice but to let me leave."

"So is she home being as unhappy as you are? Or is she fine with all of this . . . this?"

Now, more depressed than ever, Riordan said, "I don't know how she is, Mum. I haven't spoken to her, or anyone about her. I felt it best to just try to move on and get on with our lives."

Almost sounding a bit exasperated, his mum quipped, "Well, Riordan, I don't think that's working out so well for you." Then, sounding more positive, she said, "You need to call Josh."

"Why do I need to call Josh?"

"You need to call Josh and find out if Mormons are really the only Christians in the world who don't believe in Christ's saving grace. In repentance. Because I think you're wrong. All the Mormon commercials I've ever seen demonstrate repentance. I think the Mormons believe that Christ's atonement is bigger than even your years of bitterness and all of your supposed heathenness. Which, frankly, I think is a crock of wallaby euke. I think you're a wonderful, good, honorable man and I'm proud to have been your mum. But that's beside the point. Why would the Mormons throw out the main premise of Christianity? Call Josh."

"Fine. I'll call Josh."

"Call him now."

"We're just going to have lunch. Dad's probably starving."

"Fine. But right after lunch."

"Okay, but why is this such a big deal right now?"

"Because frankly, your father and I are sick to death of watching you sink deeper into the Pit Of Despair." She said the last three words with a raspy dramatic deep voice like the albino in The Princess Bride and for the first time in days, Riordan finally smiled.

Airily, she added, "And if you think I'm good with letting you walk away from the love of your life, just because of some misguided sense of self deprecation, you're off your rocker! You and Jessie will have adorable little grandchildren for me! Now eat, so you can call Josh!"

Riordan rolled his eyes, but then felt like he needed to level with his mum. "I'll call Josh, Mum, but I don't think I'd get my hopes up for grandchildren just yet. If I'd thought it was possible to make it work with Jessie, I would have."

She pushed a plated sandwich with a dill pickle spear and some chips across the table to him and then leaned to wake up his dad, saying, "Roy, hon, would you like a bite to eat? And just look at those mountains!"

His dad woke up and stretched his leg out in front of him for a minute and then exclaimed at the view out the window, "Glory be! Now that's a mountain range!"

His mum pushed a plate across to his dad as well and asked, "What would you like to drink with that, dear?"

"An iced tea. Thanks."

His mum got up to get the tea and asked, "Do Mormons drink iced tea, Ri? And what do you want to drink?"

"No. It's against their health code. Why? I'll take an A & W."

His mum came back to the table with two A & W root beers and a bottled water. Setting them all three down in front of her

Jaclyn M. Hawkes

husband, she said, "Riordan and I were just talking about joining the Mormon Church, Roy. What would you think about that?"

Warily, Roy looked from one to the other of them. "You were talking about what? Have you lost your bloomin' mind? Why the Mormons? Riordan, would you say grace on the food?"

Riordan grinned at his mum and they all bowed their heads. After the prayer, his father started right back in. "If this means I can't have iced tea, then no. You'll have to join the Mormons without me. Although, I do admit that their operations are impressive. But you better double check that they treat women the way you want to be treated.

Crunching into a pickle, his mum cracked open the second A & W and set it next to his father's plate and then nodded. "Jessie didn't appear too downtrodden to me, Roy. Did she to you, Riordan?"

Watching his dad taste the root beer, Riordan said, "No, Mum. The Mormon women aren't down trodden. Dad, you can have iced tea if you want."

Taking a big swig, his dad said, "The root beer is fine, Ri. It'll make me burp and then she'll get after me and that's worth not having tea anyway. What brought on this sudden need for Mormonism?"

His mum patted his father's hand and then said, "Well, hon, I thought it was the lesser of the two earth shattering subjects to start with."

At that, his father choked on his root beer. After she had handed him a napkin and he'd quit coughing, he asked, "What's the second?"

Smiling cheerfully, Caroline Kane asked, "What would you think of moving to America, hon?" His father was still speechless when his mum said, "Hurry and eat, Riordan, so you can call Josh."

Chapter 27

Jessie Benn drowsed in her hammock, listening to the creek burble and the crickets start up their evening chorus. The little lights in her flower vines were starting to twinkle on and the smell of the creek was a magical scent in the deepening dusk.

She pushed off with one bare foot to make the hammock barely swing and took a deep breath. There was something to be said for having given up on dating. Yeah, she'd probably be the maiden aunt to all of her brothers' adorable children, but even that wouldn't be so bad. She could be an amazing aunt. Heck, she'd take aunthood to a whole new level.

At least her evenings were less hectic. Lonely as can be, because she always missed Riordan so much, but still, it seemed like she missed Riordan the most when she was with some other guy she didn't really care for, and they were both trying too hard to find emotion that wasn't there. After the crazy sweet emotion she'd felt with Riordan, she knew she could never settle for humdrum. It wouldn't be fair to either her or a guy and it wouldn't work anyway. She knew a marriage needed true, strong emotion to work.

It was sad, really. For years, she'd made an honest effort to find Mr. Right. She truly had. And she'd truly wanted to have a wonderful happy marriage, like Josh and Lucy's, and Brennan and Suki's. She'd still love that. But, she'd finally gotten honest enough with herself to admit that maybe happily ever after wasn't going to happen for her. Falling in love with Riordan had been a huge mistake. He had ruined her for everyone else.

She wiped at a tear that seeped out of her eyes. It was one thing to give up on the idea of happily ever after. It was another not to mourn that dream. It made her so, so sad.

A late bee buzzed past on its way back to her dad's beehives and she focused on the sounds of the twilight. The water over the stones in the creek soothed her sad heart and she took a deep breath of the smell of cottonwoods and water. She was going to be okay. Sometimes she had to remind herself of that, but it was true. Somehow, her Heavenly Father had a plan for her and if she just worked hard, and stayed strong, she'd be fine.

She pulled her long hair off her neck and took another deep breath and let herself drift off to the sleep that she knew would bring peace. She loved the way her little oasis smelled. She gave a last yawn. It was nice here on her patio.

It was the aroma of basil and Canadian bacon again. She slowly came aware, and then opened her eyes, wondering why she would be having the pizza dream again. But there was Riordan, wearing different shorts and another t-shirt without sleeves, standing beside her hammock, holding an opened pizza box in front of her and carrying root beer and napkins again.

Jaclyn M. Hawkes

For a moment, she only blinked. She was dreaming. She knew that. And later it would make her sad and she'd try to make herself be a responsible adult and try to get past how much she cared, but right now, she was going to enjoy the heck out of Riordan standing there in her dream, the soft light from the vines setting off each muscle. Riordan was simply too attractive to even be a dream. She put out a hand and touched him on his bicep and then pulled her hand away and mumbled, "You even feel real." She closed her eyes again and gave a happy sigh. Such a vivid dream was nice.

She heard Riordan's laugh and then heard him say, "Yeah. Still completely real."

For some reason, the sound of his voice woke her up and she opened her eyes and then sat up so fast she nearly upset the hammock. It was Riordan! He was real! She was so shocked that she suddenly felt a little bit shy.

She stood up from the hammock and in confusion said, "Riordan?" She reached out to touch him again and then ran her hand down his arm. Still sounding sleepy, she asked, "Is it really you? I thought you'd be in Wyoming by now. What are you doing here?"

Setting the pizza and soda on the little table, he moved over close and stood looking down at her, while she stood looking up at him, wondering if she was still somehow dreaming.

He put his hands on her shoulders, and then without answering her question, slowly leaned down to kiss her. Just once, but so deliberately and sweetly that she closed her eyes and basked in his kiss for a long, long moment. She reveled in the feel of his firm mouth and his hair in her fingers, and his taste and breathed in that scent that had haunted her for weeks now. Man, she had missed him. Missed this. As foolish as it was—and it was definitely foolish to fall in love with someone who you have little in common with, who can just up and go walk-about—she had missed this.

But then, reminding herself that he had indeed been able to pick up and leave her, she needed to know what was going on. She needed to understand why, out of the blue, Riordan was back here in her arms, and dreams, and actually kissing her on her patio. Much as she loved it, she knew by now it would only make the wounds she was already struggling to heal, fresh again. Yeah, she adored him, but that was a huge mistake. She felt like her life was still reeling from falling for Riordan the last time. Her heart was ragged. And the last thing she wanted was to be Riordan's American toy.

Almost sadly, she slowly drew away and let go of him, then took a step back, looking at him for some explanation. She loved this man, but in a way, she was mad at him as well. Or maybe it was mostly sad, not mad. He'd been so darn attractive that she'd fallen foolishly in love with him.

Then he'd left. She knew he'd had every right to go road tripping, but when he actually did it, she'd had to face the fact that she hadn't mattered enough for him to consider staying. Even though he had asked her to go, probably knowing that she couldn't, that stung. It made her a little hesitant.

She sat down on the porch swing and gave him a tentative smile and asked, "So, what are you doing here?"

Sitting down beside her, he said, "I had to come back."

She nodded, not sure she understood. Maybe he'd had more meetings or something. In a way, she didn't care why he'd come back, she was just thrilled that he had. And in a way, the fact that she was so thrilled frightened the dickens out of her. She wished she'd had some warning so she could have been trying to get her defenses up against caring so much for him.

They sat there in silence for a few minutes, and then he asked, "Would you like some pizza?"

She nodded again. "Sure. Thank you."

He handed her a piece of pizza on a napkin and then cracked a soda and gave that to her as well.

Taking a bite, she chewed it and then finally asked, "What did you have to come back for?"

He put his arm along the back of the swing and touched a strand of her hair and said softly, "Because I love you."

She looked up at him so fast that she nearly spilled her soda. He met her eyes and his honesty made her almost feel a bit panicky. She'd suspected that he loved her before he left. He had always been so kind and considerate of her. But she'd never dreamed that he'd come back and admit it to her. And now that he had, she had no idea what to say to him.

She loved him too. She'd fallen for him ridiculously fast. But even though they had both felt it, it hadn't been enough. Loving each other didn't fix all the seemingly insurmountable issues between them.

Not wanting to leave such an honest admission hanging, she said, "I love you, too, Riordan." She gave him another hesitant smile and took a sip of her soda.

With a gentle touch, he lifted her chin to get her to look up at him, and asked, "Why does that make you sad, Jessie?"

She looked away and wiped at a stupid tear as she tried to figure out how to answer him. All these years she'd hoped that when she finally fell in love with someone it would be happily ever after. It had actually turned out to be painfully sad. But she didn't want to admit that to him.

Instead, she said, "I just . . . You . . . We're . . . I guess I just missed you. Did you want some pizza?"

He stroked the strand of her hair again. "No. I'm too nervous to eat, thanks."

That made her confused. She'd never known Riordan to be nervous and she looked up at him. "Why are you nervous?"

Now playing with the strand of her hair, he looked at her and said softly, "Because, I think this is probably the most important conversation of my whole life."

Her soda stalled on the way to her mouth. "What are you talking about? What conversation?"

He gave her a mellow smile. "Oh, you know that conversation where I say, I know we've only known each other for a little over a month, and I know we live on the back side of the earth from each other, and I know you totally have a life of your own and a business, but I love you. You make me happy. I don't want to leave you. But we've only known each other for a little over a month. And even if we could overcome all of those things, you're a Mormon, who wants to marry a Mormon, and I'm a spiritual disaster and could never be good enough to marry you, and we've only known each other a little over a month anyway."

He gave her a smile that was a bit sad, "But maybe, just maybe, the atonement is enough to rescue even a spiritual disaster—at least Josh says it is, but how can we be sure that I'm joining the church because I believe it's Christ's own church, and not just because you make me happy and I want to marry you? And really, this whole conversation is insane, because we've only known each other for a little over a month. You know that conversation?"

Jessie knew her eyes were huge, but she couldn't help it. She felt herself blink in utter shock as she tried to wrap her brain around what he'd just said. *Holy my oh my!*

Finally, she replied casually, "Oh, that conversation. That's the conversation we're having?"

Riordan nodded. "Yeah. And it's making me crazy nervous."

He didn't even hint at humor as he said it and it finally made Jessie smile, but at the same instant, tears welled into her eyes.

This time, they weren't sad tears.

She turned and set her pizza and soda aside and grabbed another napkin. Putting it to her eyes, she leaned into Riordan's chest and buried her face and he wrapped his arms around her and pulled her close. Gently, he began to rub up and down her back like he had when she'd been so motion sick.

After a few moments, he pulled back and tipped her face up to look into her eyes and quietly ask, "Are you okay? I didn't mean to make you cry."

She nodded, but didn't say anything. She couldn't yet. Hesitantly, he asked, "Are you totally mad at me?"

She shook her head and smiled again through her tears. "Mad? Riordan, why would I be mad? Are you crazy?"

He tipped his head and shrugged. "Obviously. But I blame it on you. I wasn't the least bit crazy before I came to America. And now look at me."

She laughed, but leaned back into him and he pulled her close again. Looking up at him, she put a hand to his cheek, smiling, even though she was still teary. She reached to kiss him and then closed her eyes and finally let herself give in to the joy of being back in Riordan's arms. She did love this adorable man, and with his one nutty, vital conversation, that probably was insane because they'd only known each other a little over a month, he was back to being the most comfortable friend she'd ever had, who warmed her heart and miraculously dried her tears.

And tasted like happiness. He was still a marvelous kisser.

A little while later, when they stopped kissing and she was lying against his chest again, she finally whispered, "Did you mean to say all those things?"

She could hear the smile in his voice as he said, "Yes."

Still without looking up, she asked, "Even the M word?"

He leaned down and kissed her again, this time just a touch fiercely and nodded. "Even the M word."

She finally looked up and gave him a full blown teasing smile. "No wonder you were nervous."

Rubbing a thumb across her cheek, he smiled back. "Yeah. Definitely, no wonder."

After some more incredibly happy kisses, she snuggled back into his neck and breathed in his scent mixed with the magic of the cottonwoods and the stream, and gave a happy sigh and asked, "How do you say don't be nervous in Australian?"

With his lips on her hair, he said, "Mmm, something like, no worries, mate."

She looked up and put a hand to his cheek and smiled, "Then, no worries, mate. We'll figure it out," and she kissed him again.

Epilogue

Jessie Kane drowsed in the big hammock, her back spooned against Riordan, listening to the creek burble and the crickets start up their evening chorus with the occasional sound of children's voices in the background. The little lights in her flower vines were starting to twinkle on and the smell of the creek was a magical scent in the deepening dusk.

She pushed off with one bare foot to make the hammock barely swing and took a deep breath to savor the moment. There was something to be said for the peace and quiet of early evening in May.

Suddenly, there was the sound of water splashing and then a dog barked. At the bark, the tiny baby on the blanket lying beside them let out a whimper that slowly gained velocity until she finally let out a true cry. In Jessie's ear, Riordan whispered, "Ah, but wasn't that peace beautiful while it lasted, love? What were we thinking to have three children in four years?"

She smiled with her eyes still closed and enjoyed the chills from his breath against her neck. Giving a dreamy sigh, she

Jaclyn M. Hawkes

finally opened her eyes and then sat up suddenly and said, "James, Daniel, please stop plastering your cousin in mud!" She pulled at her shirt to straighten it."Oh, my word, Jacob looks like a two year old Aborigine. Lucy is going to want to murder us, although he does look adorable that color."

Beside her, Riordan rolled to sit up beside her. He picked up the crying baby, snuggled her close for a moment until she stopped fussing and then handed her to Jesse and said, "Apparently Jennifer woke up hungry enough to attempt to eat her own fist. You feed her. I'll see to hosing off the aboriginal cousin. My mum always warned that I'd have a child just like me. She never mentioned I'd get two of them."

As he went toward the stream, he said, "No! Not the dog! You know Mum hates it when you let the dog in the house muddy! And what happened to your swimming togs? Did you let them go down the stream again? Boys, that's the fourth time. Remember how we talked about how you might make a fish downstream choke? We're working on being kind to the fishes, remember? And keeping the stream clean. That's what Daddy does, you know, help people all over the world with clean water. Plus, remember how Grandpa Ken says stuff gets stuck in his culvert?"

Jessie watched the three little muddy faces look up in penitence and laughed as Riordan said, "What are you hiding behind your back, Daniel?" Riordan held out a hand and added, "Give me the togs."

Daniel smiled cheerfully and put a dripping wet glob of mud into Riordan's hand and Jessie smiled again as she got

342

ready to nurse the baby. She watched her handsome husband patiently and gently line up three little boys and one muddy golden retriever and hose off the bulk of the mud.

She laughed again when the dog suddenly shook and flipped water over the lot of them, making the boys all squeal and laugh, and spattering Riordan's shorts and golf shirt as well. Then she tried not to laugh when she saw one-year-old Daniel casually begin to take this naked watery opportunity to relieve his bladder in an arc that matched Riordan with the hose. Of course, all three boys went into gales of laughter. Riordan forbade the other two from joining in the waterworks just as Josh and Lucy came around the corner, at which the still whizzing Daniel cheerfully waved at them.

Lucy raised her eyebrows, but Josh only laughed and said, "That's an awesome aim you've got there, Daniel!"

Shaking her head, Jessie grinned and said, "Don't encourage him, Josh. I swear, he's got a touch of Uncle Quinn in him. Riordan is already worrying that we're in over our heads and I still need a couple more of these rugrats."

Josh grinned at her and said, "Oh, yeah, like Riordan would ever deny you anything you want."

Picking up three towels from the basket on the deck, Lucy headed toward her child who still somewhat resembled an Aborigine, handed Riordan two of the towels and said, "When you have this cute of children, Riordan, you can't stop at three."

Riordan turned off the hose, wrapped James and Daniel in the towels, then picked up a child in each arm, grinned and said, "That's what I'm afraid of."

An hour later, miraculously, all three Kane children were fed, and the boys bathed and snuggly asleep in their beds. On her way up from putting the muddy towels in the washer, Jessie let the still damp dog in the back door and then watched Riordan tenderly tuck the sheets around his two little dark curly headed boys. He met her at their bedroom door, where she held tiny Jennifer and he leaned to kiss Jessie lingeringly on the mouth.

As he pulled away, they looked back at the two sleeping boys and she asked, "Aren't they marvelous?"

Putting an arm around her, he followed her out of the room, saying, "They are absolutely marvelous. And thank heavens the good Lord made little children need lots of sleep, no matter what continent they're on."

They paused to lay the baby in her crib and Riordan reached in to touch a soft little pink cheek with a gentle finger and say, "She's growing up so fast."

"Riordan, she's two months old."

"But she'll probably grow up just as fast as the boys have."

"Yes, I hope so. The boys are fabulously healthy. So is she."

He stroked Jennifer's baby cheek again. "But when I see them asleep and so tiny and trusting, it brings this almost primal need to protect them."

She nodded. "It does. If I think too much about it all, it makes me worry. But then I try to remind myself that they're Heavenly Father's children as well and that He's helping us watch over them."

Riordan turned to her and looked into her eyes and said, "And they're sealed to us. For eternity." Jessie nodded as she looked into his fascinating eyes and he added, "Thank you for that. It's every bit as priceless a gift as you knew it was. I would never have made it here without you. Thank you for welcoming me back that day."

Jessie nodded again and blinked at a tear. "You're welcome. I would never have made it here without you, either. Thank you for coming back to have that conversation."

He leaned in to kiss her and then grinned and said, "I couldn't not."

The End

About the author

Jaclyn M. Hawkes grew up with 6 sisters, 4 brothers and any number of pets. (It was never boring!) She got a bachelor's degree, had a career as a cartographer with the federal government, and traveled extensively before settling down to her life's work of being the mother of four magnificent and sometimes challenging children. She loves shellfish, Meat Lover's pizza, the out-of-doors, the youth, and hearing her children laugh. She and her extremely attractive husband, their younger children, and their happy dogs, now live in a mountain valley in northern Utah, where it smells like heaven and kids still move sprinkler pipe.

To learn more about Jaclyn, visit www.jaclynmhawkes.com.

Author's Note

The epilogue scene with the mud and the golden retriever and the naked children waving as they uh hmm hmmed into the stream, was taken directly from one of my own children, who shall remain nameless.

I have a beautiful stream that meanders through my yard beside my front porch with a quaint little bridge, just the right size for two-year-olds to sit on and dangle their feet in the water. One fateful summer day, when the cousins were visiting, there came a knock on my door. It was my crusty old farmer neighbor and as I greeted him, he said, "There go the swimming suits. You'd better catch them before they go through the culvert."

On glancing out, there on the bridge stood two very naked, muddy two-year-olds, and a muddy golden retriever. (The golden retriever was naked too, but that's beside the point.) And yes, the cousin really was smiling and waving at the passing traffic as he whizzed into the stream. Of course I immortalized the moment on camera.

My child and the cousin try to accuse me of ruining their lives by taking that photo, but it's great black mailing leverage now that they're teenagers. I'd put it here, but this is not that kind of a book! Trust me, it's priceless!

I did save the swimming suits, but the neighbors probably still think we're lunatics.

Jaclyn